The Seven Perfumes

of Sacrifice

A Novel

Amy Logan

Though 99% of the facts in *The Seven Perfumes of Sacrifice* were drawn from scholarly research, the story is a work of fiction. All characters, with the exception of well-known figures herein, are products of the author's imagination.

Logan, Amy, 1966-

 The seven perfumes of sacrifice : a novel / Amy Logan

 ISBN-13: 978-0-9853080-1-8

Published in the United States by Priya Press, San Francisco

Printed in the United States of America

To Vaughan

meae dimidium animae semper

ACKNOWLEDGMENTS

My gratitude to the Israeli Department of Tourism for the fam trip that started this whole journey; Al Badeel; Kayan Feminist Organization; Interights; Al-Fanar Palestinian Feminist Organization; The Palestinian Human Rights Monitoring Group; Amnesty International; El - Manahel Assn of Arab Druze Women; Equality Now; Gabriel Ben-Dor of the University of Haifa; HRA - The Arab Association for Human Rights; Isha L'Isha; Israel Women's Network; WIZO; Women Against Violence Israel; Women's Center for Legal Aid & Counseling; Na'amat; the Laguna Beach Library; the Broward County Library System; the Orange County Library System; Inter-Library Loan; the British Library; the Laguna Beach Police Department; the International Women's Health Coalition; Prof. Robert Segal at the University of Aberdeen and Prof. and Provost Brian Copenhaver at UCLA, for information on Hermes Trismegistus; Associate Prof. C. Bruce MacDonald, MD, at the University of Tennessee, for assistance with acoustic trauma; Prof. Emeritus Roger Just at the University of Kent, for suggesting a reading list about honor; Dr. Efraim Lev at the University of Haifa, for assistance with Israeli traditional medicine; Rana Husseini at the *Jordan Times*, Joseph Campbell, Michael Meade and Jeanne Brescania for inspiration; Robert McKee and Dara Marks for story-telling lessons; Tremper Longman and the late Huston Smith, for guidance on the *Song of Songs*; Mordechai Beck and *Parabola* magazine, on "threshold"; Jon Schwartz, for anthropological insights; and David M. Frost, for permitting my use of his joke.

I could not have created this story without most of the 150+ sources I have listed in my bibliography, which can be found on my website – www.7perfumes.com.

I had countless interviews and several homestays with Arabs, Druze and other Israelis who don't wish to be acknowledged by name for the essential help they provided this controversial project.

My deepest appreciation to my patient, professional editors: John Paine, May Wuthrich, Dara Marks and Mary Logue. And to my early readers who offered invaluable insight and support: Amy and Michael Corley, Jackie and Hal Watson, Gayle Hudgens and Harvey Davis, Betty X. Davis, Joyce Cushing, Joy Tipping, Karen Moser, Sherry Jones, Jheri St. James, Anne Cushman, Dan Howard, Jan Johnson, JoAnne Tompkins and Cheryl Richardson.

Thank you to Karen Kimsey-House, John Vercelli and the Willows, for giving me the final push to put this out in the world.

Thank you, Robert Logan, for your support of my dream to write this book, and Vaughan Logan, who missed his mommy during the many writing days.

Thank you to my parents and step-parents for believing in me. I love you!

I, the mind of the past, to be driven under the ground out cast, like dirt!"

— The Furies, Aeschylus' *The Eumenides*, 458 BCE

1

The afternoon my life blew apart, at the bus stop near the Jaffa clock tower, a Palestinian teenage girl was staring at a young couple kissing. Under her black headscarf, the girl's face betrayed none of her feelings, but she shifted on the bench, crossing and uncrossing her legs. She couldn't keep her eyes off the lip-locked pair in shorts and tank tops, probably Jewish Israelis. What could she be thinking? Disgusting? Disgraceful? Maybe she was envious. Or taking notes.

With the new concrete and ancient stone of Yefet Street acting like a convection oven for the June heat, body contact seemed unbearable to me. After a few minutes, the Palestinian remembered herself and lowered her gaze from the couple, covering her face with the end of her headscarf.

Finally, the bus headed for central Tel Aviv arrived. Holding hands, the lovers boarded first and headed for the back. As I scooted into the seat behind the driver, I noticed a young woman running up to the bus holding a white scarf on her head – my friend, Leila. Without a word, she cut in line in front of the Palestinian girl and jumped on the bus.

"Fereby, that one's going directly to the central station," Leila said, pointing to another bus that was just pulling up in front of mine. She stood in the stairwell, blocking the entrance, and shielded her eyes from the sun with purple paint-mottled fingers. "Come with me. This one will stop many times before it gets there."

This unmannerly behavior, so unlike her, confused me. The bus driver glared at us.

"It'll be faster. I'm going there myself," she entreated. "Come." She reached out and pulled me by the hand.

As I stepped down to the curb, I bumped shoulders with the Palestinian girl, making her drop her bus fare on the sidewalk.

"I'm sorry – *slikha!* I mean, uh, *as-fa*," I finally said in the right language.

She glanced at me, startled by my using Arabic or perhaps that I had spoken to her at all. Her pale eyes, not exactly blue nor green, surprised me. We both bent down and gathered up what few coins remained in reach.

"Quickly!" Leila pleaded.

I handed the money to the girl, plus another coin from my pocket, and she nodded her thanks, eyes lowered. I ran to catch the other bus, following Leila's billowing white *foutta*, fumbling for more *shekels*. We bought tickets from the driver and sat down in the first row. Soon, the bus pulled out into Yefet Street.

"Thank you, Leil–" The loudest noise I'd ever heard caromed through my head. All around me, windows collapsed.

"*Ya Abu Ibrahim!*" Leila cried as she covered me with her arms, pushing my head down with her cheek, like a mother.

Crumbs of glass poured into our laps. People started screaming. I jumped up; every cell in my body felt as if it were ablaze. I didn't know what was happening, but my body was moving without me. Leila seized my upper arm and pulled me toward the exit, the *foutta* falling to her shoulders. We pushed against the door, but it wouldn't open. People yelled and pressed on us. Desperate elbows and hands surged at me, burrowing for any vulnerable place to grip and overtake. Someone grabbed my long hair, which yanked out one of my hoop earrings that was caught in it. Bodies urged us out, but we had no place to go. The only impulse inside me was *Get out!* It was pure energy, no calculation needed. I didn't seem to be in charge of my mind or body anymore.

A hot wave of metallic air funneled through the broken windows. Someone's shoe dug into my heel as glass crunched underfoot. So many voices that didn't seem to belong to any language resounded in my head. A cell phone rang and rang. As my body began to fold under the weight of the crowd, a blend of guilt and shame – my default emotions in any crisis – overtook me.

Leila must have felt me collapsing behind her. Suddenly, she threw her head back hitting me in the face, screaming "*Shahada!*" It was more the cry of a fanatical dictator than a panic-stricken girl. The crowd recoiled at the Arabic word like another detonation. In those seconds of release, Leila thrust her body into mine, pushing me back just enough to reach her arm behind us and blindly find the button that opened the door, which the driver, evidently, was still too stunned to push himself. The accordion-style automatic door folded hard into Leila, knocking her into me, but she shifted around it as if it were a small nuisance and pulled me out into the frenzied street.

We were hauling somehow – Leila's one arm around me, the other gripping my closest elbow – but locomotion was tricky for me. My feet tangled on themselves, as though she were teaching me a complex ethnic dance. She was pushing us onwards to try to lead us away from the scene, I finally realized. "In case there's another," she yelled in my ear at point-blank range, though it came through in muffled tones as if she were shouting at me from far away.

Leila's head jerked back and forth, her long swath of black hair flying into my eyes. I looked back and, for an instant, saw flames shooting out of a dark mass of mangled metal down the block, black smoke pouring out into the air above.

"What's happening?" I yelled.

Leila grabbed my neck to steer me forward and didn't let go until we had crossed an intersection. Eyes flashing, she inhaled as though surfacing from a free dive. I turned to look again, felt myself unhinging and Leila's grip righting me again.

Many people rushing in our direction were bleeding or crying. Others came out of the shops around us, throwing their hands up in the air or covering their mouths. One word echoed through the street: "*Pzaza!*"

"What're they saying?" I shouted at Leila over the din.

Leila yelled back, though I strained to hear her.

"What?" I yelled.

"Bomb!" She repeated.

Most of the windows of our bus lay in tiny shards on the asphalt of Yefet Street, glittering like quartz under the Mediterranean sun. Somewhere behind it, black smoke unfurled into the transparent sky. I stepped onto the sidewalk to try to see around our bus. People dashed back and forth, blocking my view; in between, I caught glimpses of fire. What had been bombed?

I felt cotton in my ears; I stuck a finger in each but found nothing. We both looked toward the flames and smoke. A terrible, strange smell hit me. You needn't ever have smelled burning human flesh before to recognize it: sweet, sour and charred, as if something in nature has gone cataclysmically wrong.

"That was the first bus you were on, Fereby," Leila said.

I heard her, but not as well as I should have. A tremor shuddered through me; I scanned the street for its source, my gaze coming to rest on a pink plastic grocery bag in the gutter. Then I noticed the street and sidewalks were otherwise spotless. I was fixating on irrelevant things. What was wrong with me?

I turned to Leila. "How did you know to get me off that bus?"

She regarded me for a long moment. *"Qada'an wa-qaddar."*

"Huh?"

"Fate and destiny. You're shaking," she said. "Are you hurt?"

She examined me for signs of injury, then had me shake the shards of glass out of my hair and off my clothing. "Don't try to brush it off with your hands. You'll just get cut."

She saw me looking at her suspiciously.

"How did you know?" I asked.

"You're yelling...I *didn't!* I mean, sometimes I sort of know things before I know them, okay?" she said. "I can't explain."

To my knowledge, the Israeli Druze had never been involved in terrorism against Israel, but I couldn't help but wonder now about Leila. I'd met her less than a year before when I was on assignment in Israel with *National Geographic* covering the Druze, Leila's culture, an Arabic-speaking minority. I was the first American Leila had gotten to know and she was mesmerized by my stories of traveling the world alone, working at what I loved and living independently as a woman in the U.S. Perhaps because of this, she trusted me enough to share her secret life – painting nudes, lovers and goddesses – taboo subjects in her conservative culture, a thousand-year-old offshoot of Islam – and selling them in a gallery in Jaffa. She'd taken me to an art show where she was anonymously exhibiting a provocative installation piece that had caused a commotion all over the country about the treatment of women in traditional cultures. I desperately wanted to write about her, but couldn't without endangering her. Though a friendship had been born, I realized now there was much I still didn't know about her.

Sirens filled the sky. Leila walked me several blocks before I thought to ask where we were going.

"The Central Bus Station. That's where you wanted to go, right?" she said, her arm linked with mine, leading me through intersections, not waiting for pedestrian cross signals.

"Yes. No! It's too far to walk. I have to get to...I don't – " I stammered. *What am I doing?* I stopped. I had to fly home to the States – yeah, that was it. Running out of money.

"Are you okay?" Leila held my elbows.

I rubbed my forehead and ran my nails along my scalp. "I don't know. I...I'm–" My head swam as if I were struggling to come out of anesthesia. I felt porous. "I can't hear that well."

"Neither can I," she said, clutching my arms now, speaking slowly as if I were very old or dim-witted. "It will probably go away in a few days; we weren't that close. You were going to the airport, right?"

I sighed. It was too bright outside to be real. "No," I said, shaking my head. "Not yet. My flight's not until one a.m."

Leila held me at arm's length now, staring at the lower half of my body. Everything beyond our twosome was out of focus, something less than pure.

She looked up at me with concern. "Where are your clothes?"

I glanced down, feeling for my pants. They were still on, thank God.

"No. Your *clean* clothes."

I blinked at her, still not following.

"Where is the luggage you're taking on the airplane?" she pressed.

"Oh. At the hotel." I was staying in Tel Aviv, just adjacent to Jaffa.

"We need to get it now."

Her eyes returned to my lower half. I looked down again at myself, bending over farther this time. A dark stain emanated from my crotch all the way down to my ankles.

Leila tied my jacket around my waist to conceal the accident and hailed a taxi to take us to my hotel on Hayarkon Street. I'd lost track of where we were and how long it had been since the explosion, but Leila was in charge, shepherding me.

In the hotel restroom, I cleaned myself up and changed into some khaki slacks while Leila waited in the lobby. Since the bombing, it had been like the patchy consciousness of a drunken night out – lost chunks of time, mundane objects commanding undue attention, lucid moments of humiliation and suspicion. I considered that, in three decades traveling the globe, I'd found the single-most embarrassing experience that all cultures share is soiling oneself in public. Wetting one's pants should certainly come in second, but after nearly being killed, I couldn't care less.

The bombing also put something even more important into proper perspective: I had long dreamed of being published in *The New York Times* but, since I'd been in Israel for the past nine days, all the freelance articles I'd written for them had been rejected. I was leaving that night because I couldn't afford to stay any longer without a sale. I shook my head at myself in the bathroom mirror, incredulous that I'd hit the jackpot of surviving a terrorist attack. But I still couldn't let go of how exactly Leila managed to save me.

When I emerged, Leila looked nervous.

"You're coming home with me for dinner before going to the airport," she said, her slightly hooded eyes, soot-colored with flecks of green, leaving no room for debate.

"I don't know –"

"You won't be late," she said. "We'll drive you to the airport and have you there in plenty of time for your flight."

Flight. My heart pounded so hard, I glanced at my chest. Just the idea filled me with dread.

"I just need to ask my parents," she said, pulling a silver cell phone out of her shoulder bag. She dropped it back in, fished around some more, then pulled out a black cell phone and began to dial.

"I don't know, Leila –"

"You'll be afraid if you're all alone." She turned her back to me as she put the phone to her ear.

We took another taxi to the Central Train Station in Tel Aviv, but when we got in line to buy our tickets to Haifa – the closest stop to her college, where her brother would be picking us up – my heart hammered again.

"Leila," I whispered. "I don't think I can take the train."

She regarded me with studious compassion. "It's almost four o'clock and Fadi will be at school in one hour," she said in a kind but firm voice. "I cannot be late, or I'll be in big trouble. I don't see how else we're going to get there."

I knew she wasn't supposed to be in Tel Aviv – she'd told me her family would kill her if they found out she so much as visited the city on her own, let alone painted risqué art and sold it there. She was only able to manage such complex deception with the help of one of her college professors. "Because of Devrah, I can paint what I want in Haifa, sell in Tel Aviv, and live as a good Druze girl in Atabi," she'd confided.

"What about another taxi?" I suggested.

"It's far, more than 100 kilometers. It would be close to three hundred *shekels*."

I tried to compute that in U.S. dollars, but nothing happened. "I'll pay for it."

She blinked at me, either insulted, impressed or unsure if I was actually good for it.

"Let's go," I said.

Two minutes later, we were pulling out into a traffic jam in a taxi. Leila dug into her bag again for her black cell phone and turned it off.

"Don't you want to call your family...or someone?" she asked, giving her *foutta* a shake.

I looked down at my lap, which came into peculiar hyper focus. I glanced at my watch to calculate what time it was in California where both my parents and I lived. Numbers swam in my head and I gave up. No matter: I couldn't tell my mother, and therefore, I couldn't tell my father. They couldn't keep such secrets from each other. Werner, the guy I was dating, was fishing somewhere in the North Sea. We hadn't seen each other in three weeks and the few conversations had been strained. I had no one to call. I fought to stifle the knot of despair forming in my chest.

"Not right now," I managed, and turned my attention to the congestion outside.

When we reached the coastal highway and turned north, the Mediterranean shimmered its obnoxious beauty as if nothing could be wrong with the world.

Leila frowned at her watch, then craned her neck to assess the traffic up ahead. The driver stole frequent glances at her in the rearview. Her beauty, overwhelmingly Arab, was on the order of a semi-feral sultana. Men, women and children alike stopped to ogle her. Leila wore no makeup, probably never had. I didn't know her exact age and couldn't begin to guess: Nineteen? Twenty-two? Twenty-five?

She leaned forward and told the driver in Hebrew what must have been, "Would you kindly step on it?" because he immediately accelerated. She turned to check on me.

"How are you?"

I closed my eyes and exhaled. "Just this morning I cancelled an interview with a member of the Zaka task force." The Zaka were the *haredi*, the ultra-Orthodox Jews, who collected body parts and spatters of blood for burial after a terrorist attack. One of them was writing poetry about his work that was receiving international acclaim.

"Yes," she said, as though that kind of creepy coincidence was to be expected here. "Why did you cancel?"

I looked out the window and shifted in my seat. "*The Times* passed on all my stories. Didn't really see the point."

"Why didn't they take them?"

I didn't know. I'd interviewed an 87-year-old Auschwitz survivor in Jerusalem who'd sent her reparations check to a young German whose grandfather had executed her husband in the war. She wanted him to have the money for his foundation that was trying to eliminate the Neo-Nazi movement in Europe. I'd reported on Palestinian Buddhists. I'd found a folk cure for pancreatic cancer from the Dead Sea with actual doctors backing up its efficacy. I'd gone spelunking in Qumran with some modern Essenes.

"The editor told me to go where the locals tell you *not* to go," I said. "He said, 'Talk to the finance minister of the Israeli mafia. Get 'embedded' with a bounty hunter for fugitive terrorists. Find out something new about the child prostitutes trafficked from Eastern Europe.'"

"That would be interesting," Leila said. "Tel Aviv's the brothel capital of the world. It's a billion dollar slave trade."

"I know, I know," I said, a prickle of guilt at the nape of my neck.

"Well, now you've got quite a story to tell."

I looked at her and swallowed hard. I hadn't even remembered to take pictures after the bombing, let alone call my editor. I could no longer deny it: I wasn't cut out for the higher realm of this business. I lacked ambition for lurid stories because they seemed to be told mainly for their spectacle, not their meaning. I felt my livelihood slipping away from me and I was the one pushing it. A brew of alarm and anger stirred inside me.

The radio blared guttural vocals and static as the driver fumbled to find a station.

Leila pulled both her cell phones out of her bag again and began punching buttons. "Raziel didn't even try to call me." She dropped them back into her bag and tilted her head towards Jaffa. "The bombing was so close and he knew I was on my way home."

Raziel was the owner of Mujun, the art gallery where she sold her work in Jaffa. I had just been there minutes before the bombing to say goodbye to Leila before I left the country. She and Raziel were arguing when I arrived, the gallery full of tension. It was not the best time to hang out, so I'd left after a brief visit.

I still couldn't shake a funny feeling. "You have two cell phones," I said.

A guilty smile turned up the corners of her mouth. She combed her hair with her fingers and tucked it behind her ears. No earrings, no piercings, no nail polish, no rings. Just dried purple paint on her fingers from making art.

"I guess I can tell you," she said. "One phone is secret. My boyfriend gave it to me so we can talk and my family won't know."

This was interesting: Dating was forbidden by the Druze, even between each other. She smiled more radiantly than I'd ever seen her, then her face fell. "Fereby, please don't tell anyone. You know what could happen. And he's not even Druze."

The Druze, who were neither Muslim, Christian nor Jewish but had their own religion, didn't recognize marriage with outsiders and seemed to have a number of such restrictions to keep their religion as pure and secret as possible. The rare woman who dated or married outside the faith was usually hunted down and "dispatched." Men sometimes met the same fate, or, at least, were excommunicated.

"I'm not going to tell on you, but I'm curious – is he Palestinian?" I asked.

"No."

"Jewish?"

"No, American – not religious."

She told me her boyfriend collected art for his own foundation in New York City and had acquired a number of works of emerging and well-known artists from around the world. His curator saw Leila's work in a Tel Aviv exhibition the previous September and bought several pieces. Since she showed her work anonymously, it took him several months of persistence to find her. After several long conversations, he flew out from New York to meet her.

"How do you see each other if you can't go on dates?" I asked.

"He visits me at school when he's in town. Sometimes he takes me places far off-campus."

13

Suddenly, she leaned forward and listened to the radio broadcast.

"They've counted twelve dead already from the bombing," she said. "Many more seriously wounded."

The report ended and the driver turned off the radio, leaving us in an unbearable silence. I could barely breathe. I stared out at the Bolshevik-inspired box buildings going by, their lines repeating into a blur. I imagined the kissing lovers who had boarded that bus ahead of me, their blood-soaked tank tops, suntanned skin gaping from shrapnel. My abdomen felt like twisted metal. Leila folded my hand into hers. I watched palm trees whiz by, ruins of Roman aqueducts and fields of Shamouti orange trees. Was she involved somehow? Haifa's working class port finally broke the view as fertile Mount Carmel rose to the east.

"We'll be at the university soon, Fereby," Leila said, arranging her *foutta* back on her head. "Fadi will pick us up. We're about twenty minutes late. This is our story: I was not in Jaffa or Tel Aviv. You were in the bombing, not me. You then came to school to find me. I invited you home for some Druze hospitality after your trauma before you leave the country tonight. I'm not an artist. Nothing about a gallery. There's no boyfriend."

"Got it," I said, my unstable mind stirring up facts, fiction and memory like a dangerous potion.

I knew her brother, Fadi, had to drive her to school because she wasn't allowed to have a drivers' license like many Druze women. She said he never asked her what she did away from home so she wouldn't have to lie.

After crossing the *foutta* under her chin and flipping the ends over her shoulders, Leila handed me her secret silver cell phone from her bag. "There's no time for me to go to Devrah's office first where I keep my things at school…and I don't like to take this home with me. You keep it until the airport and then slip it to me and I'll hide it somewhere afterwards."

"I don't know if that's such a good – "

"My mother will search my things while I'm gone to take you to the airport or later when I'm asleep," she said, pressing it into my palm. "She mustn't find it and Fadi doesn't know, either."

Reluctantly, I tucked it into my backpack.

2

The higher we rose, the more densely the pine trees grew, the safer I felt. The University of Haifa's campus was located on the top of Mount Carmel, its sleek skyscraper rising ridiculously out of the wilderness. Leila directed the driver to let us off at a different entrance from where Fadi usually picked her up so he wouldn't see us get out of the taxi.

We took a shortcut through the student center. Outside, along a circular driveway, a tall police officer leaned against a white car, arms folded across his chest. When he saw us, he bolted in our direction, shouting at Leila in Arabic. I felt a wave of fear until I realized it was Leila's brother. In his crisp, black Border Police uniform with a gun holstered on his belt, Fadi looked much bigger than when I'd first met him with Leila ten months ago. She yelled back at him, unintimidated. Their words ricocheted like ammo through their fierce gestures. She motioned me onward with one hand while she held up her other to shush him.

Fadi's jaw line followed the same oval shape as Leila's, but his eyes were the lightest of brown – almost golden – made more remarkable next to his brown skin, several shades darker than Leila's. He was as beautiful as she.

Leila pulled her black cell phone out, looked at it in surprise and showed it to him. He snatched it from her and turned it on. She grabbed it back, shaking her head. She was pretending she'd left her phone off by accident – her excuse for not receiving his calls when she was late.

He looked over at me finally and Leila used the moment to depart from their argument.

"Fadi, you remember Fereby."

As though forced by decorum, he shifted his gaze and nodded at me, distracted by his anger at Leila. I tentatively offered my hand to shake, which he squeezed with his nearest hand – the left one – as though he couldn't be bothered to shake politely with the right one, which hung by his side.

Glaring at Leila, he threw my pack in the trunk of the car, an old, dirty coupe that didn't fit him at all. Soon we were on the other side of Mount Carmel, Fadi coaxing a loose clutch and straining accelerator. Scarlet poppies and white parasols of cow's parsley waved from the shoulder.

A few minutes later, past the entrance to Carmel National Park, we approached the first buildings on the outskirts of Atabi, their three-hundred-year-old village. Fadi pointed out the only bar in town, a small, cinderblock dive with no sign. The village's modest business district huddled up to both sides of the main street. Half the buildings seemed to be suspended in some stage of remodel or demolition. Cars were parked haphazardly. A man in an embroidered skullcap leaned against an old olive press in the main square. Men with bushy mustaches and white turbans strolled down the dusty street in long black robes. (The pious were easy to spot – they always wore head coverings.) Narrow dirt roads led out of the square to flat-roofed, thick-walled stone and concrete houses clustered across the slopes. Atabi possessed an astonishing absence of color. *Don't mind me*, it murmured.

Fadi slowed as we passed a building with a narrow old road that split it down the middle and said it was the *khalwe* of Shaikh Hayyan, the head of the Druze Religious Council of Israel – Atabi's claim to fame.

"It's like Druze church," he said.

"Can we go in?" I asked.

He and Leila exchanged glances. "If a non-initiated Druze goes in, they will be killed," Fadi explained.

I looked back at the unassuming building with newfound wonder.

"If a woman goes in the man's side, even if she's Druze, same thing," Leila added, picking at some purple paint on a finger.

Fadi kept driving. Some homes were situated on a lower level of the ridge so that their flat rooftops were level with the road. An empty baby's walker sat stranded in a puddle of brown water on a fenced-in roof. A yellow terrier was tied to some rebar protruding from an unfinished floor on another. Clotheslines hung from something at every house. If there wasn't cement on the ground, there was dirt as pale as sand.

But then I saw a little valley that swept down one side of the road and afforded a view of a nearby hillside terraced with vines and wide-spreading figs. Phone lines sagged from a leaning concrete pole. A wrinkled woman in a navy shawl stooped over a wood-fired oven on her patio. She removed a massive disc of pita to a metal platter that sat atop an overturned green plastic crate.

Fadi slowed as we neared a dead end and pulled into their crumbling driveway. The Azzams' stone house was covered with crude patchwork from what appeared to be generations of homemade repairs. A huge gnarled gum tree, planted behind the house, shrouded most of its roofline; I caught a whiff of its antiseptic scent as we followed Fadi through an opening in the garden wall at the far side of the house.

Mature fig trees had made a primordial bower of the courtyard, vines curling through bricks and over the wooden loggia. He cautioned me around a loose stepping stone, then continued toward the back of the house, past a young potted apricot tree on the patio. He stopped at the edge where the Azzams' modest orchard spread out behind the house, down a gentle slope of terraces. The sun was setting in tones of orange, casting a warm glow across the leaves. Beyond them was a thick forest of pines that disappeared down a gorge into the wilderness. This was the very spot where we'd first gotten acquainted almost a year ago.

"Leila, Leila!" An excited voice came from the direction of the house and a door slammed. We turned to see a little boy, whom I presumed was Qasim, Leila's six-year-old brother, running towards us carrying a blue ball of fluff with both hands. His wide grin revealed two missing front teeth.

Leila stooped down for a cuddle. I felt a familiar pang in my heart – my own brother was that age last I saw him before he died. Qasim held out a baby chick whose downy coat had been inexplicably dyed blue.

"Qasim, you remember me telling you about Fereby," Leila said, repeating it in Arabic.

The black-haired boy held the anxious chick up to his cheek, hiding his eyes behind its tiny body. He peeked out for a moment and said, "Hello," then covered his eyes again with blue down.

"Hi, Qasim. *Key fak*? What's your friend's name?" I asked.

"Bamba!" he answered. We all laughed. Bamba was my favorite Israeli snack food, a kind of peanut butter puff. I pulled my stash from my daypack.

"Does Bamba eat Bamba?" I held the opened bag out to him.

Qasim eyed it with a wicked smile.

"Would you like to feed him some?"

Leila translated.

"Thank you," he said.

We watched the chick peck at the puff in Qasim's hand while Qasim yelped each time the chick missed and got his palm.

"I need to get inside and help with dinner," Leila said, suddenly anxious.

"May I help?" I asked.

"My mother won't let you."

Qasim left the chick in a little basket outside and we followed her in. The room we entered first was a simple, small dining room with a large table set with bowls of colorful salads, creamy dips, stuffed grape leaves, olives and crumbled feta. Mismatched wooden chairs surrounded it like members of a multigenerational family. Leila rushed to set the table as her mother, Dima, came out of the kitchen in a long navy dress and flip-flops, sputtering orders to her flock in Arabic.

She was a dark, billowy woman, with eyes that drooped into brown weathered bags over high cheekbones. Black wavy hair stuck to her forehead like rickrack sewing trim. Her *foutta* hung around her neck and she fussed with it, uncertain how much to cover.

She scolded Leila in their language until Leila interrupted to introduce her to me. Then Dima held my hands, looking back at me every few seconds as they discussed my plight. Her long nose pointed down to a small thin-lipped mouth, which she held as if she could barely contain her disapproval.

"She's very sorry for your terrible experience today," Leila said. "She wants you to sit down."

"I'd rather join you all in the kitchen," I said.

I was allowed to see what was being prepared and meet Leila's older sister, Iman, who was chopping more parsley than I'd ever seen one recipe require. "Druze girls are always making *tabouli*," Leila explained. With long black hair and light skin like Leila, Iman was almost as beautiful as her sister, if it weren't for her lazy eye. Leila had told me Iman had left school early and never learned fluent Hebrew, let alone English.

As the two girls bickered under their breath, Dima opened the oven to show me what was baking – lamb and potatoes in a thick tomato sauce. An aroma so earthy and complete infused the air that tears filled my eyes.

"Potatoes Soniya," Leila announced, pouring mint lemonade into several glasses.

Dima saw my emotion and put a fleshy arm around me.

"I'm sorry," I said. "I'm so…"

I sighed and willed a veneer of composure, but Dima ordered me to go rest, so I followed Leila with the drinks into the dining room.

A large, winsome man with straight cropped grey hair and Leila's sultry eyes emerged from a back room.

"Missus Jones," he said, smiling broadly. "An honor to meet you. Kamil, Leila's father."

I reached out to shake hands, but he placed his hand over his heart.

"Forgive me, my religion prevents me," he said, turning so I could see the Druze skullcap on the back of his head.

"I'm so sorry," I said, withdrawing my hand, embarrassed at my lapse. Religious Druze wouldn't touch people of the opposite sex they weren't related to.

"Don't worry," he said, smiling. He barked at Leila, who handed me a glass and ran into the kitchen at her father's command.

"We heard about the terrible event," Kamil said, shaking his head. *"Ma sha'allah.* You are flying home this evening?"

I nodded and tried to push the thought of it out of my mind. He motioned me into the living room where Fadi and Qasim were playing cards on a brick and navy patterned divan on the floor. Qasim invited me to join them, but Kamil vetoed it with a wave of his hand. He gestured for me to sit down across from them on a well-worn blue velvet sofa. He spoke to Fadi for a full ten minutes in the curious blend of Arabic and Hebrew the Israeli Druze speak. I sipped lemonade, wondering why they couldn't speak in English since it was our one common language. (Leila had told me Kamil learned English from his father who grew up during the British Mandate of Israel.) But I was more than content to watch Fadi and his muscular, graceful hands moving the cards around.

Suddenly, the escalating blare of a siren outside turned our heads. Fadi went to the window and exclaimed in Arabic. He and Kamil rushed for the door.

"There is an emergency at our cousin's house," he told me.

Kamil called out to the women in the kitchen. They came out, startled, wiping hands on aprons.

An ambulance was in the road outside in front of a modest, one-story concrete home with a white porch swing. I hung back in the yard with Iman and Qasim as the others crossed to check on their relatives. Neighbors came outside with concerned expressions. I had no idea what was happening, but I'd had one too many emergencies for one day. I sat on the stoop and closed my weary eyes.

Within minutes, the paramedics brought a large, young woman out on a gurney, loaded her into the ambulance and sped off. The Azzams spoke to some elders at the house for a few minutes before returning.

"Our cousin's wife has gone to the hospital to have her baby," Fadi explained, walking up to me.

In a recent e-mail, Leila had mentioned that Ru'yah, wife of her first cousin, whom she was very close to, was expecting soon. "Ru'yah?"

He nodded. "Everyone is scared because the baby is one month early, but it's a full moon tonight. That can happen."

Leila's face was filled with worry as she crossed the road.

"Do you think they're going to be okay?" I asked when she approached.

"Yes," she said, not so convincingly.

It was about six-thirty when Leila called us to dinner. Much of the evening's conversation was passed in their dialect. I still couldn't hear everything anyway, so I kept to myself as I ate the delicious food, complimenting Dima as expected when I tasted something new. I noticed I was trying to read lips to compensate for my muffled hearing and lack of language comprehension. Fadi often met my gaze when he spoke to his family, as if I might actually come to understand some Arabic before the night was over. Occasionally I inserted myself into the conversation at inappropriate moments, completely off-topic or a little too loud, like a hard-of-hearing granny. Leila attempted to ease my clumsiness by explaining what they were talking about. I tried to listen for words I knew in Arabic. I heard the children frequently address Dima as *Omm*, "mother," which made me think about the Sanskrit syllable I often chanted in yoga class. My teacher told me *Om* is the sound the universe makes when it's happy with itself. It's what creates and sustains life, like a mother. In India, I'd seen newborns ritually bathed and the sacred syllable *Om* written on their tongues with honey.

My mind wandered to my impending flight. I felt a surge of panic. How was I going to get *inside* an airplane and fly over the ocean for many hours when a mere city bus ride was out of the question? A public transportation phobia could be disastrous for me: Not only was traveling integral to my livelihood, but some of my best writing was done on a moving train, plane or bus.

Out of the blue, Dima raised her voice and pulled herself up from her chair. She pointed at Leila's white collar. Everyone leaned in to examine it and Leila strained to see it, too. Fadi glanced over at me.

"What is it?" I asked.

"It looks like blood," Kamil said.

"It isn't blood, *Ab*," Leila said. "It's paint, from school. I was working with red paint this morning." She held out her fingers for inspection, but they had purple paint stains. "And other colors."

Dima clenched her jaw and pulled Iman into the kitchen.

The conversation drifted back into sounds that meant nothing to me and I coached myself about the virtue of patience. Iman emerged with bowls of red and yellow cherries and slices of watermelon and juicy white cantaloupe. Then Dima carried out a tray of coffee service and some ring-shaped cookies she said were filled with dates. Qasim brought a special plate of fruit over to me and whispered to Fadi.

"Qasim wants to know if you can come to Leila's wedding," Fadi said.

I looked at him in surprise, then caught myself and glanced at Leila, but she had lifted her glass to drink so I couldn't make eye contact. She hadn't mentioned this little detail.

"When is that again?" I asked as casually as I could.

"Two weeks," Kamil said. "We would be honored to have you as our guest."

"I wish I could, but I'll be working in Latin America then."

When my response was translated for Qasim, he stuck out his lower lip and looked down at his plate.

Fadi passed a coffee to me. "What a shame," he said, holding eye contact with me long enough to mean something but I wasn't sure what. My stomach flip-flopped.

Leila wouldn't meet my gaze.

After dessert, Qasim yawned and climbed into his mother's ample lap. I watched them snuggle and whisper confidences. She looked relaxed for the first time all evening. Soon Qasim came over to say goodbye to me, his little pinkish-brown mouth turned into a pout. I shook his hand and told him when he got older, he could come visit me in America. His eyes lit up and he regarded his parents excitedly.

"What a nice invitation, Qasim," Kamil said.

"Thank you for a beautiful meal I will never forget," I said to all of them.

Dima handed me a bulging plastic grocery bag and asked Leila to explain its contents.

"In case she isn't back from putting Qasim to bed before you leave, she wants to give you some things to take home…some *za'atar*, an herb we use…some hummus and pita sandwiches for the airplane…some pretzels rolled in sesame seeds…and a *foutta*."

Leila put the white head scarf on me and everyone exclaimed. I wondered if I looked ridiculous, my long, light brown, curly hair bulging through the thin fabric, refusing to be tamed. I winced and looked at Fadi to gauge his reaction. He held my gaze, folding his arms across his chest in assessment and nodded at me with appreciation. That was rousing enough that, when I next suggested taking pictures of the family, I almost dropped my camera because my hands were shaking. I let Qasim take a few of Leila and me, too.

"*Nawwart il-beyt*," Dima said to me afterwards.

" 'You've brought light to this house,' " Fadi translated. "It's what we say to *special* visitors." He smiled.

"*Shukran*," I said. Thank you. "How do I respond?"

"*Kifaya nurak* – your light is sufficient," Leila chimed in.

I repeated the phrase, making them laugh and clap at my poor intonation. Dima and Qasim said goodnight to me and disappeared into the back of the house.

We lingered at the table over coffee. Iman pointed to my untouched cup, my apparent faux pas, when the back door flew open.

A wild-eyed young man entered, pointed at Leila and spat bullets of Arabic so fast he tripped over his words.

"*Ayb!*" Iman gasped, clapping her hands over her mouth.

Fadi and Kamil jumped up and implored him to stop, indicating my presence at the table. He glanced over at me and his expression turned to alarm. Leila remained still as a stone. Did this have something to do with the bombing?

"Please forgive us, Fereby," Kamil said. "Tamir didn't know you were here."

I felt slightly relieved they knew this guy, but Tamir was shaking with rage. Of medium, muscular build, he wore his clothes more fitted than other Druze men I'd seen, with capped sleeves to show off his toned biceps. He could hurt somebody if he wanted.

"I need to get to the airport anyway," I said, unwinding the *foutta.* "I'll call a taxi outside."

"No, I'm driving you," said Fadi, patting his pocket for his keys.

Leila stood up, her face ashen, and came around the far side of the table to me, away from Tamir. She paused at my side, taking hold of my hand. "I'm going, too," she whispered, eyes lowered.

As I started for the door with her, Kamil grasped Leila's arm, scolding her.

"I have to stay," she said, her mouth barely moving when she spoke. It seemed she wanted me to protest this, but I couldn't disregard her father's authority.

"It's okay," I said, not sure at whom I should look. "Thank you so much for all that you've done for me today." I hugged her stiff, trembling body and felt her face contort against my shoulder. She held on after I let go. I felt many eyes on me pushing me out the door. "I'll be in touch when I get home." She slowly released me and I squeezed her hands in mine. She nodded in slow motion, eyes still lowered, not letting go.

Tamir was pacing by the window, hyperventilating and running his fingers through his sun-streaked hair. I said an awkward goodbye to Iman and Kamil, who separated Leila from me, and then I followed a grave Fadi out the door.

3

Fadi drove faster than before, staring straight ahead. As we descended Mount Carmel, the clouds moved off the full moon, which lit up the port of Haifa in shades of grey. I was so tense, when my ears popped, adrenaline surged as if it was life threatening. My flight was in five hours and it was an hour or two trip to get to the airport, depending on traffic.

I turned to Fadi. "Who was that guy?"

Fadi wiped his upper lip on his shoulder and straightened his arms on the steering wheel. Before dinner he had changed out of his uniform into jeans and a white button-down shirt, sleeves rolled to the elbow.

"Tamir. My sister's husband."

"Iman's married?"

"No," he said, checking the side mirror by me. "Leila's husband."

I stared at him, confused. "You mean her fiancé?"

"Druze are considered married upon signing the contract, but don't live together until after the wedding party."

I stared at the oncoming car lights whizzing by on the freeway. That icky feeling was resurfacing in my gut.

"He was sure mad about something," I said, looking at Fadi.

Fadi changed lanes to pass a truck. Adjusted the rearview mirror. Checked his cell phone.

We rode in silence for a mile.

"What does *ayb* mean?" I asked.

"*Ayb?*" he said, in a better accent.

"Iman said that after Tamir came in."

Fadi squinted at the dials on the dash and fiddled with something there. "It means 'shameful'."

"What was shameful?" I prodded.

He accelerated as if the one thing that mattered in this world was getting me to the airport. I felt my insides hardening again. The only thing worse than going somewhere you don't want to go is doing so in a huge hurry.

"Fadi, we're not going to be late."

He kept his eyes on the road.

I thought about flying again. Three hours of security hell. Boarding the plane. Heart palpitations. Buckling up. Hundreds of people coming in, surrounding me. The doors closing, locking. Engine noise. Not enough air. Used air. Dirty air.

I tried to breathe deeply to calm down. Fadi glanced over at me just before I felt the blood rush out of my head. I tried to put my head between my knees, but the seat belt caught me with a jerk.

"What's wrong?" He touched my arm, then instantly withdrew it.

"I…feel…really…sick," I moaned, holding on to the dashboard.

"Are you going to…?"

"I dunno…"

He pulled over on the shoulder and hopped out so fast his seat belt hit the window glass with a loud pop that made me jump. He opened my door and reached across my lap to release my seat belt. Gently, he took my hands and pulled me out of the car.

The fresh night air felt disagreeably erotic on my flushed face. I squatted at the edge of the asphalt and hung my head. I felt him a few feet behind me.

I hated to say it, but I had to: "I can't fly." I glanced up as he knelt in front of me. He watched me intensely, blinking his thick lashes when passing headlights flashed across his face.

"I'm so sorry, Fadi," I said. "Is there any way you could take me back to a hotel near your house? I'll postpone my flight."

"There are no hotels in Atabi or any of the Druze villages," he said. Traffic hurtled by in loud *whooshes*. "You will stay with us."

"No, no. I've already imposed enough – "

"Not possible – "

I steadied myself with my hands on the road and looked at him directly. "I'm not going back there tonight, Fadi."

He gazed out beyond me for a long moment, glancing left and right. "There's a Carmelite nunnery a few miles from the National Park that may still run a hospice."

"A hospice?" I imagined the yellow smell of the dying.

"They rent simple rooms in a separate hotel area. It's pretty late for nuns, but we can try."

The hospice-hotel was located in a forest clearing and resembled a small private school campus. A very short nun with enormous jowls made more so by her tight wimple met us at the door, looking back and forth at us in contempt, as though we were lovers looking for a room by the hour. My face heated at the notion. Fadi spoke to her politely as she scrutinized me; he must have told her about the bombing to gain her sympathy. I paid for a single dorm room for one night. Fadi said he and Leila would check on me in the morning. I thanked him with an awkward handshake (he was not religious yet – many Druze became religious in middle age) under the reproving eye of the grouchy sister, who jingled her keys until Fadi was out the door. She slammed it behind him and locked it up tight.

My room was as small as a Castilian prison cell, but had its own bathroom and bathtub. A large, bloody crucifix and framed Arabic prayers, yellowed and slipping from their mats, were displayed over the bed. I dropped my pack and collapsed on the pillow with a screech of bed spring. The bed sagged pitifully, making me suddenly so homesick. I lived very simply in an upscale trailer park in Laguna Beach, California – the last bastion of hippies and artists in town – and I was home barely half the time, but it was still more comfortable than this. Leila was right about one thing: Being alone after the day I'd had absolutely sucked.

I reached in my daypack for my phone and saw Leila's phone, too. I'd forgotten to give it back to her, not that I'd even had a chance. I'd have to find a way tomorrow. I called El Al and rescheduled my flight for the next day, not feeling at all confident I'd be up for it then either.

I fell asleep sometime after three, but awoke at the slightest suggestion of sunrise. I put on my running clothes and tucked my hair into a baseball cap, slipping Leila's cell phone into my pocket with my own. I headed for the main road and ran towards Atabi. It felt good to sweat, to immerse myself in physical exertion. A few stretches of the road had sidewalks, but mostly I ran through the dust at the edge of the pavement.

The bombing replayed itself in my head, including some fresh details about trying to get out of the bus: An elderly man praying aloud in Hebrew, hands on his forehead, tears wetting his face. The woman who pulled my hair had blood dripping from one elbow. The bus driver frozen by the trauma, white knuckles still on the steering wheel. Leila moving like a cat through the chaos. I stopped running to record these memories on my smart phone so I wouldn't forget anything. That's when I realized I was writing a story about the bombing. Evidently, I wasn't done with *The New York Times* yet. More doubts about Leila crept into my mind.

By the time I got to Daliat-al Carmel, the largest Druze village on Mt. Carmel, it was light enough to see the obstacle course of holes, pipes, shredded tires, barbed wire, puddles and scrap lumber on the shoulder. No one else was jogging or even so much as riding a bicycle. Vehicles slowed as they passed. I felt self-conscious, but continued to the village of Isfiyeh to Atabi's turn-off. A few minutes later, two police cars sped past me towards Atabi, their lights casting otherworldly patterns on the forest that hugged the road, sirens screeching through the morning's serenity.

Atabi was starting to stir. Several cars honked as I approached the square, drivers flashing peace signs with their fingers to each other, which seemed nice but odd. Two old bearded Druze men greeted one another in front of the café, grasping right hands, raising them up to their faces and kissing the backs of each other's hand.

Of all things, a traffic jam spilled out from the Azzams' little dead-end dirt road. Dozens of spirited pedestrians clapped and cheered as they walked in the direction of the Azzams' house, as though celebrating something. The birth of Ru'yah's baby? The bombing? I slowed to a walk and followed the crowd. Close to the end, lights flashed from several police cars. My heart fluttered. Whatever was happening, it was taking place right in front of the Azzams' house.

I hurried up to the mob. A dozen men stood in a circle in the road. They seemed to be trying to organize the holding up of a continuous chain of blankets, but I couldn't tell if they were trying to keep something inside or outside their barrier. Some women stood on porches, holding up their fingers in the peace sign. Was it some kind of Druze holiday ceremony?

I craned my neck, but still couldn't see. A short man standing next to me scowled.

"What is this?" I asked in my limited Arabic.

He frowned up at me. "*Jarimat sharaf.*" He walked away, shaking his head.

I had no idea what that meant. Frustrated, I looked around for the Azzams, but couldn't spot them. I walked closer toward the circle of blankets and caught a glimpse of what was inside. My breath caught in my throat. A woman lay in the road. The dirt around her head was wet and dark. Her bloodied face was turned up, eyes open, but not seeing. It was Leila.

4

The realization hit me like fire engulfing my body.

"Leila!" I screamed. "Leila! Noooo!"

I tried to shove past the men to reach for her but they held firm and blocked me. The blanket barrier hit me about hip-level and when I attempted to push through it, I fell forward into the road, ripping the blanket out of the men's hands. There was shouting and then I felt my shoulders being seized with sudden precision and my body lifted up and away by at least two people.

"Stop!" I cried, my arms flailing. "Leila!"

My mind was moving at light-speed, but under the horror, I was useless. Outside the barrier, forceful hands put me up on my feet, but my legs collapsed and I fell again. From the ground, I was afforded another view of Leila between the legs of a man who had dropped his blanket. There was a puzzling line across her face. Then, I realized what it was: Her headwound had bled diagonally across her forehead, down the inside corner of one eye and over her cheekbone before spilling on the ground. The trail of blood on her skin was dry and dark now.

Someone threw a dirty quilt over Leila, wafting dust into the air. The only part of her left exposed was an arm. The sleeve of her black dress had fallen back to bare her delicate, bloody forearm, bent up at the elbow.

Someone caught me in the armpits and pulled me up. Every face was turned on me now, shouting in a clamor of Arabic. The crowd was heading into a frenzy. Terrified, I struggled and tripped as I was dragged backwards, away from the circle around Leila. Dust rose from the road, stinging my eyes.

A moment later, the hands tucked me into the back of a car and slammed the door shut. I felt a moment of relief until my panicked brain looped nonsense over the intolerable sight I'd just witnessed. *Leila!* People were staring in at me, shaking their fingers as if I'd done something awful. What was going on?

Suddenly a door opened and a cop got behind the wheel. I was in a police cruiser.

"What happened to her?" I cried.

He adjusted the volume down on his police radio, but didn't answer.

"*Bi tit kalimi ingleezi?*" I stammered. Do you speak English?

He glanced at me with disinterest. "Who are you?"

"Fereby – Fereby McCullough Jones," I stammered. "Friend of Leila's. What's going on?"

He picked up a clipboard from the front seat. "We wait for remove the body." His accent was heavy.

"What happened to her?" My voice broke and I noticed I was crying and it hadn't just begun.

The cop flipped through his paperwork. "We investigate."

"Why are they cheering?"

He shook his head. "Leila make trouble for her family," he said flatly.

"*What?*" Had she gotten involved with terrorists?

A loud rap on the window to my left jolted me. A brown-skinned woman wearing a tightly wound muslin *foutta* held a chubby infant. The cop rolled down the windows and she stuck her head in. I moved to the other side of the backseat.

"*Ayb!* Why you cry for her? She *shameless!*" the woman yelled at me, shaking her finger.

"Could you please roll the windows back up?" I asked the cop urgently.

The woman slapped her palm on the door. "God's will! *Ma sha'allah!* God's will!"

I turned my back to her, but there was a man on the right side shouting at me in Hebrew. I scooted to the middle, starting to panic.

"Please roll up the windows!" I shouted, as more began to crowd around the vehicle, raising their voices. My face blazed.

He hit a few buttons and up they went. "Visiting Israel?" he asked nonchalantly, as if this kind of thing happened every day.

"Yes."

"American?"

"Yeah. Can you get me out of here, please?"

"Where are you stay?"

"The Carmel Hospice."

He got out of the cruiser without another word, locked the doors and disappeared into the crowd. I clutched my shaking hands in my lap and rested my head on them as people yelled unintelligible indignities at me. I'm the only one here who's grieving, I thought. How could that be? What did Leila do? Did they know about her boyfriend?

Finally, some minutes later, I heard the door next to me opening and I jumped. The cop shoved a plastic crate that appeared to carry police supplies next to me in the backseat, then picked up something off the ground and tossed it on top before getting into the driver's seat. I glanced beside me and, to my horror, he'd thrown a *bloody* rag – obviously from the crime scene – in right next to me. *Leila's blood.* I stared at it in disbelief.

He turned the engine on and drove through the crowd, blasting the siren. I felt like screaming and kicking the back of his seat or clobbering him, but instead I cried as silently as I could, watching the circle of men around Leila until they fell from view.

My last vision of beautiful Leila was her blood-washed hand, facing up, as if she were waving goodbye.

The officer, who said his name was Detective Metanis, dropped me off at the hospice hotel, speaking with the grouchy nun, who eyeballed me suspiciously for my spate of bad luck. The hallway to my room was surreal with chatty tourists. The cafeteria comfort food smelled sacrilegious.

I climbed onto my bed and lay face down on the pillow. My breath was shallow and quick, as if I was prepared for action on short notice. Every muscle in my body felt tense and depleted. I kicked off my shoes and crawled under the scratchy sheets, curling my knees up to my chest. Anger was an emotion I infrequently allowed myself; I could rationalize away most every situation that called for it. A familiar, awful fear was working its way to the surface and I knew why: Grief was the most dangerous condition – you let your guard down and terrible things happen. And what I feared most, I needed equally – someone safe to hold me.

I thought about Werner and buried my face in the covers. This wasn't the first time my career had interfered with a relationship. I didn't miss *him* per se, or any of the other stunted and irregular connections I'd had with men. It was much bigger than that. An ache began in my chest and pushed its way into my skull. *I have nobody.*

I rolled over to blow my nose and felt Leila's phone in my pocket. I pulled it out and turned it on. What was Tamir so mad about last night? What happened after I left? Why did that woman at the crime scene say Leila was shameless? The phone beeped with new messages. Were they from Leila's American boyfriend? He probably didn't even know she was dead yet. I started to look for his number in the contact list, but the phone was programmed in Hebrew. I stuck her phone in my backpack.

Loneliness surrounded me. I dialed Werner, but his voicemail picked up. I left a brief message, trying not to give away my despair.

I tried to force myself to sleep, but I couldn't shake the intolerable image of Leila's face, her bloody hand, her *dead* body in the dust. And the painting she had shown me yesterday, just before the bombing. When I'd walked into the gallery, it was the first thing I'd noticed: A nude woman with impossibly long hair, lying dead in the road, her violet eyes open, staring out like the forsaken. A small child crouched beside her, clutching his voluptuous mother, suckling her breast. In one hand, she held half a glistening pomegranate, which stained her pale skin like blood.

I sat bolt upright in bed, my mind racing back over what happened. Leila had propped open the door of the dark gallery, letting sunlight pour in over the painting, which was laid out on three panels – a triptych. An iridescent out-sized scimitar moon, like a slice of pale cantaloupe, and a single star illuminated the dark sky behind the mother and child. She said it was Asherah, one of the original Mother Goddesses worshipped across the Near East in ancient times, and she'd been murdered. She tapped the crescent in the sky. "The moon is feminine consciousness – she is both our inner child *and* our inner mother – how we protect ourselves and make ourselves feel secure and comforted." Leila's finger slid down the canvas to the beautiful, dead Asherah. "Middle Eastern women have become disconnected from their ancient Mother, thus sacrificing the deep nurturance of themselves and their children."

Here she is, I had marveled: A Druze woman, painting pagan *pietà*. And selling it in a public gallery.

"They never could get rid of Asherah," she said with a smile, closing the gallery door again. "The Jews and Christians had considered her a rival, but many Jews adored her, especially the poor farmers. She found her way into Jewish ritual in the form of angels. Few people know this anymore, but angels represent our intuition. And you may sometimes hear Arabs say '*Niswan naksat 'aqel wedin*' – women lack intelligence and piousness. Arabs believe God and the angels are men because they are unaware of the history."

With my promise the pictures would remain in my confidential possession, Leila let me photograph her in front of her painting of Asherah with child, which she called "Death of the Future."

I felt nauseous. I turned on the light in my room and pulled my camera out of my backpack. I scrolled until I found the picture of her in front of the triptych. I stared, sick and incredulous: So self-possessed. Generous. Fiercely intelligent. She was gone. Dead. I prayed she wasn't involved in anything criminal. I laid my head on the pillow and closed my eyes. So much didn't add up.

Sometime later, I awoke startled to a noise in the hall that seemed at first to emerge from the recesses of a dream. I thought about calling my parents and saw that it was about eleven p.m. in Riverside, California. They'd still be up. They wouldn't take the news well, though.

My parents were both scared to death of losing me in some freak accident abroad. They'd been full-time missionaries, taking my brother, Cary, and me around the world to convert "unevangelized peoples," until Cary's death in India. We were living outside Delhi, visiting some friends in Jaipur at a hotel that had once been a maharajah's palace. I was twelve, Cary was six. The two of us were exploring the lush gardens of the hotel when a Doberman came out of nowhere, knocked Cary down and crushed his throat with its jaws. I screamed and threw rocks at the dog, which did nothing but cause a gardener in a fuchsia sari to stop her weeding and stand up. Some guests looked over, but made no effort to help. The police said the mauling couldn't have been prevented because of the epidemic number of stray dogs in India that could not be euthanized legally.

Then, a few weeks later, while Mom and Dad were immobilized by grief and Indian bureaucracy, Pat, an eighteen-year-old American boy I idolized who led the local missionary youth group, seduced me in my vulnerable state. It was impossible for me to hide it from my parents; the twin losses ended my parents' missionary work and nearly broke up their marriage. Dad gave up his faith and Mom melted into a fundamentalist group, occupying her time volunteering at an orphanage down in Baja. Ironically, I pretty much raised myself from then on, feeling like an orphan.

I wasn't allowed to go abroad again until I did it in college without permission. I became tolerant of other ways of life to a fault. In order for me to survive, there couldn't be anyone to blame for what had happened to Cary or the injustice of it would have killed me. All cultures are relative, I decided. Their dangerous artifacts are like natural disasters: The devastation is nobody's fault. Relatives of murder victims who sought redemption by forgiving the killers became my benchmark for absolution. I blamed mostly myself for Pat's seduction.

I dialed ambivalently, as always. When Mom answered, I told her about Leila and my discovery of the crime scene. I didn't mention the bombing.

"You barely knew this girl," she said. What she meant was I had no right to be sad about anyone dying but Cary. Her callousness still shocked me even after all these years.

I mumbled something about how special Leila was. She changed the subject to a mission she was planning in Baja to help kids born with club feet, as though my crisis were nothing more than another story I was covering.

After we hung up, I felt a sort of relief, but not the kind I'd been looking for. A mute sorrow settled in my chest. I turned on the shower and let the water drench my sweat-dried hair. I stood soaking in the stream trying not to think about Leila and her bloody hand, but all I could replace it with was the panic and bleeding people after the bombing.

As I lathered my hair, a sharp pain glanced from my scalp. I felt around until I located a tender place on the top of my head. What's that? I wondered. When I rinsed out the shampoo, I watched a small scab swirl around and go down the drain. I got out of the shower and tried to locate the wound in the mirror. I pulled a few hairs at a time away from the raw place on my scalp. Fresh blood came off on my fingertips. *The spot of blood on Leila's collar.* I held up a mirrored compact so I could see the cut in the bathroom's wall mirror. It was about half an inch long. I sat down on the toilet and pressed a washcloth to my head. It was official: I'd been injured in a terrorist attack. I was a statistic.

5

I wrote out my rough, personal account of the bombing and rescue and read it through. With the question of Leila's involvement still up in the air, it was clearly incomplete. I did shiatsu on my forehead where it was starting to throb. I was supposed to leave Israel tonight, but I felt Leila pulling me back to the crime scene. I closed my laptop.

A little after ten a.m., as I was leaving the hospice-hotel, I noticed a stack of *Jerusalem Posts* in the lobby. A familiar face in the lead photo stopped me as if I'd crashed into a wall. I grabbed a paper and gaped at the image: The girl with pale eyes. The Palestinian teenage girl I'd bumped into getting off the bus yesterday! She had to be dead now. The caption said her name was Hanan Barghouti. Sixteen years old, from Gaza. She was the bomber.

A chill swept down my body and my legs went weak. I eased myself into a nearby chair. The grouchy nun barked at me in Arabic to pay her for the paper, so I dug out some *shekels*. Eighteen dead, twelve injured I read. I scrutinized Hanan's face. Delicate bones, polite, humble eyes. Acid gathered in my stomach. How could I have looked her in the eye – *made physical contact with her* – and not known on some level what she was about to do? Had my years of studying human beings around the world not provided me any instinct for such things? Journalists never think it will happen to them. And worse: I facilitated the carnage by giving her back the bus fare I'd knocked out of her hand.

I called a taxi to take me into Atabi and had the driver drop me at the beginning of Leila's street so I could walk in less conspicuously. Everyone was gone now. The crowd, the police, Leila. The Azzams' brown station wagon was parked in the driveway. I noted a pang of disappointment when I saw Fadi's car wasn't there. A man was hosing down the dirt road in front. I stopped behind a parked car several houses away to watch him. He pulled the hose up to the Azzams' yard and carried it through the opening in the wall to their courtyard below the fig bower. I strained to see what he was doing until I realized another man across the street had come out on his porch to eat seeds out of a whole, dried head of a sunflower and was eyeing me. I pretended to talk on my phone, trying to look unconcerned with the Azzams' house. I glanced back and saw the first man hosing off the stepping-stones that led out from the courtyard. Pink water ran down the crumbly driveway into a muddy puddle. I quickly snapped a picture with my phone, knowing I was too far away for it to be much good. The man with the sunflower was staring at me now. And he knew I'd noticed. The other turned the water off and went in the house with the white porch swing where Ru'yah, Leila's cousin, lived. Was it Ru'yah's husband? Then I remembered Ru'yah and the baby and wondered if they were okay.

I desperately wanted to talk to the Azzams. I put my phone back in my pocket and steeled myself as I walked past the part of the road where Leila's body had lain. I went up to the Azzams' house, getting a shot of unwelcome nerves before I reached up to knock on the front door. No answer. I couldn't find a doorbell. I knocked again, louder. A woman in a *foutta* came out on her porch next door and pretended to sweep, scowling at me.

Suddenly, the man with the sunflower was at the bottom of the Azzams' front steps ranting at me in Hebrew. He pointed to my pocket where I'd put my phone. I asked if he knew English or French, the two languages I could speak that were most likely to be spoken here, but he shook his head. There are few things more frustrating to me than knowing several languages but being unable to communicate in a foreign land. I was glad when he gave up and took off in the direction of his house.

I walked to the entrance of the Azzams' courtyard and peeked inside. The patio and stepping-stones were freshly washed. The top half of the trunk of the baby apricot tree was bent perpendicular. I snapped another picture.

"Hello," I heard a voice say behind my back. I swung around. A skinny teenage boy stood before me, his hands tucked into his jean pockets. "The Azzams are not accepting visitors yet," he said kindly.

"Oh, I see. Th-thank you."

He stood his ground, waiting for me to leave. I began walking back the way I'd come. He got into a car, but didn't start the engine.

An old couple in long, dark robes strolled down the dusty road and went up the steps to Ru'yah's house. The man I'd seen with the hose answered the door and welcomed them in. The couple must have been paying their respects for the safe arrival of the baby...or so I hoped.

Leila had told me Ru'yah had recently graduated from a women's college to become an English teacher. She was probably either still at the hospital or in bed, but maybe there was someone else at her home who knew English, too. I crossed the road, the teenager's eyes on me the whole time, and knocked on the door. A woman about my mother's age answered, tucking some hair under her headscarf. I quickly ascertained we had no language in common. The man I'd seen outside with the hose sat on the couch talking with the old couple. I thanked the woman and turned to leave. *I'm like a helpless infant here.*

On the many extended missionary trips I took with my parents as a child, I picked up language quickly to make friends. I learned bits of Romani from the Balkan gypsies, some Kammuang from the Muang, and a few colorful phrases in Chechen. I became fluent in Spanish in Uruguay, in French in the Congo. Unlike many academic subjects, language came easily to me; its nuances thrilled me like mystical revelation. To know another's tongue is to know the secret code to the collective unconscious of their people. I tasted every word in my mouth as I said it for the first time. I rarely forgot one.

At university, I took languages as electives, but double-majored in geography and English (ironically), minoring in religion. I took a fellowship in Spain where I developed a working knowledge of Basque, a language isolate that may date back to the Stone Age. After a year in Bali (not missionizing, much to my mom's chagrin – her efforts at indoctrinating me never did take. This was one paradise that's never been "saved" that I desperately wanted to see for that reason), I pulled off a respectable grasp of Balinese and Bahasa Indonesian. Unfortunately, I was never exposed to Hebrew or Arabic since my parents' missionary work wasn't welcomed where those languages were spoken.

In the months following 9/11, I got a recruitment call from the newly formed Homeland Security. Desperate for linguists, they offered to put me through accelerated Arabic, Dari or Pashtu training, which I declined. Now I was imagining if I'd taken advantage of that...but then again, I'd be interrogating prisoners at Gitmo right now. Or worse: Translating intercepted wiretaps from a cubicle in some God-forsaken place.

I walked back to the square in frustration to get directions to the police station. Maybe the police had found witnesses to Leila's death or spoken to the Azzams. I went into a café; a table of religious men turned and glared at me. Suddenly, the holes worn in the knees of my faded blue jeans seemed resplendently slutty, my unfettered, long, curly hair an open invitation for sex. I got directions from a waiter and left.

"Miss Jones," said Detective Metanis, after the receptionist had kept me waiting for twenty minutes to see him. He reached out his hand and I shook it, but then he continued to hold my hand and clasped his other one over it. "You feel better," he said.

I nodded vaguely, wondering if that was a question or a statement. And did he mean I felt better *to him*, touching me like that? Was that intimate handshake a custom I was unaware of? Maybe he was trying to show how sorry he was for how he treated me earlier. Or was being disrespectful in the guise of politeness.

He finally let go of my hand and motioned me to sit by his desk. Several other cops in the office eyed me.

"Do you know what happened to Leila?" I asked.

"No, sorry." He opened his desk drawer and rummaged around. "It was probably an accident, Miss Jones."

"I was at the Azzams' home last night for dinner," I said. "A little before eight o'clock, Leila's fiancé – or, husband – Tamir, arrived and he was furious with her."

Metanis exchanged glances with the cop sitting at the adjacent desk.

"I left because it seemed like a family crisis," I went on. "Her brother, Fadi, drove me to a hotel."

Metanis met my eyes and his brows went up.

"He dropped me off," I added, in case he inferred something else.

He shot me a phony smile. "Anything more?"

"Well, yeah," I said. "Were there any witnesses? Have you spoken to the Azzams yet?"

He stood and motioned for the door. "I not authorized to talk of open investigation with the public. So sorry."

"Oh," I said, confused. *That's it?* "I'm glad to answer any questions you have."

Metanis opened the door for me. "We contact you if we need."

I was reluctant to say anything about the bombing if he was being this evasive. I stood up. "You know, Leila was my friend."

He stood in the threshold with a puzzled look on his face. "How you became friends with her?"

I hesitated, then walked through the doorway. "I met her when I was working in Israel last year."

"Why you are here now?"

"For work...I met Leila in Jaffa yesterday and she brought me home for dinner."

"*Jaffa?*"

I nodded.

"She was there with her family?"

"Nnn...no." Just as I said it, I realized I shouldn't have.

He stifled a grin and muttered something to the other cop.

"Look," I said. "Do you know when the funeral will be?"

He shook his head. "No funeral."

"Won't she be buried?"

"Yes, maybe tomorrow. But no funeral."

"Don't Druze have funerals?"

He sighed, as if holding this door open was getting to be quite a burden. "Yes, but not for her."

"Why not?" *Do they think she's a terrorist?*

He rubbed the back of his neck. "It's...her parents' wish. Now–"

I heard the muffled ringing of a nearby phone. "The burial is rather soon. Isn't an autopsy being performed?"

He came all the way out into the lobby and closed the door behind him, walking me to the exit of the station.

"It's family decision because Leila is minor and female," he said, apparently working hard to deal patiently with someone as difficult as myself. "Probably no autopsy." He looked at my bag as the phone rang again.

It wasn't my ringtone – it must be Leila's phone, I thought. What if it's her boyfriend? I was dying to answer it, but couldn't in front of Metanis since it was evidence I shouldn't have even had. Then I realized what he'd just said. "What do you mean, a *minor*?" I said. "Under twenty-one?"

"Under *eighteen*," he said.

"She wasn't *eighteen* yet? She'd been in college for...a few years, I think."

He nodded, eyes closed, as if this was all he could bear.

Riiinnggggg.

"You must answer," he said, retreating back into the station.

"How old *was* she?"

He sighed. "Seventeen. I must use telephone now–"

"Sir. With all due respect, why does the family get to decide whether or not she gets an autopsy?"

"Druze custom." Metanis turned away.

"Excuse me," I called out, as politely as I could, pulling a business card out of my backpack. "Here, in case you get any news or think of anything to ask me."

I handed him the card.

"How long you stay in Israel?" He asked, glancing at the card, which said I was a freelance journalist. He flipped it over to a list of media outlets I contributed to.

"I don't know."

His mouth slackened and he shot me a look of apprehension. "Who you report for here?"

"Uh...well, I wrote a bunch of stories for *The New York Times*, but – "

"You did not say you are newspaper woman before! You should told me."

"I – I'm sorry," I said. "I'm telling you now. I'm not even sure there's a story here yet. I don't have an assignment. As I said, Leila was my friend."

Metanis opened the lobby door for me. "I be in touch, Miss Jones."

I was surprised by his sudden respectful tone. Why couldn't I have had that before he thought I had credentials? As I left the stationhouse, I glanced over my shoulder. He was still in the threshold, stabbing his finger at the dial pad of his cell phone.

6

I plodded towards the highway that led into Haifa, a wave of exhaustion passing through me like a drug. My head ached from trying to follow Metanis' impervious accent. Why wouldn't Leila's parents want to give her a funeral? Everyone in Atabi seemed to dislike Leila. Why? And she was only 17! I thought of her favorite professor at school who was privy to her secret life and knew I had to find her right away.

The mere thought of public transportation unnerved me. A jeepload of army guys let me hitch a ride with them, a common practice in Israel. I considered enlisting them to help me use Leila's phone since I couldn't decipher the Hebrew, then thought better of it. I had them drop me off at the university.

"Monsters!" Devrah Stavi yelled, slamming a chisel down on the wooden table, when I gave her the news about Leila. It had taken an hour to track the red-headed hippie artist down; she was in a courtyard of the arts building, which appeared to be set up for a stone carving class. "How?" she demanded.

"They said probably just an accident of some kind," I said. "But they wouldn't give me any details or reasons why they think that."

Devrah sunk down on a stool and hung her head. "I just knew this would happen someday."

My heart skipped. "How come?"

She looked up at me as though she'd forgotten I was there. Her earlobes sagged under the weight of huge Egyptian gold disc earrings. "Leila never mentioned you before."

"I met her last year…I had dinner at her house last night and—" I pulled out my digital camera and showed her several pictures at the gallery and the Azzams'.

She glared at me. "I've known her for two years and I've never been invited to her house."

"You know that bus that was bombed in Jaffa yesterday?"

She nodded quizzically.

"Leila pulled me off of it just before it blew up."

Her eyes widened and she cursed in Hebrew. "Are you okay?"

I pointed to the cut on my head. "Got lucky. Leila took me home with her afterwards."

"Was she injured?"

"No, no. But why did you say you always thought this would happen?" I asked, fearing the worst.

Devrah's face disfigured into grief and she sobbed into her hands.

"I'm so sorry," I said, afraid to try to comfort her more. She didn't seem receptive.

"I have to teach in fifteen minutes," she said, ripping a paper towel off a roll on a nearby table and wiping her face roughly, smearing blue eyeliner on her freckled cheekbones. "Her whole life she's been trying *not* to get killed. I've been afraid she would be murdered in an honor killing."

A newspaper headline with those words – "honor killing" – swam in my memory. "What's that?" I asked.

"Arab families sometimes kill their women for not taking orders or for having lovers," she said, rolling her eyes.

I described Tamir's outburst, my departure with Fadi, the hostile crime scene and what Metanis had shared with me.

Devrah shook her head, eyes closed tightly, as if to prevent a horrible image from materializing. Then, suddenly, opened them wide with fire, squaring them on me. "Why the *hell* did you leave her there after Tamir arrived?"

Her anger entered me like a surprise piece of shrapnel. My breath caught. Leila's ashen face flickered in my mind. I heard her words again: *"I'm going, too."* Her grip on my arm. *"I have to stay."* That last hug. I heard my own voice, but detached from me, speak to me with words as indignant as my father's: *She was holding on to you for dear life and you pretended not to know!* I saw my brother Cary's limp body, bright red blood glistening on the hand-cut grass. Something barreled up from inside my bones. I began coughing.

Devrah patted me on the back until my breath evened. "I'm sorry," she whispered. She smelled of paint solvent and patchouli. "I *hope* it was an accident."

I pulled away from her and wiped my nose on my sleeve. A warm tear dribbled down my cheek and fell in my hand.

After she'd given me tissues and a drink of water, Devrah pulled her stool up next to me.

"Devrah, is there any chance Leila was involved in some kind of resistance against Israel?"

She looked at me as if I was nuts. "Like terrorism?"

"I'm just wondering how she knew to get me off that bus, and if that was somehow related to her death."

She shook her head. "Leila had a strong sixth sense, but she would never harm anyone. What you might not understand is how nice and tight Arabs keep their women reeled in." She made a fist and pulled it in close to her chest. "Their precious 'honor' is everything to them. If a woman does the slightest thing…" She grabbed a chisel off the carving block and made a slicing motion by her neck. "The bloodier the killing, the bigger a hero the guy is."

I stared at her and thought of Leila's bloody arm they left uncovered on the street. A shiver went down my spine.

"Her family's been ashamed of her since she was a small child. She's used to living under a constant death threat," she said. "She joked that all Arab women have a lifelong *fatwa* on them."

"Why were they ashamed?"

She sighed. "She only spoke of it once, but before she was school age, she was attacked and left for dead. Women must be virgins until marriage or the whole family's disgraced."

My stomach clenched. "But she was a child, for God's sake!"

"Try telling *them* that," she said as she made stab marks in the soft wooden table with the chisel. "An old woman found her in the woods behind her house and took her to the hospital. Her family didn't want her back, but had to take her, and her whole life's been a living hell since. She wasn't allowed to leave the house for years and she still can't drive or leave her village without a male relative."

Devrah pulled a handful of small identical carving tools out of a large pocket in her smock and looked at me gravely. "They could've killed her."

"Why now?"

"The family's been under a lot of pressure with her wedding coming up…and Leila was dreading her marriage."

"Was it arranged?"

"No," she said, slipping the tools into a ceramic mug. "More like *forced* – to her *attacker*."

"*Tamir* was her attacker?" I felt myself going numb.

She nodded. Tamir couldn't be more than ten years older than Leila. He would have just become a teenager when he assaulted her.

She got up to stack stone, a chunky, hennaed braid swinging across her back.

"Why would they make her marry *him* of all people?" I asked.

"To cleanse the family honor!" Devrah cried. "They've been waiting all her life to do it!"

"Make an 'honest woman' of her?"

She flung some stone scraps to the ground. "I guess."

I imagined myself marrying Pat, my Tamir equivalent, and had to shake my head to clear the vile image.

"So, what set him off this time?" she asked.

"I was going to ask you. I couldn't understand anything he said. Could he have found out about her secret boyfriend in New York?"

Devrah looked at me as if I'd just launched into Yiddish. "She told you that? Sounds like her fantasy – Escape to New York!" She fanned her hands out in the manner of a magician. "Or maybe it's an Internet thing. I'm sure she would have told me if it were real."

I wanted to pull out Leila's secret cell phone and ask Devrah for help finding his number, but I wasn't sure I could trust her. If Leila hadn't told her about him, maybe she didn't trust Devrah completely either. Or had Leila lied to me about her boyfriend and what that phone was for?

"But why would she be killed to restore her family's honor just weeks before her wedding would have accomplished the same thing?" I asked.

"Hell if I know." She shook her head bitterly.

"The police told me Leila was only 17."

"Yep." She glanced over when the first student arrived for class. "She would've been 18 in a fortnight."

"How was she already in college – and for a while?"

"Leila's a genius, Fereby. Or was." Devrah tried to shake new tears off and made herself go back to setting out equipment. "Her family didn't let her start school until she was nine and, by the time she was 15, she was ahead of everyone else in her high school – even with all her illnesses."

"What illnesses?"

"Chronic pain." She pointed to her pelvis. "And ulcers. Just since I've known her, she's been in the hospital at least three times and missed a lot of school. She was always going to the clinic for something. Probably from abuse, but she'd never say so… sometimes I think she just checked herself in to get away from home."

"I'm surprised her family let her go to college," I said.

"She was bored in high school. Her parents worried it would make her misbehave, so they got her engagement set, and then let her study here when she was sixteen to get her teaching certificate. She was supposed to go to the Gordon Seminary where all the Druze girls go for teacher training, but she was so advanced, the University of Haifa gave her a full scholarship. Her parents were quite progressive in permitting this, but Leila still had to agree to the marriage and to having Fadi or another male relative drive her to and from campus."

"I thought she was an art major."

"She was. My best student. But she had to tell her parents she was studying to be an elementary school teacher because it's one of the few professions the Druze consider suitable for their women because they can work in their own village isolated from outsider males."

"Didn't her parents look at her report card and notice what classes she was taking?"

"I doubt they bothered. Before college, she did 12 years' worth of school in seven."

"It's kind of hard to hide that you're a painter," I said, pointing down at her nails.

"She told her family she was learning to teach kids art. They have no idea she was a real painter. They could have killed her just for that."

What elaborate – and dangerous – deception Leila had to orchestrate to be her true self. "Where's all of her art?"

"Some is in the storeroom," she said. "Collectors have several canvasses and so does Raziel."

"Can I see what's here? Maybe they would help somehow in putting this whole puzzle together."

Students were beginning to set up their workstations.

"Let me just get them started and I'll take you upstairs," she said.

"Arab folk painting is a dying art and they don't seem to mind," Devrah said, leading me into the storeroom, which was lined with floor-to-ceiling shelves of art supplies. We stepped around large stones on the floor to get to a stack of canvasses leaning against the back wall. She thumbed through them and pulled out a few.

"These are a few of the paintings from what turned out to be her last series," she said. " 'The Seven Perfumes of Sacrifice.' "

Leila had emailed me about the series months ago when she'd started it. 'The Seven Perfumes of Sacrifice' referred to the incense used in an ancient ritual. Each of her seven paintings used one of the incense materials as metaphor for something Middle Eastern women had lost. "I imagine the women I'm painting as the aromatics – earthy, powerful and unpredictable – and when the incense is burned in sacrifice, the smoke is the women's prayers," Leila had said. But I'd never gotten around to asking her about the origin of the reference or the purpose of the ritual.

"Where exactly does the title of the series come from?" I asked Devrah.

"Some old book...I don't know." She held up a canvas to show me. "This is 'Submission.' "

It was a nude reclining on a bed, looking back over her shoulder, like Ingres' "La Grand Odalisque." Only this woman was tied to the bed, bleeding from what appeared to be whippings and sporting a black eye and a gag in her mouth. The painting held both a raw, almost tribal intensity at the same time as a lyrical softness, like anger giving way to sadness.

"It's about the sacrifice of women's sexual autonomy," Devrah said. "Leila mixed costus oil into the paint for her body."

"What's that?" I asked.

"One of the ancient aromatics...it was a prized root from Kashmir that smells like violets and was used to heighten libido." Devrah stroked the woman's painted hair with a fingertip.

Leila had incorporated the actual aromatics into each painting somehow, either in the paint, stuck on the canvas or burned as incense while she was painting. I sniffed the canvas, but only smelled oil paint.

Devrah set that painting aside and lifted up another: A veiled woman with hands in prayer position, surrounded by rose bushes, squatting on the ground. " 'Sub Rosa Shame'."

On further inspection, I saw she was bleeding on the ground from her vagina. "What's that about?"

"*Hirman issala* – the polite Bedouin term for 'menstruation' – literally 'that which forbids prayer'." Devrah pushed some frizzy pieces of hair out of her face. "Leila said Bedouin women are forbidden to participate in religious activities when they're menstruating, but she has gone out into nature to bleed and pray and wait patiently until she can return to society."

"Even though she's not supposed to."

She put her finger to her lips as if to say "Shh." " '*Sub Rosa*'."

A red rose implied secrecy at least as far back as Greek mythology. If a rose hung in council chambers in the Middle Ages, all present were pledged to keep the meeting confidential.

"Are roses the aromatic?"

"No, it's cassia." Devrah touched the ground in the painting. "You can feel the crushed bark Leila added to the pigment. Long ago, people extracted a very holy anointing oil from cassia bark. It smells like cinnamon when it's fresh."

"Does it symbolize something?" I asked.

"Hermes, the messenger god, was associated with cassia. Arab women have been cut off from open communication...they have to live secret lives and secrets are kept from them."

Leila knew all about living a secret life. I tried to imagine how she managed to procure the bark and how she must have relished the direct, tactile work on her canvas.

Next, Devrah pulled out a painting of lovers on a bed, about to make love – the man climbing on top of the woman. But the woman was looking forlornly out the window at a bright star in the sky.

"Here is 'Initiation'." Devrah let out a disconsolate sigh, as if this wasn't going to be fun to explain. "Most women in the Middle East have lost an instinct for and access to pleasure. The husband is about to consummate this forced marriage, which is rape if the woman doesn't want it. For comfort, she is gazing at Venus, the planet of Aphrodite, the Goddess of Love, of course. Leila said spikenard, her aromatic plant, was originally associated with eroticism – it's mentioned in the *Song of Songs* as a symbol of the intimate nature of the woman's love. It's the perfume of the Lost Garden of Eden. It only emits its scent when its hairy stem is rubbed."

We exchanged smiles.

"So how does this fit with marital rape, then?" I asked.

"In more recent times, spikenard was used to heal deep-seated grief and help with the transition from life to death. I think Leila was commenting on the irony of its former erotic meaning contrasted with its current use."

"How'd she use it?"

"The flowers, which look like the tail of an ermine, are crushed into a rich, red, fragrant ointment. It's part of the marriage bed."

The bed the couple were lying on Leila had painted red. I leaned over and sniffed.

"It smells like moist earth," Devrah said. "A little pungent."

The paint did smell different from ordinary oil paint. I was amazed what heavy insights against her own culture Leila had already developed at her tender age. If the Atabi or Israeli Druze community had known of her position on these issues, I could see why they wouldn't like her. But her secret life was supposedly secret.

"Where's the rest of the series?" I asked.

"At Mujun or sold, I guess."

"What's going to happen to these?" I eyed the canvasses.

She shook her head. "I don't know. Her family doesn't know about them."

"Maybe they found out and that's why she's dead," I said.

Devrah got a funny look on her face.

"What?" I said.

She stared at me as she thought. "Leila had been moody lately…and she asked me to take her to pick up some paintings at Mujun next week."

"So?"

"Well, once we take them there, they sell. We've never brought them back."

"Why'd she want to do that?"

"I asked her, but I never got a straight answer. I could tell there was something she wasn't saying."

7

Outside on the university quad, I found a shady bench and searched the Web on my phone for anything on Leila's childhood assault. Nothing. I Googled "honor killing" and got 197,000 hits. The United Nations reported that more than five thousand women and girls were victims of honor killings around the world every year. Amnesty International said most victims were ages 15 to 30 and the majority of honor killings occurred in Muslim countries of the Middle East, South Asia and North Africa – but there had been reports in Israel (including among Druze, Palestinians, Israeli Arabs and Bedouins), India and increasingly among Muslim immigrants to the U.K, the U.S. and Europe, as well as in a Punjabi Sikh family in Canada.

An *L.A. Times* piece reported that it was usually the close male relatives that did the deed: "Brothers are the most frequent perpetrators, followed by fathers, cousins and uncles." A terrible, sickening feeling swept over me as I considered the real possibility of Fadi having done it.

According to Human Rights Watch, honor killings were carried out for a variety of reasons – losing virginity before marriage, adultery, rape, disobedience, divorce, resisting a forced marriage, or mere rumors of such. The victim was the source of disgrace to her family and the only sure way to reverse it was to kill her. The bloodier and more public, the better to prove the men could control their female relative's behavior. Somehow, that would cleanse the shame and all would be right again. But why? I hunted for an hour with no success – none of the articles went into much depth and the chat rooms spewed bigotry against Muslims I couldn't stomach.

Since talking to Devrah, I was feeling less suspicious that Leila was involved in the bombing. I considered editing my article as it was and turning it in, but finding out what I could about Leila's death before I left tonight was more urgent now. I needed to go to Leila's gallery – the owner Raziel had to have some insights about what had been going on with her. And he had her last paintings.

After renting the cheapest car I could find (a manual Fiat Punto for US$36 a day, with an Israeli cell phone thrown in), I drove two hours to Tel Aviv and then it took another half hour to find my way through Jaffa and to Mujun, Leila's gallery, thanks to my incompetence in Hebrew (few signs were in the Roman alphabet, let alone English) and my determination to avoid Yefet Street where the bombing had occurred.

The gallery was unusually dark, as if they'd had to make do in a power outage. Tall glass jars of candlelight illuminated paintings crammed mosaic-style on the walls. Peeling paint hung from the ceiling like molting snakeskin. "Death of the Future" was missing from the spot on the wall where I'd seen it hanging yesterday, which sent me into a small panic. I sensed Leila's presence here so potently, it took me off-guard. The blend of rose tobacco smoke, musty room and oil paint was Leila's scent. I stood in the dark entrance wondering how I'd get through this conversation.

At the back of the narrow room, two men lazed on a burgundy divan sharing a large *nargileh*. As my eyes adjusted, I saw it was Raziel and a man I didn't know. Vines of smoke swirled through the half-light from a high row of dirty windows. Raziel stretched out an arm to reach the *nargileh*. The other guy passed the mouthpiece, which was attached to a long, multi-colored hose that connected to the water pipe. Raziel patted his friend on the back of the hand in customary thanks and took a puff. Just yesterday, Leila had sat there with him instead. I took a deep breath and willed myself forward.

They jumped up hastily when I said hello and, as Raziel greeted me, his friend took off. It didn't seem he'd heard the news about Leila, so I asked.

"Yes, one of her teachers at school called me." He shook his head and took another puff. He wasn't even pretending to be sad. Raziel was a dark, stout man with a fleshy face and black hair shorn close to the scalp, thirty-something perhaps, but prematurely aged. I felt my temper flare.

"You know...She pulled me off that bus that was bombed yesterday 30 seconds before it blew up. She was disappointed you didn't call to check on her after the explosion."

"I know hundreds of people in Jaffa – I couldn't call all of them!" he said.

I sniffed. "Look, can you help me? I'm getting nowhere trying to get answers about her death."

He stood up, apparently relieved to change the subject. "Walk with me. I need to pick up some lunch. Are you hungry?"

We strode down an old, narrow road of bricks bleached the color of salt.

"Leila came in every other week, if she could," Raziel said, putting on a pair of black sunglasses. "The last time I saw her was when you came in."

"You two were arguing."

"Mmm," he murmured, wiping his upper lip with a handkerchief. "She said she was going away for a while and would need to take her paintings with her, whatever hadn't sold by next week."

"She was ending your arrangement then?"

He shrugged with his lips. "She didn't say that."

I looked at him.

"I asked her, but she was very, uh, secretive about what she was planning. I didn't expect her to tell me much. The Druze and their *taqqiyah* – they've raised confusion to a fine art."

Druze were famous for hiding their true feelings and intentions to safeguard their community. On my last trip here, I'd asked an elder if dishonesty wasn't against their religion. He said: "A man's shirt doesn't change the color of his skin."

"So why the argument?" I asked.

"Last week, she brought in four paintings from this series she was working on. I was waiting for the rest and expected her to bring them in yesterday. Instead, she said she would come back to get her remaining paintings and any money I owed her next Monday."

Raziel waved at a guy hauling large rectangles of glass on a hand truck into a studio.

"You got mad?"

"I have a few interested collectors that I've sold about a dozen of her paintings to. Each one's now going for over a thousand dollars U.S. I expected her to triple that in the next year. This series is her best work to date."

He stopped at a corner stand and ordered us *falafel*, insisting on paying for mine.

"Do you think she was quitting art because of her marriage?" I asked as we walked back.

"I don't know. Her husband probably found out about her asshole boyfriend."

I stopped. "You know about her boyfriend?"

He nodded and reached over to a trash bin on the sidewalk to drop a napkin in. "New York snob."

"You've *met* him?"

"He came in the gallery with her several times."

So he *was* real. "Do you know how to reach him?"

He shook his head. "She called him Duncan. Don't know his surname. I call him The Asshole."

"Why?"

"He was always trying to cut Leila a bigger deal with me."

Back at Mujun, I asked Raziel about 'Death of the Future', the painting of the dead Asherah with child trying to suckle at her breast.

"Sold," Raziel said, plopping himself down in a worn leather chair that squeaked under his weight. "Just today."

I felt a pang in my chest. "Isn't there 'The Birth of Eve' or something?" It was still packaged up when I was at the gallery yesterday, so I hadn't gotten to see it.

"'The Birth of Hawwah' – or 'Eve.' Sold to the same collector. *That* one's from her last series – collector's coming back for it." He pointed behind me on the opposite wall to a painting of two snakes curled in an embrace, as a caduceus, one of them inflicting a fatal bite to the neck of the other. Their bodies were more sculpted than brushed with paint, in thick layers, the background red as ochre. It was "Sacrifice of the Goddess-Queen," one Leila had shown me yesterday, from the Seven Perfumes series. It was about women losing their very lives. The 'perfume' was the resin styrax, a symbol of death, according to Genesis, and burned during frankincense harvesting to drive away snakes. Leila said she couldn't figure out how to incorporate the hardened resin into the painting, so she burned it as incense every day while she painted the picture.

I thought about the paintings Devrah had shown me and these. "I know of six of the seven in the series," I said. "Do you have another?"

"Sold 'Resurrection' to that collector, too."

"Which one is that?" Leila had described most of them to me.

"Tree with face and hands of a girl in the roots with a big sun behind. He took it today."

I hadn't seen it yesterday, probably because I'd left so quickly since Leila and Raziel were arguing.

"Do you know where she got the title of the series from?" I asked.

"Some very old source," he said absently, sorting through a mess of papers on his desk. "I meant to ask her last time I saw her."

"What will you do with the rest of her paintings?"

"Keep selling them until they're gone, I guess." He laughed, then caught himself.

I headed back towards Atabi worrying about the fate of Leila's paintings and missed my turn so I had to go directly through Haifa and pass the Bahá'í Temple. Its terraced gardens stretched down the mountain like a sinuous Persian carpet. My throat tightened. I last visited a Bahá'í shrine the day before my brother Cary was killed in India. My family spent some time at the Bahá'í house of worship in New Delhi, he and I playing around the grounds for hours.

Coming in to Atabi, I passed the *souk* and caught glimpses of copperware, bamboo furniture and blue ceramics. Blousy pants and tent dresses hung from a shop ceiling, blowing in the wind like disembodied souls. Two obese ladies in long robes and flat slide sandals carried distended plastic shopping bags, their *foutta*-wrapped heads bobbing side to side as they ambled down the sidewalk.

I bought some pistachios and a few apples at a produce stall. On my way out, Leila's mother, Dima, brushed past me without acknowledgement. I was shocked to see her out, so soon after her daughter had died. I watched her fill a paper bag with peaches and fuss over some large bundles of greens. She was still wearing her navy apron, perhaps so people would think that, as a proper Druze woman, she had just rushed out for a vital, spur-of-the-moment errand. Casual shopping for women was still considered brazen by traditional Druze.

Then I saw it: For a few seconds, her *foutta* hung open at an angle exposing a spectacular purple bruise extending from her left eyebrow down across her eyelid to the top of her cheekbone. She turned her back. Had her husband, Kamil, hit her? Had she tried to intervene on Leila's behalf and been beaten for it? I felt the urge to dismiss Fadi as a possible assailant, feeling guilty for even thinking it. She opened her change purse and counted out some *shekels*. Her hunched, draped body seemed a visible apology for her very existence. Leila's Arabic 'La Grande Odalisque" woman with a shiner in her "Submission" painting flashed through my mind.

"Dima," I said softly.

She glanced up in alarm, then ducked, pulling her *foutta* across her cheek.

I put my hand on her arm. "Dima. What happened?" I pointed to her bruise.

She whispered something unintelligible to me in Arabic, not meeting my gaze. I tried to put my arm around her, but she shuffled over to the cashier to pay, then darted out.

"Someone hit Dima Azzam in the face," I told Metanis back at the police station. I wasn't confident he'd do much after stonewalling me before, but I didn't see any better alternative.

He didn't look up from his computer screen. "Did you see it happen?"

"Well, no," I said. "But she had a terrible bruise around her eye."

"Did she say someone assaulted her?"

"No," I said. "We can't communicate." Not to mention I wasn't the Azzams' favorite person anymore, so she probably wouldn't have told me anyway.

"It could have been caused by something else," he said.

"She tried to hide the bruise from me, as if she was protecting someone."

He smiled at me like I was a silly child.

I sighed angrily. "She left the *souk*. Maybe she went home. Why don't you send someone, Detective?"

"If they call," he said, and began typing something.

I rubbed my temples, willing patience. "Have you learned the cause of Leila's death yet?"

"Still no news, Miss Jones."

"Has the body been released to the family for burial yet?

"Soon." He squinted at his computer monitor.

If the authorities still had her body, maybe they were doing a postmortem. "Was there an autopsy?"

"It is right now," he said.

I tried to hide my satisfaction. "Why did they decide to do one after all?"

He picked up his cell phone and started tapping it.

"Have they told you how she died yet?" I pressed.

"Perhaps later today we release that."

"Well, has anyone come forward with any leads about her death?" I tried.

Metanis exchanged glances with another cop sitting nearby as if I was their private joke. He didn't seem to care that I could see this. "I cannot say," he said.

"Were there any witnesses? I'm not asking for their identities or what they saw or heard. I just want to know if you're getting any closer—"

"You are also policewoman in U.S., Miss Jones?"

"No."

"Hmmm," he said, sitting back and folding his arms. He was finally looking me in the eye. "Our work is difficult for you to understand. You know everything when we tell public. You not look well again. You need to go to hotel for some nap."

"When will the burial be?"

"I tell you later."

Annoyed and frustrated, I started walking back to my car at the *souk*, when a loud, brown Subaru station wagon passed and I saw a finger pointing at me from the front seat. Suddenly, the car pulled over onto the shoulder in front of me. I stopped, my heart pounding wildly, and watched as Kamil came out of the driver's side and slammed the door shut. The front passenger door opened, and I could see Dima's draped arm holding the handle, but Kamil shouted something at her and she shut it again. Had he hit her earlier? Not knowing what to expect, I braced myself as an unsmiling Kamil stormed toward me.

8

H e stopped a stranger's distance away from me, clenching his fists. Tension I hadn't felt last night at the Azzams' house now swelled between us.

"I'm so sorry for your loss, Kamil," I said nervously. "I came by earlier, but no one answered your door."

"Leila was in Jaffa yesterday with you," he said. "You met her there, not at school."

Metanis had squealed evidently, as he was the only one who knew that.

"Yes," I admitted.

"What was she doing there?"

"I don't know," I lied. "Shopping? Does this have something to do with her death?"

"When did you meet her?"

"After the bombing, I called her," I said, thinking fast.

"Where did you meet?"

"A few blocks away."

"Who was she with?" he asked.

"She came by herself to meet me."

Why was he so concerned about logistics when she was dead?

Remembering Dima, I peeked at his hands, searching for signs of injury but finding nothing.

Kamil glanced at the ground, then turned to go back to the car.

"She wanted to help me," I called out, but he wouldn't look back. "What happened to Leila?"

He opened the car door.

"Sir, will she be buried tomorrow?"

He frowned at me and ducked into the driver's seat.

"Wait!" I yelled, running towards the car. "What about Dima's eye?"

The door slammed and he peeled away, wheels spinning dust into the air, stinging my eyes. I had to cover my face with my hands until it settled back down to the road.

Back at the *souk*, I wandered deep in thought. If there was any chance Leila had something to do with the bombing, I should probably not be lying about related circumstances lest it implicate me somehow or hamper the investigation into the bombing. There were so many questions still unanswered and new ones arising every hour. If I stayed a few more days, maybe I could do this story justice. I didn't want to fly tonight anyway. My chest and shoulders felt tight, my skin slightly prickly – a familiar feeling from a different context. Another compelling reason to stay was working its way into my consciousness, but I couldn't admit it to myself just yet.

Unable to concentrate on the decisions I needed to make, I was relieved to find a distraction – a building that had "House of Druze" printed in English on its sign. I drifted in to the windowless room, redolent of a flea market, which appeared to be a sort of homemade museum, every fragment of wall space filled with artifacts. A striped flag and dusty scimitar hung from the ceiling. A dozen visitors sat on *divans*, captivated by a young man lecturing in Hebrew. I tried to disappear against the displays of ancient Druze lore on the wall.

There were yellowed documents behind glass and a grand old *nargileh*. Sepia photographs depicted men with white beards as long as their turbans were tall, like men I'd seen in the village. I paused in front of a daguerreotype of a striking warrior with pale eyes whose lids were smudged black with kohl. His Wild West handlebar mustache had a certain Eastern European flair like the ones worn by some farmers I'd seen in the Hungarian countryside. Another picture showed him on horseback with a jeweled sword surrounded by dozens of dagger-waving warriors in flowing robes with braided hair. By the looks of him, he'd either been a shaman or a lunatic.

"*Ze Atrash*," a voice behind me said. I turned to find the young man who'd been giving the talk smiling and holding a cup of espresso out to me. The group had disappeared. "Welcome to House of Druze. I am Mustafa, your very own Druze Guide. You have found the great Sultan Pasha Atrash, the infamous war lord of the Druze, with his hundred bodyguards."

I graciously accepted the cup and asked him to tell me more. His eyes lit up as he relayed how the Syrian Druze fought the Ottoman Turks and raised the Arab flag over Damascus upon their defeat. When the French took over Syria in 1925, it was Atrash who led the revolt, making world headlines.

"We Druze care more about rebellion than victory," he said. "We sacrifice everything for the battle."

I took a polite sip of coffee. "Why is that?"

"We believe a person's fate is fixed from birth. There's nothing he can do to change it, so there's no reason to fear danger."

"Was honor important to Atrash?"

"Of course...It's like air," said Mustafa, spreading his hands out as if referring to something holy.

I spotted a photo of some amply-covered, 19th-century Druze women at a well. "Why are women always the ones killed for transgressions of honor?"

"They're not – it depends on the crime," he said. "In the Djebel, during Atrash's time, there was a custom for dealing with blackened *sharaf*, one kind of honor. A Druze who proved cowardly during a fight was never scolded, but the next time he shared coffee with the other warriors, the host would spill it on him, thus pronouncing his death penalty. In the next battle, the coward had to sacrifice himself to the enemy. If he survived, his whole family was disgraced. Also, a man must be killed if he attains his honor through his mother."

"Well, what if the offense has to do with...a woman?" I asked. I didn't dare say *sex*.

"That is the other kind of honor – '*ird*. You might say 'purity.' "

"She's always the one that's killed, isn't she...not the man?"

"Not always," Mustafa said, licking a finger and dusting the top of a frame with it. "About a hundred years ago, a carpenter came from Syria to build new furniture for a client in Lebanon. When the job was nearly done, the son of the village *shaikh* went to where the carpenter was staying and raped his wife. She told her husband and they left in the night. The client went after him and learned what had happened. He then went back and told the *shaikh* the village had lost its honor. In front of the *shaikh*'s son and village elders, the client asked the *shaikh* if someone was guilty of such an offense, what punishment should he receive. 'He should be sentenced to death!' said the *shaikh*. 'Even if he were your own family?' asked the client. 'As I said, he should die!' said the *shaikh*. The elders agreed. The carpenter and his wife were brought in to point out the guilty one and the *shaikh* killed his own son right on the spot!"

Mustafa folded his arms, satisfied he'd proven his point.

"So, why wasn't the carpenter's wife killed?" I asked.

He blinked at me for a long moment and a look of bewilderment swept over his face. "Oh, I'm confused. I forgot, she and the carpenter were Christians."

9

The sun was beginning to set and storekeepers in the *souk* were closing up shop now. Metanis hadn't called about when the burial would be or cause of death and I didn't have the courage to call the Azzams, who probably wouldn't tell me anything now. I phoned Metanis, but got his voicemail. Then, on the fly, I caught the assistant editorial page editor at *The New York Times* whom I'd tried to write for before. I knew I just had to go for it.

"Stephan, there's a story here I want to cover. That suicide bombing in Jaffa yesterday? I was *in* it. A friend saved me from being killed."

"Uh-huh," he said, as if he was unsure if he should believe me. "Doesn't sound like your kind of piece, Fereby."

"I know, but I want to do it, in first-person."

I heard fast typing. "Do you have any exciting color?" He sounded bored.

I shook off my revulsion. "Yes, and my friend who saved me, her body was found this morning in the street. I'm trying to find out if there is any connection to the bombing."

"Okay, well get it over here ASAP before everyone's forgotten about it," he said. "It's strictly spec. Hang on to your receipts, but if we don't buy the story, you eat 'em."

A new kind of energy welled up inside me as I edited the first draft of my bombing story in the corner of a kebob restaurant on the main street. This assignment could be a significant break for me – if I could deliver. The problem was confessing to the world I had thwarted – and then assisted – a suicide bomber, albeit unawares. I didn't send the story in, telling myself it wasn't finished yet...that I still needed to talk to Duncan, Leila's boyfriend in New York, who might know something essential. To call him, I needed his last name or to find someone trustworthy to get into Leila's phone for his number.

After dinner, as I headed back to the hospice-hotel, I passed the bar on the outskirts of Atabi that Fadi had pointed out. What could the only drinking establishment in Atabi, which was barely tolerated, be like? Did the lowlifes of Druzedom hang out there? It might be just the place to uncover some helpful clues – if it seemed safe. Plus, a beer sounded good. I turned around on the shoulder.

The small bar was dim and redolent of licorice tobacco. About a dozen young men sat in cane-back chairs around low tables and looked over when I entered. I scanned for any recognizable face among them, but, to my disappointment, found none. I sat on a stool at the empty bar and ordered a Maccabee beer from the young bartender. Exotic musical instruments were tacked to the walls. French-Arabic pop music was playing; a wall-mounted TV behind the bar aired the evening news, muted with Hebrew subtitles. I sipped my beer and tried to figure out what the stories were about. Another suicide bombing. Iraq in ruins. Insurgents in Afghanistan. A checkpoint. Old file footage of Ariel Sharon shouting into a microphone. Something about Harry Potter.

I called El Al to cancel my flight reservation. After my ordeal with El Al security getting here (a three-hour search/frisk since I was suspicious: a freelancer with no health insurance going to interview Palestinians) followed by my rescheduling and canceling, they'd probably never let me on another plane.

I still hadn't heard back from Werner and it had been five days since we'd spoken. I called; he answered on the first ring. He was at a bar himself, in Aberdeen, Scotland, post-fishing trip, sounding drunk and detached. I didn't tell him what I'd been through. It was obviously over between us. We hung up after few words. I felt a quivery hole open in my gut, as if I was falling.

I stared at the TV watching nothing. I couldn't have it both ways, once again. It was as if there was some piece of humanity missing from me, but no one could tell me what it was. I never picked the right men. Or maybe it was just me. My thoughts turned to Fadi, his bedroom eyes, tenderness, intensity...and possible guilt. It pained me to even consider that he'd hurt Leila.

"You're Leila's friend," a voice suddenly said.

I looked up, out of my trance. The bartender was drying a glass in front of me.

"How'd you know?" I said.

He tried to suppress a smile as he wiped the counter. "Everybody knows."

I stared down into my beer. This might not be good news. "You know Fadi?"

"Of course. We went to school together." He moved a plastic tub of dirty glassware into a sink and turned on the water. "He comes here a lot."

"Do you think he was involved in Leila's death?" I asked.

He squirted some detergent into the water. "Fadi was in the habit of forgetting."

"Forgetting?"

"The man who forgets or delays his duty is not a man."

"What duty?"

He turned his head abruptly, as if to shake off a feeling. He licked his lips. "We say that nothing can help you accept something bitter except something more bitter."

I knit my brow.

"Only his fear of shame made him do what his sense of honor could not," he said, swishing two glasses in the soapy water.

A knot was forming in my stomach. "Do what? Finish her off?"

He shrugged. "Somebody did. If they hadn't, the Azzams would have nothing now."

I froze, my insides hardening. Someone *killed* her. Deliberately. He'd said it out loud.

"What do you mean?"

"They sold off most their land just to survive and spent their life savings on Leila's wedding. All they have left now is their tiny orchard and their honor."

A man sat down next to me at the bar. I got up and went to the restroom. Resting my elbows on the sink, I let the cold water flow through my fingers. My face looked fragile in the mirror. *I hope it's not Fadi.* I washed my face and rinsed out my mouth.

When I came out of the restroom, a group of young men had gathered at the bar, jostling one another. To my shock, Fadi was in their midst, holding a bottle of beer up as the others toasted him. I couldn't believe what I was seeing. I quickly left some *shekels* on the bar and headed for the door, avoiding eye contact with Fadi. As soon as I hit the warm night air, I felt my arm being grasped from behind.

"Fereby," Fadi said as I turned. "I thought you went home to America."

He was already drunk. I yanked my arm away and kept walking.

"Fereby?"

He came after me. I kept going, but regarded him over my shoulder. "What could you possibly be celebrating the night after your sister's death, Fadi?"

"You don't understand! Wait!"

I reached my car and opened the door between us. "How *could* you?"

A stark floodlight backlit him, making me squint to see his face. His skin glistened with light perspiration; some locks of wet hair stuck to his forehead. His eyes weren't focusing quite right.

"Okay, just calm down," he said, reaching for my shoulder.

"Don't touch me!" I spat.

"I'm sorry." He stumbled, righting himself on the driver's side mirror, sober enough to look embarrassed. He whispered now, but loudly, like a drunk. "Fereby, listen to me, please." He pointed towards the bar with his head. "They think I killed her, but it wasn't me. I'm not celebrating. They are."

"Someone killed her on purpose...or by accident?" I asked.

"Can I get in so we can talk?" He glanced at my car, which he was leaning on.

My shock and fear must have been apparent in my expression. He swallowed anxiously, his face distorting into an ache. "I loved her, Fereby," he said, his voice breaking.

It was hard to see him so vulnerable. He tried to squeeze around the open door.

"No, get in on the passenger side," I said, against my better judgment.

Holding the hood for balance, he lurched around the front of the car, then fumbled with the handle until I reached over and opened the door from the inside for him. Once seated, he leaned into my space, reeking of booze.

"That's close enough," I said, putting my hand out to show him the boundary. I cracked my window. "So, you claim you didn't kill her, but someone else did...on purpose?"

He dropped his head to his chest and covered his face.

I felt my eyes well up, but I refused to cry in front of him. "She was *murdered!*"

He shook his head and gazed up at me, eyes wet with tears. "You don't know what we've been through! People's *words*...shame followed us wherever we went..."

"It was an honor killing, wasn't it?" I seethed.

He let out a huge sigh, dropping his head. A chill set off a race of goose bumps down my arms with this terrible, unspeakable truth.

"Tell me who did it, Fadi."

He buried his face in his hands.

"Tell me!" I yelled.

He sobbed.

"I saw your mother at the market today, Fadi. Looks as if someone beat the crap out of her."

He looked up, swallowing. "I didn't see her," he cried, then glanced toward the bar. "Can we drive away now, please? Let me."

"You can't drive like this," I said, starting the engine.

I headed out of town toward the hospice-hotel for lack of a better plan. He didn't even seem alarmed about his mother's injuries.

"Will your mother be *next?*" I asked.

He closed his eyes and shook his head.

"Tell me something, Fadi: Why is *violence* the answer when honor is damaged?"

"Because shame is violence," he said, more lucid now. "Repairing damaged honor is like picking a dunam of olives and then trying to put them all back on the right stems. Leila dishonored us, but our failure to make it right was even worse."

"Why didn't you deny that you killed Leila to all those guys at the bar?"

"They think I'm a hero now."

I looked at him with disgust. My phone rang. As I reached to answer it, Fadi grabbed it out of the car's cup holder first.

"You can't talk without hands-free," he said.

"What?"

"It's against the law."

"Like that's a big concern for you," I said, snatching it out of his hand and answering it before it could go into voicemail.

"I am Amir Metanis," said a familiar voice on the other end.

I prayed Fadi wouldn't talk so Detective Metanis wouldn't know I was with him. He'd make any number of assumptions I didn't want to have to dispel. Fadi helped himself to my bag of pistachios in the empty ashtray.

"The autopsy say Leila maybe hit by car," Metanis said. "Maybe suicide, but please not to tell anyone. The family Azzam feel shame."

If I wasn't supposed to have this privileged information, why would he share it with me? Why would the Azzams be ashamed if she killed herself? That would've been the most helpful thing she could have done for them – she's history and nobody goes to prison. Could Fadi have hit her when he drove back from taking me to the hotel? Or someone else? Was she running away? Why was the blood in the yard? Or maybe he drove me to give himself an alibi. I didn't remember seeing any glass on the ground. I couldn't very well ask Metanis anything with Fadi sitting right there.

After I hung up, Fadi mumbled through a mouthful of nuts. "Dishonor isn't always answered with violence."

"No?"

"Some years ago, my father went on a trip. Everyone in our house was so excited to be free for a day to do whatever we wanted. He had banned my mother and sisters from leaving the village while he was gone, but I talked my mother into going with me to visit the shrine of her favorite Druze saint in a nearby village – I didn't see what harm it was if I went with her. When my father returned, he was angry that she went against his word and ordered her to leave the house for disobeying him."

"Where did she go?"

"To her parents' house."

"He obviously let her come back."

"After about three days, he forgave her."

"So, forgiveness is possible with transgressions of honor."

"It depends on the offense and the family." Fadi rubbed his eyes and yawned. "Take me back to my car."

Leila's secret cell phone rang in my backpack in the back seat. Fadi glanced down at the two phones I already had on the front console.

"How many phones do you have?" he asked.

"Many."

We arrived at the hospice-hotel and I made a U-turn in the parking lot.

"Are you going to answer it or not?" he asked.

"Not," I said, though I desperately wanted to.

Grouchy Nun was walking toward the front door with a huge ring of keys as we passed by and I prayed she wouldn't see me. I headed back toward the highway.

"What was Tamir so angry about last night?" I asked.

He stared out the window for a long moment. "Money."

"Not honor?"

He watched the headlights of cars coming towards us, following them as they passed. "You're a terrible driver, Fereby."

"What's wrong?"

He grinned. "You don't know how to accelerate on the incline. You have to push the pedal down all the way to the floor to get the car to shift gears."

He demonstrated on his side. Sheepishly, I tried it and we picked up speed.

Suddenly, he grabbed the steering wheel and turned it so we swerved towards the edge of the road.

"NO!" I screamed as we hit the shoulder heading for the forest, pistachios flying.

10

Before we collided with the trees, Fadi yanked the wheel back and we swerved back on the highway.

"Jesus!" I cried, seizing the wheel from him, my heart pounding out of my chest. "Are you out of your mind?"

He shrugged. "We practice this in police training."

"I don't care! Don't *ever* touch my steering wheel again!" I yelled. "Or me!"

Was this normal for him or just the alcohol and stress? Did he do it to avoid having to answer my question about Tamir? He stared out the window, steadying himself on the dashboard.

I finally calmed down and refocused, but was still worrying what he might do. "Why was Tamir mad about money?"

Fadi looked more disconsolate now. Leila was probably the only woman that had ever confronted him until now. "He's a pig."

"Why?"

"He would have gotten half of my family's orchard after the wedding," he mumbled. "That was the deal. He'd spent about ten thousand *shekels* preparing the house they would share and bought her some gifts."

So, why was he mad last night then? She was still alive – the wedding was still on. We drove in silence for a few minutes. *And then it hit me:* Unless…he thought she wasn't planning on going through with it.

"Did Tamir kill her?" I asked and turned off the highway onto the road to Atabi.

"No," he said, unbuckling his seat belt and trying to get down in the floorboard, but he was too tall.

Was this guy nuts? I tried to keep a firm eye on the road. I didn't know if I could believe anything Fadi said. "What are you doing?"

He tried to make himself as small as possible.

"What, *you* don't want to be seen with *me*?" The irony.

Fadi laid his head back against the passenger door and closed his eyes.

"I'm taking you home." I said.

"No!" He popped up to look out the window. "Stop at the bar!"

"You're not driving like this, Fadi."

He shot me a hateful look. "You don't rule me! Stop at the bar!"

That hurt more than it should have. We were just coming up to the bar and I feared he'd reach up and grab the steering wheel again if I didn't comply. I turned into the parking lot, which had emptied out somewhat since our departure.

"Where's my car?" he said, looking around. "There." He pointed to the dirty white coupe.

"You'll kill yourself or somebody else, Fadi. Please. You're a *cop*. You could lose your job. Permanently."

He took the keys out of his pocket and scratched his head with them. "You know, I'm just too sleepy to drive. Take me home."

I went along as though it was his idea. When I drove over the spot on the street in front of the Azzams' house where Leila's body had lain, a huge pit opened in my stomach. As I turned around at the dead end, Fadi reached over and hit the release button on my seat belt. I punched the brake hard to give him a jolt. He looked stunned into my glaring eyes. I couldn't find any words to address his behavior.

"Oh, I forgot. You're not coming in. Never mind," he said cheerfully, as though it were customary to unfasten a woman's seatbelt for her.

I stared him down.

He reached over to re-buckle my seatbelt and I slapped his hand away.

"Well, goodnight then," he said sweetly. "Drive safely, *habibi*."

As he closed the car door, he kissed his fingers and waved them at me, then stumbled through the fig bower.

The grief poured out of me as I drove back to the hospice-hotel. Most likely, Leila had been murdered for honor. But why? And by whom? Leila had put together a plan, a way out. She hadn't told me about her wedding because she wasn't going through with it. And Tamir must have found out about her escape plan somehow. Could he have killed her out of anger or revenge? Or did he tell her family and then Fadi did it? Or another Azzam? Or maybe something went wrong and Leila decided to kill herself rather than marry Tamir. Only one thing was absolutely certain: I was going to find out.

11

The mythologist Joseph Campbell said when you meet someone who is going to be of deep significance in your life, somehow you know it right there in the first meeting. Ten months ago, I'd felt it with Leila and Fadi, if only as a breath beneath my consciousness. I'd spent the latter part of the day in Atabi, their three-hundred-year-old village on Mount Carmel, wrapping up a thirteen-hour schedule of interviews via interpreter. The full moon followed a rare late summer rain and, as I was driving out of the village, I saw something out of the corner of one eye – something indistinct but out of place in the night sky. I glanced over, seeing nothing but the crinkled void of trees. Then, through a clearing for a second and a half: a diffuse semi-circle of light bent over the horizon. I made a U-turn on the muddy shoulder. "Thirteen," I said to myself.

Few people ever see a single moonbow in their lifetime, but now I'd seen more than a dozen. As I headed toward it, fragments of a dim memory tried to organize themselves in my head...*wet grass beneath me...my first moonbow, floating out of focus in the monsoon air...I'm out of my mind with grief, confusion and – this is the hardest part to admit – desire... I never think of protesting...then he's on top of me.*

The Atabi moonbow seemed to be positioned on the northern side of the village, so I took the first road I thought might reach the highest part of the facing ridge. I grabbed my camera bag and knocked on the door of the last house on the dead-end street.

A striking young Arab with seductive eyes answered the door. When I asked if I could walk through his property to take pictures of the moonbow, he answered "yes, please" in English, called to his family and, to my disappointment, led me through a shadowy side patio to the back of the house. I was exhausted and wanted to be alone.

The white moonbow straddled the valley that fell below us and spanned the horizon. Above the milky arc, the sky was dark; below glowed an iridescent blue. I smelled orange blossoms and looked down to see the silhouettes of dozens of rows of trees spread across the barely illuminated valley.

As I set up my tripod by moonlight, Fadi introduced himself and told me the orchard belonged to his family. Some of the olive trees were over five hundred years old. Talking with him became awkward inside such a voluptuous night. Druze men didn't have innocent conversations alone in the dark with unrelated women. Fadi wouldn't make much eye contact with me. To fill the silence (and justify my late intrusion), I told him about my photos of moonbows spanning Bolinas, California, and the Chachai Waterfall in the jungle of Madhya Pradesh, India.

As I pulled a filter out of my bag, a young woman slipped next to Fadi. In the faint gleam of the moon, all I could make out were her large, intelligent eyes. Fadi introduced me to his sister, Leila.

"This is extremely rare," I said, pointing to the moonbow. "Even if there's enough moonlight and the moon isn't higher than forty-two degrees, more often than not, the sky isn't clear enough. Usually there has to be a waterfall involved instead of rain."

I listened to them whisper in their tongue while I took pictures, wondering if they considered themselves Arab in spite of the Palestinian connotation most Druze in this country wanted nothing to do with. I was enchanted by what I'd found of their culture so far – with little geopolitical ambition of their own, they lived in peaceful co-existence with the Jews and seemed to be thriving for it.

"Look over there," Leila said.

Behind us, the full moon was surrounded by multiple pale halos – *circular* moonbows. We stood still and witnessed the radiance as though it were a visitation. I watched them, their faces lit up in this angle of moonlight, and was startled by their opposite beauty – Leila's face, shining with awe; Fadi's desolate eyes. It was as if the vision was somehow extracting his life force and infusing it in her. A grown brother and sister together: I felt a familiar twinge as I thought of Cary and what he might have looked like as a young man. Would we have resembled each other as Fadi and Leila did? I turned my camera around and caught them, their heads tilted toward the crown of light.

"This is why we call it Atabi," Leila whispered.

"How so?" I asked.

"Atabi means 'threshold'," she said. "The early inhabitants passed down a story of a flood of shooting stars on the occasion of a miracle and, since then, people have noticed many such coincidences…we say Atabi has a thinner boundary to the heavens, that we're at God's doorstep."

While I photographed the circular moonbow, Fadi muttered something cynical-sounding to her in Arabic; then his voice became cross. He hurried past me, disappearing towards the house.

"He's mad because I forgot my *foutta*," Leila said. "He's going to try to get it without my parents noticing."

We watched the twin moonbows, silently memorizing the effulgence no technology could fully capture. We chatted about her painting, my photography, our writing, until a low, livid voice boomed from the direction of the house, echoing across the valley.

"*Leila!*"

We both started.

"My father," she whispered. "I must go. Come see my work sometime in Jaffa. It's at Mujun Gallery."

The forbidding voice repeated its urgent order. As suddenly as she had arrived, Leila slid back into the night. After the door slammed, I looked up in the sky again. The full moonbow was vanishing. Creatures in the forest below began to stir as they awakened to the darkness.

12

Since it was after ten when I returned to the hospice-hotel, the front door was locked and I had to wake the grouchy nun to let me in. Given what she knew I'd been through in the last twenty-four hours, I wouldn't have blamed her if she'd refused.

Curled into my pillow, I tossed the evidence back and forth in my mind. When a battered woman is on the verge of leaving her abuser, it's the most dangerous time for her. At least that was true in the U.S. Yet, the police suspected suicide. Maybe a coerced suicide was a way the Druze avoided prison sentences for what would otherwise be a homicide – sort of a cultural adaptation to living in a Western-style democracy.

Fadi claimed he didn't do it, but he was the only one I knew for sure was in a car that night. And he fit the profile to a tee: A brother to the victim, between 18 and 25 years old, unmarried and no kids to support.

Kamil was less likely, being his family's primary breadwinner, but then again, if the police didn't charge anyone, there wouldn't be any prison time.

Iman and Dima were as improbable: I'd read women rarely took part in the actual murders, though their gossip often instigated them. Sometimes they helped organize them or cover them up, but it would be another dishonor to the family if either were imprisoned. And I doubted Dima or Iman even knew how to drive.

It was usually the youngest brother of the victim who was pressured into doing the killing – or at least to confess for it. But Qasim was only six, couldn't drive and went to bed before everything came down.

Nothing added up. The whole point was for the killer to get the credit so their family honor could be restored with the most prestige. If the killing wasn't done in public, then the killer often turned himself in. That hadn't happened here.

Honor killing or not, I couldn't shake the unbearable feeling that Fadi must at least know much more than he was letting on. He might be nothing but Leila's innocent and beloved brother or he could be a raving homicidal maniac. Either way, since Druze romances with outsiders were forbidden, he was the most dangerous crush I'd ever had.

I had to find a way to contact Duncan, Leila's boyfriend. His number was in her secret love phone. Who could I get to help me?

I was working on a story about Leila now and it was clear that my bombing story was separate and probably complete. Time to send it in. My chance to get published in *The New York Times*. What was holding me back? Anyone would have done the same thing I did with the Palestinian girl. Wouldn't they?

I went to bed without finishing it, my body feeling sore and brittle. I didn't wake up until nearly noon the next day. I was shocked when I saw the time, thinking my phone was on the wrong time zone. My thoughts turned to the crime scene again, but I was trying to imagine it now through a different lens. How could anyone drive fast enough toward the space at the end of the cul-de-sac to kill someone without either also wrecking their car in the trees beyond the dead end or making a very loud screeching noise when they hit their brakes? Would the braking have made a noise on a dirt road, alerting the neighbors? Would the tires have left marks in the dirt? I needed to go back there.

On my way out of the hospice, I pored over a new *Jerusalem Post* until I found the headline I was looking for: "Druze Teen Killed on Mt. Carmel." It said the autopsy indicated Leila was likely struck by a speeding vehicle, but no suspects had been remanded. Several villagers speculated it was an honor killing; one man said, "She finally got what she deserved." The women I'd seen holding up their fingers in a "V" weren't making a peace sign at all – the article said it was a "victory" sign to show support for the killing!

In the Azzams' dusty road, two boys were kicking a deflated soccer ball. I drove slowly, surveying potential damage on cars, wary of being observed. The area where Leila's body had come to rest had been hosed down after the incident, leaving no trace of its memory. I looked around. Only the boys at the other end of the road were in sight. I rolled my window down and hit the accelerator. As I neared the Azzams' house, I slammed on the brakes. *Whooooosh!* went the tires, followed by a brief scraping sound as I slid to a stop. It was barely audible compared to what you'd expect on a paved street. Or was my hearing still a little muffled? I got out of my car and looked at the road around the tires and under the car. There was a shallow indentation where the dirt dragged along before the car stopped, with bunching on the edges. I got back in the car and rolled backward over the tracks. I peered over the hood. They'd disappeared. Any evidence would be long gone.

I contemplated knocking on the Azzams' front door. What I needed was to talk to Leila's family, especially her mother and sister, who didn't speak English. I slapped my steering wheel in frustration. Did any of the neighbors witness her death or know something relevant? Could they speak English or French? I looked from door to door, considering what each might hold. I shook out some nerves and approached Ru'yah's house.

Still not knowing what had happened to Ru'yah and her baby, I was relieved to see a young woman answer my knocks on the door. After introducing myself in English – luckily, Leila had mentioned me to Ru'yah – Ru'yah let me in and led me through a musty-smelling sitting room and another room, whose precise purpose I couldn't ascertain, to the kitchen at the back of the house. I smelled meat cooking.

"How's your baby doing?" I asked.

"Still in the hospital," she said. Ru'yah had probably once been pretty, but her black eyes were drawn and bloodshot. There were some small broken capillaries on her cheeks. Her *foutta* was slung around her neck in a meager nod to tradition. Long dark hair hung down her back in a ponytail.

"I hope she can come home soon," I said. "What have you named her?"

"Khadija," she said.

"Blessings to you and your husband."

"Thank you. After I cook, I'm going to the hospital to see her."

I was surprised to see her up and cooking so soon after the birth. Her kitchen, circa 1965, was brimming with eggplants, a large bowl of bright red tomatoes and enormous bunches of parsley hanging off the counter. The back door was open and I could see a *taboon* oven on the patio. Sunlight shone through pale yellow curtains over the sink. Ru'yah poured me a cup of coffee and lit the oven with a long wooden match.

"This was my husband's grandparents' house until they died," she said, as if she were embarrassed about the old appliances. She spread a strong hand across a shiny eggplant and began to slice.

"Leila brought me home for dinner night before last," I said.

The skin around Ru'yah's eyes twitched, but she carried on with her task.

"I'm so sorry about Leila," I said. "She told me you were special to her."

Ru'yah nodded and pinched her lips.

I hesitated, but gathered my courage. "What happened, Ru'yah?"

Ru'yah set the knife down on the counter and closed her eyes. "We don't know," she said in a nervous, loud voice. "I was still at the hospital after Khadija was born…Rushdi came home at dawn. As soon as he drove up, he saw her body in the street. He went to see if she was breathing, but she wasn't. When he checked her pulse, he knew she was dead just by her cold skin. He went over to their house and Dima came to the door. Then she woke up the rest of the family and called the police. Fadi came out and covered her up."

How strange. I was to believe that Leila was somehow hit by a car in the street one evening and her body wasn't found until the morning? As if her family wasn't going to notice she didn't go to bed? They hardly let her outside in the daytime by herself.

"I saw a man hosing blood off the Azzams' property after the police left," I said. "Afterwards, he went into your house."

"That was Rushdi," she said, lining up tomatoes to slice next. "The police were finished."

"You don't know how she died…or who else was there?"

Ru'yah shook her head. Expert circles of shiny tomato dropped from her blade.

"Did Leila ever mention that someone had hurt her? Someone in her family?" I asked.

Ru'yah took her time pulling a large cast iron casserole out of a low cabinet. "That is very rare for Druze."

"What about threats of honor crimes?"

She shook her head. "Not anymore."

"No?" I watched her face closely. She was clamming up on me.

"Well, they *could* happen… under rare circumstances." She poured a shallow layer of tomato sauce in the pan.

"Like what?"

She sniffed and wiped her hands on her apron. "Oh, maybe if an unmarried daughter became pregnant. Something like that. But it's ancient history."

"What do you think happened to Leila then?"

Ru'yah looked up at me with blank eyes. "Probably just a very unfortunate accident."

She knew more than this. If she cared for Leila, why was she hiding something? I watched her lay the eggplant slices in the tomato sauce. I was afraid to push too much harder.

"Did Leila ever come to you? About her…uh, family problems?" I asked.

She flinched. Perhaps I had crossed some line. She wouldn't look at me. "Once she asked me if I knew the law."

"What for?"

She placed a slice of tomato on top of each slice of eggplant. "She wanted to know her rights."

I tried to soften my tone and seem more curious than desperate. "With respect to what?"

"I don't really know."

"What'd you tell her?"

"That maybe she should call the Women's Center for Legal Support in Jerusalem. I saw a TV commercial for it."

"Did she call?"

Ru'yah shrugged and drained the browned ground meat in the sink. She added it to a saucepan of tomato sauce and then poured the mixture into the casserole around the vegetables. She finished by tossing pine nuts on top of each eggplant-tomato stack.

"*Mtabak*," she said, holding out the heavy dish for me to see before she placed it in the oven.

I noticed I wasn't invited to dinner.

13

I *can't do this, it's too much,* I told myself as I drove more than two hours to the Women's Center for Legal Support in Jerusalem. *But if you don't do this, who will?* When I showed the receptionist the *Post* article about Leila's death, she made a call, then led me back to the attorney who'd met with Leila.

"How do we ever win at this?" Adam Rubin cried, cursing in Hebrew and slamming an open palm on his desk. With his tiny silver hoop earring, black Chuck Taylor sneakers and blue jeans, he looked more American Gen-Y webpreneur than Israeli attorney.

"Why'd she come here?" I said, standing in his doorway. Chatty women employees rushed past, talking loudly. Adam seemed to be the only male in the office.

He pulled his hands through his shoulder-length black curls and sighed. "Come in." He motioned to a threadbare chair for me to sit in across from his desk and then dropped into his own.

"She was looking into the possibility of asylum to the U.S. due to the threat of honor killing by her family," he said.

More confirmation. I sighed and pulled out my notebook. "Asylum? I thought the culture of the country had to be discriminatory to qualify for that."

"There's some evidence it is," he said, cocking his head to one side.

"What – Israel's culture *persecutes* women?"

"A lack of state protection is enough to support an asylum claim," he said. "Parts of the government are surprisingly tolerant of honor crimes. If a girl who's threatened by her family goes to the police, they often refer her back to her family or to the *shaikhs* – the religious leaders – who send her home where she's often killed."

I tried to make sense of this somehow. "Do the police sympathize with the perpetrators somehow?"

"Partly," he said, drumming a pen on his desk. "Most cops in the Arab villages are Arab, likewise with Druze, and many of the cases in Israel go unsolved. There were fourteen cases in the past fourteen months; charges were submitted on only four. I expect three to convict."

"Don't they usually have confessions, though?"

Adam's phone rang. He reached over and hit a button to turn off the ringer. "Sometimes that's not even enough evidence to raise charges," he said. "The real perp is often not the one confessing. And there are almost always accessories to the murders the police don't bother to investigate."

"What about witnesses?"

"The whole village compels the killing, so who's going to come forward? But even when perps do get charged, the charges are sometimes reduced from murder to manslaughter, negligence or assisting a suicide. And, of course, lots of them are labeled accidents."

Indeed – Metanis and Ru'yah had tried to convince me Leila's death was probably an accident. The fluorescent light above us flickered and we both glanced up. The dull ache in my head was coming back.

"See, the problem is worsened by the police taking cues from the courts," he said. "If a case goes to trial, the perp is often acquitted or gets a reduced sentence because the jury figures he killed because of the 'Arab mentality.' Technically, an honor killing earns a sentence of life imprisonment in Israel. On average, offenders only get four years behind bars."

"Seriously?"

Adam lit a cigarette and rolled his sleeves up to the elbows. His ashtray already had a dozen cigarette butts in it.

"In Israel – even among Jews – family members spend *half* the amount of time in prison as strangers do for killing a woman. The rate of convictions is lower when the vic is a woman, and the jail sentence two years shorter. Even Arab members of the Knesset have said publicly that honor killings are not murder. That's not just an absence of state response – that's complicity."

"This sounds politically suicidal," I said, trying to disregard the smoke.

"People don't know. Or care." He leaned back in his chair, bumping a bookshelf bowing from the weight of legal books piled on it. "The U.S.A. probably has plenty of similar unmentionables."

I ignored the dig as I scribbled notes. "Why would Israel do this?"

He exhaled and leaned in. "Some politicians figured out if they let select honor killings slip through unpunished, they get support of certain tribal leaders and secure votes. In '98, the president of Israel, Eizer Weizman, was going to give amnesty to many imprisoned honor murderers for Israel's fiftieth anniversary, but women's groups went nuts until he backed down."

Adam reached up and pushed his door closed. "Honor is the Arabs' vulnerable spot and Israel knows it." He sat back in his chair and clasped a hand behind his neck. "Do you know why so many Palestinians fled their homes in '48?"

"I assume they were afraid of getting killed," I said.

"Sure, but more importantly, they feared Zionist soldiers would rape their women and violate their honor – a fate worse than death for an Arab. Our guys made the most of this by not denying they *might* have raped some women to get families to abandon their homes…Nowadays, as a political tactic, Israeli cops arrest young Palestinian girls. After they're released, their families often kill them or marry them off at twelve if anyone will have them. If they run away, their families put ads in the Palestinian newspapers to hunt them down."

My head was spinning. "Did you file a request for asylum for Leila?"

"We offered to, but battered women asylum seekers have a tough time getting into the U.S. – and that's where she wanted to go. New regulations were proposed back in 2000, but are stuck in limbo between two agencies. And the Board of Immigration Appeals is known to overturn asylum grants in this category. See, you have to prove state persecution due to membership in a social group, political opinion, race, religion or nationality. They don't seem to see that battered women are a social group or that their protesting their own beatings is a political act."

Adam took a long hit off his cigarette, exhaling a contrail of smoke up towards the aging light fixture. With the exception of a few computers, the whole center seemed to be stuck in 1978.

I scratched my head. "So what happened with Leila?"

"It was going to take too long. With all the documentation she'd have to get from the police and courts, she was sure her family would find out and kill her just for applying and bringing more attention to her situation."

"Wouldn't she have had to flee to the U.S. before she applied, though?"

"Yes, but she thought they'd come after her. After our initial meeting, she never came back."

"Did you refer her to some sort of shelter or safe house?"

"I would have if she'd returned or called again," he said. And he apparently didn't follow up. The smoke was collecting in the tiny office.

I reached over to open the door. "Where does a Druze girl turn for help?" I asked.

"Well, they could come here, but that rarely happens. There isn't a shelter just for Druze, but they are welcome at the mixed shelters. Usually, they check in to the hospital for a while, but don't tell the real reason."

That's what Devrah had said about Leila.

"Sometimes they'll try going to physicians or counselors, but often they refuse to help these girls out of fear of reprisal by the family."

"Where does honor killing come from anyway?"

He shrugged. "Some say a Bedouin tradition of blood revenge, but who knows? In the old days, the lover or rapist used to be killed along with the woman. The guys are lucky now."

"Does Islam have a role?" I asked.

Without saying a word, a middle-aged woman in tall black patent leather boots came in, dropped a stack of files on Adam's desk and left.

"Not directly," he said. "The Qur'an recommends state execution for adulterers, but only if there are four eyewitnesses. The problem is Islamic clergy rarely denounce honor killings and some have even said publicly that if the practice ended, families would fall apart."

"Seems like most honor killings are in Muslim families, though."

"That's probably true – they're more prevalent in the territories and among Israeli Muslims than with Druze – but not all Muslims subscribe to the practice," he said. "It's virtually unheard of in Indonesia, the largest Muslim country in the world."

I felt dizzy from the smoke. "Is the U.N. on top of this?"

"The U.N. didn't even address honor killings formally until 2000. Israel ratified CEDAW – the Convention on the Elimination of All Forms of Discrimination against Women – but with reservations...Israel doesn't want equal rights in family law for women."

I shook my head in disbelief.

"But lots of groups are pushing for reform."

"I figured Israel was pretty much like the U.S. with respect to women's rights or maybe even ahead given the women have to go to the army."

He looked at me with scarcely masked indignation and put his cigarette out in a cup of melting ice. "Are you aware that yours is the only industrialized nation in the world that hasn't ratified CEDAW, Miss Jones? The U.S. joins the ranks of Iran, Sudan and Somalia on that one. You also didn't ratify the Convention on the Rights of the *Child*, which Israel did."

I stared at him, mortified.

"And you have one of the highest rates of femicide in the First World."

I nodded. *I should know this.*

"Nevertheless," he went on, seeing my embarrassment. "Israel's got its issues. Look at what I'm working on right now." He lifted up a thick accordion file and pulled out a magazine with Hebrew lettering. He turned to a bookmarked section and handed it to me. In the photograph was a staged scene of what appeared to be a Nazi pouring gasoline over the naked, emaciated body of a dark-haired woman who lay next to an open oven, like the kind I'd seen at Auschwitz.

"Jesus, what's that?" I said, horrified.

"Holocaust pornography."

I looked at him, uncomprehending. I turned the page to a scene of a packed train. A naked woman was squatting and defecating.

"Oh, my God!" I thrust it back to him. "This is sick."

"I'm working on a case where three Russian women were trafficked over here and forced to appear in these pictures."

I thought of the story on human trafficking an editor at *The New York Times* had suggested I pursue – and Leila's encouragement. "Holocaust pornography," I repeated.

"Yeah, isn't it nice? It positions Jewish men as the Nazis and Jewish women as the victims, with scenes of sexual violence even the Nazis never imagined. It's very popular here."

14

Anger pulsed in my temples as I drove back. It was a catch-22 for women and girls to retaliate. It seemed to be a conspiracy every step of the way. I imagined Leila leaving Adam's office months ago in despair, realizing there was almost no way out. Why did the men need to hold the women down so hard? What were they afraid of? And, more perplexing, honor killing didn't seem to be strictly attached to one race, religion, nationality, culture or geography. What was the common denominator?

I cursed myself for forgetting to enlist Adam to help me search Leila's phone, but then felt relieved since he was a lawyer and my possession of it was probably a felony he'd have to report – or lose his license.

I stopped into a *pelephone* store to buy a hands-free device for my own cell phone so I could use it legally in the car, then looked for a better local map and a beginner's guide to learning Arabic in a used bookstore across Moriah Boulevard. I wasn't too confident I would get very far very fast, though. A friend in the Foreign Service had told me Arabic was one of the most difficult languages for native English-speakers to learn. It took two years to be trained in as a diplomat – twice as long as other languages.

I walked back to my car, the sun blinding, the air unusually calm. *La mujer honrada, la pierna quebrada y en casa* – the honorable woman: locked in the house with a broken leg. I'd heard it years ago when I'd traveled through Andalusia, where they'd made a fetish of virginity and chastity. They called loose women *los sin vergüenza* – the shameless ones. And put them in the same moral caste as the gypsies. They'd say, "*Dime con quién andas y te dire quién eres*" – tell me whom you associate with and I'll tell you who you are. A person's honor and his family's honor went hand in hand. Since women were thought weak, no one expected them to stay wholesome without help. It was their male relatives – not their lovers – who were scorned if they got out of line. If girls had sex out of wedlock, it proved the men failed to defend their honor. Spaniards had been saying 'Glass and a man's honor shatter at the first blow,' since the Middle Ages. Perhaps a vestige of the Moors, the North African Muslims who occupied Spain for 800 years.

But, my God, why the death penalty for sullying Druze honor? Surely their religion addressed this issue, but how was I going to find out? Once the Muslims persecuted them, the Druze closed their faith and kept much of it secret, even from the uninitiated Druze. I'd never heard of a renegade Druze defecting to confess the secrets. And the anthropological fieldwork published on them was scanty since no one had penetrated the sect.

I knew a lot, having researched them for *National Geographic*, but my knowledge was not without its gaps. Their founding prophet, Al-Hakim bi-Amr Allah, the last of the great Fatimid caliphs, was quite a character – he nixed Nile booze cruises, abolished slavery eight centuries before America did, and outlawed polygamy, alcohol and some vegetable for a reason no one seems to remember. He even let his subjects choose their own religion, which is how the Druze faith got started in Cairo in 1017. Their religion was purported to be a complex mixture of neo-Platonic philosophy, Gnosticism, Sufi mysticism and Isma'ili tradition. Someone called them the Zen Buddhists of the Middle East. My favorite theory was that the name "Druze" came from the Greek root *drous* (to know, be wise), from which also came the Western European "Druids," the priestly caste of the Celts. Old Egyptian spiritual ideas that influenced the Druze could have arrived on the west coast of Ireland via trade with the Carthageans. Both Druze and Druids held that the soul could not miss an earthly breath between two lives, unlike in Hinduism or Buddhism. Each time a Druid or a Druze died, their community celebrated a birth. Was it just coincidence that they are the only known cultures to share those exact beliefs about reincarnation?

Druze ethnic heritage was equally mysterious: Most Druze said they were Arab, while others claimed to trace their lineage back to Assassin bloodlines, the ancient Hittites of Anatolia, the European Freemasons (with a similar emphasis on secrecy) or the lost tribes of the Jews.

I spent half an hour looking for a place to park on the Haifa university campus, and resigned myself to following the lead of several students who had parallel-parked halfway up on a curb. I knew the Druze held the Old Testament, the Gospels and the Qur'an sacred, but read them more metaphorically for hidden meaning. *Kitab Al-Hikma* (the Book of Wisdom), the Druze's sacred text, represented their culture and tradition and was the book they most often used. If I could find one, perhaps it would offer a clue to their position on honor killing which could help me get to the bottom of Leila's murder.

As I headed toward the main library in hopes of locating an English translation of the *Kitab*, I became aware of two guys walking a few yards behind me talking in Arabic. "I *looove* American women," one of them said in English. When I glanced back, they laughed and pushed each other. I picked up my pace. "Where do you think she's going?" I heard one ask. "There's no brothel here, doesn't she know that?" Uncontrollable laughter. I walked faster, pushing past some students waiting outside a class and took a shortcut through a building to lose them, but they followed me. When I got to an exit, I started running and didn't stop until I got to the library. *What was that about? How did they know I was American?*

I located the reference librarian, an older bald man who lectured me about why the Druze don't want any non-initiated Druze to read their holy books: "They feel the scripture must be protected from unfit persons. If not, they'll learn the truth of God and life and, if they fail to adhere to those responsibilities, it's worse than if they'd remained unenlightened. A Druze will sacrifice his life to ensure this knowledge doesn't fall into impure hands."

He told me the only copies of the *Kitab* were in Arabic, all hand-written and they didn't own one. But there were half a dozen copies in European libraries that had been found after earthquakes in Syria in 1759 or stolen during the Egyptian invasion of Lebanon in the 1830s. Even if I could get hold of a copy, there was no time or budget with which to translate it.

"Do you know them?" the librarian asked me, pointing with his glance behind me. I turned to see the two Druze guys who had followed me standing about five yards away by the door watching me, not laughing anymore. They saw me looking and one motioned to the other to have a seat next to the door. What did they want? Were they going to confront me when I left?

I carried on with the librarian, who found in the computer a sort of primer on the Druze religion, a set of five volumes called *The Tawhid Faith*, published in English by the American Druze Society probably meant for American Druze kids who couldn't read Arabic. What could be more perfect for me? But then he spotted a notation that they were checked out about three years ago for the last time. They were never returned and the borrower was never located. Maybe I could find them somewhere else.

With his word that he wouldn't tell the Druze guys what I was looking for, the librarian showed me some back stairs so I was able to sneak out and lose them. Hidden in the crowd in the quad, I phoned Devrah, Leila's professor, to see if she knew a way to reach the Bedouin woman who took Leila to the hospital after the attack when she was a child. Maybe she knew more about the Azzams and how the whole conflict got started.

"I think Leila said the woman was a nomad in the Judean desert, or maybe it was the Negev? I'm sure she only speaks Arabic. If she's still alive and you can find her," she said.

I'd never needed a language as much as this before; I cursed my lost years of learning so many useless tongues. Devrah didn't know her name off-hand, but told me about a large painting Leila did of her hanging in the lobby of the Jewish-Arab Center on campus. She said she'd search for a contact number in one of Leila's notebooks. Meanwhile, I got her to order the *Tawhid Faith* books for me from interlibrary loan under her name with a faculty rush on it.

Still looking over my shoulder for the Druze guys who'd followed me to the library, I walked into the lobby of the Jewish-Arab Center. The canvas, perhaps six-feet tall by five-feet wide, was the most prominent thing in the room. The woman depicted in the painting had sunken cataract eyes, high protruding cheekbones and many missing teeth. She had to be at least a hundred years old. Black and white fabric draped everything except her face and hands. Her roped and knobby fingers, sporting gold rings, poked out of the cape like exposed roots of an heirloom olive tree. She was a Nabatean crone.

A girl, whom I could tell was Muslim from her headscarf, stopped nearby to open her backpack so I asked if she could translate the little sign next to the painting. She leaned in to read the fine print. "Badi'a," she said. "*Hakima*. She's a sort of Bedouin healer. Painted two years ago. Oil on canvas. The artist is Leila. No surname."

Leila's nod to anonymity. *Badi'a*, I said to myself. Her haunting face was older than consciousness, reminding me of my visit several years back to the three longest-lived tribes in the world. Badi'a, in oil paint, could have been the grandmother of the centenarians I met on those trips. I photographed her portrait and went up to Devrah's office.

"Here's Leila's stuff," Devrah said, carrying a large box out of the storeroom. She set it down on a paint-splattered worktable in her office and locked the door. Her face was tense, holding back grief. Inside was a handwritten calendar, some sketchbooks, paints and paintbrushes, several library books and a wooden box. Why hadn't Devrah shown these to me last time?

I flipped through a sketchbook. In the middle was a meditation on snakes…snakes as meandering rivers, vines, roots of trees, umbilical cords, snakes in deep crevices in the earth, shedding, forming a circle to bite its own tail (the mythical *ourobouros*), a coiled cobra atop a pharaoh's headdress, Adam and Eve with the snake coiled on the tree, the double helix of DNA like two snakes entwined. On another page, Egyptian hieroglyphs, many in an "S" shape. Even Leila's Arabic script looked serpentine.

"This must have been the study for 'Sacrifice of the Goddess-Queen,' her caduceus painting," I said.

"That's right," Devrah said, peering over at the drawings as she pulled her thick red hair into an elastic band.

The sketchbooks turned up nothing about Badi'a. But I wanted to spend more time looking through Leila's most recent sketchbook, so Devrah let me borrow it. She'd scour her Leila files for anything on Badi'a later today.

Leila's library books were in Arabic and Hebrew. Devrah turned one over. "A critique on the *Song of Songs*."

"What was she using that for?"

"Her last series. She said it's one of the few pre-biblical literary relics that wasn't destroyed."

"The *Song of Songs* is pagan?"

"It comes from ancient love poetry and sacred marriage rituals of Egypt and Sumeria," she said. "Leila mentioned the Sumerian Goddess inviting the king into her 'garden.' "

We exchanged smiles.

"What's this?" I held up the wooden box, which was about a foot long by six inches tall. It looked rather old, with oxidized hardware and most of its dark brown varnish worn off, exposing weathered grey wood.

Devrah lifted it out of my hands and unfastened the catch. Inside were numerous small manila envelopes with string-tie closures. She opened one up, peered inside and took a sniff.

"These are the leftover aromatics from her last series," she said, holding the envelope under my nose.

Its contents smelled of cinnamon. "There's writing on it," I said.

Devrah turned over the envelope. "I can't read Arabic, but I know these are malabathron leaves. She used them for her 'Birth of Hawwah' painting."

We opened the remaining envelopes and looked at the raw ingredients for the ancient incense, Devrah trying to guess each one. There were dried red flowers, a musky-sweet resin, a heady-scented bark, a root redolent of wet dog and dirty-looking resin with no aroma at all.

"It's myrrh," Devrah said of the last one. "It was too dark to mix with the paint for the moon, which is what it's associated with, so Leila actually burned some myrrh as incense while she painted 'Death of the Future.' "

I held some of the brown resin up to my nose.

"It has no aroma until it's smoldered," she said. "It was used for immortality."

Too bad that didn't work for her, I thought.

One envelope had a small bottle of frankincense oil inside.

"She put this in 'Resurrection,' " Devrah said. "It was the most cherished perfume in ancient times," she said, unscrewing the lid and pouring a drop on her finger. "It was symbolic of the sun and revealed God." She daubed some on my throat and then on her own. A spicy citrus scent rose to my nostrils. "The story goes that the sun seduced a king's daughter. When the king discovered it, he killed and buried her. The sun tried to revive the dead princess unsuccessfully with his rays. He promised her she could still come up to see him in the sky so he covered her body in a sweet-smelling nectar that melted away, filling the earth and sky with its fragrance. The spot where her body was buried was where the first frankincense tree grew."

"That's great," I said. "One of the most prized substances of the ancient world was inspired by an honor killing."

When we were done with the box, I pulled out Leila's secret phone and turned it on. It beeped with many new voicemails, but Devrah couldn't tell who most of them were from because they were blocked, identified by an odd-looking phone number (too many digits) or a company or last name only. Leila's voicemail was password-protected, so we couldn't listen to her messages, either. To make matters worse, there was no one called Duncan in her contacts list so she must have had him under a pseudonym.

"By the way, an administrator came to my office yesterday to collect Leila's art and personal things," Devrah said.

"What?" I said, putting the phone down. She's just now mentioning this? "Why?"

"To return them to her family."

"*Oh my God!* What did you say?"

"I told him I didn't have anything."

I sighed in relief. That was at least a misdemeanor. "What are you going to do with them?"

"Take her paintings to Raziel this weekend."

Cold panic hit me. "Raziel?"

She looked defensive. "He offered to keep them at Mujun."

"When did you talk to him?"

"When I called to tell him of her death."

"Oh," I said. "His was a short mourning, I guess...He'll just sell them, you know."

"If her family gets them, they'll be destroyed."

"Well, if you take her paintings to Raziel, you're probably trafficking what is, in effect, stolen art to be sold under the table. That's a felony. And we'll never see them again."

Her eyes widened. "I guess I'll just keep them hidden in the back of the storeroom for now."

I struggled to fall asleep that night at the hospice-hotel. So many questions and worries about Leila's death swirled in my head and I couldn't stay in Israel forever trying to get to the bottom of it. Scenes from a novel I'd read a year ago kept playing themselves out in my mind. In preparation for an interview with Gabriel Garcia Márquez at his home in Colombia, I'd read several of his books, including *Chronicle of a Death Foretold*, which told of a kind of honor killing in an unnamed country like Colombia, where a man was murdered by two brothers whose sister the man had seduced. Someone said of the anticipated murder: "There's no way out of this. It's as if it's already happened." Another one's mother said, "Honor is love." The townspeople didn't try to stop the murder because they considered it a family affair, sacrosanct from outside intervention. But, unlike in Leila's situation, the adulteress was not, in fact, killed, and her and her family's honor was recovered after the murder of her lover.

I turned on the light and made a few bad sketches of the crime scene to help me remember details. I talked to the audio recording app on my phone. I tried to write, but couldn't. I fixated on Tamir's possible role in Leila's death. What exactly did he do to Leila in the woods when she was a little girl? I imagined the worst and then jumped up to physically shake it out of myself. I knew I couldn't be less qualified to investigate this. I turned my thoughts to Fadi: How curious that, according to Ru'yah, he had covered up Leila's body – a respectful, loving, gesture – but it was uncovered when I joined the crowd in front of her house. Why? My mind kept straying away from the investigation to analyze nuances of eye contact we'd made, the few times we'd touched, words he'd spoken that could in any way indicate his attraction to me. Now I really couldn't sleep.

I checked Leila's secret phone, but there were no calls I'd missed and barely any signal here in the boonies of Mt. Carmel. It would be running out of battery power soon. I took a Benadryl to make me sleepy and edited pictures for an hour until it kicked in. As I was tucking under the covers feeling woozy, my phone rang. It was Stephan, the assistant editorial page editor at *The New York Times*.

"I need your story pronto," he said. "The Israeli Defense Force shelled the home of your suicide bomber's family in Gaza."

"Huh?"

"Killed eleven of her family members in retaliation."

"Oh my God."

"Send me your piece. You got two hours."

Crap. I edited it as best as I could in my condition, somehow remembered to spell-check and emailed it off. Something told me I shouldn't, but I wrote off the feeling as lack of confidence or drug-induced paranoia.

When I finally fell asleep, I had erratic dreams. In one, I needed to cross a river, but couldn't find a way. In another, I surged through the circle of men hiding Leila's body and pulled the blanket off. She lay on the ground in a pool of blood, the color of shame, her hair sticky and matted from her head injury. But, to my further horror, my brother, Cary, lay next to her, a gaping wound to his throat. Leila rubbed her eyelids with the fingers of her bloody hand, reddening her skin like the Neolithic red ochre burials. Then they both opened their eyes. When they saw me, they said in unison: "You're too late."

15

To shake off the nightmare, I forced myself to jog at dawn, as though that would normalize things. My neck felt unreliable from fitful sleep, but at least my hearing seemed to be restored. I picked up a *Jerusalem Post* at a newsstand in Daliat. An article about Leila's murder indicated the rumors in Atabi leaned towards honor killing, but "no clear motive or obvious suspect has been established, two criteria usually self-evident in honor killings." Her burial was scheduled for that morning, but no services "per the family's request."

I didn't have the nerve to ask Kamil, so I phoned Metanis at seven a.m. for the burial time. I wanted to go; correction – I needed to go. But I got no answer. I finished writing a story on Palestinian and Israeli Jewish Buddhists I hoped to sell to *Mother Jones*, then dialed the newsroom of the *Jerusalem Post* and got David Cohen, the author of the article about Leila, on the phone. I told him I was a freelance journalist and Leila's friend and wanted to talk to him about the case. He was going to be tied up all day on deadline, but invited me to dinner in Jerusalem that evening. I hoped he could give me some insight into what was going on at the police department.

There was one person I had avoided so far whom I knew had information I needed. I dreaded this duty, but if I really wanted to do the right thing by Leila – and advance my career to the next level – I had to make myself go.

~ ~ ~

A very old Druze, a huge sphere of a woman, sat alone on the porch in a rocking chair. I'd gotten directions to this home after asking around town; it hadn't been easy to find with no numbers on the houses. I approached her and, having practiced with my phrasebook, asked in Arabic, "Does Tamir Shahin live here?" Naturally, since I'd asked in Arabic, she answered in Arabic, and I couldn't understand a word after *ay-wa* – yes.

"*Bi tit kalimi inglizi?*" Do you speak English? I tried hopefully.

She shrugged, watery brown eyes twinkling. "*Non, mais je parle français.*"

"*Moi aussi!*" It was my lucky day.

She smiled and motioned me up the steps.

"I lived in the Lebanon during the French Mandate," she said in French.

That was, what, 1920 to 1940-something? "You are much too young for that," I said.

"*Mais, non!*" she exclaimed, revealing a few missing front teeth. "I even remember when the *Ottoman* Empire fell! I was a young girl. We lived in Syria on the mountain – the Djebel Druze. Come. Sit." She waved me over.

I seated myself on the bench beside her rocker. A rusty ironing board was pushed up against one wall of the house on the porch, its ancient iron with a fraying cloth-covered cord plugged into an uncovered outlet.

"My father lost both his brothers fighting the Turks," she said. "Then my brothers and cousins led the Syrian revolt against the French in '20. We Druze had our own state for about five years, *inshallah*. My husband fought the French, too, but we lost, you know. We brought our children to the Lebanon and then to Palestine in '46."

"Is Tamir in your family?" I asked.

"He's my great-grandson."

"Then you knew Leila Azzam."

She frowned and pulled at the *foutta* where it was wrapped tightly around her chin. "*Bint hara. Bint hara.* Girl 'of the neighborhood.' When I was young, we said" – she leaned forward and unintentionally spat on me a little while saying "*la lessive de l'honneur ne se coule qu'au sang.*" The laundry of honor is only bleached with blood.

Her openness was fascinating; I resisted the urge to interrupt her with a barrage of embarrassing questions.

"The trouble today is we're losing our traditions that keep girls pure, you know. I was a *shattra*, a *bint beit* – a decent girl. Most girls were. But now, it's changing."

She looked out to the road. A few houses over, a neighbor watered flowers on her porch as a toddler climbed backwards down the steps.

"What is done about the *bint hara*?" I asked, as though I didn't know.

She raised her eyebrows as she looked down at her black dress and picked a piece of white lint off her enormous bosom. She shook her head as if saying the word was even more than she could bear.

"Must they be…stopped?" I asked.

She nodded. "*Oui.* A woman's *ayb* descends in the female line, you know. How many children do you have, *Madame?*"

"None."

She looked alarmed and took up my hand in hers. "What a terrible sadness! Sitt Afifah will keep you in her prayers."

I assumed she was Sitt Afifah and smiled.

She looked down at my hand she was holding. "You're so thin, *Madame.* You must eat more to have babies!"

"I promise."

She let my hand go and I followed her gaze toward the neighbor who emptied the used water from a dishpan off a balcony into the garden below.

"It hasn't always been this way, you know," she said ruefully. "During the time of the clans, land was more valuable than honor. But since the occupation, after the Druze began losing land, many families reversed the phrase 'land before honor' to 'honor before land.' "

"I heard that long ago, both the man and the woman who were in a forbidden relationship that sullied the family honor would be killed to cleanse it," I said.

She nodded. "That rarely happens any more."

"Why not?"

She regarded me with indignant surprise. "Blood feuds, my dear! If you kill a man from another clan, it will spark violence that could go on forever," she said, punctuating the last word – *toujours* – with two raps of her cane on the wooden floorboards of the porch.

"So why kill the woman?" I asked.

"Then, it's over." She dusted her palms off each other to illustrate.

"But is it?"

She glared at me. "*Oui!*" She scratched her head through the scarf. "Well…it did use to be simpler when the Turks were in power."

Suddenly, she bolted upright, startling me. I had no idea she could move so quickly. "Wait! I want to show you something!" She pulled herself out of the chair with a cane.

I rose to help her.

"Don't leave!" She said, waddling inside.

When she returned several minutes later, Afifah was carrying what appeared to be a faded red woolen sock, about four feet long, with something very stiff inside. She eyed the object with a sort of secret pride and laid it reverently in my hands. It was heavy and solid, like a weapon. The cover was knitted closed.

"When I was a young woman, I knitted this cover. Then, I presented this dagger to my husband on our wedding day."

"Was this your wedding gift to him?" I asked, bemused.

"No, *I* was the gift. The dagger means the death penalty for infidelity. The cover symbolizes the most sacred law of the clan: If I was unfaithful, my husband could not unsheathe the knife unless all my own male relatives were dead. He had to return me and the dagger to my father or brothers who would carry out the punishment."

The front door opened and out came a middle-aged woman in a *foutta*, followed by Tamir. When they saw me and the sacred heirloom I held, they both froze, then glanced from Afifah to me to the sword and back again, as though treason were in progress. I placed the relic in Afifah's lap and stood up.

"I'm so sorry about your loss," I said to Tamir.

Tamir grabbed the sword and handed it to the woman he'd come out with, whom he called *Omm* (mother), ordering her inside. Then, he knelt at Afifah's side and whispered to her, trying to help her out of the rocker. She refused his gentle exhortations until he gave up.

"She's not of sound mind anymore," he said, turning to me. "You shouldn't bother her."

A cricket chirped happily underneath the porch.

"I came to talk to you, actually," I said, relieved he could speak English.

Tamir's mother returned to the porch carrying a white button-down shirt with sweat stains under the arms and went to work at the ironing board.

To my surprise, Tamir lit a cigarette. Tobacco was forbidden to religious Druze, and I'd read that two Israeli Druze women had been killed by their families for smoking. I'd have thought he would at least be discreet about it. His sun-streaked brown hair and strangely Slavic blue eyes stood out next to his olive complexion. Every move he made required a swagger. *Handsome guy, for a child rapist.*

"What happened to Leila?" I asked.

He glared at me and took a long drag. I waited for him to answer, but he continued to smoke, not taking his eyes off me. Was he checking me out? Trying to intimidate me? I glanced over at Afifah, but she was engrossed by the cricket, which was on the porch by her rocker now. Tamir's mother ironed an armpit of the shirt and an acrid odor rose in the air.

"Can you tell me *anything*?" I pressed.

"*Hish! Hish!*" Afifah said to the cricket, trying to shoo it away.

Tamir exhaled. "A dog gets what it deserves."

"Why'd she deserve it?"

He smiled vaguely, revealing a tiny dimple on his left cheek. "Are you married?"

"What?"

"Do you have a *husband*?" he snapped.

"Yes," I lied.

He smiled wider. "Your husband lets you come all the way from America by yourself?"

"Sure."

"He must not love you very much if he lets you travel alone."

I willed my focus. "You were angry when you came to the Azzams' house the other night."

"He realizes that you could easily cheat and still lets you go." Tamir rested his rear on the porch railing, as if we were having a neighborly chat.

Afifah didn't seem to understand anything, but was eyeing our exchange with an interest that was anything but senile.

"What upset you, Tamir?"

"Are you going to tell your husband you were visiting me at my house?"

"Are you going to answer any of my questions?"

"You know *nothing* about Druze," he said.

"I know a little," I said. "But I'd like to know a lot more – if you'll be good enough to share."

Tamir stared at me – contemptuously or lasciviously, the line between seemed blurry at best. Afifah muttered something aloud and they bickered in a short burst of Arabic.

A pretty young woman opened the front door and came out onto the porch with a tray of coffee. Tamir waved her off, but behind his back, Afifah beckoned her to set it down on the low table next to the door. Tamir's mother held up the ironed shirt. He rested his cigarette on the porch railing and let her help him put the button-down on over the T-shirt he was wearing.

The cricket hopped into the center of the porch and sang. Tamir picked up his cigarette and leaned down towards the insect. He pressed the burning end onto the cricket's back, sending it leaping and then falling onto its side.

"*Ay!*" the women exclaimed.

Tamir laughed and looked up at me before I could hide my disgust. He watched me as he stepped on his cigarette and began to button his shirt.

"Here's your first Druze lesson, so pay attention." He leaned in close to my face.

I felt my chest muscles quaver with nerves. I took a deep breath, afraid to exhale. He was so close.

"A man's honor lies between the legs of a woman," he said, tucking in his shirt. Then he stepped on the cricket and sauntered down the steps.

16

I walked around the *souk* contemplating my collision with Tamir's family, cataloguing the aromas of lamb, coffee with cardamom, roasted pistachios and yeast in the market. Such approachable, friendly smells, a part of the culture the Druze allowed a stranger. As I passed through the crowd, loneliness yanked hard on me.

I went to Ru'yah's without phoning first. When she opened the door and saw me, her eyes dimmed with regret and she looked behind her for some excuse not to let me in.

"What if someone sees you here?" she whispered. The circles under her eyes looked deeper.

"No one's home at the Azzams," I said, pointing to the empty driveway across the road. "Please."

"We're in enough pain already with Leila gone. Can't you just let us be without the shame we had to bear for so long?"

There were so many things wrong with that question, I didn't know where to begin. And Ru'yah wasn't very convincing.

"I wish I could be of help to you, Fereby," she said, untying her apron. "But I must go to the market."

I leaned on the doorjamb. ""How's Khadija?"

"A little better." She sighed and pulled a photograph out of her apron pocket and handed it to me. It was a tiny black-haired baby hooked up to half a dozen hospital machines. She had little pink, heart-shaped lips.

"She's beautiful, Ru'yah."

"I miss her all the time I'm not at the hospital," she said.

"I'm sure you do."

We both looked at the picture.

"Ru'yah, I know you loved Leila. I'm not confident the authorities are trying to solve this case. I could really use your help."

She smoothed her skirt.

I wanted to reach out and touch her arm but something stopped me. "You're afraid. There's something you want to say."

She glared at me. "Yes, but this isn't the United States, Fereby. And we don't want it to be. You can't just storm into our village like the Marines and take command."

I took a deep breath. "I really don't mean to do that."

She stood her ground. "Let me explain something. The Israeli Druze are in a very delicate position right now. We're traditional, living in a modern country. There's been a lot of change in the last forty years that's very frightening to our elders. Did you know that in the '80s, no Druze woman could even shop at the *souk*? They could only go to town to see a doctor. In the '70s, half the Druze girls were illiterate. But not long ago, Druze women started going to college – a Jewish orthodox one that keeps men and women separated. This was fine until women wanted more…then some became active in local politics…That's when the problems started." She looked away, shaking her head.

"What kind?"

"The more our women get out in the world, the more strangers they might talk to," she whispered, wiping sweat from her upper lip. The sun was already beating down on us.

"And then they want to leave the villages or marry a non-Druze," I added.

"The religious view it as westernization, which angers them," she said.

"And that's why the violence."

Ru'yah pulled an elastic off her wrist and put her hair up in a ponytail. "People don't know how to behave. Some are holding on to tradition while others are trying to move forward."

"Why was Leila killed then?"

She rubbed her forehead in exasperation. "There's an ancient saying: 'The wound of words is worse than the wound of swords. The wound that bleedeth inwardly is the most dangerous.' If a woman defiles the family honor and isn't killed, the men are thought cowardly. Isn't it preferable for only one person to die than for an entire family to die from shame?"

"But girls have been killed even when they weren't involved with a man," I said.

"Yes, if men talk about a woman enough, or if she acts or dresses too boldly, she causes shame."

Well, that fixed me squarely in the slut camp. "Sounds like a full-time job for the men, making sure the women aren't fooling around or becoming too confident."

"And for the women," she said. "Mothers must keep a very close eye on their daughters. If they're bad, it reflects mostly on the mother's character."

"So they tell their daughters it's for their own good to keep their heads down?"

"Well," she said, looking back down at the picture of Khadija. "It is."

I was surprised she was opening up to me, but realized I had to take advantage of this opportunity. I was done with gentle persuasion. "Look, if you know anything about Leila's death and you don't come forward, you're committing a felony and could go to prison." I had no idea if this was true.

Ru'yah gaped at me, a blend of dread and loathing in her eyes.

"I won't tell anyone where I got the information," I said. "You have my word."

She inhaled, shutting her eyes for a long moment, as though she were reaching for something so contained, it required extreme concentration to retrieve. Finally, she waved me inside the house.

The kitchen was dark today; no meal was cooking. She pulled out a chair for me at the table.

"You understand what will happen if you tell anyone," she said.

I looked her in the eye. "I won't endanger you."

"I only have fifteen minutes."

"As you wish."

She put a pot of water on for the mandatory coffee and leaned against the counter, hands in the pockets of her black skirt. She looked as if she could use a two-week vacation of nothing but sleep.

"As far as we know, Leila was the first Druze born in Israel by Caesarean section done by a male doctor. Her mother almost died – Dima was in labor for two days before Leila's father took her to the hospital."

I raised my eyebrows.

"They say her head was very big."

Probably to accommodate her estimable brain. "Why'd he wait so long?"

"Druze are very traditional about such things. Births had to be attended only by women back then."

She pulled two brown coffee cups out of the cupboard and looked inside them. "That was the first indignity. And then she was born with – I don't know what you would call this…something over her face?" She spread her fingers wide and waved them across her face, bringing them together down at her neck.

Amniotic sac? I thought for a moment. "A caul?"

She nodded. "They took extraordinary care in burying it and the afterbirth deep in the ground down in the forest. Everyone predicted that she would be dangerous."

I almost laughed. "That *she* would be dangerous?" In Medieval Europe, cauls were considered good luck talismans, a sign that the child was destined for greatness or psychic powers. Sailors spent hefty sums buying cauls to protect them from drowning.

"Almost everyone considers the Azzams the victims here," she said. "They were respectable before Leila. They lived in a state of disgrace for almost eighteen years."

"Not just because of the male doctor who delivered her."

She turned her back to spoon ground coffee into the boiling water.

"I heard about the assault when she was small," I added.

Ru'yah turned the fire down and leaned on the stove with both hands, her back to me. She took a deep breath, then found something needing washing in the sink.

"Is the disgrace over now that she's gone?" I asked.

"It seems so," she said. "What a pity she didn't marry Tamir last year. She'd still be alive and her family's honor would be recovered."

"Was that an option, marrying him earlier?" I asked.

"Tamir and Leila became engaged when she was sixteen. Druze usually wait a year before signing the marriage license, then have the wedding ceremony and party a year or two later. Their families sped up the process, having them sign the marriage license a few months after the engagement. The wedding was supposed to take place this past year when Leila turned seventeen, the legal age to marry in Israel. But when our *shaikhs* found out, they made her family wait until she was eighteen due to her special circumstances."

"Being…everything we've been discussing?"

She blinked a dubious agreement. "Her family was very upset."

"Why?"

"They felt it was more unfair punishment. Because of Leila, they haven't been able to find a suitable husband for their older daughter, who's already twenty-three. They struggle with money. It's hard to sell produce when people despise you."

She opened a small jar and added something light brown to the coffee. The scent of cardamom rose in the room.

"So, they planned the wedding for her eighteenth birthday, the first day they could," I said.

She nodded.

"And if Leila had married Tamir, her honor would have been restored?"

"Not exactly. A girl's honor – her *'ird* – can only be lost, never regained." (*'Ird* was pronounced a lot like *'ard*, the Arabic word for land, I noticed.) "The family would have cleansed its shame and resumed its place in society, not without the memories, but better than it's been."

"Why would marrying Tamir fix things?"

She poured a cup of coffee and set it in front of me. "He's the one who defiled her. It would close the matter. And it was better than killing her. The Azzams could never truly retrieve the status they once had. Leila was a daily reminder of this."

So he really did rape her, the freak. "Was Tamir ever punished?" I asked.

"He was only thirteen at the time, but because of her young age, he spent five years in a prison-school for boys."

"Was he rehabilitated when he got out?"

She shrugged. "He refused mandatory army service, called it prison. The army arrested him in the middle of the night, taking him out in chains, humiliating his family."

"Did he serve then?"

"Not the full three years. He was caught assaulting Palestinian prisoners in the Shatta detention camp. Harassing female soldiers. Fighting with male officers. He was often moved around. He put a picture on the Internet of another IDF soldier taking a picture of Tamir standing over a dead Palestinian that he said he'd shot. Then he shot and killed an American peace activist and that was it. "

I felt my stomach lurch. "What's he doing now?"

"The family woodworking business. On the highway to Isfiyeh." She pointed in the direction.

I stroked the coffee cup absently. "So, what happened to Leila Monday night?"

"I guess someone in her family finally killed her."

"Not Tamir?"

She shook her head. "I doubt it."

"Is there any chance it was a suicide?"

She looked puzzled and shook her head.

"Do you know who, then?"

"There is not a practical choice."

Except for Fadi, I thought sadly.

"And no one has confessed, which is unusual, especially since last time...the word around the village was all the same."

"*Last time?*" I said, putting my coffee down.

"It was about five years ago. Fadi tried to kill her."

My heart sank into my gut.

17

H ow?" I asked.
Ru'yah shook her head. "The Azzams kept it to themselves. Leila only told me that he cut her."

I winced as a horrific image passed through my mind. "Was it reported to the police?"

"No."

"So what would have provoked the murder this time?"

She got up, looking for something to wash. "People are saying she...was involved with a man. An American."

"Do you know anything about him?"

"No." She looked down at her hands.

"They'd murder based on a *rumor*?"

"Honor's not about truth, Fereby. It's about perception."

She looked up at the clock on the stove. I was keeping her too long. I stood up to go.

At threshold of the front door, I turned to her. "Why did Leila have to die? Wasn't there some other way?"

In the daylight, the circles under Ru'yah's eyes shone like bruises. "With Tamir, she had a chance to get on with her life."

"Being married to Tamir is not a life."

We glanced over as some children shrieked with laughter in the street.

"Where were you during all of this?" I said. "Where were Leila's mother and sister?"

Her eyes welled up. "I saw an honor killing in Daliat when I was a teenager, Fereby. A woman named Ibtihaj Hasson was stabbed to death on the street by her younger brother."

"Why?"

"For living on her own."

"Not for something sexual?"

She shook her head. "They hung her body on the street as a warning." Ru'yah looked scared.

"Leila's mother couldn't even stand up for her after she was *raped* at four, for God's sake?" I said.

"Fereby, you don't understand...she wanted to help – all mothers of rape victims want to help their daughters, but they need their family's honor back. If they take their daughters' side, all females in the family are then at risk. And when a girl is raped, everyone accuses the mother of not teaching her daughter to protect herself."

"Don't just blame the victim – blame the victim's *mother*?" I said. "That's insane."

Ru'yah wiped her eyes with her apron. A strange, emboldened look appeared on her face. "It used to be different."

I looked at her curiously.

"About a thousand years ago, there was a girl imprisoned for disgracing the family honor. She'd run away with a boy her father disapproved of. When she was released years later, the men of her tribe were going to stone her to death since she wasn't a virgin anymore. But the women in her family somehow whisked her away to a secret location. She became a legend, a symbol of romantic love." Ru'yah's expression had softened and I noticed her beauty for the first time.

"Now, if a preschool-aged girl is raped, her life becomes worthless," I said.

"Rape is the worst thing," she said, tensing again. "In the Galilee, there was a nineteen-year-old Druze girl who was raped by a Jew. Her family quickly married her to a Druze man in his mid-sixties."

"That's an option?"

"Sometimes. In some countries, a girl's only choices are to live in a prison for her own protection or become a prostitute."

"They send the *girl* to prison – not the people threatening her?"

She nodded and took a step outside the threshold.

"Do you see that two-story house with the red roof?" She pointed her eyes down the road.

"Next to the darker tan house?"

"Yes. There's a woman living there who was molested as a young teenager in 1962. Her family hid her in the attic and have never let her out."

No wonder women stopped sticking up for each other. As I left, I drove slowly past the house with the red roof. It was unremarkable. Not dilapidated or even unkempt. Same as all the rest.

A memory I hadn't thought of in years came back all the sudden: In the '70s, the early part of my mother's missionary career, she visited a tribe of Nigerian Igbo that had a women's council called the Inyom Nnobi that represented a supreme Goddess. If a girl was raped or even sexually harassed, it was considered an assault on all women and an injury to the Goddess herself. All the women of the village would stop the cooking, housework, sex with their husbands and parenting. They'd just pick up and blow out of town together with only their nursing infants. They'd return only when the men promised justice would be served.

What would happen if Druze women went on strike like this?

It was ten-thirty a.m. when I dropped in on Metanis at the police station. He walked out to the lobby, probably so it would be a shorter distance to get me out the door.

"When's the burial?" I asked.

"Soon, but do not go." He busied himself flipping through a logbook on the receptionist's desk.

"What time?"

"Half-past eleven maybe," he said, not meeting my eyes. "Do not go."

"Why not?"

"No one going."

"So, it was a hit-and-run."

"It appears to be an accident, but we're still investigating."

"A hit-and-run suicide or hit-and-run honor killing?"

He looked up, startled at my directness and reached for the door to return to the secure area.

"May I see the autopsy report?" I pressed.

"It is police evidence only until it get to court."

"Can you just tell me where on her body she was struck?"

The receptionist regarded me warily.

"This is sensitive matter," he said in a quieter voice, walking me to the outer door of the building. "Please allow us to complete work on the case."

"I read in the paper you don't have any suspects yet."

He remained poker-faced.

"Did you know Fadi was thrown a hero's party night before last at the bar?"

He looked skeptical.

"I was there."

The corners of his mouth turned up the slightest possible smile as his eyes narrowed.

"They were celebrating."

"Maybe for something else," he said. "You must excuse me." He turned and walked back inside the station, his posture stiffer than necessary.

In the *souk*, inspired by Leila's painting "Sub Rosa Shame," I bought a dozen long-stemmed red roses from the flower merchant to take to her grave.

It was eleven a.m. when I arrived at the cemetery on the other end of the village and parked across the road. A six-foot-high stone wall surrounded the graveyard on three sides. A small shed with corrugated tin roofing sat off to one side, probably used as a mourning tent. There were no headstones, only piles of rocks, and not a single flower to be seen, either, except the ones blossoming from weeds taking over the plots.

Three men were hand-digging a grave, piling up dirt as they went. A large tan pickup truck idled nearby. I climbed into the back seat of my car and pulled my camera out of my backpack. I crouched down and watched what was going on through the zoom lens.

Twenty minutes passed. Another man suddenly popped up from the hole and climbed out. It was Leila's father, Kamil. I strained to see his face. He dusted his hands on his pants and motioned to the others. They all walked over to the truck and together lifted a plain wooden casket out of the back. *Leila.* I snapped pictures as I felt my throat close. Why wasn't Fadi there? They carried the casket down into the grave, then filled it in with the dirt until it was a mound. Lastly, Kamil threw a rock on it. He began walking towards the road, his head down. I glanced around and saw his car across the street from mine. I ducked way down so he wouldn't see me. A minute later, he had gone. The other men were standing by the truck next to the grave sharing a jug of water.

That was Leila's funeral. Metanis had either lied to me about the time of the burial or was mistaken, but I would've missed the whole thing if I hadn't gotten there early.

After the men left, I made sure no one was around before I walked over to the cemetery. I approached Leila's grave with my bouquet. There was no marker, only the one stone on top. Others had dozens. I knelt down, clutching the roses, and found several stray stones and lay them on her burial plot.

"Leila," I said aloud, swallowing hard. "You saved my life...I knew something was wrong, but I couldn't do anything. I didn't know what to do. I failed you...I'm sorry!" Sobs came forth and I bent myself toward her grave until I could speak again. "I don't know what happened to you, but I'm going to find out. And I'm going to make them pay!" I wiped the tears from my cheeks and held up the roses. "I brought you these roses, ancient symbol of secrecy, that the mystery of your death may be revealed to me." I tore some petals off a blossom and, as I cast them onto her grave, a loud voice booming behind me made me jump out of my skin. I turned just as a blur passed across my eyes. A thick arm reached down in front of my face and tore the roses out of my hand, thorns ripping across my skin. I lurched back to see the purest fury igniting his face.

18

K amil began to revile me in Arabic or Hebrew – they start to sound alike at a certain velocity – shaking the roses with each angry gesture.

"What the – " I cried, stumbling on Leila's grave as I leapt to my feet.

"Forbidden!" he yelled, shaking the flowers violently over his head. Crimson petals floated down onto his head and shoulders, oblivious the ritual was over.

Instinctively, I crossed my hands over my heart. "Am I not supposed to be in here?"

"*La!* Flowers forbidden!"

Well, that explained the complete absence of floral arrangements in the cemetery.

"I'm sorry!" I said, backing away. "I didn't know."

"Prayer forbidden!" he scolded.

"Prayer?"

"For *her*!" He shook a weather-beaten finger at the grave. "Who are you coming here to intrude on us with your American ideas? *Im-shee!* Go home!"

Kamil started to walk away with the tattered roses, muttering in his language.

I braced myself. "Your daughter was murdered, Sir," I called. "And she was my friend."

He turned and his eyes shot loathing through me. "You. Have. *No. Right!*"

I blinked at him, debating how to handle this, my heart drumming in my ears. "Are you *defending* her murder, Sir?"

He started back towards me and I feared how close he would come, what he would do.

"Before Leila, we left our doors unlocked all night and no one dared come in. If I left town, no one dared to pass through my door. Dima walked by herself in the village and men were afraid to look. Adulterous women are the greatest threat to our survival. If men cannot find such women, they live moral. Women *must* be taught self-discipline! Leila's death sets the example."

I willed myself to stay focused. "How do you *know* she committed adultery, Sir?"

He narrowed his eyes at me. "You. Know. Nothing!"

"Leila didn't deserve to be murdered and, in any case, murder is wrong."

"Killing is the worst sin but if it's done to remove a disgrace, and done for love, not hate, we accept it. Shaikh Amin Tarif said so. Any proud Druze would do the same thing to protect his family name."

"How is it okay to kill someone for disobeying the norms of society?"

"The U.S.A. has the death penalty for disobey some of your laws, Miss Jones."

I couldn't argue with him there. I noticed half a dozen people standing in front of the cemetery watching us. I walked wide around Kamil and lowered my eyes as I hurried past them to my car. When I drove off, he was still standing in the same place, one fist clenched by his side while the other kept thrashing the roses, spilling petals over Leila's grave.

Trembling, I headed toward the square, chastising myself. I should've known not to bring flowers there. My left palm was bleeding from several long, deep scratches the rose thorns made when Kamil ripped the bouquet from my grip. I couldn't think of another time I'd made such a glaring cross-cultural faux pas.

I drove around for a while, ashamed and angry at my lack of understanding of these people. Still, I knew Leila should have a real funeral and I promised her right then I'd give her one somehow, someday.

Even though most of the evidence seemed to point to Fadi as the killer, and I wanted more than anything to nail down a probable suspect, I couldn't shake a feeling that said no. He'd had a million opportunities to kill her from the start of his family's disgrace but only tried once – and couldn't pull it off. Why not? Or maybe my inexplicable fondness (or unmitigated lust) for him was keeping me in denial.

If the police and the Azzams and Tamir weren't going to help me get to the bottom of this, I needed to go over their heads. And I was in just the right place for that. I pulled over at the House of Druze as Mustafa was preparing for an afternoon tour group. He sketched me detailed directions to the house I was looking for, less than half a mile from the Azzams'.

None of the homes on the street had address numbers. The one I thought resembled the home Mustafa described was a one-story, humble, white concrete affair that seemed to be attached by breezeways to several other homes, in a sort of compound. Bony old trees twisted and stooped in the front yard like statues of crusty, revered ancestors.

I buttoned the top two buttons on my blouse and pulled my hair back in a ponytail. When I knocked, a little old woman in a long, black dress, not one hair showing under her *foutta*, answered the door.

"*Ahlan wasahlan ya Hagga,*" I said. Hello, Ma'am. "*'Ismee Fereby McCullough Jones. Awza ashoof Shaikh, min fadlik. Mumkin?*" May I see the *shaikh*, please?

"*Lahza,*" she said, in a tiny voice, then turned and closed the door halfway. I heard her walking away and calling out. Perhaps she'd told me to hang on, she'd go get him.

When the door opened again a few minutes later, a short, elderly man with a bushy white mustache and a long, white beard stood in the threshold. Wearing a long black robe, billowy black pants and a white turban was Shaikh Fouad Hayyan, the head of the Druze Religious Council of Israel. He looked like an Arabesque Santa.

"Shaikh?"

He nodded, expressionless.

"Fereby McCullough Jones. *It sharraf na,*" I said. Pleased to meet you. I didn't dare try to shake his hand.

"Please come inside, Miss Jones," he said in thickly accented, but perfect English.

Relieved that he could speak my language, I followed him into the kitchen, where the old woman stood by the stove. The kitchen was the color of stale bread, painted white probably twenty years ago, with no decoration whatsoever, as if someone had taken pains to keep it as utilitarian as possible. A doorway off to the right side revealed a sparse bedroom with twin beds. I'd heard that Druze *shaikhs* could ask their fiancées to marry them without conjugal relations and wondered if that was the case here.

There was a large living room beyond the kitchen appointed with two red sofas and several red armchairs all pushed against the walls, leaving the middle of the room empty. White lace doilies lay over the backs of the furnishings.

The *shaikh* waved to a sofa for me to sit on and then eased himself into a chair by the window with the help of his cane. The sun coming through the window at an angle backlit his white beard like a swath of raw silk. He looked at me for a long moment, unselfconscious of the pregnant pause. His eyes were at once innocent and certain, like pure water. "What brings you to honor us with a visit today, Miss Jones?"

"I am the one who is honored, thank you. I'm visiting from the United States," I said, feeling nervous about my manners; he demanded that level of formality. "I'd like to learn more about the Druze."

"We prefer the name *Muwahhidoon*, Miss Jones." He spoke in an assured voice, but quiet enough that I had to sit forward to hear him. " 'Druze' came from Nashtakin Darazi, a heretic of our sect, whom we try to forget. Unfortunately, the name has held fast through the centuries."

"I'm sorry," I said, feeling my face flush. I knew this from my previous research, but no one had corrected me until now and many Druze called themselves Druze. "I'm finding it difficult to locate information."

"Our religion is private," he said in a sterner tone. "We do not reveal it to outsiders. Did you not learn enough in preparing your article on us last year?"

I knew my *National Geographic* article had been translated into Hebrew, and Leila said many Druze had read it, but I was impressed that he remembered my name from the byline.

"Yes, Sir – Shaikh. I did, but now I'm on a personal quest…I would appreciate hearing more about the part of your religion that is not secret, if there is anything you can share."

"The most valuable knowledge illuminates the path towards immortality," he said, enunciating as if he were reciting a poem. "And that must not be casually revealed."

I strained to catch each word he spoke, which had a precious, primeval quality to it, made more so by his accent and hushed tone. I ached to get out my phone to record him or my notepad, but didn't dare.

"I will tell you a story that is not in our scriptures," he said. "After God created the universe, humans began to sin. God decided to send prophets to help lead them back to honorable living. First, he sent Noah, but only his family followed him. Next, he sent Abraham, but only his tribe followed him. Then came Moses, and all the tribes of Israel followed. He sent Jesus, and the gentiles went. He sent Mohammed and the rest of the world followed – except the *Muwahhidoon*. So, God sent the Angel Gabriel and, speaking through him to the *Muwahhidoon*, said: 'I have sent many true prophets and the whole world has accepted one or another. You, however, have followed none.' The *Muwahhidoon* sent a message back through Gabriel: 'God is enough for us.' "

I smiled.

The old woman emerged from the kitchen with the compulsory tray of coffee, tottering over to a table next to the *shaikh*. She bent over slowly and he reached out to help her put the tray down.

"You have met my wife?"

"*It sharaf na*," I said.

Her *foutta* concealed most of her chin and mouth, but I could detect an impish smile pointing up from it. Neither offered her name.

"Mulberries from our garden," the *shaikh* said, holding out a bowl to me.

I tasted one, still warm from the sun. The stark white walls of the sitting room were festooned with colorful crocheted discs framing photographs of children. In the center was a fabric wallhanging depicting a turbaned man, a Druze flag and an old stone building, images familiar to me from the House of Druze. An old photograph of a man that resembled the *shaikh* was framed above the wallhanging.

"Are you religious, Miss Jones?" Shaikh Hayyan asked, cradling his cup in one hand.

"Well, when I was seven, my aunt who was a nun told me I was thinking too much about religion."

His eyes twinkled.

"Now I would say I'm spiritual, but I don't say set prayers or go to church."

"The Prophet, peace be upon him, believed that one hour's contemplation on the work of God is better than years of obligatory prayer. Most people don't suspect their own divinity."

"Are we divine?" I asked.

"Of course. Human beings, God's most magnificent creations, are brought to life by a divine spark. We mortals have two natures – the mortal and the divine, the body and the spirit. We must affirm our divinity and, at the same time, do no harm to any man."

I wondered if that included any woman, too. "Shaikh, could you explain to me the place of women in *Muwahhidoon* society?"

He gestured to his wife. "*Muwahhidoon* women are the center of the family and the keepers of tradition. As such, they command their own chastity and modesty. Woman is the sacred cup of honor passed down from the ancestors."

"What if the cup is chipped?" I was shocked at my own boldness.

He stared at me for a very long moment and I feared what would happen next. "Did you know that glass was first invented not far from here about five thousand years ago?" he asked.

I nodded.

"A woman's reputation is like glass. Once broken, it is ruined. It cannot be fixed or repaired. Whatever happens to woman is the most visible – it is a reflection on the whole family."

I recalled the almost unbreakable glassware the Druze were famous for making. A salesman had demonstrated it in the *souk* by dropping a cup that just bounced off the tile floor. "We cook it *ten times*," he boasted. "Nothing weaker is acceptable!" Just like their women.

"What happens when a transgression occurs to a woman – by no fault of her own?" I asked the *shaikh*.

His mustache twitched slightly as his mouth tightened underneath it. "It is a very serious concern."

I waited for him to go on, but he didn't. "How important is honor to a *Muwahhid*?"

Shaikh Hayyan folded his hands in his lap and appeared to give some consideration to this question. "You are familiar with Pythagoras?" He pronounced it as the French do – PEE-ta-gore.

"He's a saint to the *Muwahhidoon*," I said.

He nodded. "In Pythagoras' time, Greek culture suffered because of the issue of inherited guilt. The Greeks believed the mistakes of the father controlled the fate of his children."

"Like Oedipus," I said.

"Yes. This idea was logical for some period of time, when the family unit was very critical in society, but it began to lose its worth as Greek culture started to change in about the sixth century before Christ. It punished the morally innocent without logical cause. Pythagoras was an Orphic shaman and Orphic doctrine taught that there was a part of every person that was divine and eternal that could leave the human body — the soul. Pythagoras claimed every person contained a wholly good and perfect immortal soul confined to a wicked body."

Was that his answer about honor? "So, then...what does that mean exactly?" I asked.

"Pythagoras said there are three kinds of people in this world: lovers of money, lovers of honor and lovers of knowledge. A true *Muwahhid* is a lover of knowledge of the truth."

But what was *his* truth? He seemed to be talking around it. I thought of the old Arab adage, "It is good to know the truth, but it is better to speak of palm trees."

"Does your Tawhid faith sanctify life?" I asked.

He nodded solemnly.

"I know that the Qur'an is a holy book for the Druze." I opened my notebook to read. "There's a *sura:* 'Men have authority over women because Allah has made the one superior to the other because they spend their wealth to maintain them. So good women are obedient, guarding the unseen parts as God has guarded them.' And another that says, 'As to those women on whose part ye fear disloyalty and ill conduct, admonish them, refuse to share their beds, beat them.'"

He looked at me as if I'd said nothing he needed to defend.

"Those *suras* seem to encourage punishing women for the kinds of behavior that is considered dishonorable," I said.

"Because the language is vague, it has been open to many interpretations."

"With all due respect, Shaikh, what's vague about 'beat them'?"

"That is English, Miss Jones. The Holy Qur'an is not meant to be translated."

"I've also read that the status of women in pagan Arabia was higher than now."

"No. In fact, the Prophet banished the murder of newborn baby girls."

"But what about the traditional Islamic punishment of stoning for adultery?" I pressed.

"Some Islamic states have practiced execution for crimes such as adultery. Tawhid interprets the Qur'an esoterically, Miss Jones. You must remember that while we descend from Islam, we are not *of* it."

"Well, isn't honor killing the same as execution?"

"Honor killing is an extra-judicial killing and is done to spare families the shame of public execution."

"But Israel doesn't execute anyone for adultery and honor killing happens here anyway," I said.

The front door opened and slammed closed hard enough to shake the walls a bit, startling the *shaikh*. We both looked up to see a short man enter and stop to speak to the *shaikh*'s wife, who was now drying and putting away dishes.

"My grandson," he said. "Full of energy, like a bull."

A dark man with a tentative smile strode into the living room, greeting his grandfather first. The *shaikh* introduced me to Jabr Hayyan, who surprised me when he reached out to shake my hand – not what I expected from the grandson of the religious leader of the Druze here. Jabr took a seat next to his grandfather. The *shaikh*'s wife delivered a bowl of almonds and took an unobtrusive seat on the opposite wall.

"We have been discussing *'ird* and the place of women in our society," the *shaikh* told Jabr.

Jabr's black eyebrows, which grew together under a broad, Hellenistic forehead, went up. "*Muwahhidoon* women enjoy prestige in our society. They are honored for their commitment to the success of the family and community," he said.

"Are men and women equals in your society?" I asked.

"Tawhid law requires a husband to treat his wife with affection and as an equal," Jabr said. "Spouses have equal rights and must share their possessions with each other."

"Women may become religious initiates automatically," added the *shaikh*, waving towards his wife. "They are considered pure until proven otherwise, but men must undergo a process of initiation."

"What does the law say about how women must treat their husbands?" I asked.

"In return for being treated with equal rights, the wife is obliged to obey the husband's legal rights emanating from the marriage."

I almost laughed. "Well, how can two people be equal if one has to obey the other?"

"Men are not given any advantage over women in Tawhid," said the *shaikh*.

"With all due respect, sir, it's certainly an advantage to be encouraged, both legally and scripturally, to govern your spouse. And I understand few women are permitted to work outside the village or even get a driver's license."

Jabr dismissed my words with a wave. "No, restrictions are for protection and vary with the family and village. There's a lot of outside political pressure to suppress progressive movements."

"But you live in Israel," I said. "The average Jewish woman here certainly has more freedoms than Druze women."

"Precisely," said Jabr. "We live amidst many Western-style people. We don't wish to become Westernized. We must hold the reins in as long as we are surrounded by this foreign culture to protect our women."

He was contradicting himself.

"But girls who are molested *inside the village* are treated like despicable criminals and are often killed for honor as a result," I said. "That's the opposite of protection, isn't it?"

They both froze at my audacity. I was shaking and trying to hide it. The *shaikh* broke the silence. "Every *Muwahhidoon* woman is in a position of influence if she is a mother."

"But do they ever reach your status, Shaikh?"

"Tawhid is the only monotheistic religion that allows women to serve as spiritual head and to fulfill all its religious functions," said Jabr.

I knew most Episcopal churches had voted to accept female ministers. Many other Christian denominations did. But I wasn't certain that women were permitted to fulfill all the religious functions of their churches.

"So there are female Tawhid leaders?" I asked.

They looked at each other and exchanged some quick words in Arabic.

"Omm Nasib was head of religious affairs in Sami'a from 1919 to 1979," said Jabr. "When she died, her granddaughter took her place."

They looked at me as if that occurrence in one village proved the rule.

"I heard that, a few years ago, Atabi had its first female on the town council," I said.

They nodded proudly.

"But she resigned after a few months because she was getting harassment around town."

"No, that's not true," said Jabr. "I'm head of the town council. My wife knows her very well and she said she quit to spend more time with her children. Women are free to do whatever they want so long as they remain true to Tawhid."

"Oh," I said. "Then, could I speak with your wife about some of these issues?"

"Oh, no," he said, shaking his head. "Not her."

19

My visit with the *shaikh* and his grandson had gotten me thinking again about Leila's paintings – her way of protesting against the strictures of her culture. But what did the name of her last series, "The Seven Perfumes of Sacrifice", refer to specifically? Devrah said some ancient ritual, but why did Leila care about that? If I could find out, I had a hunch it might offer some insight that could help me somehow, but I didn't know why.

On my way to meet *Jerusalem Post* reporter David Cohen for dinner, I stopped in an Internet café in the crumbling Byzantine alleyways in the old part of Jerusalem to see if my story had been posted at nytimes.com and do some quick research since my phone wasn't finding a Wi-Fi connection. My story was there, edited, but not too much, along with my byline. I was ebullient. I texted a friend in New York to buy me ten copies off a local newsstand. I wanted the real deal. Google only returned one single entry for "The Seven Perfumes of Sacrifice," but it was quite on target, translated from a French book entitled *La Révélation d'Hermès Trismégiste*, by Festugière: "It is this very book [the *Book of Moses*] which Hermes plagiarized when he named the seven perfumes of sacrifice in his sacred book entitled *The Wing*." Next, I searched for *The Wing*, but found nothing that seemed relevant. I'd seen the name "Hermes Trismegistus" yesterday in the table of contents for *Kitab al-Hikma*, the Druze holy book, on the library's computer. So "The Seven Perfumes" *did* have a Druze connection. Now I just needed to find out how.

I was twenty minutes late to the restaurant and impatient going through its metal detector to guard against suicide bombers. How soon we forget.

It was a Moroccan place and our table was in a candlelit nook, too romantic a setting for a business meeting. Cohen, who looked about mid-career, with a receding hairline and starter pot belly, was finishing a red cocktail. Another red cocktail waited on my side of the table. Cohen insisted on ordering our food, too, which he did in Arabic (to impress me, so it seemed), then asked me lots of questions about my freelance journalism career, with particular interest in my contacts at *The New York Times*. I'd done my homework on him this morning. He'd been covering the Arabic-speaking minorities of Israel at the *Post* for eleven years and, from what I could tell, writing the same stories year after year.

"So, how is it covering the Druze?" I asked.

"Oh, they're great. Friendly, polite, very hospitable," he said. "Supported the creation of the State. Tolerant of other religions. Pretty much keep their heads down. Fight for Israel." He leaned forward, whispered, "And they're the most civilized Arabs – a breath of fresh air, you know? Next to the Jews, they're the classiest people in all the Middle East."

I blinked at him, unsure how I should take him. I disliked his eyebrows, which arched sharply above his glasses, like A-frame roofs, giving him an ever-surprised look. He might have been handsome fifteen years ago and was probably baffled that women didn't find him so anymore.

The waiter brought us *pastilla*, thin phyllo pastries stuffed with almonds, cinnamon and Cornish hen.

"So, are you writing about the Druze?" He asked through a mouthful of *pastilla*.

"Not sure yet. Mainly just trying to investigate the death of my friend."

"Don't write about Druze women or girls, whatever you do."

"Why not?"

"Taboo." He wiped his mouth with the back of one hand. "Over a decade ago, a Druze journalist from Daliat, guy named Mosbah Halabi – who leaked in '73 that Druze believe in reincarnation – published a book called *Diary of a Young Druze Girl*. The Druze religious elders made him publicly burn every copy."

"A *book burning?*"

He nodded.

"What was in it?" I asked.

"Oh, just some stuff about how they get past some of the rules – sneaking behind their parents' backs... guys going to Tel Aviv to sleep with Jewish women and stuff."

"Do you have a copy?"

He shook his head. "Threw it on the bonfire with the rest of 'em."

"You *did?*"

He shrugged. "Gotta cover them for the *Post*."

I took a slow sip of my martini and remembered that Plato – a prophet to the Druze – urged the city fathers of Athens to exile the poets and storytellers because they were a threat to society. "So…I guess you've found your niche, then."

"Actually, I'm ready to move on," he said, setting down his drink.

"To?"

Cohen pulled an envelope out of his jacket hanging on the chair and pushed it towards me. "In case your editor at the *Times* is interested."

I peeked inside. His resumé and clips. As though I had any pull. Something wasn't right. "You prepared this before? But I just mentioned I'd turned in my first piece to them."

"I confess…I heard about you yesterday when I was in Atabi covering a court case," he said.

"You heard I write for *The Times*?"

"That you're a senior investigative reporter there."

I laughed and shook my head. "That's not true."

He smiled at me doubtfully.

"Why would I lie? Google me."

He shrugged. "I did. I assume you're undercover."

I smiled and shook my head.

So," he said, pursing his lips. "What can I do for *you*?"

I couldn't stand this guy, but I needed some information out of him. While I told him an abbreviated version of my last five days, he mowed through the *pastilla*, washing them down with another red martini.

"I think it was an honor killing, not some sort of random hit-and-run," I said.

He laughed through a mouthful. "Of course it was an honor killing."

"Why do you say that?"

"Everybody in Atabi knows that. Her family has wanted her to go away since she was four. The real story is how she made it *this* long!"

"Then why did the cop I talked to say it was possibly a suicide hit-and-run?"

Cohen guffawed, which turned into a coughing fit. I didn't know what to think.

"Excuse me, I'm sorry…" He slapped his chest. "Who told you that?"

"Metanis."

He smiled and shook his head. "That fits."

"So, he flat out *lied* to me?"

"He never said it was *definitely* one way or the other?"

"Well…no. I guess not. He keeps saying they're investigating it."

"One thing you should know about the Druze," he said, swirling the ice in his water glass. "They've made a fine art of political correctness. Drink up! You're behind."

In another room, a band started up a Berber rhythm.

"Do you know how she died?" I asked.

"I saw the autopsy report."

I put my fork down. "How'd you get that?"

He smirked with heady satisfaction. "How do you think I've managed to cover these people so well for so long?"

"Can I see it? You've got to show it to me!"

"I just got to read it at the station. She – and this is *totally* off-the-record – was hit a *lot* of times...had facial abrasions from being dragged. Clearly a novice."

I felt my heart waver while I tried to get my mind around his words. "She wasn't hit by a car?"

He waved the notion off as if I was naïve to have ever even considered it.

"Then what was the official cause of death?" I asked.

"Blunt force trauma to the back of the head causing skull fracture and massive internal bleeding. She was probably knocked unconscious on the second or third blow. Her right hand and fingers were bruised and two left fingers fractured, probably defensive wounds. The perp gave her a good whack to the side of the face as well. Bashed in her cheek and forehead."

The waiter arrived with our carrot salads and ginger-scented lamb *tajines*. I looked up at the stone archway over the doorway to try to keep tears from falling down my cheeks. I blotted them quickly with my napkin when the waiter placed the food on the table. He gave Cohen another martini.

"But you know what the best part is?" Cohen said, oblivious to my emotion. "They're officially calling it an *accidental death*!"

"But they're still investigating it."

He shrugged, his pitched-roof brows rising, and dug into his *tajine*. Adam at Women's Legal Support had warned me about political favors. Cohen had to know.

"How can they get away with that?" I said.

He reached across the table to pat me on the back. "*Tabtabeh.*"

"What?"

"Lip service."

Which side was this guy on?

"Look, it's a rare event for a Druze – especially a female – to get an autopsy," he said. "Be happy they did that much."

I took a sip of my martini, a storm building inside me. "What kind of crime scene investigation did the police do?"

He scratched the back of his neck. "I'm sure I already said *entirely* too much, thank you martinis."

"Oh, come on, David."

"That's *really* confidential information even *I* wasn't supposed to get."

"I *really* need to know," I said.

He sighed, running a hand through his hair. "I could lose all my inside contacts at the police. Or worse, my job."

"I thought you *wanted* to lose your job," I said, waving the envelope he'd given me.

"Not that way."

I looked at him squarely. "All right," I said, wiping my mouth on my napkin. "I've got an early morning meeting–"

"Wait," he started.

"It's okay," I said, reaching for my backpack. "I'll find another way."

"You know I can't tell you that, Fereby," Cohen protested.

I stood and put on my backpack. "What beat interests you at the *Times?*" Might as well take advantage of my phony prestigious credential.

His eyes widened; he licked his lower lip. "The Jerusalem bureau'd be fine, or, hell, I'd even write obits…if I could be in New York. Please sit down."

I stood my ground and we looked at each other a long moment. He knew the price of admission.

"Okay," he said, glancing at the ceiling in surrender. "Sit and I'll tell you."

I obeyed. The waiter dropped the check in front of him.

"It wasn't even perfunctory," said Cohen. "The cops took a few pictures. CSI didn't come. Or the medical examiner. He issued his report the next day, once the body was in the morgue."

"Did anyone search for evidence?" I asked.

"Search? The local cops don't work that hard on cases like this!"

"So how are they planning to support their theory of it being accidental?"

"By lack of any other evidence, I guess."

"How would that hold up?"

"Just fine…" He locked his eyes on me. "Unless they're *unexpectedly* challenged."

"A fly in the ointment," I said. *Me,* in other words. "What do you think's going on?"

He pulled out a pack of cigarettes. "Mind if I smoke?"

"Actually, yes."

He put them away. "Well, it's…complicated. This family…Tamir Shahin, Leila's fiancé-husband – is in the largest clan in Atabi. His great-grandmother is the elder of the clan."

"Sitt Afifah?"

"Yeah."

Who knew? Crazy Afifah was the Queen of Atabi.

"And the Azzams are related to Afifah's clan," he said.

"I didn't know that."

"I think Tamir and Leila have grandparents that are brother and sister."

So Tamir *was* a blood relative of Leila's. He could have been inclined to kill her for honor, too.

"And then you know Leila's brother, Fadi, was a decorated IDF soldier who's now in the Border Police."

"Are you suggesting there could be political reasons the police aren't doing their job?" I said.

"I'm not suggesting anything," he said, feigning innocence.

"What I don't understand even more is why they killed her *now*," I said. "Was she pregnant or something?"

"*Pregnant?*" He smiled incredulously. "Only if it was the immaculate conception!"

I blinked at him in confusion. "You mean…she was a…*virgin?*"

Cohen smiled and downed his drink.

20

How could the autopsy show Leila was a virgin if she had been raped as a child? Who was lying? And, as importantly, why? At least her family couldn't call her an adulteress anymore and use that as an excuse for her murder. With Leila buried, the police evidently corrupt and the case, in effect, closed, I had to get answers quickly by some miracle or Leila would be utterly forgotten.

An ambulance flashing its emergency lights idled in front of the hospice when I pulled into the parking lot that night. Another patient had passed away. No wonder Grouchy the nun was grouchy.

My phone rang. Fadi was on the line, drunk again, wanting to see me. I wanted to see him, too, and figure out if I could believe in his innocence, but not tonight in his state. I worried he could be dangerous again, especially intoxicated. As I watched four paramedics leave the hospice with a yellow body bag, I agreed to let him pick me up the next day at two, after he got off work.

A call from Adam, the attorney at Women's Legal Support in Jerusalem I'd met with, awakened me in the morning. He said the *shaikh*'s grandson Jabr was quoted in the local Arabic-language paper saying Leila's killing was justified. "He said she didn't follow the law of the Druze and received the 'appropriate consequences.' This could constitute incitement of murder."

I asked if the "law of the Druze" was written down anywhere and he said, if anywhere, in their hidden holy books. I had to get a hold of the *Kitab*.

"It's not just Druze," Adam said. "Since the U.S. invaded Iraq and Afghanistan, about the only place these men feel they have any power is in their families. And, since Israel put up the fence, Palestinians have committed more honor killings."

He said they were being committed off-site in secret more frequently with no announcement because of the family's fear of prison time, which made them harder to solve. He also mentioned a new trend in Lebanon: *Husbands* committing honor killings against their own wives.

My mind raced: *They had to cover their asses!* "The police were expecting a confession for Leila's murder, Adam! That's what they've gotten used to, right? They knew it was an honor killing, so perhaps they didn't bother with much evidence collection. When no confession materialized, they found themselves in a bind. They *had* to call it a hit-and-run."

"You think that's bad?" he said. "In the West Bank, almost daily a man kills his daughter, then fills out a death certificate at the police station with whatever cause of death suits him. Usually it's 'fate and destiny' – and that's enough to close the case."

Newly fueled by my *New York Times* piece and Jabr's incitement, I headed to Atabi's police station to turn up the heat. En route, my mother called from California.

"Fereby, I need a favor. We're opening the orphanage's new wing Monday and our PR volunteer has left us in the lurch. Can you get *The L.A. Times* and whatever TV stations are important to come?" She hadn't even asked me where I was in the world or how I was doing.

"Mom, I'm still in Israel."

"Oh." She sounded annoyed. "Are you still fussing over that poor dead girl?"

I felt heat flash out through my skin. "Yes, Mom, I am."

"Well, can't you just make a few calls? "

"I can't *make* them cover an event," I said.

She exhaled too close to the receiver. "You don't think this is important."

"Mom," I said, willing patience. "Trying to talk my contacts into covering a minor event in Mexico that's not newsworthy to their local audiences is only going to harm my relationships with them. And they're not going to do it."

"Not *newsworthy?*" She spat the words out as if I'd been malicious.

"Mom– "

"Never mind, Fereby. I don't know what I was thinking. Why would you care? God bless you." She was gone.

~ ~ ~

"What are you doing to find Leila's murderer?" I asked Metanis in the lobby of the police station, our standard meeting space now. "Have you talked to any witnesses?"

"Miss Jones, you know I not allow to talk about investigation."

"What investigation?" I ached to tell him I knew it had already been officially ruled an accidental death, but that could jeopardize Cohen, a source I still needed. "Have you even questioned Fadi or any of the Azzams?"

"He has alibi, you know." Metanis was regarding me differently somehow. "He was with *you* when she die."

I wanted to feel some kind of relief at this, but I didn't trust him with the time of death, or anything else for that matter. And his eyes said that Fadi and I'd been in the throes of fornication instead of navigating my nausea on the highway.

"What about her husband, Tamir, or her father, Kamil?" I asked. "Or Leila's cousin, Rushdi? He's the one who admits to finding her body, and I saw him hosing blood out of the Azzams' courtyard after the body was removed. How did the car get up in the courtyard without making any tire tracks?"

He narrowed his eyes. Two other cops had come out of the back office to speak to the receptionist; all three watched us with interest.

"Everyone knows this was an honor killing," I said. "The Azzams know who's responsible and you know it."

"You have no evidence, Miss Jones."

"Because all the physical evidence was destroyed when Rushdi washed it away with your permission!"

He stared at me with loathing unprecedented in my lifetime. "Evidence is *never* destroy, Miss Jones."

"Have you even talked to anyone who could be involved?" I said. "The Azzams had a very strong motive, ample opportunity and a long pattern of violence against Leila. The crime scene was *on their property*! And what about Jabr Hayyan? He was quoted in *El-Medina* officially excusing the killing! That sounds like incitement to me."

He turned and saw his colleagues watching an American woman putting him in his place. His face was purple with rage. Now I was afraid.

"I warn you, Miss Jones," Metanis said, his voice shaking in his clenched jaw. "People talking about you all over Mt. Carmel."

I already knew I was seen as a threat. An independent, educated, unmarried female, seven thousand miles from home, traveling alone. This put me off the chart of any category of female most of them had probably ever met. Never mind what I was doing there. "So?" I said, smiling, faking bravery.

He blinked at me, caught off-guard by my unexpected nonchalance. "They saying you not a journalist now. You spy for America."

I laughed. How flattering they'd give me so much credit given my incompetence here!

He narrowed his eyes, taking my laughter for ridicule. "They say more, but you must find out yourself."

What – that I'd slept with half of Atabi? I shook my head in disbelief and turned to walk out the door. I paused in the threshold and looked at him over my shoulder, all bravado. "You know what I'm a lot more interested in finding out, Detective? Who's policing *you*."

His eyes spat hatred at me. "I report you to Immigration, Miss Jones."

Great. Now I had to figure out who murdered Leila and why before I was deported or the truth would never be revealed. I was shaking on the way to my car. With disturbing clarity, I heard in my mind the voice of the manager of the hotel where my brother was killed telling my parents how helpless he felt about the law that protected all the stray dogs: "We have a saying here in India – 'If a dog goes mad, it can be chained; but what can be done if the chain goes mad?' "

I felt my rage move into an unfamiliar and frightening place. My heart hammering, I gripped the steering wheel, trying to calm down, my teeth chattering incongruously.

Out of nowhere, other memories began to pour themselves out...A small, secluded courtyard...an empty house...the bodily-fluid stench of the Delhi summer hanging in the air... *You're so beautiful, Fereby...It hurts so much to see you sad*...I was so grateful for his attention...my first open-mouthed kiss, repulsive and enthralling...I needed so much, I didn't know what I needed...*I need you so much, Fereby...let me take your pain away...it will be our own unbreakable spiritual union, yours and mine...together forever*... It never occurred to me I could refuse him – he was supposed to be a safe place.

Then, something seemed to fall out of my subconscious: Maybe I wasn't "seduced" after all. He was eighteen. I was barely twelve, back when twelve was still innocent.

Maybe I was molested.

My mouth fell agape as I began to cry, but no sound came forth. How open and good I thought I was to only see the light. Being value-neutral was the sacred balm that had worked for me for two decades. I realized now, clutching this cheap piece-of-shit steering wheel whose plastic cover was peeling off, my conviction of tolerance wasn't proof of my healing – it was a mask to protect me from experiencing loss. How my parents coped and what that teenager did to me cut off my mourning. I never finished grieving for Cary, for me, or for the spiritual death of my whole family. To do so meant inviting that dangerous vulnerability back into my heart.

I ripped the plastic cover from the steering wheel, tearing and pulling it until it unwound and fell off, leaving black gum on my palms. I screamed and pounded my fists on the dashboard. I hit the rearview mirror, which, infuriatingly, didn't go far. I kicked the underside of the dash, stomping my feet on the floorboard, bumping my knees on the stupid steering wheel. Why'd he have to have me? I threw my backpack into the backseat and hurled the bag of pistachios against the windshield. I tore up a newspaper that was on the front seat, shredding it into a hundred pieces, like confetti, in honor of the cry of a lifetime. Why couldn't they just control the fucking dogs? I gasped and wailed and sobbed the excruciating sob I owed Cary, I owed me – a score of tears washed out of me.

21

S weating, I leaned my head against the window. The plastic steering wheel cover lay in a self-conscious spiral on the floorboard, like a molted snakeskin. I felt an unbidden release in my body and knew without a doubt that I wasn't just here for Leila. I needed to do this for Cary, too, for both the people I had cared for, let down and lost. I needed to do it for me.

I dialed the Atabi station and asked for the station commanding officer, Metanis' boss. Safwan Sa'd el Din was in a meeting, so I asked for his boss, the northern district commander in Haifa. I had to leave a message for Joshua Shuman. Now what?

I closed my eyes. I'd talked to everyone I could. I'd learned enough to enrage me, but not enough to solve Leila's murder. I'd angered more than a few people in Atabi. I still had more questions than answers. Now I was at a dead end. *Leila, what do I do?* I tried to quiet my chaotic mind. *One breath at a time....*The paintings. I opened my eyes. It seemed a bit of a stretch, but I was out of clues and leads. *Yes, get back to the paintings.*

On my phone, I Googled Hermes Trismegistus, the fellow associated with the seven perfumes of sacrifice and mentioned in the Druze's holy book's table of contents. Sometimes equated with the androgynous messenger god, Hermes, Hermes T. probably lived around the time of Moses and was a wise magician who got credit for authoring many Gnostic books on esoteric philosophy, magic and alchemy, including the *Hermetica*. His mission was to help people become immortal, which was possible when the purified soul was absorbed into God, so that when the person was reincarnated, they could be considered a god. Hermes' symbol was the caduceus, two entwined snakes, one of each sex. Now we're getting somewhere, I thought, remembering "Sacrifice of the Goddess Queen," Leila's painting of the intertwined snakes, one fatally biting the other. I found the text of the *Hermetica*, but there was nothing about "Seven Perfumes of Sacrifice" anywhere in it. I searched for "incense," "aromatics" and other variations. Nothing. There was nothing called *The Wing*, either.

Feeling lost, I was about to give up when I came across something that made the hair on my arms stand up: Kamal Jumblatt, a major Lebanese-Druze politician and contemporary of Sultan Pasha Atrash, the crazy Druze warlord Mustafa had told me about, claimed the Druze traced their lineage back five thousand years to Hermes Trismegistus.

Leila's cell phone rang, startling me out of my thoughts. Finally! But the caller-ID was in Hebrew.

"Hello?" I answered.

There was a long pause. "Leila?" It was a man's voice, sounding bewildered.

"Who's this?"

Another pause. "Who's *this*?" He asked, sounding American.

"Fereby."

"Why are you answering her phone?" A New York accent? It had to be him. *Oh, God! He doesn't know yet!*

"Duncan?"

"Who're you?"

"Leila's friend."

"Put her on."

"Uh, I…uh…she can't come to the phone."

"I've called and emailed a dozen times and she hasn't answered or called me back. What's going on?"

I heard someone speaking what sounded like Hebrew in the background.

"*Toda raba*," Duncan said, away from the mouthpiece, thanking someone.

"Are you in Israel?" I asked.

"Yeah, I was so worried I got on a plane…why can't she come to the phone?"

"She's…not here…she asked me to hang on to her phone for a bit so her parents wouldn't find it."

"Oh," he said. "You're American?"

"Yeah."

"Well…I'm just about to arrive in front of the student center. Is she here?"

He was at the university! "Can you wait and I'll be there in five minutes?" I asked. "I'll…um...take you to her."

"I'll be at the west entrance," he said. "In a limo."

Jesus Christ. I called Devrah, Leila's professor, as I sped to school. She was in the middle of class, but said her office was unlocked and I could take Duncan there to talk in private.

A black limousine, its windows as dark as its paint, was parked illegally in front of the student center. I approached it, my heart hammering in my chest, dreading this duty. He wouldn't be here if he didn't love her. I was about to destroy his world.

The back door opened and an elegant man stepped out, speaking English into his cell phone. His blonde hair was parted on one side and slicked back businesslike. He wore wire-rimmed glasses and an expensive dark green suit. Probably mid-thirties. Duncan looked more Teutonic banker than New York art collector.

He slipped the phone in his pocket. "Fereby?"

I nodded.

"Duncan Ramsay," he said, reaching out his hand.

We shook. He didn't smile.

"Follow me," I said uneasily. I was a terrible actress.

"Where?"

"Up to Devrah's office," I said, trying to hide my nervousness.

He looked uneasy, but gestured for me to lead the way.

I took the stairs to avoid the awkward elevator time with him. Classes had just broken for lunch and students bounded down as we climbed the four flights up. I led him into Devrah's office and closed the door. He took a quick look around and turned towards me like an impatient New Yorker.

"Where is she, for God's sake?"

I felt my throat tighten. His face blurred in the prism of my tears. I tried to blink them away, not wanting to lose sight of him. His grey eyes followed a tear that rolled down my cheek. Mystified, he met my eyes again. In the silence between us, I watched his comprehension form.

"She's dead." I heard the words come from his mouth, but his lips didn't seem to move.

My neck hurt as I nodded in concurrence. I felt my face rearranging itself into an ugly sorrow.

Duncan's fair skin flushed as he stood there, his arms hanging at his sides. His head dropped to his chest and his whole body began to tremble. A gasp released from his throat. He grabbed his head. "No, Lei-la! No, no, no, Lei-la!" He shook his head back and forth. "Leila, no," he whispered. "I'm so sorry, my love…I'm so sorry. I'm so sorry…"

Watching this was as awkward as walking in on a couple making love. I stood in front of him weeping, Leila's mandatory expulsion from the world hitting me almost fresh. *I am so over my head.*

I grabbed a box of tissues off Devrah's desk and held them out for him while he cried, trying to avert my eyes to give him some semblance of privacy. I had to watch him, though, as if I were in a room with someone on the verge of dying or being born. Comforting him seemed somehow oppressive; stopping this outpouring of grief a violation of nature. Duncan needed nothing I could offer. This elegant tower of a man had been brought to his knees in an unscheduled initiation in a dirty, reeking art studio. He obviously loved Leila in a way I had never been loved. I put the tissues down on the desk next to him and started for the door.

"I knew something was wrong when I couldn't reach her," he said.

I turned. He pulled off his glasses, his face awash with pain.

"I'm so sorry, Duncan."

"They aren't getting away with this."

I hadn't said anything about the circumstances of her death yet.

"Which one did it?" he asked, fury rising in his voice.

"I'm not sure," I said. "No one's confessed. The police haven't arrested anyone."

"They're *incorrigible*...How'd they kill her?"

I described what I knew, as well as the story the police were sticking to, each word feeling like a blow to Duncan as I said it.

He closed his eyes and rubbed his brows. "When?"

"Monday night."

He was quiet for a long moment.

"Do you want to know why some are saying she was killed?" I asked.

He looked up at me, his eyes growing larger. I don't think he did.

"I think they found out about your relationship."

He looked back and forth at my eyes, searching for an exit. "God!" he fumed, facing a corner of the room and running his hands through his hair. "We were never even *intimate!*"

"Was she leaving to join you in the U.S.?"

He turned and looked at me. "Yes."

By killing her, maybe the Azzams were doing preemptive damage control, hoping to quietly cleanse the future dishonor by preventing her from leaving with Duncan.

"So, that's why she was going to pick up all her paintings from Mujun," I said.

He nodded. "Did she get them?"

"No...you know that Druze girls aren't allowed to even befriend unrelated Druze men, let alone outsiders. That's enough provocation."

"There's *no* justification for murder!" he boomed.

"I agree, Duncan. I'm just trying to figure it out from their point of view."

He leaned against Devrah's desk and rocked himself, eyes squeezed shut. Then, suddenly, he moved towards the door.

"Where are you going?"

"To the Azzams'."

"No, no, no!" I cried. "Please don't do that, Duncan."

"Why not? They *murdered* her, Fereby."

I followed him out of the office. "Duncan, please wait! Please don't go yet!"

He ran down the stairwell.

"Stop!" I followed him as fast as I could. "They could have you arrested for intent to kidnap or worse!" I yelled over our echoing footsteps.

He stopped on the landing and turned to me.

"If they can prove you were dating her, you could be charged with statutory rape or corruption of a minor," I said.

"She wasn't a minor!" He said.

"She would have been until her next birthday."

His brow furrowed. "What nation doesn't consider someone a legal adult at twenty-three?"

"Twenty-three? You think Leila was twenty-three?" We stared at each other, the tension locking our eyes together. "She was seventeen, Duncan."

His mouth slackened and his face drained of color. *"Seventeen? Impossible...are you sure?"*

I nodded.

He looked down the stairwell and shook his head. "She said she was twenty-three."

"But how, at seventeen, would she have been able to travel out of the country with you without her parents' permission?" I asked.

"I don't know." He scraped his fingers back along his scalp, disheveling his gel-stiffened hair. "She kept delaying the date. I was worried she'd get cold feet to leave with me if she waited until her wedding day, with all the excitement and pressure and guilt."

I wondered if he knew Leila and Tamir were already technically married, just not ceremonially. "She was leaving with you on her *wedding* day?"

"I was going to come in a day before, and she was going to sneak out so we could fly together in the morning before the ceremony could take place."

"Well, her wedding day – the twenty-first – was also her eighteenth birthday," I said, "which means she would have been legal to leave the country with you."

He gaped at me, his mind racing. "That's why she kept delaying the departure date...she knew she couldn't travel abroad as a minor without her parents' consent...Why would she lie to me about her age?"

"I don't know. Look, let's focus on who killed her. Did Leila ever mention any threats? Did she ever speak of someone in particular? Like Fadi or Tamir?"

He shook his head. "Most all of them threatened her physically or verbally at some point."

"Did she say what the reason was?"

He wiped his chin. "She said that when she was three or four, she had some strange memories."

"Of what?"

"Like past lives or something. It caused a huge scandal."

"Really," I said. "How so?"

"The family's reputation. The whole honor deal again. She couldn't remember much. Or wouldn't tell me."

"Did it have anything to do with the...assault?"

He looked confused. "The one on Monday?"

I cleared my throat. "No. I think she was sexually assaulted at about the age of those memories."

His forehead wrinkled up. "*Raped?*"

"By Tamir.

He rubbed his eyebrows hard. Something in his mind seemed to calculate and click, while something else severed and flew apart. "So that's why her mother told her she had no reason to live. She said she was twenty-three, but she was really seventeen. She told me she was a virgin, but she was raped? She said she wanted to wait to be intimate with me until she was safely in the U.S. What was the truth? What else did she lie about? That she loved me? God, what a *fool* I am! She was just using me to escape!" He swung his fist and pounded it against the exit door to the second floor. The bang reverberated up and down the stairwell.

"I don't think so, Duncan. She could've forged a document with her parents' permission, but she didn't want to put you at risk. She may still be a virgin. The autopsy report supposedly claims she was, but others say she was raped. I don't know who to believe."

He turned and ran down the stairs.

"Where are you going?" I yelled, half a flight behind him.

"Home!" he said, pushing out to the lobby.

22

I couldn't blame Duncan for feeling duped, but I couldn't believe he was just going to bail like that without giving the whole thing more deliberation. This was the woman he supposedly loved, after all. Didn't he want to see justice done? Maybe Raziel was right. Maybe he *was* The Asshole.

The district commanding officer, Joshua Shuman, returned my call as I drove back to the hospice-hotel.

"Someone would have been arrested already if there's enough evidence," he said.

"Sir, my concern is that evidence was deliberately not collected in the first place."

"At my Atabi station? No, it's one of the top-notch stations. And the Druze villages are among the most law-abiding in the country."

"Do you routinely send in your crime scene investigation people when there's a suspicious death?" If I told him that I knew it was an honor killing because Leila was planning to skip the country with her American boyfriend, I could get Duncan in some kind of trouble for plotting to traffic a minor.

"Of course."

"So that was done in Leila Azzam's case?"

"I-I'm sure it was," he said.

"You might want to double-check that, sir."

I parked on a side street off the main road of Atabi near the bank so I could use the ATM. When I returned to my car, I noticed the elementary school across the street was having recess. I crossed over and approached the chain-link fence. A blur of children in matching navy uniforms played ball on a black top. I scanned the swings and the slide. Two little girls in the sandbox zoomed toy helicopters through the air. A small boy sat up on his knees and dive-bombed something in the sand with a rocket ship. It was Leila's little brother.

Qasim met my gaze as though I'd called to him. I smiled but ached inside. I'd once been the kid at school whose sibling had just died. He stood up, still watching me, and his face contorted in anguish. He looked over at two teachers standing by the building. Was he checking to see if they saw me? I hoped he wanted to come over and talk to me. He looked back at me and I gave a little wave. He began to bawl. I stepped back from the fence. A confounding fear rose up in me and I darted to my car. I sped off feeling filthy with guilt.

Fadi was driving up when I arrived at the hotel. He had no plan for where we were going and we bickered over who would drive which car. Finally, I insisted on driving my own. "If you touch my steering wheel or my seat belt, or interfere with my driving in any way, you're getting out wherever we are and walking home," I said.

Fadi fiddled with the seat adjustment, settling on lower and more reclined than necessary. He lay back and put some sunglasses on. "Do you want to go for a hike in the Carmel? There's an easy trail."

Did he think this was a *date*? I thought he wanted to talk to me about Leila or my confrontation with Kamil in the cemetery. I figured we'd just go somewhere like a coffee shop. A hike would put us really alone together and I still didn't know what he was capable of. "No. How about a tour of Atabi? You can show me everything."

"That's boring," he said.

"Don't you want to show off your home town to an interested foreigner?"

"I know something you'll like."

"You just don't want to be seen with me by any Druze, do you?"

He shook his head as if I were hopelessly paranoid. "Just keep on this road. It's not far."

Pink flax spilled out of the Carmel wilderness as we made our way down the highway.

"You can go faster," he said, helping himself to what was left of my bag of pistachios. "We're going to Ein Hod, an artist colony in the Carmel forest. It was once a retreat for Crusaders before becoming an Arab village," Fadi said, sitting up. "It was one of Leila's favorite places."

We parked and walked down a dusty, meandering path. Gnarled olive trees and overgrown briars grew out of crumbling stone walls. Bougainvillea climbed over Moorish archways and through wrought-iron gates. Rough-hewn signs pointed down scraggly trails toward artist studios. Visitors strolled along the tree-shaded road, pausing to take in the view of the sea.

"Leila was allowed to come here?" I asked.

"No, but I brought her occasionally. She dreamed of living here one day."

I wondered if he'd ever seen any of Leila's paintings, or even knew she was a painter. "Would that have been possible?"

"No," he laughed. "Druze women, their house is their tomb."

Fadi walked under an artist's tent to look at some paintings.

"You've returned to your job at the Border Police," I said, following him.

"Yes."

"Where do you work?"

"Usually I patrol the western border of Judea and Samaria. I do assignments wherever they need me. Tomorrow I go to the Lebanese border at Rosh Ha'Nikra."

He ducked out of the tent and I followed him back to the path. He was quiet, or perhaps just sober.

"There's a bench with a view of the sea this way." He cut off the path and stepped through a broken fence in the yard of one of the artists' residences.

"Are you sure we're allowed to—"

"Follow me."

I dismissed a funny feeling in my gut as I walked behind him through the overgrown yard to a narrow trail that hadn't been pruned back in at least a year. I climbed under some wild roses. Fadi held a tangle of thorny stems out of the way for me. When he let them go, a barb stabbed him in the back of the hand. He wiped away the blood with his thumb as if he was cleaning a smudge on a window.

The bench was fashioned out of an old door and a couple of wine casks and set into the side of a grassy patch of the slope. The Eastern Mediterranean spread out before us, the sparkling sea of so much history. The sum of many seas: Lord Byron's haunted, holy ground. I joined him somewhat warily on the seat. From this isolated spot, he could throw me off the cliff or make love to me and no one would know. How did he ever learn this was here?

He stared straight ahead at the sea, leaning his elbows on his thighs. We watched the water for a while, and I tipped my face up to the sun, enjoying an unexpected moment of peace. He made no move to open any conversation. I began to feel anxious.

Fadi clasped his hands. "You've been to see Shaikh Hayyan."

"He's a kind man," I said, knowing I was in trouble. "Very intelligent."

"It's a pain to have religious leaders. They're not as educated and experienced in the modern world as the youth are. And they decide everything important in our villages."

"You'd rather a less traditional environment."

He nodded, anger pulling at the corners of his mouth.

"That's a tall order for a Druze village?"

He studied the sky. "The elders won't change. The youth rarely question them because they think it's not worth the risk. No one looks inside themselves, so we stay tribal."

"You have a good job outside the village. You could move out."

He faced me. "I'm a Druze, Fereby. We don't fit in anywhere else."

"But it seems the Druze get along well here for the most part – which is quite an accomplishment in Israel."

"We're an island of a hundred thousand in a sea of six million. The Palestinians don't trust us because we support Israel. The Jews don't trust us because, at the end of the day, we're still Arabs."

"But don't the Jews respect the Druze for serving in the army?"

He let out a cynical laugh. "Oh, yeah, they love our military sacrifices. But if I'm not wearing my uniform, I'm nothing. Like your blacks who fought in the Second World War. When they returned, they gained no more respect...One day I took my aunt to the hospital in a Jewish town for surgery on the way to my post in Jerusalem. The receptionist was friendly when I dropped my aunt off, but when I came back wearing civilian clothes to pick her up, the receptionist didn't recognize me and was extremely rude."

His expression had turned into a sneer, but at least we were talking.

"My father tells me not to complain because it used to be worse. He lost his younger brother and sister in 1963 from the German measles outbreak that hit Atabi. There were no roads into town, and no medical care. I think a dozen infants died. After that, the government started to notice us."

A falcon with a glinting white beak glided by, landing somewhere below us.

"How did Leila feel about Atabi?"

He shook his head. "It's not a question for a Druze girl."

"Why...'cause they're stuck, regardless?"

He nodded.

"Did she want to leave?"

"There's no place to go. Except another Druze village."

Unless you have a wealthy foreigner who's in love with you and willing to assist.

"What about Iman?" I asked.

"If she can marry, she'll be satisfied."

"Fadi, why do Druze permit honor killing?"

He held his breath for a long moment, then let it out all at once. "He who takes off his clothes, stays naked."

"Huh?"

"If you do something wrong, you can never be right again."

The falcon floated in the wind fifty yards away. We both watched until it glided downward again.

"There's a story every Druze hears as a child," Fadi said. "In the far north, there is a lake, Birkat Ram, in an extinct volcano where there used to be a village long ago. A traveling prophet stopped to ask for a drink, but was repeatedly refused. Eventually, a respectable woman felt sorry for him and offered him a drink. But her husband was disgusted by her forward behavior and killed her on the spot. The prophet was so offended by the villagers' inhospitality, he flooded the village, destroying it forever. Her corpse turned into an exquisite fig tree shaped like a woman that grew beside the lake. My grandparents talked about visiting the tree until it disappeared about fifty years ago. If you cut into the bark, its sap would bleed red like blood, not white, like ordinary fig trees."

"What happened to it?" I asked.

"There were a few years of heavy rain. The water rose in the lake and the tree rotted and floated away."

I wondered if that was the original honor killing fairytale of the Druze. The frankincense tree legend Leila had painted seemed even older. We sat silently for a minute as a bee explored each of us before moving on.

"Why are you hanging around here?" Fadi asked, not looking at me.

I glanced at the Mediterranean and the blurred line where it met the sky. "I can't just let this go."

He shook his head. "Please don't bother Shaikh Hayyan again. Or our neighbors."

We stared at each other. His face contained a baffling range of emotion; I couldn't tell if he felt rage or compassion or agony or some feeling that was beyond my experience.

"Fadi, Leila saved my life the day she was killed. She got me off that bus in Jaffa just before it was suicide-bombed."

"I know. I read your article."

"What?" I was shocked. "How did you know about it?"

"Word travels fast. So you owe her something now?"

"It's more than that." I wanted to say, *And I have to figure out if you're the murderer or not because I've fallen for you.* "So, who killed Leila, then? You? Kamil? Tamir?"

He shot me a severe look. "Why do you keep asking everyone such things?"

"No one else is!"

He covered his face with his hands, drawing his fingers through his hair in frustration. "*Yalla*." Let's go. He stood up.

We climbed out of the cliffside seat and back through the overgrown foliage without speaking. He walked with a businesslike gait to the car, not looking at me. Halfway through the drive back to the hospice, he demanded I pull over. I was afraid he'd pull his steering wheel prank again, so I did so. He got out of the car and came around to my side.

"I'll drive the rest of the way," he said, motioning for me to get out of the driver's seat.

More out of curiosity than concern, I traded places with him. He probably didn't want anyone he knew to see him being driven by a woman.

Fadi drove through upper Haifa past the university and on towards the hospice. He turned off the engine before he'd pulled all the way into a parking space, letting the car roll into place.

"What," I said, his stare with those gorgeous golden eyes making me pleasantly uncomfortable.

"You're not married, are you?"

My stomach flipped. "No, why?"

"I heard you were, but I didn't believe it."

"I told Tamir I was married just so he'd back off."

A smirk turned up on his mouth for a moment. "Did it work?"

"I don't know." I looked down at my hands, feeling self-conscious and a little turned on.

Fadi rolled down his window.

"Why didn't you believe I could be married?" I asked.

He gave a cynical snort. "You...you're..." He looked outside, resting his arm on the door, tapping the side mirror with a finger. "Like a cluster of stars in the sky."

I laughed. "What does *that* mean?"

"You can't be reached."

"Hmm," I said, not sure if I should be flattered or not.

"Nothing wipes your tears away but your own hand."

It felt like a sucker-punch, but I shrugged it off and hid my hurt. "Right now, it would be hard to settle down since I travel so much."

He looked at me. "Or maybe you travel so much so you can't settle down."

I raised an eyebrow to say *touché*. True, my barely used trailer in Laguna Beach didn't exactly lay out a welcome mat to a potential partner. "I would like to marry someday, but it will have to be for love," I said.

He looked at me for a long moment. He was younger than me, probably still in his twenties. I thought for a millisecond that he might lean over and kiss me. A butterfly caromed through my belly. Instead, he looked back out the window.

"Have you ever loved a man?" he asked.

"I don't know," I said. "There've been moments where I thought so. Have you ever loved a woman?"

"Love," he spat, as though the word itself tasted bad. He shook his head in disgust that I didn't buy.

I thought of the line from *Chronicle of a Death Foretold*: "Is honor love?" I asked.

"No," he answered quickly. His face seemed somehow to go numb. "It's more."

23

A package from Devrah was waiting for me at the hospice-hotel desk when I got back. In my room, I tore it open and pulled out a stack of slim softcover books, the books on the Druze religion she'd ordered me through interlibrary loan. Ironically, they'd come all the way from UCLA. I was elated. I stayed up until after ten poring over them for several hours and forgot about eating dinner. Then I called Devrah.

"Listen to this: 'Tawhid prohibits the use of force in facing its adversaries, except in cases of self-defense or in defense of one's land and *honor.*' "

"They actually *wrote* that down?"

"I also found conflicting stuff in here...one should support 'basic human rights for all citizens and nations alike.' And 'when someone does wrong, first reprove (but not condemn) them.' If that doesn't work, then 'blame and reprimand them.' If that still doesn't work, it says to 'part company.' "

"Is 'part company' a nice way of saying 'murder'?" she asked.

"I doubt it. The inner circle of the *uqqals*, the initiated religious, has never let a convicted murderer into its ranks. So they've got to disapprove of honor killing on some level."

"But what if you kill someone but you're not *convicted* of it? Is that okay?" She asked.

"Or maybe they just don't consider honor killing murder."

~ ~ ~

The next morning, a knock on my door I mistook in my sleep for an explosion awakened me with a surge of adrenaline. As I sat up in bed, heart racing, I heard a woman's voice outside in the hall calling my name. I opened the door to Ru'yah, looking distraught.

She gave a quick and heavy exhale, as if she'd forgotten to breathe on the way over. "Qasim's been arrested for Leila's murder!"

I looked back and forth at her eyes, as though they might rectify this insupportable news – Leila's six-year-old brother, a killer. "*Qasim?*"

"Early this morning, the police came to the Azzams' house and took him away!" She covered her mouth with trembling hands.

"That's crazy! He's a little kid!" I motioned her inside. "What evidence do they have?"

"He confessed."

In shock, I dropped down on my bed, the springs squealing. This was not a scenario I'd ever envisioned. I looked up at Ru'yah as the tears skidded down her cheeks. Palestinian children had been manipulated into becoming suicide bombers, but a Druze kid killing his own sister?

"Do you think he could have done it?" I asked.

She closed her eyes. "I don't know…"

"I saw his love for Leila. And hers for him. I saw his sweetness," I said. "I don't believe it. He's too young. I just don't see how it's possible. And, besides, he was asleep when Tamir came over."

She sat down next to me and clutched her hands in her lap. "But it was his fate and destiny."

"Why do you say that?"

She swallowed, staring at her skirt. "He was conceived to save the family."

I bent my head to try to get a look at her face. "Save the family? I don't understand."

"I guess after Fadi refused his duty to kill Leila, Kamil felt they needed another son. They got one and Qasim has been trained from birth that he must put the family honor first – more strictly than is even usual. I always feared this would happen."

I couldn't believe what I was hearing. My body ached all over. My brother Cary, same age as Qasim when he died, was as loving as a child could be, and not physically or emotionally capable of hurting anyone – unfortunately, he was no match for the Doberman. But, then again, there was an eleven-year age gap between Leila and Qasim. That he was conceived for such a mission seemed plausible. I recalled Qasim crying and reaching for me in the schoolyard yesterday. Was he feeling the crushing centripetal force of honor, his family pressuring him to confess?

"I don't believe he did it," I said. "Even if he *was* groomed to be the pinch-hitter. Ru'yah, I need to talk to Rushdi."

Her eyes flew open in fear. "No, Fereby! He mustn't know we've been talking –"

"He doesn't have to," I said, taking her hands in mine. They were cold for summertime. I looked her in the eyes. "I just need you to translate. I'm not going to endanger you."

"It may be too late for that," she said. "All the men are talking about the article you wrote about Leila saving you from the bomb. They're saying you're making us look bad, showing the world our women are brazen and defiant. They said Druze women should *never* be allowed to befriend Americans because they are a threat to the Druze community. I have to go to the hospital now to visit my baby before someone notices my delay. Please stay away from me or something terrible could happen."

I had to think of something drastic now. I threw my clothes on and drove north for a little over an hour before I could see the white chalk cliffs rising above the sea – Rosh Ha'Nikra, where Fadi said he'd be posted today. The stiffness in my chest and shoulders felt like skin stretched over a drum. I asked some Israeli soldiers at the Lebanon border fence where I could find him and they pointed to the cable car that went down to the caves.

At the bottom near the sea, I had to hike along a path pocked like the moon on the edge of the cliffs to get to the cave entrance. I gripped the metal railing as I went, the wind whipping my hair across my face, water splashing up over the edge.

Inside, a veil of damp, warm air clung to me. I smelled dead fish, mildew and guano. The cave was dim, but when I glanced at the bright opening to the sea, I had to squint. I could see evidence of the railway tunnels the British had drilled to link Europe and Egypt, but the project was never finished. The East and West, it seemed, were never really meant to be connected.

In the next chamber, Fadi leaned on the railing, watching the waves pour inside through a wide hole. He was in uniform and wore a rifle across his chest as the soldiers had. My stomach fluttered as I approached him. He was startled for a moment, seeing me in this unexpected context, then his expression turned into a glare. We were never exactly allies, but something had declined since yesterday.

"What are you doing here?" he barked.

"Qasim was arrested!" I cried.

Fadi closed his eyes and turned back to the sea. He obviously knew.

"He didn't do it! He confessed under duress, didn't he?"

Fadi shook his head, which I could have taken either way.

I grabbed Fadi's arm to make him look at me. "Fadi, how can you let him take the fall?"

He glanced at my hand on him and his eyes flashed with fury. "I didn't see anything. I wasn't there when Leila died! I was with you!" He shrugged me off him.

I wasn't about to sell out Ru'yah, revealing what she'd said about Qasim's 'fate and destiny.' "He's not capable of it, Fadi. He's *six*! Even if he were brainwashed, how could he kill someone twice his size? He's being used as the scapegoat since he's so young and won't get as much prison time...You've got to *do* something! Your family's falling apart!"

Fadi's eyes seethed as he hit the metal railing with an open hand and his rifle clamored hard against it, echoing through the cave. "My family's falling apart because of *you*!" he snarled.

Fadi shifted his gaze to the cave floor as a couple of laughing tourists traipsed past us. I felt a charge of warm air coming from behind me and looked up to see a pair of bats flying over us.

"You've stuck your nose in *our business* and ruined everything," he continued under his breath. "And now the whole World Wide Web knows my family's shame thanks to you! Please, Fereby, I'm begging you: Leave us alone. Go home before they deport you – or worse! I don't want anything else bad to happen."

"Fadi, if you don't think Qasim killed Leila, you *have* to go to the police and tell them! This is so unbelievable – you *are* the police! *You know* this is traumatic for him to be in custody and to be forced into this by his own family...this is *sick*!"

"I can't, Fereby!" he whisper-yelled back through his teeth.

"Why not?" I yelled.

Waves crashed hard against the inside of the cave. Seawater misted us. I tasted salt.

"You could confess, Fadi. Even if you didn't do it. Make them let Qasim go."

"I wish I could, but now it's too late for that because the police know I was with you."

"You could have done it after you got back from being with me," I said. "Why has no one but me thought of that?"

He shook his head and sighed. "They won't believe me. Fereby?" He reached out as if he were going to touch my face, but remembered himself inches away. "Please go home. Don't write about us anymore, I'm begging you. Don't visit the *shaikh* or my cousins or Tamir anymore. Or the police."

"Nobody's doing a damn thing anyway," I snapped.

"Maybe you don't understand that we do things differently than in Caul-ee-*for*-nya," he said, pronouncing the state exactly as Schwarzenegger does.

"Look, Fadi. I've traveled. I know that."

"Yeah, you've traveled the world, but you don't *live in it*," he said.

Somehow, he knew just what to say to hurt me. I took a deep breath.

"I don't believe these cops are doing their job even by Israel's standards, Fadi. I'm not an expert on police work, but it doesn't appear that they're even *trying* to find the real killer. Sounds to me as if you don't want justice for Leila either."

"I loved my sister, Fereby. I miss her…*so much*." His voice broke. "But it's not so simple."

"Why not? Did *you* kill her?"

He locked eyes with me. "No, Fereby…You should know by now what the sensitivities are. Your visit to the cemetery – let that be a warning to you how people feel. You were lucky that time."

"You can't pray at a cemetery?"

"Druze don't pray for someone who's committed one of the big sins – murder, adultery and sacrilege."

"Leila committed one of those?"

"Heed the warnings. If two tell you your head's not on your shoulders, feel for it."

"An innocent life was taken and everyone here just seems to want to forget about it," I said.

"That would be the best thing for all of us, including you."

I wanted to slap him so bad. "How can you *say* that, Fadi? If you really loved Leila, why don't you want the truth to come out?!"

"Nothing good can come of it…you know what I heard someone say about Leila and you in the café? 'Don't rejoice over she who goes before you see she who comes.'"

24

I drove back to Haifa mad as hell at Fadi, and unnerved by his insinuation that it was my fault Qasim was arrested, yet, if I didn't back off, I could be in danger myself. There was no way I was going to let them put that beautiful little boy away for a heinous crime I know he didn't commit without a fight. I couldn't.

But why would Qasim have confessed now, particularly if he didn't do it? Why would he have been coerced? Weren't they content with how the case was going? The police had their phony hit-and-run theory, a bogus "accidental death" case that would soon grow cold, and the Azzams were getting away with murder. The only reason they'd offer up a confession is if they *had* to. Qasim's confession came shortly after I told Shuman to check on CSI. Could the police have feared getting busted because of my suspicions? The only way the Azzams could know the hit-and-run theory had failed was if the police had alerted them. *God. Who can I go to now?*

It was time to go higher up the chain of command. I was scared they'd put me on the next flight home, but what choice did I have? I made my case for Qasim's innocence to the northern district commander Joshua Shuman in person, but he wasn't buying it.

"Why haven't the Atabi investigators interviewed me yet?" I asked.

"They're probably just busy on another case, Miss Jones."

Shuman was a bald, short, burly man of about forty with the posture of an admiral. His office was a glassed-in corner room overlooking the Port of Haifa.

"It's the only murder there's been there in three years," I said. "They have something better to do? Why doesn't *your* office just take over the investigation?"

Shuman folded his thick fingers on his desk. "Miss Jones, out of respect for their cultural differences, we allow the Druze villages some sovereignty in solving their own problems. I'm sure you can understand the sensitivity of the situation."

"So, in other words," I said. "It's not your problem."

Out on the street, I left an urgent message for Yael Simon, the district attorney in Haifa.

Imagining Qasim suffering made me think about my brother Cary's death; I wanted to climb out of my own skin. I couldn't avoid it any longer: I needed to call my parents and tell them exactly what I was doing. I phoned home on my drive back to the hospice.

"It's about friggin' time somebody had the balls to bring these Muslim cowards to justice, but not *you*, Fereby!" Dad yelled. "Someone with more power, more knowledge and more competence…Who do you think you are – a Navy Seal?"

"Dad, I told you, the Druze are not Muslim, nor is honor killing, and I will not tolerate your bigoted language – "

"You said so yourself most of those murders are by Muslims!"

"Yes, but most Muslims don't kill for honor. Honor killing is no more Islamic than pedophilia is Catholic, Dad. Neither comes from the religion per se, but they've each found a shelter within it."

"What's that – their slogan?…Look, do you actually think you're going to somehow *change* these people, Fereby? Have you learned nothing from Iraq or Afghanistan? These people aren't even…human!"

"I won't listen to this, Dad."

"Well, call me crazy, but where I come from, when a woman's honor's insulted, it doesn't matter what she's done – her men family are gonna beat the living daylights out of whoever did it! The Arabs, well, they find their *woman* and beat the hell out of *her*! Imagine if our Southern states were Muslim."

Dad suddenly affected a southern drawl. "That, Suh, was an insult to the honuh of mah wife! Ah regret Ah shall have to demand satisfaction!"

Now he switched to a southern baritone: "Very well. Pistols?"

"No," he said, back to the first drawl. "Ah think Ah'll just beat her to death with the shovel."

I didn't laugh. I could only think about Pat, the eighteen-year-old who stole my virginity at twelve. "Then why did you whip *me* after you found out about Pat?"

I heard the roar of a televised baseball game on the other end. "Well...that's different. You were only a kid, for God's sake, Fereby," he said. "It was discipline. So you wouldn't run around *doing* that sort of thing! I wanted to whoop the hell out of Pat, too."

But he didn't even say anything to Pat or his parents because Pat's parents were the lead surgeons of the mission that provided sight to hundreds of impoverished blind Indians. Evidently, that family was above reproach.

"Look, Fereby, my point was, this honor killing thing's a lost cause, honey. Please come home now."

"I told you, I can't get on a plane!"

He sighed. "Well, when do you *have* to be back?"

"I'm supposed to go to Ecuador at the end of next week."

I was doing a feature on several places where ancient languages were about to vanish – central India, Papua New Guinea and the Ecuadorian Amazon. I'd already been to the first two spots to talk to the elders who were the last speakers.

"Fereby." My mother had grabbed the phone. "What are you trying to prove, dear?"

"Nothing, Mom."

"If you really want to help, you mustn't judge people."

This from my mother who'd made a lifelong, global career out of converting heathens to her Christian worldview.

I sat up on my elbows on the bed. "They're judging their own culture, " I said. "Arab women are protesting on their own."

"I haven't exactly heard of any Arab women burning their bras." She laughed.

"The suffragettes went into a voting booth and pulled a lever as an act of civil disobedience," I said. "Rosa Parks sat in a white person's seat. Maybe an Arab woman does something else...like fall in love with an American man. Or paint whatever she feels like. Or something subtler. I'm not doing anything at least some of the women here wouldn't if they weren't so intimidated. They're already pushing for change on their own. Why else would they need honor killing?"

"You're starting to sound like a vigilante," she said. Mom liked everyone to just toe the main line, never veer off-course.

"Sometimes that's what's called for."

She sighed. "Aren't you concerned for your safety?"

"I'm an American. If someone tried to hurt me, it wouldn't go unnoticed."

"That's what that peace activist Rachel Corrie thought, too," she said. "She was sure her 'international white-person privileges' would protect her from harm. And they were *Israeli soldiers* who ran over her with a bulldozer."

I hated it when she tried to chip away at my confidence like this. But I knew this was her agenda. *Stay true to yourself, Fer.*

"Fereby, honey, you're overlooking the most important point of all."

Here we go. "What, Mom?"

"You're fighting a battle you can't win."

"How do you know that?"

"Leila's death, like everyone's, is God's will."

Something sharp zigzagged in my gut. *Ma sha'allah: God's will.* That woman at the crime scene had yelled that at me through the car window about Leila's death. Fury ignited up and out of the top of my skull.

"Like *hell* it is, Mom!"

For the first time in my life, I hung up on my mother.

25

I need a translator fluent in English, Hebrew and Arabic," I said to Raziel, the gallery owner, by phone that night. "Hebrew'd be a bonus." I couldn't afford the interpreter I'd worked with for the *Geographic* piece and thought Raziel might know someone cheaper since he lived in Jaffa, which was a mixed town of Arabs and Jews.

"Sounds like you're getting serious," he said.

"It's just a small client project," I lied.

"I'll ask around and call you back tomorrow morning. Oh – by the way...that Duncan guy came by the other evening."

"*Duncan?*" I said. "When?"

"Saturday, I think."

The day I met him and told him of Leila's death.

"He was in a big hurry," Raziel said. "On his way to the airport to go back to the States."

"What did he want?"

"He bought every last one of Leila's paintings."

Raziel was right – Duncan was The Asshole. Grabbed what he wanted and bailed. I needed to call and confront him. I pulled out Leila's secret love phone and turned it on. I still couldn't figure out which was his number.

Finally, I gave up and Googled "Duncan Ramsay" on my own phone and found his foundation. I called, but had to leave a message with his assistant.

I'd planned to go running when I woke up the next morning, but I'd been awake half the night worrying about Qasim and brooding over my disillusionment with Fadi while I tried to study Arabic. Instead, Raziel referred me to a motley crew of interpreters that I spent several hours auditioning: A competent Palestinian guy who refused the job once he learned it was for the Druze. A Jewish co-ed majoring in Arabic who could speak English well enough to be confident, but not well enough to be understood. And a Golan Druze who'd been dismissed from his job in the Israeli military courts for making too many errors. I was starting to think that Raziel didn't want me to have an effective interpreter and had given up on him when he phoned.

"Moshe Mansano's on his way to see you now."

"Is he actually qualified, Raziel?"

"Oh, yeah, sharp guy. Performance artist in Tel Aviv. Israeli Jew born in Morocco. Fluent in Hebrew, Arabic and English. He's kind of different but I think you'll like him."

I tried not to get my hopes up as I waited for Moshe in the hospice-hotel lobby under the suspicious eye of the grouchy nun. Suddenly, the door opened a few inches and a pair of dark sunglasses poked inside.

"*Shalom! Eyfo ha hospis, beseder?*" Where is the hospice, please?

To my surprise, I understood. The immersion was starting to take. "*Po,*" I said. Here.

Then, this creature swung the door all the way open and entered with a flourish. He wore a thin peach T-shirt, skintight to reveal a lean, muscled torso, faded bellbottom jeans and stacked-heel combat boots, and carried a bronze hobo purse over one shoulder. He stopped in front of me and pulled off his sunglasses. He was wearing false eyelashes.

"Fereby?" he said.

I nodded, speechless. He flashed a dazzling smile and thrust his hand out to shake.

"Moshe Mansano!"

Moshe tucked his shoulder-length black hair behind his ears and arranged his sunglasses on his head. His nails were painted pale peach. He even smelled like peaches.

Grouchy had a look of stiffened horror on her face.

"Why don't we go...*out,*" I said. "I think there's a place to sit around the corner in the garden."

We found a bench in the courtyard, where several hospice patients in wheelchairs watched some finches play in a birdbath.

"Raziel told me you're a performance artist," I began.

Moshe roared with laughter, slapping his thighs. "*That* was kind of him! Ouch, that hurt…" He rubbed his leg.

"Well…then, what do you do?" I asked uneasily.

He draped one arm languorously over his crossed legs. "I'm a belly dancing star in the gay ghetto of Tel Aviv."

Ah, of course. "I didn't know there were male belly dancers," I said.

"Oh, sure…but I actually dress as a woman."

I cleared my throat. "Why do you want this job?"

"I got fired a few weeks ago and I really need the cash."

I sighed. Why was Raziel wasting my time like this? Maybe *he* should be a suspect.

"I think you'll actually love me," Moshe said, flashing his showgirl smile. It wasn't hard to imagine him in sequins and a long wig. "If you give me a chance."

Moshe had a handsome face in a kind of mischievous way; when he smirked, which was often, his eyes looked as if he had a delicious secret.

I scratched my head.

"I'll work for cheap. First day's on me!"

He was so earnest and energetic. I was so tired.

"We'll drive my van! Raziel said you have a rental car…you can turn it in and just pay for my gas."

"You'll be driving back and forth between here and Tel Aviv every day?"

"No."

"You have a place to stay?"

"Uh-huh."

I didn't want to inflict him on the dying patients in the garden, so I took Moshe back inside to look for hotel guests we could recruit for an audition. The grouchy nun blocked our way past her desk, though, a tirade exploding from her tiny mouth.

Moshe quickly calmed her down with some mannerly Hebrew.

"She says there's no way I'm going inside," he said to me, bemused.

"Tell her you're not sleeping here."

"She doesn't care."

"Tell her we're just going to talk to some people in the lounge," I said.

Grouchy was looking back and forth at us, bracing herself for further entreaty.

Moshe switched into Arabic and within moments, Grouchy's demeanor began to soften. She spoke back to him in Arabic and, in under a minute, she even *laughed*.

"What happened?" I asked.

"She says it's house rules that visitors can only be in the lobby, and she'd get into serious trouble if she got caught flouting that again. I told her no problem, I understood," he said, winking at her.

"Well, I guess that covers our interpretation audition, too."

I walked Moshe outside to the parking lot where he led me to a purple van that had plainly been through several incidents. I noted a significant dent in the driver's side door, a side mirror knocked out of kilter and hardened candle wax in a rainbow of colors spilling out over the back fender. And that was just one angle.

"You know Arabic from living in Morocco?" I asked.

"It's my first language," he said. "I *am* Arab."

"An *Arab* Jew?"

"Yes."

How does that work, I wondered. "Do you think you can interpret successfully for some Druze and a Bedouin?"

"Of course," he said. "I know all about the Druze: they're a little bit Muslim, but not really Arab...they like Jesus, but think it was an imposter who was crucified...they're gifted soldiers, but positively brutal toward Palestinians...they worship a golden calf, Druze widows can't remarry, and they bury old people in the walls."

"They stopped burying people in the walls about a hundred years ago," I corrected. "They're an offshoot of Islam and consider themselves Arab in every country they inhabit *except* Israel. Druze widows can remarry but rarely do because they'd lose their children to the former husband's family."

"Well, hello Wikipedia.com!" he said. "Did you know they call the toilet the House of Good Manners? And do you know why they wear baggy trousers?"

"No."

"They believe the Messiah will be born to a man, but they don't know whom, so they wear baggy trousers to catch the baby in case they unexpectedly give birth!"

"That sounds like an old wives' tale."

Moshe frowned.

"How is your English so good?"

"I lived in San Francisco for two years growing up."

"So, what do you want to be paid?"

"Nine hundred *shekels* a day," he said, brightening.

"*What?!*"

"Five hundred?"

"Try two hundred," I said.

"Four," he said.

I shook my head. He couldn't be older than twenty-five tops.

"I'm worth every *shekel*."

"I just don't have the money."

"Okay," he said. "How about fifty U.S. dollars a day – paid in actual *dollars* – plus gas and food?"

"Not food," I said. "You'd have to eat anyway."

He rolled his eyes. "Fine."

"Oh. One stipulation of your employment," I said. "You can't wear makeup...or women's clothing."

"That's two stipulations, but *whatever*...I have a stipulation, too: I have psychoanalysis three times a week in Tel Aviv."

"*Three times?*"

"It's subsidized by the government."

"What am I going to do for transportation when you're gone?"

"You'll have the van," he said, patting it lovingly. "I can take the bus or train."

I looked at the van and felt reluctant. At least there wasn't a sign on it for his belly-dancing business. "Okay."

"A basketful of eyes for a blind man!" He jumped up and clapped his hands and when he landed, shimmied his bottom for a few seconds so fast it seemed electricity had to be involved. "When do we start?"

"Right now," I said. "I need to find a witness to a murder."

Moshe followed me in his van to return my rental car. On the way to Ru'yah's, I told him what had happened with Leila. At red lights, he removed his false eyelashes and changed shoes.

As we were getting out of the van in front of Ru'yah's house, a clanging vehicle came down the road toward the cul-de-sac. The Azzams' brown station wagon bounced up into their driveway.

"The Azzams," I said to Moshe as I searched for Fadi, but he wasn't with them.

Iman hurried inside the courtyard without looking at us, while Dima lowered her gaze and hastily carried in some groceries. Kamil eyed us with baffled contempt.

Ru'yah answered the door. She looked at Moshe and me with equal shock, apparently struggling to determine how we came to end up on her front porch simultaneously. I introduced them and Moshe asked her in his gracious Arabic if we could speak to Rushdi. I cringed, noticing he still had on eye shadow. He was really quite a pretty man – great bones, dimples. When he smiled, his real eyelashes pointed out like stars.

"We're about to eat dinner right now," she said, looking nervous.

Rushdi came up behind her and regarded Moshe with barely concealed alarm. He was short, the same height as Ru'yah, with thick black hair like Fadi's and a boyish energy. When Ru'yah stalled, Moshe made introductions.

"Moshe, ask him who told him to wash Leila's blood down the sewer," I said.

Moshe shot me a look as he reluctantly translated my question. Ru'yah pretended not to hear. Rushdi answered in a solemn tone.

"He says the police told him he could...he doesn't remember specifically who. They were finished," Moshe said.

"Did you witness the murder when you came home from the hospital?" I asked.

"No, it was already done," Moshe translated.

"What time was that?" I asked.

"Sunrise." Ru'yah had said the same.

"Who killed Leila?" I asked.

Ru'yah looked nauseous. Moshe winced at my simple, indelicate question before rendering it into Arabic. Rushdi's eyes narrowed. Ru'yah opened her mouth to speak, but Rushdi quieted her with a hand on her hip I wasn't meant to notice. Rushdi spat a slew of heated Arabic. Ru'yah didn't seem to be listening at all. In fact, her eyes weren't completely in focus, and her face had grown pale. Her hand came out awkwardly at me; instinctively, I stepped back. Her knees gave out and she fainted.

26

We all jumped forward to catch Ru'yah. Rushdi pulled her into the house, cursing us, and slammed the door behind him with his foot.

Moshe and I looked at each other.

"She knows something," he said. "And he had some things to say about you."

"What?"

"He called you a menace to Druze society."

My article had really ruffled some feathers. And all I did was mention Leila's rescuing me and then being killed, possibly in an honor killing.

"Well, let's go see if we can talk to the other Azzams," I said.

"The pay's good, but the path's troublesome," Moshe said.

"Huh?"

"That's what the mouse said when he was dared to take a guinea and walk on the whiskers of the cat. It's an old fable."

"Meaning?"

"They did not look friendly," he said. "I'm not going in *there*."

Moshe stayed two steps below me as I knocked on the Azzams' front door. Seconds later, Kamil opened it. He looked Moshe up and down with disdain, then regarded me vacantly.

"May I speak to Dima and Iman with my interpreter, please?"

"You had better go home to the USA *now*, Miss Jones," he bellowed.

"Not until Qasim is free and Leila's murderer is caught," I said, amazed at my own nerve.

"I am warning you!" He slammed the door.

"Hothead," I heard Moshe murmur behind me.

Moshe took me back to the hospice-hotel and we made a plan to meet there in the morning after breakfast. I worked for a while, tried to fall asleep, contemplated calling Fadi, then tossed and turned for two hours rattled about how unwelcome I'd become in Atabi. Duncan called me back as I was getting out my Arabic textbook.

"Do you still have Leila's cell phone – the one I gave her?" he asked.

"Yes."

"You've got to get rid of it...*permanently*. I don't want to be framed."

What a jerk, I thought. All he cares about is himself. Leila wouldn't have been that much better off with him.

"The police can trace any phone records," I said. "They don't need the phone for evidence."

"But if they don't know about me or that she was using it, they won't know where to look."

"Raziel told me you stopped by the gallery and did a little 'shopping' en route to the airport."

There was a long pause. "Yeah...so?"

"Your priorities were saving your own neck and making sure you ended up with her art?"

"I'm putting all of her work I have – pieces I bought and ones she gave me – into the permanent collection of the foundation, Fereby. They'll be accessible to the public always."

"Amazing you had such clarity of mind in your state of grief to think up such a brilliant plan."

He sighed. "Would you rather a bunch of unknown collectors end up with her remaining work and no one ever gets to see it – or *worse* – her family gets a hold of it?"

He was right. They would destroy it.

"I didn't even get her best pieces – the ones from her last series. They were already sold," he said.

I considered telling him about the ones Devrah was hiding, but thought better of it.

"By the way, did your good buddy Raziel mention that he charged me five grand a canvas?"

I left the hospice at six a.m. to go for a run. All I could think about was freeing Qasim. If Fadi wouldn't confess, the only way to get Qasim out of custody was to find the person who actually committed the murder. Unfortunately, this was no ordinary honor killing. My instincts said that in order to uncover *who* cleansed the dishonor, I would have to reconstruct *how* and *why* the honor got besmirched in the first place. I couldn't ignore my intuition that Leila's final series could help me somehow. Her paintings revealed her deep psyche and perhaps the conflicts of her family, community and culture that led to her murder. I still didn't know what ancient ritual the seven perfumes were used for that Hermes Trismegistus wrote about...or what it meant to Leila. I shouldn't have come down so hard on Duncan last night before getting any details out of him about those paintings, whatever he knew. Having the series split up – and not even knowing who had most of the paintings and why – was gnawing at me. If only I could locate the rest of them...and their owners.

Moshe's van was parked in the lot in the same place when I'd left him last night. I peered into the front seat through the windshield. No Moshe. I couldn't see into the back of the darkened van. I glanced around the parking lot; there was no one around. I rapped on the door. A little shriek came from inside. Moments later, the side door of the van slid open and a disheveled Moshe squinted out from under a pink blanket. I smelled stale *ylang ylang* incense.

"*Boker tov,*" he croaked, covering his eyes.

"What are you doing *sleeping* here?"

"Why should I drive somewhere else to sleep in my van?"

"You said you had someplace to stay."

"I do." He fluffed his pillow up underneath him. "Do you mind if I finish my beauty rest?"

When I returned from my run, Grouchy Nun was fit to be tied. She began a tirade I couldn't follow, but as it turned out, I only needed to grasp several telling words: "man," "leave," and "key" – the last one she said with her hand out.

Evidently, I wasn't the only one who'd discovered Moshe camping out. I showered and packed in twenty minutes. From the hospice steps, Grouchy scowled as Moshe and I took off in his van. I felt bad leaving on such terms.

"Look how adorable she is, Fereby," he said, giggling. "Roll down your window and blow her a kiss." We did.

Moshe drove me to Jaffa to confront Raziel in person about price-gouging Duncan and to try to locate Leila's other paintings from her last series. After therapy, Moshe would come back to pick me up.

When I walked into Mujun, I startled Raziel, who was lying on the divan, hands resting on his protruding belly, holding the end of the *nargileh*. He sat up and scooted over, motioning me to sit where he'd been lying. The cushions were still off-puttingly warm with his body heat. I recoiled to the edge as he relit the tobacco.

"Do you know how to get in touch with the collectors who bought Leila's 'Seven Perfumes' paintings? " I asked. Before I left on bad terms, I'd get something useful out of him.

He scratched his head. "Why?"

"I'd just like to see them before I go," I lied.

"Name's Ira Binyamin. He owns all four."

"Could you call him for me, please?"

He got up and thumbed some stacks on his desk, though his eyes looked loath to help me. He placed the call, then jotted something down.

"He's home now, expecting you." Raziel gave me the address and picked up the *nargileh* again.

I hadn't forgotten that he'd begged Devrah for the rest of the Seven Perfumes series in the same conversation he'd learned of Leila's death.

"Thanks...So, you've sold all of Leila's paintings now, from the last series and earlier work," I said.

He nodded, relighting the pipe.

"What are you planning on doing with Leila's share of the earnings?"

He glared at me.

"Which is what – half your take?" I asked.

He exhaled. "She got eleven hundred fifty *shekels* a picture until her prices went up just last week and then she was going to get eighteen hundred."

"But she gets a percentage of what you sell them for, not a flat rate."

"What business is it of yours?"

"You owe that money to her estate."

"Her *estate?*" He laughed. "Druze women own nothing, Fereby. Most of them volunteer to give up their inheritance to their sons or brothers. They're not going to have anything to settle. Would you want those creeps to have her cash anyway?"

"Leila wouldn't have given up her inheritance on her own volition," I shot back. "Regardless, that money belongs to her estate and should be put in a safe place – a bank account – and we'll figure out later whose it rightfully is."

He smoked without speaking for a while, gazing at the disintegrating ceiling. "You're right, Fereby," he said. "Don't worry, I'll take care of her share."

I walked toward Yefet Street fretting about Raziel's trustworthiness. On the block where the bombing had occurred, I stood motionless, my stomach churning. A bus's brakes screeched at the red light. Cars honked insults at each other. The clock on the tower was keeping correct time. A Muslim woman walked past me with her cell phone tucked into her tightly wound headscarf so she could use it hands-free. There was no broken glass, no charred remains, no odor of burned flesh, no blood splatters, not even flowers or cards or candles placed as a memorial. Other than a few shops with boarded-up windows, it was just another day in Mediterranean paradise. "Remove the sacred to let the profane return," the Zaka task force poet had written.

A new pang of sadness entered me: With Leila, my confidante, my co-survivor, gone, there was no one to compare the nuances of the bombing experience with. No one who knew how it felt, what it meant. No one to rectify the memories with as they unfolded their madness. And finally I felt I could speak of it.

Pedestrians sauntered down the sidewalk oblivious to the terrorist event that had killed eighteen people just last week. I searched the faces of the people who waited at the bus stop. Did they hide their fear and grief behind a mask so the enemy couldn't see? No one just stood and gaped as I did. Was I the crazy one? I hadn't looked this closely when I had been waiting for that fateful bus.

We never really look until we can see.

27

Moshe picked me up in front of the Jaffa clock tower. It was a relief to have someone else driving and navigating for a change. On the way to Ira Binyamin's in lower Haifa, I Googled him and learned he'd been a professor of archaeology at Hebrew University in the '60s and '70s, his last publication in 1978. His work had focused on the archaeology of the Mid-East's ancient goddess cultures.

We found the Professor's austere apartment building in a western suburb of the city. When we walked up to his door, we could hear an old man shouting on the phone inside. I knocked. His conversation continued. I knocked again, louder. Same. Moshe was getting restless.

"Must be hard of hearing," I said. "But Raziel told him I was coming soon."

I rang the bell and knocked again and again as Moshe passed the time practicing belly dance moves.

"What are you doing?" I asked.

"Hip isolations."

"What if he opens the door?"

"That would be a miracle."

I heard the professor say goodbye and hang up his phone finally. I rapped on the door and Moshe lay on the doorbell with his rear-end.

Binyamin swung open the door. "Sorry, sorry, sorry!" he said and hurried us inside.

He was a small but spry, bespectacled old man, with longish silver hair that floated off the top of his head when he rushed around, his only speed of locomotion. He sat us down in his fusty living room of vintage 1950s furniture that was lined on all sides with floor-to-ceiling bookshelves. More books, an old Hebrew typewriter and a chess set covered the dining table. I sensed Mrs. Binyamin was long gone. There was no real art to speak of – or room to hang it – and I had to wonder what a man of such apparent modest means and taste was doing with some of Leila Azzam's last works of art.

Binyamin brought out a bottle of mineral water for us and poured it into chipped glasses from tourist destinations in Israel. His English turned out to be good enough I wouldn't need Moshe to translate.

"I understand you own some of Leila Azzam's paintings," I said.

"Yes, yes, I do," he said and cleared his throat.

"You know, of course, about her death."

He shook his head. "I can't believe it. Breaks my heart."

"How did you come to take an interest in her work?" I took a sip of the tepid drink.

"Yes, well, I often take my weekend walk in old Jaffa because I enjoy the galleries. I buy as many paintings as I can afford that I think are important, which isn't many. She was there the day I first saw her paintings, actually. I only met her that once. She was so kind and told me all about her art. We talked a long time."

"You think Leila's paintings are important?"

"Oh, yes," he said protectively, pushing his glasses back up on his nose as if to see my offensive person better. "She was documenting a part of history that was nearly wiped off the planet."

"What do you mean?"

He knit his thick, silver brows. "She was your friend and you don't know what she painted?"

I glanced at Moshe. "Our friendship was just beginning," I conceded. "I haven't seen all of her paintings…Are you speaking of the Goddess era?"

"Well, of course."

"What's your interest there?"

He sat back in his chair and crossed his arms. "I doubt Miss Azzam ever knew of my work since I couldn't publish most of what I found, but she painted some of the ideas I have studied and dreamed of for more than half a century."

"What sort of…ideas?" I asked.

He jumped up and retreated down a hallway. Moshe and I exchanged quizzical looks. He returned with two framed canvasses, which he tenderly leaned against his dining table so we couldn't see them.

He turned the first one around. I immediately recognized "Resurrection" from Raziel's description – a huge orange-red sun on the horizon behind a frankincense tree with the face and hands of a beautiful girl in its twisty, low branches. "She mixed frankincense oil into the oil paint for the tree," said Professor Binyamin. "The sun, as the giver of life, symbolizes our conscious mind. It's our basic identity, our self-realization. Leila was saying that women in her culture have lost their creative life force and their own purpose."

It was breathtaking, the colors and the girl as part of the tree, especially in light of the circumstances of her death – an honor killing – as Devrah had described.

Binyamin turned around the other painting. "I present 'The Birth of Hawwah.' Here is the Great Goddess who has created the first human – Eve," he said reverently. "Adam, as you notice, is nowhere in sight. She was not born from his rib."

There was the lovely violet-eyed Asherah, giving birth to Eve (Hawwah in Hebrew), whose feet were still inside the birth canal, umbilical cord still intact, as she suckled the breast of the Goddess. I was stunned. Moshe's eyes were full of wonder.

"Professor, do you know how Leila used the aromatic in this painting?" I asked.

"Indeed! She crushed malabathron leaves and mixed them with the paint for the baby's body. Malabathron is Zeus' substance and his planet, Jupiter, represents hope and possibility."

"So, what was Leila saying women sacrificed here?"

He gazed lovingly at the canvas, then back at me. "Their potential, my dear."

I gazed at Asherah and baby Eve – the Mother Goddess and the First Woman – one of the most starkly empowering images I'd ever seen.

"She also sneaked in some lilies for fertility," he said, pointing to the white flowers in Asherah's hair. "Just as the Angel Gabriel carried lilies when he appeared to Mary in the Annunciation. Of course, lilies are in the *Song of Songs* and the *Hermetica*, too, which are dear to the Druze."

I sat forward in my chair. "You know the *Hermetica*?"

"Oh, yes." He eyed the bookcase behind him, perhaps searching for a copy. "We go back a long way."

"By any chance, are you familiar with *The Wing* then?" I asked.

His eyebrows seemed to rise about three inches. "I haven't heard anyone mention that in years!"

"So you are."

"Well, just from the legend. I've never seen the book, of course."

"What legend?"

"You know of *The Wing*, but not what comprises its infamy?"

I shook my head.

"Oh, well, let's see," he said, scratching the silver scruff on his chin. "Clement of Alexandria believed the Egyptians had forty-two sacred writings of Hermes Trismegistus, which he supposedly wrote five thousand years ago somewhere in the Eastern Mediterranean at the time of the invasion by the patriarchs. In one of them, *The Wing*, Hermes is said to have predicted the conspiracy to suppress the Goddess religion, feminine values and women's rights. He said the invaders would, in effect, give the Goddess a sex change operation and turn her into a male God, inverting nature to have woman created from man."

Moshe perked up and met my glance.

"Why would they want to do that?" I asked.

"To destroy the matrilineal power structure, of course," he said. "The patriarchs wanted control of the government, land and other resources and, to get it, they had to upturn the system. The high priestess held the divine right to the throne, and kinship and property had always been passed down through women. The Canaanites didn't pay much attention to who their fathers were and patriliny doesn't work without that. So, the patriarchs had to start controlling paternity. To establish the idea of male superiority, they inserted their male creator god into the existing creation myth as though he had been there from the beginning. Then, they revised other stories – like Adam and Eve – to underscore that women are less than men and naturally immoral. Finally, they transformed the sacred sexual rites of the Goddess religion into something terrible."

"That's all it took?" I asked, half sarcastically.

Moshe looked as if he had a bitter taste in his mouth.

"Oh, no. It was a long, bloody war," Professor Binyamin went on. "Both the old Goddess religion and the new religion – what we now call Judaism – co-existed for thousands of years. Asherah was worshipped right alongside Yahweh as his spouse in the Temple in Jerusalem for almost three hundred years. Imagine convincing Hebrew women to be their husbands' property when their pagan neighbors were free! Ha! That had to be tough, if you know Jewish women today! It took everything they had – violence and suppression and destruction of everything Goddess, to get rid of Her. They were so thorough, there's not even a word for Goddess in Hebrew."

Moshe seemed to be barely containing himself. This was obviously some sensitive stuff for him.

"Of course, there had already been invasions into the region throughout the Bronze Age by violent Indo-European pagans who didn't worship the Goddess," Binyamin admitted, noticing Moshe's agitation. "The revolution was long and slow. The writing of the Old Testament was merely the climax. After several generations, people were successfully brainwashed to buy into the new system."

Moshe got up and walked over to the window. I blinked at Binyamin, a strange sensation growing in my gut. Turns out distorting the divine feminine by associating her with prostitution and evil was already a tried-and-true political maneuver when the Vatican besmirched the memory of Mary Magdalene, turning her into a harlot.

"How did I get an advanced education and not learn this?" I said.

Binyamin cocked his head. "Few people do. It doesn't serve the powers that be."

"But getting back to *The Wing*—" I said.

"Yes, yes," Binyamin sputtered, pushing his glasses up on his nose. "It called for men and women – the survivors and the enlightened ones, mind you – to carry on their worship of the Goddess secretly, to never give up, and wait until the tide turned again. Hermes said we would know Her resurrection was underway when the battle reached its lowest moral point … 'Into the Underworld goeth thine Soul.' He predicted it would start in approximately five thousand years and it would take a thousand years or so to succeed, about as long as it took to contain."

Moshe faced us, his mouth open. As I did the math, a slight chill slinked over my scalp. "So," I said. "That new era...would be arriving...*now.*"

Binyamin smiled knowingly and nodded. "Naturally, the book itself was suppressed to the point that it disappeared, too."

"Do you know what in *The Wing* Leila was referring to by naming her series 'The Seven Perfumes of Sacrifice'?" I asked.

He talked to himself in Hebrew as he eyed his bookshelves, bumping into a chair stacked high with volumes. "*The Greek Magical Papyri.* That's the one."

He entreated Moshe to climb a ladder and pull down the volume.

"A collection of wonderful spells from Egypt, written from the second century BCE to the fifth century CE. It's the only place I've ever seen any reference to the seven perfumes along with *The Wing.*"

I came around to his side while he thumbed the dusty pages, obliviously licking his fingers.

"The famous Leiden papyrus mentions something called the *Eighth Book of Moses,* which might have been used for initiation ceremonies. The author claims to have found a recipe in it that Hermes stole and published in another book entitled *The Wing.* The recipe called for seven kinds of incense. But the Hermetic text may be older than the Mosaic one."

"Are the specific incenses mentioned?" I asked.

"It reads: 'Have the table prepared with these following kinds of incense...The proper incense of Kronos is styrax; of Zeus, malabathron; of Ares, kostos; of Helios, frankincense; of Aphrodite, Indian nard; of Hermes, cassia; of Selene, myrrh. These are the secret incenses'."

"Those are precisely the incenses Leila used in her paintings," I said. "What was the recipe for?"

"A ceremony meant to win one a meeting with the gods to try to achieve immortality. But it was only provided as a guise to fool the new patriarchal establishment into believing they partook of the new rituals that included the male gods. Kind of like 'when in Rome'. "

I sat back to try to absorb this. Leila had taken an ancient, traditional ritual and set of symbols sacred to her patriarchal culture (who were unaware of their subversiveness) and turned them on their head to reveal their injustice, brutality, immorality – inhumanity even – to women. She had performed mythopoetic alchemy. Her paintings might be, in fact, the most dangerous images the Druze could ever fathom. If someone had discovered them, Leila surely would have been assassinated. And what timing, if Hermes was accurate.

"So, it seems Hermes was right about the first part of his prediction – the losses," I said. "Do you think the part about the tide turning back holds any merit?"

He tilted his head, as if to see me more clearly. "Isn't it obvious, Miss Jones?" He pointed to Leila's painting.

"Besides Leila, are there people actually trying to bring back the Old Religion?"

"One could speculate that there have been for eons." He crossed his legs and got a roguish look on his face. "Why do you think Hypatia was killed? Or Digna Ochoa? Or Marilyn Monroe? Or Karen Silkwood? Marla Ruzicka or Rachel Corrie? Or Princess Diana? I could go on and on."

"You're saying Princess Diana was a Goddess worshipper?" I said.

"No, not specifically. But she was a shining symbol of the values of the sacred feminine – beauty, nurture, cooperation, reverence for nature, equality, compassion, peace and non-violence, generosity, glorious *life!* – that sustained all the cultures of Goddess. There are many more like her that never became famous…the thousands who were killed in the witch hunts…There were nearly as many men killed for the same reasons – and look at Jesus, for Christ's sake! Exalt feminine values and it threatens the hell out of the powerful."

Moshe crossed his arms and leaned his chin studiously on the back of his wrist. "Because they know it's *real.*"

Binyamin and I both looked at him in surprise. How many disparate emotions could Moshe produce in an hour?

"Correct, young man," said Binyamin. "Female power is intrinsic…profound!" He gaped at me, sweeping his arms open wide. "Your very existence is of mythic proportions with your capacity to *create* and *feed* new life with your body. Women issue blood but *do not die* from it!" He got to his feet. "Many ancient cultures believed the Goddess withheld the secret of immortality from men, you know. They saw that women, like the Goddess, reproduced themselves; no one knew for a long while that men were part of the equation. Men envied and feared women's seemingly magical powers, so to compensate, men began to try to cheat death by spilling blood and killing."

Indeed, the *shaikh* had said the only knowledge worth having was that which led to immortality. No wonder his ancestors developed the recipe of the seven perfumes.

"Many men think they must destroy something to prove their worth," the professor went on, stroking his flyaway hair back. "Women are accused of being the emotional sex, but it's normally the male who has so little mastery of his feelings that he resorts to violence to achieve his aims."

In his element now, Binyamin leaned forward breathlessly, eyes sparkling. The silver hair on top of his head floated up into a momentary question mark. "I don't think the Old Religion ever completely died," he whispered.

"How so?" I asked, taking a nervous sip of water.

"I was doing a dig near Mecca in the 1970s. I found many artifacts that prove Arabs continued to worship goddesses all throughout Muhammed's reign and beyond, in spite of his officially ending the national worship of the Sun Goddess, Al Lat. That means 'Goddess' in Arabic, the same deity as Asherah, Astarte, Ishtar. When you go home and drink a *latté* at Starbucks, think of Al Lat – the Goddess' name is the root for 'milk.' Anyway, Muhammed completed the final destruction of the shrines to the goddesses in Arabia. But the Ka'aba – that black stone in Mecca that they walk around *seven* times on *haj?* – it was originally associated with Goddess, but because it was so popular, it was left and re-imagined as a Muslim object of worship."

"Did you publish this?" I asked.

"No," he said, his face falling. "I was forced to leave Saudi Arabia without any of my artifacts or research materials. They kept all my notes. I tell you, I was too scared to publish *anything*...It's happened in other places, too. There have been massive efforts to suppress the truth. James Mellaart, who dug Hacilar, the Neolithic site in Turkey, was also ordered to halt his work."

"What did he find?"

"Evidence of Turkey's most ancient religion, from nine thousand years ago."

"Not the one the officials wanted him to find?" I asked.

He shook his head. "The worship of the Great Goddess."

28

I should be paying *you*," said Moshe when we were walking out to the van. "Catch the halter-rope and it will lead you to the donkey."

"What?" I asked.

"To get to the root of a matter, go to where it starts. It's Moroccan."

"You looked as if you were going to blow a fuse earlier," I said.

"I know...my shrink calls me a Jew of Two Minds. I guess it's true that everything contains the light and the darkness."

We exchanged a smile; I felt relieved.

My phone rang. It was Fadi again. My heart skipped.

"Everything is getting worse," Fadi said. "Now Tamir is trying to force my father to give him half the orchard even though Leila's gone. He's filed a lawsuit against us."

Why was he confiding in me? "What right does he have to it?" I asked.

"It was promised to him when they married. The contract was signed, of course, but the marriage not officially begun since the wedding never took place. He thinks we still owe it to him."

Could Tamir have killed her off just to get the property? Maybe he was planning on killing her after the wedding, to be certain it would be legally his, but had to do it sooner when he discovered Leila's affair and plans to leave. If husbands were starting to kill for honor in Lebanon, why not Israel? Especially with an extra financial motive. Or was Fadi telling me this just to throw me off?

I sighed. "Money's not what's most important here, Fadi. Leila and Qasim are."

"Could you just promise to stay out of it from now on? You tried to interrogate my family after I told you not to."

"I'm only trying to see that justice is done for *your sister's* death — something *you* should be doing, Fadi."

"The *shaikhs* are meeting to discuss Leila's death and will soon make a public statement," he said. "Then it will be over."

I doubted that would put an end to the matter unless they offered up the perpetrator, so I promised him nothing. We hung up and I felt oddly betrayed. Why had I ever thought he was something else? And how did I let myself get so drawn in? We could *never* be together and I knew that going in. My heart — and body — had other ideas, evidently.

On the way to Haifa, my phone rang again. It was Mona, my next-door neighbor in California, sounding upset. It was before dawn in the U.S.

"Some guys broke into your trailer, Fereby."

"*What?*" I looked over at Moshe in alarm. In the loosely gated trailer park where I lived in Laguna Beach, crime of any kind was rare.

"I went over to your place tonight to drop off your mail. I saw a light moving around inside." She was breathing hard and had to stop to catch her breath. "I waited to see what was going on. I went to the door when two men came out whispering in a foreign language. I said, 'Hey!' Then, one of them shoved me down and they ran off."

"My God! Are you okay?" I cried.

Moshe's eyes widened.

"Yeah...They ran down to the highway. They were gone when I got there."

"What'd they take?"

"Hard to say. They trashed the place, Fer."

I sighed and ran my fingers over my scalp. I didn't really own valuables, just books and unusual or sentimental things I'd collected from my travels.

"I called the police," Mona went on. "Paul's coming over to repair the door. They broke the lock."

"Did you get a look at them?"

"It was dark, but I think they were the same guys I saw a few days ago who might have been casing the trailer park. They seemed out of place, that's why I noticed them."

"Out of place how?"

"Well, they looked sort of...Middle Eastern."

My mind raced as we neared Haifa. In my research, I'd learned there were 25,000 Druze living in southern California. Had some been alerted to my activities in Israel and figured out where I lived to try to intimidate me? This was all unfamiliar, scary territory for me. I was determined to keep my focus. I pulled out Leila's cell phone.

"I wish we could check the messages on this," I said to Moshe. "It's Leila's secret love line."

"Really?" Moshe's eyebrows went up.

"It's programmed in Hebrew."

"Let me see."

He hit some buttons, glancing up occasionally while he drove. He fumbled around as I kept both eyes on the road for him.

"*This* might be useful," he said. "The call log. Dialed, missed and received calls."

The phone beeped several times. He frowned up at me. "Battery's dead."

Neither of our car chargers would work with Leila's phone, but Moshe was able to find a *pelephone* store on Allenby where we could buy the right one. Then he did a reverse phone number look-up online to figure out Leila's last phone calls. She had called Duncan at three different numbers, Raziel's cell phone and El Al airlines. The last ten missed calls were all from Duncan. The two days before her death, she received calls from Duncan's cell phone, Devrah's office phone, Raziel's cell phone and a number in Jordan we couldn't get any information on through reverse look-up.

"Should I just try calling it?" Moshe asked.

I shrugged. "Why not?"

He dialed and soon began speaking in his most formal-sounding Arabic. I listened intently, understanding little. After a few minutes of what resembled negotiation, Moshe hung up.

"He's a doctor of women's health care. At first he wouldn't reveal if he even knew of Leila. When I told him she was dead, he let his guard down and asked if she had hemorrhaged or gotten a fatal infection."

"As if she'd had a D&C or abortion," I said.

"Yeah. He asked how she died. I wouldn't tell him until he said what she went to him for."

"Good work. What'd he say?"

"That he couldn't answer that for patient privacy, but his specialty is hymen repair surgery."

"*Hymen repair.* What's that?"

"Many Arabs – and religious Jews, too – still believe that a woman must bleed on her wedding night for proof of her virginity. The doctor sews up what's left of the torn hymen and *voilà* — you're a born-again virgin!"

"That must be why the coroner found Leila's hymen intact despite the rape," I said. Ru'yah had told me honor is not about truth, but perception. "But a coroner should be able to detect a surgically repaired hymen, I would think."

"Not if he doesn't want to find it," Moshe pointed out.

"If she were escaping to the U.S., why would she get this surgery?" I asked.

"Maybe someone else made her do it."

"Tamir obviously knew she wasn't a virgin…as did anyone else who knew her history. But she told Duncan she was still a virgin."

"Maybe she wanted him to think so. She was *really* starting over," he said.

"Can a girl get a hymen repair in Israel?"

"Sure."

"Then, why would Leila go to the trouble to travel to Amman for it?"

"Privacy. It's a big deal."

True, she wouldn't have risked running into someone she knew. "How much do these operations cost?" I asked.

"Eighteen hundred Jordanian *dinars*. About…thirteen – no – twelve thousand *shekels*."

"Twenty-five hundred bucks," I said. "She could've saved enough from her art to pay for it."

"Or maybe Tamir forced her to go with him to Jordan for the operation so he could show everyone that she bled on their wedding night to try to convince them he never actually raped her," Moshe said.

"You're right. He could have legally crossed the border with her since they were technically married," I said. "Or, maybe he just wanted her to be a virgin again so he could relive his crime."

"That's disgusting, Fereby."

There were no hotel vacancies within my budget near Mt. Carmel, so we reserved a campsite and decided to sleep in the van. Of all things, we found a Mexican restaurant at the bottom of the road, where Moshe regaled me with stories about honor over a few Bohemias.

"The thing about *ayb* is that it's not so much what was actually done as *who knows about it*. We say, 'A concealed shame is two-thirds forgiven.' There's a famous story about a *shaikh* who was taking a nap under a palm tree. A poor Arab came upon him and took his expensive cloak. When the *shaikh* woke up and discovered the crime, his disciples went after and caught the thief. At trial, the thief said, 'I saw him asleep under the tree, so I had sex with him while he slept and then I took the cloak.' The *shaikh* replied hastily, 'That's not my cloak,' and the accused man was let go."

I laughed. Moshe took a long swig of beer, basking in my enjoyment.

"Have you ever heard an Arab answer *mastur al-hal* when you ask them how they are doing?" he asked.

"Sure," I said. "What does it mean?"

" 'The condition is covered' – everything's okay, my family and I are not being shamed."

The bartender switched the TV behind the bar to the evening newscast. A photograph of the teenage suicide bomber who had nearly killed me filled the screen.

"Moshe – it's her! What are they saying?"

"Quiet and I'll tell you," he said.

The program showed several pictures of Hanan Barghouti that I hadn't seen in the newspapers. My heart began to pound. Her smiling with a group of girls in head scarves. A serious headshot. Her ceremonial suicide bomber portrait. Next was an interview with a Palestinian man in the street.

"He says she volunteered to do the suicide bombing to cleanse her family's honor," Moshe said.

I could almost feel the temperature of my body drop.

"The Israeli police said her family suspected she had a boyfriend," Moshe continued as the TV report went on. "They feel that if a girl can betray her family, she's also susceptible to becoming a collaborator with Israel. So, they offered her a way to die with dignity."

I stared numbly at Moshe. "I don't...get this."

"She knows she's going to be killed anyway, so why not regain a little dignity while she's at it?"

Since I'd met Moshe yesterday, I'd never seen such a weighty expression on his face.

"Suicide bombings are basically just another kind of honor killing, Fereby. There's nothing more painful to an Arab than humiliation. It's living in hell every day. If you can't beat it, you avenge it. It's crazy, but I think it makes them feel high for once in their lives for the few hours they have before they blow themselves up. And their families get a buzz from it, too, for a little while. Luckily, most of the women bombers are caught before they can set themselves off. Their emotions give them away."

Then Hanan Barghouti was the exception. Her deadpan face flashed before me, as she stood in line to get on the bus, then as I foolishly returned her lost bus fare. I shook my head, searching for words.

Moshe saw my bewilderment. "Honor killing – *jarimat sharaf* – is a show of patriotism." He waved an imaginary flag. "It's a way Palestinians can flaunt their rejection of the West, but the men don't seem to see that they make themselves weaker — and therefore all of Palestine — by keeping their women down. Otherwise, they could have their own state, live prosperously and peacefully next to us and have the respect and support of most of the world."

He tucked his hair behind his ears and rested his chin in both hands for a long moment while he stared at me. "You know what's really scary?"

I took a nervous gulp of beer.

"The struggle for many Palestinians now is how *not* to become suicide bombers."

29

Back at the campsite, we built a fire and Moshe somehow pulled the bucket seats out of his van so we could sit more comfortably on the ground. He brought out this enormous empty wine jug that had been redeemed as a candleholder, with dozens of layers of colored wax arrested in artful motionless drips down its sides.

"Meet the Candle God," he said as he lit it and set it just inside the open back doors of the van so it wouldn't blow out. That explained the technicolor drips of wax down the bumper.

By fire and candlelight, we tried to decipher any clues we could from Leila's sketchbook that I'd borrowed from Devrah. While he translated, I took notes. The book was so amazing, it almost could have been published just as it was: it contained charcoal and pencil drawings of ideas she was studying (faces, bodies, hands, flowers, water, the whole snake section), notes from books she'd read and museums she'd visited, poetry she'd written, quotes she loved, lists and sketches for her last series, a prayer that was found inscribed in clay to the Mother Goddess from 5000 BC in Mesopotamia. The most heart-wrenching thing I found: "Is there anywhere on earth where women are safe from rape?" I'd never even considered such a thing. It was written on a page surrounded by the smiling faces of women and girls of all ages and ethnicities. A chain of hearts linked each face together.

Curiously, Leila reserved Arabic for the emotional and spiritual, Hebrew for the intellectual, and English (and this was a surprise, but shouldn't have been, given Duncan) for the sensual.

I turned to a page with several pairs of snakes entwined in an embrace, the caduceus motif. Leila had tested different ideas: the two in a loving horizontal embrace, then vertical; the two curled around a staff, a sword, a flowering vine; and one biting the other, which resulted in "Sacrifice of the Goddess-Queen."

Moshe pointed to the facing page. A black-and-white bird was flying away with a dead snake in its mouth. " 'Ibis: The bird of Thoth, destroyer of serpents.' "

"Thoth was the Egyptian name for Hermes Trismegistus, whom the Druze trace their lineage back to," I said.

On the next page, she had penciled a snake coiled around an elaborately branched tree, like in the Garden of Eden. Moshe mumbled the Hebrew words she'd written before he translated them aloud. "The serpent in the Tree of Knowledge."

"I expected you to say something about Eve," I said. I thought I'd heard her Hebrew name. "Didn't you say 'Hawwah'?"

"No, 'hewya.' Serpent."

"How funny. They sound the same, the first woman and the first snake."

Moshe flipped the page to a huge hand strangling a snake to death.

" 'Yahweh kills Leviathan: Psalms 74 and 89.' "

We both shrugged. I Googled the psalms on my phone. "Hmm. They seem to offer an alternative creation myth that comes before Genesis," I said. "Yahweh kills the serpent Leviathan or Rahab...thus putting Yahweh in charge."

"So, according to the Old Testament, a *serpent deity* first ruled the world?" Moshe said, puzzled.

"And God – or Hermes/Thoth, the original Druze – killed it?"

We looked at each other perplexed.

"Snakes and dragons are ancient symbols of Goddess," Moshe said.

"So, the Judeo-Christian creation story is, in effect, a myth of God conquering Goddess." I lit up as the epiphany hit my brain. "Wow, Mosh. That means they concede the Goddess was here first!"

We looked at each other incredulously.

"Let's see the last page she wrote on," I said.

He flipped to it and held it up to the light. "Look, it's a 'To-Do' list. Dated two days before her death...Pick up paintings/check at Mujun."

"Raziel must have owed her some money, too."

Moshe rolled his eyes. "Raziel owes *everybody* some money – he'll lead you to the river and bring you back thirsty."

"Keep going."

"Talk to Qasim."

"Maybe she wanted to say goodbye to him."

"Wedding dress to Mother of Rags," he continued. "Who's that?"

I shrugged. An old homeless woman? A consignment boutique?

"Find Muhyiddin Ibn al-'Arabi's *Turjuman al-Ashwaq* – that means *The Translator of Desires* – in English for Duncan." Moshe grinned. "It's a very famous volume of thirteenth-century Arabic and Sufi love poetry."

"Love poetry?" I exclaimed. "Oh my God…She *loved* him, Moshe. I knew it! She *did* love him!"

"There's one more," he said. "Visit Badi'a, A'rara. "

"The Bedouin woman," I said. The fire popped. "If Leila visited her before she died, Badi'a might know something that could help us. What's A'rara?"

"I think it's a village in the Negev desert."

"We're going first thing in the morning."

I flipped through the remaining pages to make sure we hadn't missed anything and noticed she'd written in Hebrew inside the back cover.

Moshe looked at it for a minute. "It's a canticle from *The Song of Songs*."

"She checked a book out on that from the library."

"Ooh. If her parents found out about that!" he quipped.

"Aren't they just poems about Christ's love for the Church or something?"

Moshe laughed. "It's an ancient *sex* manual, Fereby." He raised an eyebrow with a naughty smile.

I feigned a disapproving look.

"It is," he insisted. " 'My head is filled with dew?' 'My locks with the drops of the night?' Please! The well and the garden of aromatic spices are clearly the woman's genitals. The Patriarchs had to claim it was all symbolic because they consider the body evil."

"Well, what did Leila have to say about it?" I asked.

"It's a quote: 'We have a little sister, and she hath no breasts: what shall we do for our sister in the day when she shall be spoken for? If she be a wall, we will build upon her a palace of silver: and if she be a door, we will enclose her with boards of cedar.' "

"If she be a 'wall'?" I said.

"The wall's a virgin," he said. "The door's a slut."

" 'Enclose her with boards of cedar?' " I said. "Does this mean what I think it means?"

He nodded.

"Kill her," I said. "For honor."

30

S leeping in the back of a sixteen-year-old van with a gay Moroccan Arab Jewish cross-dressing belly dancer wasn't as weird as most people might assume. In fact, it was kind of fun, in a slumber party way. We tried on Moshe's belly dancing costumes and he attempted to teach me how to play *zils*, the finger cymbals, by the light of the Candle God, Moshe counting beats in Arabic and the both of us erupting into laughter at my utter void of talent.

I made Moshe get up early so we could drive two and a half hours to the Bedouin market in Be'er Sheva, the closest town to A'rara, to ask around if anyone knew of Badi'a before we went deep in the desert. I let him nap in the passenger seat the first hour while I drove and got lost in my thoughts about honor killing. I did a rough calculation of the number of women in countries where it existed and figured out that about 800 million women and girls were living under threat of honor killing. How was that possible? How long had it been going on and why? Was it truly a Bedouin tradition of blood revenge as Adam had heard or did it come from somewhere else?

As we made our way south past Kiryat Gat, I tried Duncan again. I must have caught him off-guard to his Caller-ID, because he finally picked up.

"Here's my theory: Leila had her hymen repaired from the rape so she could be a 'virgin' for you."

"Why would she do that?" he asked.

"It was symbolic – she wanted you to be her 'first.' There's no way she'd have taken such a huge risk by running away if she didn't love you, trust you and want to be with you. She knew she could never return to Israel and she couldn't stay in the U.S. without your support."

"You know what, Fereby?" His voice had relaxed into a soft sort of awe. "She *didn't* lie to me."

"What do you mean?"

"What she actually said was that she had never 'made love' before. *That was true.* And she said she wanted me to be her first."

"Duncan, do you think her paintings have anything to do with her death?"

"As far as I know, her family didn't know about them."

"Do you think Tamir found out about your relationship with Leila?"

He didn't answer.

"Because it looked as if you remembered something when I first asked you that."

I could hear cars honking and someone yelling "Asshole!" in the background. Manhattan seemed positively quaint at this point.

"Did anyone see you together?" I pressed.

"Possibly."

"Where?"

"At the university."

"You know there are a number of Druze students there."

"It was the first time we ever talked in the open. And the last."

"What happened?"

"I could never understand why she wanted to wait until *the* day of her wedding to leave with me," he said. "It was an issue between us. I was worried that if she waited until then, she'd change her mind under all the family pressure. So, I flew in unannounced a few weeks early and surprised her at school. I had a plane ticket for her to come back with me that night. She said she wasn't ready – she didn't even have her visa to visit the U.S. yet, which she'd promised me she would have well in advance. Of course, I didn't know she was a minor and couldn't leave the country with me."

"Did you argue?"

"Yes." His voice wavered.

"Did anyone see or overhear you?"

"They could have – we were outside in the quad."

"When was that?"

"Saturday. Before last."

"So, two days before…before her death," I said.

"That was the last time I saw her," he said. "I left that night and went back to New York without her."

~ ~ ~

"In kohling her eyes, he blinded her," Moshe said, after we'd hung up.

I saw the sign for Be'er Sheva and sighed. I was in no mood for Arabic proverbs.

"He hurt her when he was trying to help her," Moshe offered. "You didn't tell him about the book of love poems Leila was going to get him."

"I know." Duncan had seen Leila two days before her death and hadn't mentioned that fact when I met him. I still wasn't sure about him and wasn't feeling that generous.

The Bedouin Market in Be'er Sheva was an open-air, chaotic concoction of goats, robe-clad desert vendors, enormous bundles of green leafy vegetables, bootlegged Arabic music CDs, *nargilehs*, jewelry and spices. Women with squiggly tattoos around their eyes and mouths to ward off demons squatted by their wares.

Moshe asked a man hawking carved wooden camels for directions. He wouldn't tell us where she was until I tipped him. "Badi'a," the man said, glancing at me. "Crazy as a long night."

With dubious directions, we drove further south, deeper into the blur of heat. The Negev sky opened up as though a giant lid had been removed. The sand was turning the color of bone. Spiky plants, improbably dark green, pushed up from the desert floor. I took a picture of a man texting on his camel. I loved the desert and was relieved to be away from Atabi; the tension I had been feeling was getting to me.

We turned off the highway onto a long scratch – what Moshe hoped was the right unmarked sand road – with a herd of nervous goats blocking our path. The herder shooed the flock off the road for us.

"If my van gets stuck, we can become Bedouins and tattoo each other's faces," Moshe said as we bumped along.

We passed two women enshrouded in black near the front of the flock. Each carried a large stick in one hand, a red plastic bottle that might have held fuel in the other, and a baby on her back. They didn't even try to peek at us.

"The Bedouin women do all the work," Moshe said. "Watch the flocks, care for the children, grow and cook the food, keep the tent in order, wash the clothes, get the firewood…"

"What do the men do?" I asked.

"Watch the women."

After tottering through the Negev for several more hours, we stopped to put water in the radiator. A boy on a donkey wandered up and, when Moshe inquired of Badi'a, he pointed out a camp within view off the dirt road.

"Look for the goat-hair tent," Moshe translated. "This is gonna be cool!"

When we found it, five small children burst out to greet us. Within a minute, Moshe was the Pied Piper, every kid hanging off him like buttons on his shirt. I followed him and his entourage inside. He was affecting his old swish again with unusual flair.

"Moshe!" I whispered.

He turned and winked at me. "Don't worry. It'll help."

The huge tent could have covered ten of my trailers. One side appeared to be for cooking and had the natural desert floor, makeshift tables and small appliances. The other was spread with colorful rugs and numerous embroidered pillows. I recognized her right away; Leila's paintbrush had captured her wholly. Badi'a sat on a blanket with two younger women who were spooling blood-red yarn around a couple of chair legs. All three wore white headscarves and black dresses with red and orange designs.

After Moshe made introductions, Badi'a patted the blanket for us to sit down, and sent the other women away.

"Do you know Leila Azzam?" I asked through Moshe.

She smiled a near-toothless smile, which pushed up her bulbous cheekbones so they almost fit right into her sunken eye sockets. I wondered how much of us she could see with her cloudy eyes.

"She is the sweetest rain," she said, her voice deep and raspy.

"Moshe, just tell her what's happened. You know what to say."

He spoke gently to her, and I watched her eyes for the moment of understanding. Her mouth opened just a millimeter and then her face dropped into her skeletal hands. Moshe continued to speak until she lifted her eyes, wet with tears.

"You are planning revenge?" she interrupted.

"No," I said. "Justice."

She shook her head more vigorously than I deemed safe at her age, aiming a crooked finger at me. "Her blood cries revenge!"

Moshe put a gentle hand on my knee and spoke to her for a minute. It felt so good to trust him. A woman carried in a tray of coffee and dates.

"Fereby." He turned to me. "The Bedu believe the spirit of a person is in their blood and has a will of its own. The spirit will haunt those whose duty it is to take revenge. Did anyone guard Leila's grave from ghouls and *djinni* for five days and nights?"

"Are *djinni* the same as genies? " I asked.

"Exactly," said Moshe.

"Not that I know of."

Badi'a carried on in her mythic tongue.

"She says to look for the owl near her grave," Moshe said. "It's an old superstition, but she believes the unavenged soul of a slain person becomes an owl that lives near the grave and cries out for its revenge. She told me a story of a spirit rising up from the spilled blood in the earth and cursing the murderer."

"Ask her about how she met Leila," I said.

When Badi'a spoke, I felt the music of her language, which first took shape on her face, as conspicuously visual as everything else in the Mediterranean.

"I was in the Carmel forest...looking for lemon balm. We don't have it here. I heard moans and found her beneath a bush, her face bruised and cut. She had dirt and dead leaves in her hair. Still, a beautiful child. I guessed she'd fallen out of a tree. Then I saw the bottom of her dress soaked in blood."

Tears began to pool on the tops of Badia's cheeks.

"She looked like a wild animal close to death. I thought she might be possessed by *djinni*. Maybe she spilled something hot one night and hurt one...or perhaps one was in love with her. They take revenge, you know, by possessing you."

"What did you do?" I asked.

"I tore my robe and wrapped it around her like a tight diaper to try to stop the bleeding. I carried her out of the forest, praying. I didn't have any useful medicine with me. I was afraid she was going to die before I found help. Many cars passed us on the highway before someone finally stopped and took us to a hospital. The doctor said she'd been raped and beaten. I stayed until they found her parents. They wouldn't let me see her again."

Badi'a said she never spoke to the Azzams and the police didn't even interview her. Leila kept coming to her in her dreams.

"Later, I learned she had been released to her family. I searched for her house with much difficulty, and when I found it, her father wouldn't let me see her. He warned me to never come back. But when Leila got older, she found me. Came to visit me sometimes –"

"When did you last see Leila?" I interrupted.

She and Moshe struggled to nail down an answer. "The Bedu don't track time like we do," he said. "It's probably been months."

That was disappointing to hear. "Leila was planning her escape," I said. "She was going to visit you before she left, Badi'a."

"As she grew, I came to know that it wasn't *djinni* who caused her trouble," she went on. "No, she had *pakar*."

"What's that?" I looked at Moshe. The wind whipped up and I felt some grains of sand barb the back of my neck.

"*Pakar* is when the patient is trapped because of some wrongdoing on her part due to fate." Badi'a used the same expression – *qada'an wa-qaddar* – Leila had taught me for "fate and destiny."

"Did she ever talk about the rape?"

"She didn't remember it," Badi'a said. "Only what others told her, that it was her cousin...other children watched...the *ayb*."

173

I took a deep breath. "Did she say the name 'Tamir?' "

"Yes."

"Do you have any idea what compelled a thirteen-year-old boy to rape a four-year-old girl?"

"Of course," she said, to my astonishment. "The Druze believe in past lives, you know. Leila remembered one that disgraced her family."

I looked at Moshe. "Clarify that."

"Leila remembered her most recent past life, as some Druze children of three or four do. Sometimes the family of the recollecting child will try to verify the past life if the child can give enough details and a location. Leila begged her parents to take her to Majdal Shams, a Druze village in the Golan. Evidently they did, but it was a very disappointing trip because the person she'd reincarnated from was...well, not very nice."

"And that's a trigger for *rape*?"

"She was a *bint hara*," Badi'a said. "She brought *ayb* on her family."

31

B etween interruptions from five generations of her family who came and went, Badi'a assured us she knew nothing more of the incidents in Majdal Shams or the forest.

"Moshe, why are you acting so gay?" I whispered when Badi'a was talking to a child.

"So I could be in here with you. There are no men around camp. I'm not threatening this way."

"Where are they?" I asked. Indeed, I hadn't seen one male older than ten or eleven since we'd arrived.

Moshe asked Badi'a.

"She says you should ask your question in Arabic. 'Speak out. You can't hurt the language. It's ancient.'"

I laughed. "*Feyn rig-gel-la?*" Where are the men?

She smiled, pleased at my effort.

"Several of them work as guards or drivers in a Jewish town near Be'er Sheva and are often gone overnight," Moshe explained. "The others have gone with some of the younger women in the family to the stubble fields for the summer. She didn't say this, but I can tell you Bedouin men are notorious for spending the night away with their girlfriends, too."

"Thanks, Moshe. Now, ask her about honor."

While they spoke, I chewed on a date. I could smell food cooking and two little girls were bringing in plates of creamy dips and colorful salads.

Badi'a passed a dish to Moshe. "Our tribal leaders say a woman is an olive tree," she said. "When a branch catches woodworm, it must be chopped off, so society stays clean and pure. There's a saying: *Aakhadh eth-thar tarad el-'ar* (Moshe repeated it to me in Arabic, I guess for emphasis on the rhyming). 'He resorted to retaliation and dispelled humiliation'." It rolled off the tongue just like a rap song.

Moshe handed me a bowl of herbs and green onions to cleanse the palate.

"She says after she found Leila in the forest, she began providing secret abortions to unmarried pregnant girls to prevent their being murdered for honor."

"My god," I said. "Wasn't that dangerous?"

She nodded. "I was a midwife before the government started requiring Bedu to have babies in the hospital in order to get benefits. All the women came to me for their woman problems. I used to do the purification operations on the girls, but I secretly stopped cutting out the clitoris. I just pretend to make an incision in the surrounding fold with a dull knife. The girls aren't even sure what happened. The men don't know at all what we do in the tent."

"I've heard honor killing comes from a Bedouin tradition of blood revenge," I said.

The deep fissures between Badi'a's bald brows quivered. "They're trying to pass it off on us?" She threw some salt on the pitas and passed me the plate.

"Well, do you know where it came from then?"

She shook her head, chewing, as if I was asking her where air came from.

Her great-granddaughter served us couscous with yogurt and bits of lamb, using her hand as a scoop. We helped ourselves to salty olives with peppers and lemon. Badi'a called out *"chai!"* for more tea.

After dinner, Badi'a asked Moshe to help her stand so she could get some fresh air, which was funny since we were already in an open-air tent. She pulled her headscarf farther down her forehead to shade her eyes from the setting sun and we followed her outside to a high spot. She seemed like desert royalty, pointing out the homes of her five hundred relatives nearby, until she mentioned the dwindling water supply, a big concern for the Bedu: "Sometimes we wash dishes with just sand, the old way."

A woman carrying a bowl climbed a homemade ladder leaning against the tent and placed the bowl on the roof.

"What's she doing?" I asked.

"When a person is sick, we put a bowl of milk on the roof in the moonlight," Badi'a explained. "In the morning, the sick person drinks it and then they are shaken to get the devil out."

I looked at Moshe. "They still practice pagan rites?"

"Doesn't everybody?" Moshe translated for her. "Do you touch wood?"

I smiled.

"Years ago, I would take young Bedu women who couldn't conceive to an ancient Isis temple in the Sinai," she said. "We scraped some clay off the walls and mixed it with water for them to drink to help their fertility."

"How do you know these customs?" I asked.

"My mother and grandmother taught me."

Moshe and I exchanged knowing glances. Binyamin might have been on to something about the Old Religion never dying.

Twilight declared herself as purple poured across the sky like the 'lavender hour' in Provence. Someone fired up a generator nearby and it began an incessant *put put put*. Badi'a headed back towards the tent as the dunes turned lilac. Several kerosene lamps had been lit around the tent. Badi'a invited us to stay the night and we accepted.

A young woman appeared with a pitcher and poured a bubbly golden liquid into ceramic cups.

"Bedouin beer," Moshe proclaimed. "I didn't think anyone made this since Islam."

I tasted it. Yeasty, sour, thick, room temperature. This beverage was still alive. Why not?

As the evening grew darker, Badi'a regaled us with more Bedu stories. In time, her daughters, granddaughters and great-grandchildren joined us in the tent, bringing in drums, an *oud*, a zither, and other strange instruments.

"They're going to play!" Moshe said, clapping his hands, a sparkle igniting in his eyes.

A teenage girl began with a small drum: *Taka taka dum taka dum taka dum. Taka taka dum taka dum taka dum.* Soon another joined her: *Dum dum taka taka dum taka dum. Dum dum taka taka dum taka dum.* Someone else slipped in a fast rolling drumbeat at the end of each pattern. The rhythm changed, and changed again.

A woman kneeled in the circle, removed her headscarf and began to play the *oud*. She started to sing in her language, letting her voice keen unabashedly. Another woman sang alternate verses of the song, and they went back and forth in a sort of intoned dialogue. It felt transparent, urgent, visceral. I understood why Arabic was called a language made for poetry.

Moshe leaned over and whispered in my ear. "They're singing about Asherah…that she arrived eons ago from Arabia…where mothers were heads of clans. The Phoenicians carried Asherah to far away lands in their sailboats…"

Two women stood in the middle of the circle, tying purple scarves with hundreds of coins sewn to them around their hips. They pulled their headscarves down to their shoulders and began to stomp their feet.

"*Ay-wa!*" the audience cried out in waves, ululating their approval with one finger over their upper lips: "*Lalalalalalalalala!*" Badi'a's chin moved to the beat, her cloudy eyes haunting in the lambent glow of the lanterns, the gaze of infinity.

The dancers lifted their hands into the air, rolling their fingers delicately as they circled their wrists. Their hips joined in the beat, seeming to move independently from the rest of their bodies, at times landing on the downbeat, at times on the up. They could count forward and backward with their hips, rolling them and lifting their feet off the ground in little turns. I glanced at Moshe, who was possibly on the verge of levitating.

The music, the voices, the energy were pure emotion. My senses seemed to be overlapping each other. The movements felt both foreign and familiar, something I'd never seen before but arose so logically from the body. They mirrored nature's expressions: earth tremors, ocean waves, snakes molting, eruptions, childbirth, ecstasy, death.

After a while, I closed my eyes. I heard the rhythm of my breathing inside my head, like when I scuba dive. My chest vibrated with the drumming, but it seemed to come from inside my body, as if I were breathing on different levels of consciousness. I lost track of my body's whereabouts, as in the *temezcal*, the ancient ritual steam baths of Oaxaca.

The drums rose into an apoplectic solo, like the collective heartbeat of an ancient city on fire. I opened my eyes and saw the dancers given over to a frenzy of full-body shimmies. I recalled Leila's painting of the Bedouin woman praying while she menstruated, despite the taboo. These women would do that.

A young woman with a substantial gold nose ring pulled me up by the hand. She tied an orange scarf with a few hundred coins sewn to it around my hips. I was surprised at how heavy it was. It felt grounding, like something to push off from. Everyone cheered in their Bedu way as I entered the circle. I followed the dancers' lead, moving my hips from side to side, in a simple pattern. I looked over at Moshe, who had what could only be described as a shit-eating grin on his face. I tried to circle my hips. The dancer showed me how to lift up my heels for another effect. The music told us how to move. We did snake arms. Then camel-like undulations. Finally the shimmy. It reminded me of hoola-hooping as a kid – I couldn't sustain the movement for more than several seconds, hard as I tried. Moshe was suddenly at my side, shouting over the music: "It's in the knees! Look!" He moved his knees back and forth, slowly at first for my benefit, then faster, which caused his hips to vibrate into a blur. The women ululated and clapped in their delight. Pretty soon, my hips were rolling fast and my bottom shimmying with the best of them. It felt oddly normal, and as if I was making the music with my body.

Moshe pulled my baseball cap off, letting my wild curly hair free. Self-conscious, I scanned the audience for offended reactions, but all I saw and felt was joy. The femaleness of my body was center-stage here and these women were *celebrating* it, in the purest possible way – something I'd never experienced in my own free country, or anywhere else. I let myself go. Shame slid off me with fresh sweat. For an extended moment in time, I knew without any doubt that I was whole and beautiful and safe. What I would have given for Leila to have shared this experience with me.

Watching Badi'a across the room, I thought of my mother. If only her vision of the divine included the feminine, maybe the long ache inside her would heal. Maybe she could be happy and whole once more. Maybe she would remember how to be a mother again.

I moved to the side and gestured to Moshe, who needed little encouragement to command the stage. Someone tossed him a coin belt and some finger cymbals and he went off. His energy was stratospheric. He improvised with the musicians. He worked the audience. He exploded like a volcano. Sweat streamed off him. He was sexy, funny, skillful, surprising, awe-inspiring. Though not even in drag, he embodied the divine feminine in his passionate tribute. I have no idea how long he danced, but he put on a show the likes of which I've never seen again. From the looks on their faces, the women have probably turned him into a secret legend.

It was then and there, empowered by these bold women and Leila's memory, that I decided to give Leila a real funeral on what would have been her eighteenth birthday.

When the party was over, Badi'a led us to a section of the tent that had been curtained off for privacy. Divan beds had been prepared for us on the ground several feet apart. We curled up under the blankets in our clothes, exhilarated and exhausted.

"Fereby, thank you," Moshe said, turning over on his side to face me. He reached his hand out to squeeze mine.

"No, Mosh. Thank *you*. You were amazing."

"Dancing is the only time that I really feel...connected."

I smiled. "I never knew you could be taught that dance – I assumed it was a birthright."

"Those women can only do that when the men are away thanks to the fundamentalists who consider belly dancers prostitutes. Belly dance is the oldest living relic of the Bronze Age goddess culture Prof. Binyamin was telling us about. And it's being lost throughout most of the Arab world. American women are probably doing more to preserve it than anyone."

I sat up on one elbow to face him. "No wonder Middle Eastern men think we're all sluts."

"That's ignorant. Belly dance wasn't born as a dance of seduction."

"No?"

"It was a sacred dance of fertility that women did for each other. And, after the baby was born, to celebrate and get their bodies back in shape. It's an ecstatic prayer to the Mother Goddess. When men discovered how powerful it is, they tried to pervert its meaning."

"Somewhat successfully," I said.

Someone turned off the generator. The silence of the desert seemed louder somehow. I heard a dog baying far away and then another return with a wail. A gentle breeze stirred the walls of the tent. We listened to the desert for a while.

"Speaking of feeling connected, you never mention your family, Mosh. Are they still in Morocco?"

He shook his head, smoothing his makeshift pillow. "Mostly Tel Aviv. I don't see them much." He rolled his eyes. "They don't *approve*."

"Oh," I said. "Is that...hard?"

"They kicked me out," he said, tucking his hair behind his ears. "It was my choice. I knew there were two paths, but their path would have been a short, uncomfortable ride to insanity...Many Arabs think you have a mental illness if you're gay. I mean, some Arabs have gay sex, but would never consider themselves gay. In Morocco, you go to prison for three years. My parents were not open-minded even though Israel – especially Tel Aviv – is far more tolerant. They expected me to get married; my brother beat me twice when I refused. They forced me to see a psychiatrist who tried to medicate me. My father just kind of wrote me off. I remember when I was sixteen, my mother saying, 'The one we call Moshe – Hebrew for Moses – turns out to be Pharaoh.' "

We exchanged melancholy half-smiles as voices erupted in the distance, though no words we could discern.

"Better get some sleep," I said, turning over on my back. "We're driving to Majdal Shams tomorrow to find Leila's past-life family."

Moshe pulled a hand out from under the covers and reached over to squeeze mine. "I guess there's always the next life to look forward to."

I was on the verge of sleep when I heard the curtain to our room rustle. I heard footsteps in the darkness approaching me. I opened my eyes in alarm as a figure knelt down next to me.

"*Ana Badi'a*," a raspy voice said.

I felt Badi'a's hands on my blankets. I held my breath as her fingers searched briskly for the top edges of the blankets and pulled them up. She folded them firmly under my chin and pressed them down around my shoulders. To my unqualified astonishment, I had been tucked in.

She did the same to Moshe and puttered on her way.

32

Moshe and I ate a quick breakfast of pita pulled out from under hot ashes and dunked in tea and goat's milk. I was eager to go straight to Majdal Shams, in north-eastern Israel on the border with Syria, where Leila's family from a previous life supposedly lived, and driving all the way up north would take several hours. I wanted to know exactly what went down when Leila went there with her family at age four and their lives were turned upside down with shame.

With a dozen boisterous children hanging off Moshe, I told Badi'a about the funeral I was planning for Leila while we walked out to the van. In the morning light, her ancient face looked hewn out of the desert rock. I thanked her for her hospitality and said how sorry I was we'd lost a friend.

"Women die in these deserts every day," she said. She looked out to the dunes, as if all of Israel were such a place. "No one cares."

"I do."

She blinked at me. "You will make newspaper story about Leila?"

"Perhaps."

"You look for the ending to your *own* story," she said. "Have you ever had a nightmare, but you knew you were only dreaming, so you could wake up before it got too scary?"

A lump rose in my throat. I nodded.

She clutched my arm. "Just before a soul awakens to true knowledge, she grows more and more conscious that she's dreaming and more self-assured because she recognizes she determines the end of the dream. You must wake up. Or else!"

As we drove away, I watched Badi'a disappear in the van's side mirror. Her advice had unsettled me. She shielded her face to survey the barren tract that was her homeland. I tried to imagine what she was thinking of...a fragment of an old story, a newly sprouted medicinal shrub, a footprint she recognized. Or maybe it was something defying categorization, something between memory and myth, something she didn't have to analyze the way I did. She seemed entirely content in her world.

We were soon back on the main highway to Be'er Sheva.

"The young Arab boys seem so close to their mothers and grandmothers," I said. "Why do they end up so hostile towards women later?"

"My gay friends have been trying to figure that out for years," Moshe said.

My phone found a signal, buzzed with new messages and rang all at once. It was Professor Binyamin to see what we'd learned about Leila. I put him on speaker-phone, gave him a quick update and told him what we were talking about.

"Arab adolescent boys develop contempt for women because they have no rite of passage into manhood," Binyamin said.

"American boys don't, either," I said. "Unless you're in a gang."

"Yes, but Arabs breastfeed forever and are almost always with their mothers in the house until they start school," Moshe said. He made a gesture of slicing something with his hand. "Then, one day, it's over."

"They are forced to separate from their mothers?" Binyamin asked.

"Oh, yes," said Moshe. "They wouldn't do it on their own."

"They are never taught to become men – just thrown in and forced to swim," Binyamin said.

"Right," said Moshe.

"So, they must perpetually try to prove themselves as men, which creates a lifetime of insecurity."

I imagined their rage.

"This is why the nervous breakdowns, drug abuse and addiction, crime, oppression of and violence against women..." Binyamin said.

Moshe gaped at me. I thought of Fadi's drinking and crazy behavior. Tamir was thirteen, right on that critical threshold of manhood, when he raped Leila and left her for dead.

"Oh. My. God," Moshe said. "I'm going to fire my shrink."

~ ~ ~

We made a pit-stop in Jerusalem and I called Fadi once we got through the last checkpoint.

"I didn't know if you were still in Israel," he said. "Where've you been?"

"The desert," I said. "Is Qasim still in custody?"

"Yes."

I wasn't surprised. "Have the *shaikhs* made their statement yet?"

"No."

"I heard the shame on your family all started with a memory, Fadi."

"Who told you that?"

"What was so awful about it?"

"I don't even remember. It was a long time ago," he said, agitation rising in his voice.

"Did you go up to Majdal Shams with your family?" I asked.

"How do you know about this?"

"People know, Fadi. What happened?"

"Fereby, this is not your business! Are you going to write about this too?"

"You know how and why Leila was murdered and you have the power to do something good in her memory. *What happened* in Majdal Shams?"

Moshe shot me a look.

"She recalled a past life that turned out to be very disappointing," I pressed.

Fadi let out an urgent sigh. "*Al-nutq* is usually a wonderful experience for a family, but it was a catastrophe for mine. I don't see how this interests you —"

"What's *al-nutq*?"

"The remembering...the whole thing was a terrible waste. Everything was good until the day we met the Abdos."

"That's who you saw in Majdal Shams?"

"They're Leila's...children – the children of the woman she last was."

I jotted down the name in my notebook, shaking my head in disbelief that I was taking reincarnation this seriously. It didn't matter if I believed in it or not, though, if they did and those beliefs triggered a chain of crimes.

"Fereby, don't go and stir up something there. It was so long ago."

"Tell me what happened and I won't have to," I said.

"Is the Israeli government paying you to do this to us?"

I laughed. "If anything, they're making it harder for me."

"People are saying you're either a spy, a private investigator for Leila's boyfriend, or crazy."

I laughed again. "What will they say after I give Leila a proper funeral on her birthday? You're invited, by the way."

Moshe shot me a severe look.

"You have a death wish," Fadi said and hung up.

33

I just don't get the espionage paranoia," I said to Moshe.

"Well, Israel's security forces are legendary for impersonating journalists to get information on the resistance. The Druze might suspect you're trying to get some dirt on them the Israelis can use politically. He who is bitten by a snake is afraid of an end of rope."

We grew quiet in the thrum of the highway to Majdal Shams and I closed my eyes, trying not to think about the dread that grew inside me with each interaction I had with the Azzams and others in Atabi. Instead, I made myself focus on our next mission.

The Druze believed all human souls were created at once and the number was fixed, although none of the sources I'd consulted knew what that number was. Every Druze I'd interviewed agreed that only in a long string of successive lives would a soul have sufficient opportunity to become responsible for his or her behavior. "It's not fair or even logical for someone to be judged on only one life where they might be unhealthy or poor or ugly or stupid," a *shaikh* in Kfar Mugar had told me. With their choices, people could enhance or impair their next lives.

According to the Druze, thousands of reincarnations occur to the soul until Judgment Day, when the Tawhid founder Al-Hakim will return and confront each with the memory of all its previous lives and choices and their consequences. No one would tell me what happened after that.

"So, if the Druze are right, all souls were created at the same time, and that means we're all old souls," I said.

Moshe smiled.

"So how can they justify honor killing?"

"They have little regard for the body compared to the soul," he said.

I looked out the window to consider this. Shaikh Hayyan had said the Druze saint Pythagorus taught all souls were pure but the body could be wicked. "Yeah, but if the body isn't that important, why go so far trying to control it? And, besides, any person you might murder could have been or still could become your own mother."

We'd decided to cross the country from Hadera so we could stop at Nebi Shu'aib, one of the holiest sites for the Druze, located at the foot of an extinct volcano overlooking the Sea of Galilee. Shu'aib, or Jethro, the father-in-law of Moses, best known for fighting the pagans, was deeply revered by the Druze. The enormous shrine comprised several white stone buildings, plain except for a mosque-like dome and some Islamic archways. In the prayer hall, Moshe picked up a brochure and we made our way to the tomb, walking across hundreds of overlapping Persian carpets.

Moshe stopped at a large niche in the stone wall.

"The *Mihrab*," he said. "See the imprint there?" He pointed to the floor, and an indentation in the stone — the outline of a foot across the body of a snake. "It marks the spot where Jethro killed a snake by stomping on it. The Druze often kiss it or pour oil into it and then rub the oil over their bodies for good luck."

I traced the furrow with a fingertip. Another dead snake, symbol of the Goddess.

Our thirty-eight-mile journey through the Golan Heights featured desolate plateaus scattered with volcanic rock, former Syrian army bunkers pock-marked from the war, fields of herons and disabled tanks. We passed a jogging peacekeeper just outside Majdal Shams, "UN" emblazoned on his T-shirt.

The village, Syrian until 1967 when Israel annexed the Golan Heights to prevent Syria from having a high vantage point, spread out in the foothills of snow-capped Mount Hermon, the source of the Jordan River. Orchards of apples and cherries covered the hills. It reminded me of Atabi without the frills – prepared for violence on short notice, as occupied zones often are.

We stopped to ask a pedestrian for directions to the Abdos' house. They lived in a modest neighborhood of Majdal Shams; as we got closer, the older homes began to crumble and newer ones were arrested in partial completion.

"What I don't understand is why only some Druze children remember a past life," I said.

"This Druze guy I met in the army said children who remember usually died violently," Moshe said.

"*You* were in the army?" I said incredulously. I knew it was compulsory service, but still.

"It didn't work out real well." Moshe rolled his eyes. "But, anyway, dying violently makes them a little bit psychic, you know?"

I recalled Leila's clairvoyant removal of me from the bus and her eerie calm afterwards. She was able to save me, but not herself.

"I never hear of American kids recalling past lives," I said.

"That's because their parents ignore their child's first words as nonsense," Moshe said. "Druze remember because they're encouraged to."

He pulled into the driveway of a small, dilapidated house. "Let's go find us some reincarnation."

A cheerless middle-aged woman, head wrapped in the tight headscarf of the religious, opened the door. Moshe introduced the two of us to Umniyah Abdo in Arabic and told her we were looking for the family of the person Leila Azzam had been reincarnated from. The startling request invigorated her fragile face. She raised a hand to her mouth. Her eyes, full of trepidation, leapt to mine.

"*Omm?*" Mother? She asked.

"*La, la,*" Moshe said, shaking his head – I was not her mother.

He explained that I wanted to speak to her about the meeting of the families that had occurred over a decade ago.

She shook her head and hugged her shawl to herself.

Moshe entreated her further in his gentle way, telling her I was Leila's friend. She looked me over but then thought better of it, backing up through the threshold. She started to close the door and I feared we'd lose our chance.

"Moshe, tell her Leila's dead!"

He quickly translated my request as the door shut. We exchanged discouraged looks. Then, it opened again and Umniyah's somber face reappeared.

"My mother's soul has moved on?" Moshe translated for her.

I nodded. To my utter shock, a smile arose across her face. She clapped her hands and held them to her forehead as she seemed to say a prayer of thanks out loud.

"She's happy because your friend is now a baby with a fresh life," Moshe said.

Umniyah invited us inside and showed us to her living room, apologizing for its modesty. She explained that she had been a widow since she was twenty-three and she had only a daughter before her husband died. She said her daughter was unmarried and still lived with her; she summoned the girl from another room to make the coffee. And then she began telling us her story.

"It was about fourteen years ago. I was cooking supper for my daughter's birthday when a knock came to the door. A large assembly of people was gathered on our doorstep – a dozen at least. I was in my dirty apron. I recognized no one. I suddenly felt anxious. A woman then pushed a tiny girl forward. The men shushed one another. The little girl had the shiny black hair of a pureblood Arab, but her eyes were this startling green and just huge and fixed right on me. Then, she said in almost a whisper to me: "Umniyah. My Umniyah. *Habibi!*" I knew it was my mother and I fell to my knees, crying. My little daughter came rushing to my side, afraid there was terrible news. We hugged Leila and it was the most joyful moment of my life!

"The people who had come with Leila cheered and gathered around to hear what she said. She told me I had gotten some grey hair since she passed away. Everyone laughed and began introducing themselves and I invited them inside.

"I learned Leila had led them to my house. She recognized my daughter and told her 'Happy Birthday!' She pointed out many things in the house she remembered. She showed me where she had hidden some money behind a stone in the wall of our kitchen. All the women were crying. Leila told me she had even named her doll after me two years before."

"Leila's parents were there?" I asked.

"Yes. Dima was aloof at first, probably nervous about Leila becoming too attached to our family – most mothers who go through this are. But she was very proud, too. When a child recalls a past life, it proves the mother is spiritually pure. Dima told me that before Leila was two, she would say things like, 'Please call me Hessa. Hessa is my given name. I have four children. One of them is very ill. Pray for Walid. I want to see Walid!'

"She said sometimes Leila would be despondent over her 'husband' leaving her without any security after his death. She was very afraid of any kind of gun, even toy guns. She had violent dreams. Sometimes, when she woke up, she would rush to the mirror and check her head for an injury.

"When she was three, the family had a small barn added to their orchard and Leila took to one of the builders. She told her mother in private that he looked just like her husband, Suhail. She would sometimes threaten, 'If you don't take me to see my family, I will walk there myself!' This was when they decided to try to find us.

I smiled, imagining little Leila asserting her natural will before her culture had the opportunity to try to obliterate it.

"So after we'd visited for an hour or two, and I was still crying from joy, there was another knock at my door. Several villagers stood in my front yard. They began to tell the Azzams about my mother who had reincarnated as Leila. And then our joy evaporated."

"Why?" I asked.

She shook her head and looked down at her hands twisting on her skirt. "My mother was a good woman who had a difficult life," she said, wiping tears from her eyes. "She was the first-born child of an orphan father from the Djebel Druze in Syria. His parents were executed in the Druze uprising against the French in 1927 when he was only two. He was raised by some cousins who received shelter in British-occupied Transjordan after the failure of the uprising. He married a village girl and moved here for work. Hessa was born in 1945, the first of three children."

"Hessa was Leila's —your mother's — name?"

"Yes. She married a local young man, Suhail, and quickly became pregnant with me. This was 1967. A few months later, war broke out with Israel and my grandfather fought and died in the Six-Day War. Hessa and Suhail, as well as her mother and other relatives in Majdal Shams forcibly became Israeli residents. I was born an Israeli Druze, as were my brothers and sisters.

"In 1976, my father, who was a defiant Syrian nationalist, sneaked across the border to fight for Syria when Syria joined the Lebanese Civil War. They said he was killed by friendly fire for retreating from combat, although I don't believe it since he risked his life just to have the chance to fight in the war. The rest of us – we were still little – and Mother were, of course, shamed by the village for this dishonor. We struggled for nearly ten years just to survive the *ayb*."

Umniyah's pretty daughter carried a tray of coffees into the living room, placing them in front of us.

"Then my younger brother Walid developed a rare form of cancer on his spine. He was sixteen and the one who could bring in the most income for our poor family. Mother was desperate and took him to Hadassah University Hospital in Jerusalem for treatment, leaving us behind with relatives. Her trip was considered unchaste by most in our village. Rumors spread she was prostituting. All lies!"

"She was trying to save her son's life," I said.

She sighed, dabbing her eyes. "My younger sisters stopped going to school, it got so bad. I didn't want to leave the house. So, she and Walid had been there for about six months when, one evening, she was on her way back from the hospital to the room she rented in the ghetto and stopped into the grocery. There was a robbery and she was shot and killed."

Moshe's voice broke as he translated this.

"I'm so sorry," I said. I picked up Umniyah's trembling hand.

"And what about your brother?" I asked.

Moshe's voice was hoarse getting this piece out: "Walid...died in the hospital...three weeks later."

He grabbed a tissue and blew his nose.

"How did you manage?" I asked.

"Quietly. As expected," she said.

"What happened to you and your siblings?"

She looked out the window to her front yard, but seemed to be searching for a memory.

"The cousins we were staying with married me to a man that nobody wanted – a disabled laborer, the only one that would take me given my family's double shame. But Rashid was a rare, gentle man who was so happy to marry me. A year passed and we had our beautiful Nora." She reached out and stroked the cheek of her shy daughter, who had knelt by her side and put her head on her mother's lap. "The next year, there was a complication from the medications Rashid had to take for his condition and he passed away."

Moshe covered his eyes and bent his head. Nora went to the kitchen to get water as we stared into our tissues.

"Did the neighbors tell the Azzams that Hessa was a…"

"Yes," Umniyah said. "And about my father. The villagers punished my family for years, but that wasn't enough. They heard there was *al-nutq* going on here and they had to come to my door to punish more."

"What did the Azzams do?"

"Dima turned white as a *foutta*. Her husband, Kamil, yelled at his two other kids to come, picked up Leila and carried her out the door, screaming and crying and reaching for me."

I imagined Fadi and his little sisters as small children watching this traumatic scene unfold.

"Was that it? Did you ever see Leila again?"

She shook her head. "About two years ago, she wrote to me. She didn't remember her past life anymore, or even the visit, but had heard about it from her family."

I wondered if Umniyah knew about the rape and other aftermath. "What'd she say?"

"She wanted to apologize for coming back into my life and leaving so abruptly. She said she'd felt guilty all her life about how painful that must've been for me."

I shook my head. *Leila.* Concerned about someone else's pain, which surely couldn't compare to her own.

"Did you worry about her?"

"Every day. But I relied on my faith," Umniyah said, clutching her hands in her lap. "If her death came before mine, it was meant to be. The destiny of every human being is written in advance on his forehead. Praise God."

34

That night, Moshe and I camped in his van at the foot of Mount Hermon where the Bible says the fallen angels came to Earth. I was depressed. I'd painstakingly put the pieces together of Leila's history – why she'd been the source of shame for her family for over a decade – but I still didn't have a clue who had killed her or even, really, why. What was I missing? "To get to the root of a matter, go to where it starts," Moshe kept saying. Yes, of course, the origin. If I didn't even understand the nature of the crime, how the hell did I think I could solve it? But who would know?

The next day, we drove back to Haifa and dropped in on Professor Binyamin.

"A daughter's virginity was a *big* asset," said Binyamin. We were seated around his dining room table, which was stacked high with books, periodicals and files, eating bowls of beef barley stew we couldn't set down anywhere. "Sacrifice of the Goddess Queen," Leila's snake painting, leaned against the fireplace – he'd picked it up from Mujun. "Way back when clans had to compete for natural resources, they safeguarded every asset they had. They could gain valuable men through marriage who would help them survive," he said, chewing. "By biblical times, there were dowries. If a girl lost her virginity or had been raped, she'd be killed because she could not be married off and was thus worthless."

Moshe rolled his eyes.

"But why was virginity *in and of itself* worth so much?" I pressed, dipping a chunk of bread into my stew.

"Men aren't gonna raise a kid that's not theirs!" Moshe laughed.

Binyamin wiped his chin on his napkin and swept his tongue over his teeth. "Yes, because they wanted to be sure a woman's offspring would be loyal to their family. So only approved mates got access to women. When resources became scarce, clans were extremely insecure about their property, including women. A man in control of his property was a man of honor. A man who was not was a dead man."

"What, Fereby?" Moshe said.

I looked up at him.

"You've got a weird look on your face."

"I just realized honor killing's not a strictly Muslim...or Arab...or Druze...or poor...or uneducated...or Middle Eastern phenomenon."

They looked puzzled.

"In all cultures where honor killings occur, women are considered *property* of men," I said. "That is the common denominator. So, then, does that mean honor killings began when women *became* property of men?"

Binyamin set his bowl in his lap and put his fingertips together, tapping them against his lips. "This is a very interesting question, Miss Jones."

"Well, when exactly did we become male property?" I asked. Had it really been that way throughout human history as most people assumed?

He scratched his chin and turned to examine his bookshelf. "Certainly before literacy was widespread. I believe Hammurabi's codex, from 1750 BCE in Babylonia, is the first known law making women and children property of husbands and fathers. More than likely, the custom was around far longer, but nowhere near as long as the era before when women were free."

"When did it became fashionable to kill girls for losing their virginity before marriage?" I asked.

Binyamin thought for a moment before setting his bowl on a stack of files and reaching down to the end of the table for a thick book with a worn black leather binding. The Bible. He leaned over and opened the Hebrew book, right to left, as the silver fluff of hair on top of his head floated forward as if it were curious, too.

"Hmm. In Leviticus, if a virgin is raped, her life is spared if she marries her rapist," he said, then flipped some pages. "Deuteronomy says a bride found not to be a virgin should be stoned to death publicly." He looked up over his reading glasses. "To my knowledge, this rule was never mentioned before this."

I considered this. "So...are you saying honor killing, which most everyone presumes is Muslim in origin, turns out to be, of all things, *Jewish*?"

Moshe peered up from his stew bowl.

"The sexism and misogyny in the Bible just reflected the times," Binyamin said. "The world was changing from a place that valued the feminine to one driven by conquest. The Hebrews probably weren't the original honor killers, just the first to put the legalization of it in writing."

Moshe got up to study "Sacrifice of the Goddess Queen." He got very close to the canvas then backed away five feet, checking it out from all angles. "I always thought honor killing was some form of human sacrifice. Like the murdered girl is the scapegoat."

"Possibly," said the Professor.

"I don't see how Leila was a scapegoat," I said.

"Well, scapegoats allow competing groups to have a separate focus for their aggression so they don't fight until they destroy each other," Binyamin said.

A light went on in my brain. "That's why they stopped killing men along with the women for honor – because it caused never-ending blood feuds – *mutual destruction.*" That's what Sitt Afifah had meant.

Binyamin pretended to clap for me.

"So why not have just one honor killing and be done with it?" I said.

"The culture is reenacting a deep-seated myth every time it carries out a ritual killing," said Binyamin. "It gets a fix."

"But how can they keep doing it knowing it's just wrong?" Moshe said.

"It's subconscious," he said. "William Doty says when cultures don't understand their own myths, they're in danger of taking them literally and acting them out violently."

"How can they *not* be aware?" I said.

"The myth's origins were usually forgotten generations ago."

A tingle crawled up my spine. "You mean because, say, history has been suppressed for some reason?" I said.

"Could be," Binyamin said.

The destruction of the Goddess, I thought…*they don't know!*

"One anthropologist thinks the scapegoat sacrifice is a ritual reenactment of a founding murder in the culture – one so traumatic to its people that it was disguised in the resulting mythology."

I looked at Leila's entwined snakes, one giving the other a fatal bite to the head, and it hit me like a bolt of lightning. "Oh my God, Professor Binyamin. Every time they butcher a woman for honor, they're killing the Goddess!"

After leaving Moshe in Tel Aviv to take care of some personal business, I went back to Atabi. I saw Ru'yah on the street carrying some groceries from the market. When she saw me, she looked away and crossed the street. I pulled over and ran after her.

"Ru'yah – "

"Stay away from me! I can't talk to you anymore." She picked up her pace.

"Why not?"

"There's gossip that I could be the *next* one to die!"

"What?" I followed her as fast as I could.

"I've become too friendly with you, they say!" she said. "There's a list going around now of women who should be killed for improper behavior and I'm on it!"

She stepped back into the street, her shopping bags banging against her legs as she hurried to the other side.

A list? I stood there in mute shock watching Ru'yah disappear down the street, horror sweeping over me. Not only were the Druze ritually re-enacting their violent founding myth, they were trailblazing a more sophisticated system to ensure they'd get their spiritual fix repeatedly. And Ru'yah was blaming *me* for her shameful status. I had to find a copy of the list before another woman was murdered so I could warn them. As if I weren't over my head enough. I rubbed the bridge of my nose where a headache was forming and tried to think what to do. Who would help me with this – especially now that I was *persona non grata*?

And then it dawned on me – I knew just the person who might tell me how to track down the list.

Tamir's great-grandmother, Afifah, was napping in a chair on her front porch, her enormous body shaking with each exhalation.

"Sitt Afifah?" I said, trying not to startle her as I approached.

She awoke mid-snore and opened her watery eyes.

I smiled. *"Bonjour, Sitt Afifah. Vous vous me souvenez?"* Remember me?

"Oui, Madame Fereby. Venez vous ici." Come here.

Blinking away the sleep, she reached for my hand. I took the seat next to her and she held my hand in hers like Leila had done.

"There's cantaloupe ripe today," she said, waving a hand toward her family's field behind the house. "I will ask my granddaughter to cut us some when she comes out."

"How lucky you are to live in this climate, and on such fertile land," I said. It reminded me of my own good fortune in southern California.

"The land is everything to us," she said. "Our lives, our nourishment...when we die, we are buried in it, like a baby in a womb, to be born again."

I smiled, feeling oddly nostalgic for this moment. There were still traces of the sacred feminine in her subconscious; she might have been a priestess a thousand lives ago. I shifted and crossed my legs. I needed to ease my way into this.

"I've learned more about honor since our last visit," I said.

"Good!" she said, nodding.

"I'm curious about something, Sitt Afifah. Why is the Qur'an a holy book to the Druze and it forbids honor killing, but the Druze still permit it?"

"Islam permits polygamy, too, but we don't do that," she said. "Our religion is our own. Honor was here long before Islam. They're like air and water. You need both, but you'd die first without air."

"It must be hard living in this very Westernized country with your honor code," I said.

"Oh, yes...In the old days, we never had to worry about the police or courts getting involved."

"Are the police meddling in Leila's death?"

Her eyes widened with aggravation. "They questioned Tamir yesterday! And Kamil Azzam's brood."

I tried not to show my surprise and elation. "How'd that go?"

She snorted and gave a dismissive wave. "The police have nothing. The fight between the families, this is the big concern."

"Tamir's lawsuit?"

"Now the Azzams are trying to collect money from Tamir! He was supposed to pay Kamil in the event of Leila's death, but Tamir is trying to get out of it since they are to blame for that. Tamir's trying to get his piece of the Azzam orchard since that was part of the deal, too. The Azzams are saying Tamir never paid for anything he promised to in the marriage contract and owes them now. Tamir's lawyer warned him it wouldn't be clear the day he found out about Leila's boyfriend."

"Tamir hired a lawyer that long ago?"

"Smart boy!" She tapped her temple.

"Sure is," I said. "Sitt Afifah? I heard there's a list of the *bint hara* in Atabi. Have you seen it?"

"No, but I know a few girls who should be on it," she said indignantly.

"Who keeps it?"

"I think Tamir said the *shaikhs* have it in the *khalwe*." And, in a rare moment of lucidity, she glared at me and said, "Why do *you* want to know?"

I hoped I wasn't too abrupt leaving her after those bombshells. I didn't know what to do first: confront the Azzams, raid the *khalwe*, chastise Tamir or call Moshe. I remembered that women were forbidden – under threat of execution – in the men's side of the *khalwe*, where I assumed the *shaikhs* kept the list, so going there would have to wait until I could figure out a plan.

If Tamir had consulted a lawyer the day he learned about Duncan, he was definitely playing hard ball. My gut told me he went directly to the Azzams after that meeting – the evening he burst in with me sitting at the dining table with the family. After I left, I bet he incited the Azzams to murder.

I had to turn around three times, but I eventually found Tamir's family's woodworking shop off the highway to Isfiyeh. I parked on the shoulder and walked up past some storage shacks to the main building. The Shahins had at least a half acre of land for this business, much of it filled with stacks of various cuts of wood, from clean lumber to raw branches and trunks of felled trees. Inside was a gallery of unfinished furniture they'd built. I nodded at the Druze girl behind the counter as I wandered through the gallery, pretending to browse. I followed the sounds of men's voices and electric saws out the back door.

Tamir and two other men were trying to load a mature tree, roots and all, onto a forklift. Tamir was hacking at the roots with a knife. As I approached, they each stopped what they were doing when they saw me. Tamir wiped the knife off on his jeans and sauntered toward me as if he was picking me up for a date.

"So, it's finally my turn," he said, tucking the knife into his back pocket, a smirk at the corners of his mouth.

"Your turn?"

"You've been busy pursuing a lot of men since you've been here."

I narrowed my eyes on him and took an invisible deep breath.

"Have you told your husband what you've been doing?"

I was in no mood for his crap. "Do you really think I had to come all the way to Israel to get laid?"

That was exactly the rise he wanted from me. "Why not?" he said, smiling and raising his eyebrows as if I were engaging him in foreplay. "The European girls come to the Sinai beaches for an exotic fuck."

"How'd you find out about Leila's boyfriend?"

He cocked his head, calculating me. His eyes moved down my body slowly, fantasizing. I folded my arms across my breasts. I was burning to ask him about his seeking pre-murder legal advice, but feared Afifah would pay somehow.

"Who told you?" I pressed.

He yanked a box of cigarettes out of his shirt pocket. "Why would I tell you?"

"You turned her in," I said. "You told her family. And you *knew* she'd be killed."

"She was a whore," he said through the cigarette he was lighting.

"No, she was a *child*…You destroyed her, from start to finish."

He exhaled the smoke through his nose and spat on the ground. "I wanted to, but I didn't kill her."

"You gave her a death sentence when you raped her."

He sneered. "She seduced me."

I had to steady myself on my feet for the rage building inside me. "She was *four*, Tamir."

"She deserved no respect. It was easy."

And that's when it hit me: The twelve-year-old girl I was in India was no more seducible than four-year-old Leila; I did *to myself* exactly what they do here – blame the victim.

I forced myself to stay present. "Why – because of some supposed memory of a past life?"

"Her soul was corrupt," he said. "I shouldn't have been in prison for a minute."

"The Druze saint Pythagorus said everyone's soul is pure."

"I bet yours isn't," he said, licking his lips in a smirk.

I looked away, exasperated.

He laughed at me through an exhalation of smoke. "The *bint haras* always stick up for each other…Why don't you go harass the Pakis instead? In Punjab, they kill anyone they feel like for money, call it an honor killing and get away with it."

I looked back at him. "Tamir, have you ever had a girlfriend? I mean, one who was with you voluntarily?"

"Of course."

"A Druze?"

"Sometimes. I was in the army, so I've had plenty of Jewish girls. I've dated Christians, too." He winked at me when he said "Christians," assuming I was one, I suppose.

"How were you able to date a Druze girl? Dating's not allowed."

"Druze boys and girls meet in secret in nearby Jewish towns."

Tamir's co-workers called to him, pointing to the uprooted tree.

"What if your sister did that?" I asked. "Met a Jew in secret for an affair."

He blew the smoke out fast and put the cigarette out on the ground with his boot. "Well. First I'd get my brothers and then all our cousins, and probably my father. Then we'd each get in our cars and drive in a line to find her and pick her up. We'd drive her out to the edge of town, perhaps the parking lot at Sulaimon's. Then we'd take turns running over her."

I shook my head, incredulous this guy wasn't locked up permanently.

"What you don't understand, Mrs. Jones," he said, "is the real 'honor crime' is not the killing of the girl, it's her immoral behavior that forces her men to have to kill her... and putting the men who *have* to kill her in jail!"

I turned to walk back to the van. He wasn't going to tell me how he learned about Duncan.

"You know what I like best about American women?" he called out.

I walked faster, feeling his eyes all over my body.

"Even when they're fully dressed, they still seem naked!"

I muttered an expletive under my breath and walked around the main store this time instead of through it. As I was passing the last storage shed, Tamir came around the corner of the building ahead of me and surprised me, catching me in his arms. He grabbed my wrists and shoved me up against the shed, a grotesque smile across his face.

"Let me go!" I yelled. I dropped my car keys on the ground as I struggled to pull away from him. Amused, he pinned my shoulders with his elbows. I could smell his sour tobacco breath, his face close enough to kiss me. I couldn't move under his weight. I screamed, but he clamped a hand over my mouth. "Keep your mouth shut, whore. I have a knife."

I stopped struggling.

He uncovered my hyperventilating mouth. "Look how you American girls paint up your faces to boast of your shamelessness to the world. You're *nothing* but a piece of rotten trash," he said, his eyes glowing with exhilaration.

I bit my tongue and looked him straight in the eye. *Stay calm.*

He looked hungrily down at my breasts. His elbows were hurting me. "I could take you right now...and invite all my friends to join me. Then write about it for *The New York Times*. Get a picture, too."

I stared him down as if he was little more than a nuisance, though I was scared to death. His expression suddenly switched to loathing.

"I could kill you in about two seconds." He looked as if he was imagining it as he said it.

I remembered the cricket. My heart pounded so hard, blood seemed to be battering my eardrums with every pulse. What did he want from me? Was this the nightmare Badi'a had warned me to wake up from? I couldn't let him see how scared I was. I railed at myself internally for never taking a self-defense course – I was never in one place long enough to take any kind of regular class. Fadi was right: I didn't live *in* the world, I just traveled through it, reported it. My body began to shake in spasms I couldn't control. Tamir laughed at me. Some of his saliva landed on my lower lip.

"Let go of me," I mustered through clenched teeth.

He leaned forward and licked my upper lip.

"Ugh! God!" I turned my face away and, without thinking, kneed him as hard as I could in the groin.

He instantly let go of my wrists and doubled over on the ground, moaning.

Stunned, I seized my keys out of the dirt and ran like hell.

35

I should go home to California tonight and never look back, I thought as I peeled out to the highway. This is insane. Qasim is in custody and they created the list of women that should be murdered because of *my* intrusion! I can't bring Leila back and I can't change these people. Dad was right. I glanced down with disgust at my clothes Tamir had just had his hands on and shivered with revulsion. I rubbed my mouth hard with a napkin off the floorboard; I snatched a paper cup from behind my seat and spat in it over and over to get his taste out of my mouth. Learning about the origins of their treatment of women had done nothing to make me more compassionate. I only felt loathing for Tamir now.

Before I reached the Atabi turn-off to go to the police station, as I was leaving Moshe a voicemail, a police car put on its lights and sirens behind me.

I pulled over and rolled down the window. It was Metanis, stiff and humorless, ready for a fight. He came to the driver's side of the van.

"Tamir Shahin just assaulted me," I said.

Metanis missed no more than a beat and nodded in his usual impassive way.

"I want to make a police report."

"You must go to station."

I groaned in disbelief.

"This vehicle belong to you, Miss Jones?" As if he didn't know already.

"No, Sir. It's Moshe Mansano's."

"Where is he?"

"Tel Aviv," I said impatiently. I couldn't believe how unaffected he was that I'd been attacked.

"The registration expire," he said, writing on his clipboard. "He not pay seven parking fines. Van must impound until he pay fine."

"*What?*"

He looked up at me, solemn as an executioner.

"Tamir held me down and threatened to gang-rape and kill me! He had a knife."

"You pay fine in court in Haifa, Mr. Mansano get van back."

I felt like screaming and crying at the same time, but I was too drained by my futile efforts. I pulled my backpack out of the back and tried to cram as much stuff as I could of Moshe's – costuming, CDs, DVDs, cosmetics, the Candle God – into it and three paper grocery bags that I found under the seat.

Metanis gave me a ride to the police station; we rode together in strained silence most of the way.

"Have you questioned anyone for Leila's case?" I said, curious to see if he'd own up to interviewing Tamir and the Azzams.

"Not me," he said. "I not working it now."

"It's closed?"

"No."

"Well, then, who's on it now?"

"You must ask at the station."

Of course. I rolled my eyes and looked out the window.

At the station, Metanis took me in the back and wrote up a perfunctory report of the attack.

"So, you're going to pick up Tamir for questioning now?" I asked.

"We talk to him," he said, looking up at me blankly.

I narrowed my eyes at him. "You don't believe me."

He finished writing something in his notebook and snapped it shut. "Miss Jones, you are big problem here from start. Many people mad. Druze business not your business."

I stood up, the rage returning with magnified ferocity. "So, I had it *coming* – is that what you mean?"

Two other cops turned toward us.

"I just – " Metanis started.

"It's *my* fault Tamir assaulted me?!" I almost pounded my fist on his desk.

The cops approached slowly, but Metanis waved them away as if it was nothing.

"*You* should be the one who is ashamed!" I yelled.

I hastily picked up my awkward assortment of items and bags and ungracefully fled the police station, every pair of eyes on me.

On the main road, I called Moshe, but still got no answer. What the hell was he doing? I was homeless, car-less and almost friendless. Suddenly, someone in a passing vehicle yelled "*Fitna!*" at me out the window. The car pulled onto the shoulder up ahead, its tires grinding gravel into powdery smoke. It was Fadi and, with butterflies in my stomach, I hurried to catch up to him.

He rolled down his window as I approached.

"What'd you yell at me?"

"*Fitna.* Beautiful woman," he said.

"Oh."

"It also means social chaos," he said.

I laughed. "The same word means *both*?"

"People used to say that to Leila, too."

I cleared my throat. "Look, Metanis towed my car. Is there any way you could come give me a ride, please?"

"Where are you staying?"

"I don't know," I said. Now that he was here, thoughts of flying home tonight evaporated.

He motioned for me to get in. I put all my stuff in his back seat and climbed in next to him.

He pulled out onto the highway, heading towards Atabi. "Is there any place you haven't made yourself unwelcome yet?"

I laughed, but he didn't smile. "Let's try the cabins in the park."

"Metanis got you back," he said.

I looked at him. "For what?"

"For getting him transferred. As of Monday, he'll be working out of Shfaram."

At the cabin, I told Fadi about Tamir's assault and Metanis' hostility and indifference. He seemed unsettled by the behavior, but said it fit them both – and was a normal reaction for his culture considering what I'd done. I couldn't get up the courage to tell him about the list.

"You're lucky, you know," he said.

I hadn't thought about it that way. I wondered if Tamir saw it as a victory or a defeat for himself. Would he come after me for racking him in the balls? I shivered at the thought.

Fadi was quiet for some time. It wasn't really cold enough for it, but he began building a campfire outside. I sat on a large rock and watched the sun shoot orange across the Mediterranean as it set.

"When are you going home?" he asked.

"I don't know," I said, meeting his gaze.

He looked at me like I was nuts. "Haven't you had enough?"

I glanced away for a moment to figure out how to answer him. "I have to do for Leila what I wasn't able to do for myself," I said.

Fadi seemed to consider that, silently arranging the logs just so, taking his time lighting the fire and poking at it with a long stick with far more determination than was called for. He didn't ask me to explain what I'd said. I felt awkward sitting there, waiting for him to ask.

"How is Ru'yah's baby?" I said.

"Still in neonatal intensive care," he said, tossing the stick in the flames. He stood with his hands on his hips surveying his work. "Qasim asked about you."

"You talked to him? How is he?"

"Okay. He wanted to know if you were still in Israel." Fadi sniffed, backing away from the fire, wiping his hands on his jeans.

"I want to visit him, but they won't let me," I said.

"You've done enough visiting, yes?" He glared at me. "You went to Majdal Shams."

I nodded. "It was quite informative."

He stared blankly at me. "You are digging up many things that people just want to forget, Fereby."

"There can be no healing if the wounds just fester."

He searched my face, then let his gaze wander back to the fire. He gathered some twigs off the ground.

"Did you offer to drive me to the airport the night Leila was killed so you could have an alibi?" I asked, leaning against the hood of his car.

Fadi eyed me with aggravation. "No – it was so I wouldn't commit murder." He threw a stick at the fire hard.

"You knew she was going to be killed? And you didn't stay to protect her?" I cried. My pulse quickened in my throat. *We both forsook her!*

"No! I knew the nature of the conflict and what would be expected of me," he yelled. "I didn't think it would happen if I left."

Leila must not have either, which is why she didn't run away sooner. I rubbed my eyebrows, feeling spent from the day.

"How did Tamir find out about Leila's...other relationship?" I asked.

He threw twig after twig in the flames. "He said some guy saw her talking to her boyfriend at school."

"What guy?"

"A Druze guy who goes to the university."

I recalled the pair who harassed me at the library. "Did he hear what they were saying? I mean, how could he know it was her boyfriend?"

"They were alone, speaking English... very emotional – obviously lovers...he heard something about going to the U.S. a few times."

"Did your family verify it?"

"No."

"So, someone killed her on mere *suspicion*? On mere *rumor*?"

He stared at the fire, something rising in his body.

"Was Leila's body in the street when you got home from taking me to the hospice hotel?"

He took a few steps towards the fire and put his hands near the flames. What was he doing that for?

"Was she already dead?" I pressed, trying to distract him.

He pulled his hand away from the fire and turned his eyes to me. "Do you want me to stay with you tonight?"

A frisson shot through my belly and I blinked at him, unsure of what he was proposing.

"I– I'll sleep outside," he said. "I thought you might be scared...after today."

"Yes, please stay."

We regarded each other through the flicker of the campfire.

"Then no more questions," he said.

I didn't even want to get into bed, let alone try to fall asleep. I was still shaken from the afternoon's events. Moshe was MIA, not knowing about what had happened to me or that his van had been impounded. I had no transportation of my own and little food. I was almost out of money. There was no statement from the *shaikhs* yet. Qasim was still being held. I was worried about Ru'yah and the list and had no plan for securing it. And now I was stuck in the Carmel forest with someone I somehow needed and was inexplicably smitten with, but didn't know if I could even trust with my life. Never mind that it was against Druze law for us to be alone like this together.

Fadi had insisted he sleep outside next to the campfire in the sleeping bag he kept in the trunk of his car for desert police missions. Out the cabin window, I could see that he was still awake, sitting up in his sleeping bag, leaning on one elbow. I made two cups of mint tea on the cabin's camp stove and went outside.

"You're still up," he said, without turning around.

"So are you," I said. I handed him a cup of the steaming tea.

He sat up and we sipped our tea and stared at the fire in silence for a minute. I felt awkward. This was a dumb idea.

"Well, goodnight, then," I said, turning back to the cabin.

"Fereby."

I stopped. "Yeah?"

"You can sit," he said, patting the outside of his sleeping bag.

My gut flip-flopped. Red warning lights flashed in my head. Disregarding my instincts, I sat down next to him in the dark sea of night, as if I was being pulled down by a rip current.

36

S tars dotted the clear night sky, the scent of cyclamen spicing the breeze. The charge between us on the sleeping bag felt like suction. I stole a glance at Fadi, who had a scowl on his face.

"What's wrong?" I asked.

"We should not be doing this."

"Enjoying a campfire on a beautiful summer night?"

He shot me a foreboding look. "No, sharing a campfire *alone*. It's wrong."

"According to one set of ideas. What do *you* think?"

"It doesn't matter what I think," he said and threw a stone into the fire.

"Then, what do you *feel?*"

He sighed and looked at me sideways, as if that was safer than fully facing me. He couldn't let me see him. "Many things...things I've never felt before...both good and bad. You make me crazy." His voice was gentler than I'd ever heard, his golden eyes mesmerizing in the fire's glow. "But I can't. It's forbidden. I shouldn't even be at this campsite, let alone sharing my bed with you."

His last words sent a shudder of yearning through my belly. I wanted to knock him down and kiss him like he'd never been kissed before and to hell with everything. Instead, I very slowly leaned over and rested my cheek on his shoulder. I felt him inhale with pleasure at my touch and then suddenly his posture stiffen. He turned to move away from me, which caused me to fall into him further. We caught each other by the arms; the moment was too much for me. I leaned in to kiss him, but he turned and hugged my face to his shoulder.

"*La*, Fereby...*la*." No, he said, his fingers in my hair.

I breathed him in, intoxicating myself on his warmth. He tilted his head back in response.

"Stop," he said, catching himself, gently pushing me away. He stood up, spilling his tea on the ground. "You've got to go back inside and stay there tonight. This is foolish."

"Are you sure?" I asked.

He looked me in the eye. "They'll destroy both of us for this."

The fire was dying down. An owl called out across the slope and was echoed by a clan of crickets.

Awkwardly, I started to rise to go back in the cabin when something rustled loudly in the bushes next to us. It moved along the ground behind the flicker of the fire. I jumped up and almost tripped backwards. Fadi rose without alarm and instantly produced a flashlight from who knows where. I clutched his arm as he swept the beam across the bushes and ground until we saw them: Two snakes, each about three or four feet long, slithering into our campsite.

I stepped up on the porch of the cabin as Fadi headed towards the back of his car.

"What are you doing?" I asked.

"I'm going to take care of them," he said, pulling a long-handled axe out of his trunk.

My heart shot up to my throat. *He brought an axe?* Fadi shone the light on them with his left hand and held the axe in his right. One looked sand-colored with some brown and white patterns. The smaller one shone red in the firelight. The snakes raised their bodies halfway up, hissing loudly, and struck at each other. They slithered apart, rose up and struck again. Fadi lifted the axe.

"Wait, Fadi! Don't! I want to take a picture," I said. "I've never seen a snake fight before!" I ran inside and grabbed my camera. When I returned, the larger snake had bitten the red one around the head, holding its jaws tightly so it couldn't open its mouth. The quarry skidded and slapped its body on the ground, rolling onto Fadi's sleeping bag, trying to release itself from the death grip, but the predator held on fast. Next, it tried wrapping its body around its captor to wrestle itself free. The snakes turned over and over – making Fadi step back – spinning and spanking each other's bodies until the biting snake let go. To my utter amazement, it reopened its mouth even wider and enclosed the red one's head entirely. In this advanced maneuver, they slid, smacked against a bag of Fadi's on the ground, then spun out – dangerously close to the fire. Ash rose into the air. The dominant snake then began to take in more and more of the red one headfirst, swallowing its flesh as fast as it could. I snapped pictures like a paparazzi, following the conquest through my lens. Suddenly, the swallowing snake stopped ingesting and moved only from the force of the creature fighting for its life inside its belly. Moments later, they both lay still, one halfway inside the other. The flames of the campfire had ceased under the flying ash, allowing only the occasional flicker from the glowing, log-shaped skeletons.

Both had choked to death.

Fadi set the axe down and squatted near the snakes, shining his flashlight to examine them. I walked up behind him and looked over his shoulder.

"The big one is *echis*, native to Israel," he said. "A saw-scaled viper. Kills more people than any other snake on earth."

"Oh my God," I whispered.

"The red one isn't native to Israel, but I saw the black "V" on her forehead, so she's probably an adder. Also quite venomous."

I had no idea this forest, which had seemed so innocuous compared to Atabi and Jaffa, was so fraught with danger.

"The thing is, I have been training in Israel's wilderness for years and I have never heard of an adder here," Fadi said, picking up the axe as he stood. "And to witness a snake fight..." He looked at me warily.

Was he thinking what I was thinking – that this was too unnatural to have just happened by chance? Did someone plant them knowing I was staying here?

Fadi insisted on sleeping outside despite the snake incident. I was relieved to see him return the axe to the trunk of his car. I locked and unlocked the door to the cabin twice, finally deciding on locked. It hurt to be shut down. But I was secretly thrilled at this new revelation: even if I were taboo, he *wanted* me.

Moshe finally called me back around midnight. He'd been visiting friends, auditioning and clubbing, and had left his phone at a friend's house. After learning about what had happened to me, he didn't care much about the fate of his van, though I reassured him I'd brought everything from inside it with me. Neither of us could afford to pay all the fines to get it released. He was distressed I was resigned to using Fadi as a bodyguard, but he had no way to get out there until the next day. He offered to borrow the car of a friend who was on holiday, but wouldn't have access to it until tomorrow afternoon.

When I began to fall asleep, an image clung to me: It was Devrah, Moshe, Duncan, Adam, countless others, and me, chanting "Justice for Leila! There's NO HONOR in KILLING!" We were standing in front of the Azzams' house, demonstrating to a huge crowd of Druze. The dream roused me so, I lay awake planning what I would do until the sun lit the sky pink at dawn. Then, exhausted, I slept until nine. When I got up, the snakes were still next to the fire pit in their mortal coil, serpentine squiggles scrawled in the dirt all around them. Leila would have marveled at this grisly sight, seen its mythic dimensions and sketched it from ten different angles. It creeped me out to think how they might have ended up at my campsite.

Fadi had already left, evidently not wishing to wake me. I felt so foolish, for so many reasons. Letting my libido sabotage all common sense. Throwing myself at him. Qasim was still in jail, for God's sake. I had talked myself out of suspecting Fadi when I had no concrete evidence to support that position. And worse, I felt hurt he'd left already.

I had to get a grip on my feelings, pull myself together and come up with a plan to get the list from the *khalwe*. I made some tea. Then Fadi called.

"The *shaikhs* are done with their meetings about Leila," he said.

I put down my cup. "What's their statement?"

"They said they're not making a statement."

"What? They took a week to come up with *that?*" I was pissed.

"But I have something better," he said. "Something that will change your mind about Druze tradition being bad for women."

"I'm listening," I said, rolling my eyes.

"Meet me in Akko in two hours."

I was skeptical, but, for several reasons, it was too tempting to turn down.

Moshe picked me up in his friend's restored 1973 electric blue Plymouth Valiant. "Israeli bank robbers used to love these for getaway cars," he said, beaming. Spurred by the *shaikhs'* non-statement, Moshe and I planned to try to get in to the *khalwe* that night and find the list. I didn't mention to him all the known dangers, but told myself I would get to that later. I shared my dream of protesting against Leila's murder and he got so excited, we decided to hold a real live demonstration the morning after Leila's funeral, which was two days away. I dropped him off at the train station in Haifa to go see his psychoanalyst in Tel Aviv — he'd blown off his last several appointments and wanted to end it more humanely.

I met Fadi at an enormous truck stop outside the ruins of the ancient coastal city of Akko. He still wore his black Border Police uniform and dark wire sunglasses and insisted on driving us in his own car. We were headed to Hurfeish, in the Upper Galilee, half an hour away, to visit one of the most sacred places for Druze — the tomb of Nebi Sablan, his mother Dima's favorite saint.

As we approached Mount Meron, the land began to rise rocky and green, some hillsides covered in red poppies, others with yellow patches of flowering anise. Hurfeish spread out demurely in the folds of these slopes. Fadi gave me a quick driving tour through the village, pointing out the *souk* and a statue of the fierce Sultan Pasha Atrash, raising a sword on a rearing horse.

The shrine, a set of unadorned box-shaped buildings in white, grey and tan, stood at the top of a hill above the village. When I got out of Fadi's car, I could see the Mediterranean Sea, Mount Hermon and Lebanon as I stood in one spot.

Fadi led me down to a spring that he explained was called *Durra*, meaning "lactating breasts." He said nursing mothers whose milk was drying up came for the spring's water, which they believed helped their milk flow. The springs collected in a valley named *al-Habis*, meaning "the blocked." Nebi Sablan's enemies reportedly came to this mountain to kill him. After he prostrated himself and asked God for protection, a deluge of rainfall suddenly came down, thwarting his enemies. Sablan lived off goats' milk here the rest of his pious life.

Bypassing the saint's tomb, Fadi led me across a meadow teeming with pink snapdragons to a small grove of magnificent old oaks and terebinths. It reminded me of Leila's "Resurrection," the frankincense tree with the face and hands of the beautiful girl in her branches, the huge sun glowing behind.

"The tree's branches reach out and all the way down to the ground to protect its roots from the sun," Fadi said as we ducked underneath an unpruned canopy.

We found ourselves inside a room of boughs. It might have been as many as ten degrees cooler under the tree, as though we'd stepped into some kind of primeval chapel.

He led me under the limbs on the other side of the oak and we emerged in a small clearing. Another, grander oak stood before us, sunlight setting its leaves alight. When my eyes adjusted, I saw countless strips of fabric and items of clothing tied to its branches.

"This is *Omm i sh-sharayet*," Fadi said. "Mother of Rags."

I felt a quiver inside: Leila's note in her sketchbook about her wedding dress – she was going to bring it here.

"A sacred tree?" I said.

"The Shaikh would say blessed – the prophet is said to have prayed beneath it."

I walked around the tree studying her many decorations: grimy shreds of embroidery, a ribbon of purple *crêpe de Maroc*, leather belts, a fresh white satin handkerchief, cotton T-shirts stiff from exposure, a string of chipped plastic beads. As a child I'd seen this custom among the Lamastic Buddhists in Punjab, India, who tied clothes to trees at crossroads. In Mari El, Russia, along the Volga River, they still hung bloody belts from the trees after animal sacrifice.

"These are offerings?"

"Yes. The visitor asks for the tree's help," Fadi said. "They put an item up on the tree and make a vow for a favor. It's as if they're offering a part of themselves. Sometimes they take another rag with them that has been there awhile."

"A used one?"

"It's absorbed the holiness."

"What kind of favors do they ask for?"

"Cures for sickness. Pregnancy. Easy childbirth. Sometimes it's just to say thanks or hello."

I still didn't understand why Leila had wanted to bring her wedding dress here. "May I go in?" I asked.

He lifted up a branch as if he was holding open a door for me and followed me under. Inside Mother of Rags, there were even more offerings, including numerous items of intact clothing laid over branches or suspended from hangers.

I pointed to a pair of jeans with the price tag still on. "New pants?"

Fadi swept some dried leaves off a sleeve of a yellow button-down shirt. "They're for the needy."

"You mean if someone lacked clothing, they could come here?"

"Sure. That's the only thing that's officially acceptable here. The caretaker says you don't have to help God remember you. Your wish is enough."

I scanned the tree for a wedding dress, but found nothing. I walked all the way around Mother's trunk, dragging my hand along her gnarled bark, wondering how old she might be. Sunlight dappled the earthen floor.

Fadi was scrutinizing a dark brown dress with tortoiseshell buttons he'd taken down from a branch. He looked up in the tree again, scanning the offerings, his forehead wrinkled.

I stood beside him. "What is it?"

His mouth was curved down. "It's my sister's," he said, his voice uneasy.

I felt the soft material. "Iman's?"

"No. Leila's."

I looked at the dress. "Are you sure?"

"Yes. And so is that." He pointed over my right shoulder to a black knit top with zigzag stitching. "And that shirt." A cream-colored blouse behind me.

"Why are they here?"

He held the dress across his forearms, palms open, careful not to drag it on the ground, as though he were carrying an injured person. "She must have put them here before...." He stared at the garment, his golden eyes dim in the shade of Mother. He shook his head. "*Hitt fi al-khirj.*"

"What?"

" 'Put something into the two bags.' Leila used to say that. Shaikh Tanukhi, a follower of Al-Sayyid, who wrote the tenets of our faith, used to ride from village to village with two sacks. If he met a rich person, he'd say, '*Hitt fi al-khirj.*' If he came upon the poor, he'd offer them whatever they

208

needed from the sacks. Leila loved that story. She was so generous, especially with the poor."

I thought of my brother Cary befriending the crippled beggar boys in Delhi, talking them into teaching him how to run up stairs using only his hands and knees. He always gave them whatever coins or candy were in his pockets.

Fadi cleared his throat to quell his rising emotion. He took his time hanging the dress back up in the tree, making sure it was securely attached before letting go. I felt it so clearly at last: He truly loved his sister. I inched up behind him. When he turned around, he pulled me right into his arms.

37

I t was not a usual hug. We clung to each other, not moving or breathing at first. The intensity was scary; something I'd never quite felt before but had imagined was possible for other people. He released me slightly, then began rocking me. I laid my cheek on his shoulder, facing him, and shut my eyes to draw in his smell and heat. I felt his hand on my chin and then his lips find mine. I opened my eyes – his were open, too. He looked mystified but driven. He twisted my hair between his fingers close to my scalp and kissed me harder. I couldn't get close enough to him and there was no time to spare. We were the wretched on a crime spree, stealing whatever we needed as fast as we could. I knew I was right in the threshold between danger and deliverance, but I didn't care.

I heard a car door slam. Our wet mouths parted. This was not the time nor place for everything I wanted to do with him. Fadi ran his fingers through his hair in frustration. Without speaking, he led me out from Mother's boughs.

"Wait," I said. I looked over myself to see what I could leave behind. I couldn't do without any of my clothes, so I unhooked one of my silver hoop earrings and attached it to the stem of a leaf on a low-hanging branch. *For justice*, I prayed. I untied a tiny piece of green yarn from another branch and tucked it into my pocket.

In awe, I followed Fadi out of the grove.

I saw her first. She was hiking up from the spring of lactating breasts, screwing a lid on a clear plastic bottle while she examined the water inside.

I grabbed Fadi by the elbow. "Fadi – it's Ru'yah!"

He stopped.

"Is it okay if she sees us together?" I whispered.

"No."

It was too late. Ru'yah had spotted us and after a startled pause, continued toward the parking lot, in our same direction. She looked back and forth at us, a smile not quite suppressed at the corner of her mouth. Moshe had told me when a man and woman have been alone for more than twenty minutes, Arabs assume they've had sex. As far as I knew, neither Fadi nor Ru'yah were aware I had a relationship with the other one. What would happen?

We exchanged hellos and she smiled at me nervously. The circles under her eyes were deeper.

"How's Khadija?" I asked.

"Getting better," she said. "She's out of the incubator. I'm on my way to the hospital now."

She and Fadi spoke for a minute in Arabic before we parted to our respective vehicles.

"What was she doing here?" I asked him.

"The baby hasn't been able to nurse yet and she is struggling to keep her milk supply."

I watched Ru'yah get into an old white station wagon and tear off down the hill.

"Is she going to tell on us?"

"Possibly," he said, starting the engine. "But she's only allowed to go back and forth to the hospital by herself. She wasn't supposed to be here, either."

Fadi had to go to work, so we parted in Akko without mentioning what happened under Mother of Rags. He didn't kiss me goodbye. It was as if nothing happened. The excursion to Nebi Sablan hadn't been the panacea he had hoped for with me, but it was encouraging to see that even the Druze hadn't fully excised the divine feminine. What I really wanted to know was why Atabi had not publicly condemned Leila's murder. There must have been people who disagreed with this...why weren't they speaking up? Did *Kitab Al-Hikma* say more about killing in self-defense of one's honor?

I brooded the whole hour driving back to Atabi, then dropped in on an old friend I needed to have a word with.

"You realize it appears that you and the other leaders approve of the killing if you don't publicly denounce it," I said to Shaikh Hayyan, seated across from him in his living room.

He patted the end of his cane. "What outsiders think of us is of very little concern to us, Miss Jones. We have been criticized for a thousand years."

I took a deep breath and clasped my hands together. "Your silence is loud, Sir."

He remained in a mutual stare with me, proving both of our points.

"Even Islam is officially against honor killing. Why not the Druze?" I asked.

"If women followed our rules, honor killings would disappear," he said.

Ugh! "Why must there be such rigid rules regarding relationships?"

"Integration is more dangerous for us than war, Miss Jones."

I winced at that bleak reminder that Fadi and I could never be together. "I'm not suggesting the *Muwahhidoon* should join the melting pot and die out," I said. "Couldn't you create positive incentives for marrying within the group instead?"

"We have many," he said. "And we forbid the marriage of a girl against her will."

"Leila didn't want to marry Tamir, but she was coerced into it by her family," I said. "They would have killed her if she didn't – they *did* kill her because she'd decided not to."

The *shaikh*'s wife motioned to his cup of coffee. He dismissed her by half-opening a hand.

"Not everything can be seen with the naked eye," he said.

A door slammed and his grandson Jabr came in through the kitchen. "My grandfather needs his rest now, Miss Jones." He motioned me toward the door, skipping the small talk.

I looked at the *shaikh* and his wife. Had she phoned Jabr as soon as I'd arrived to come "save" them?

"I'm very sorry, Miss Jones. I am taken with fatigue," said the *shaikh*. "Please excuse me." He pushed himself out of his chair with his grandson's help.

Jabr led me outside as if I was being escorted out of a building by security. I walked down the front steps.

"Miss Jones, my grandfather is becoming frail and I fear your meetings are too stressful for him. If you must ask a question, please come to me."

He handed his business card down to me from the porch. The English was hand-written on the back.

"Okay," I said. "The *shaikhs* met about Leila's murder and then had nothing to say about it. Can you explain that?"

"There is nothing to say – maintaining honor is a woman's responsibility."

"What is a woman – or girl – supposed to do if a man assaults her? If she even tries to defend herself, she'll be killed. If she turns him in, she'll be killed. And don't tell me only *bint haras* get assaulted, because we both know that's untrue."

His face caught fire with indignance. "I will not engage you in such a Western discussion of contaminated ideas!"

"This is *not* a Western discussion. It's a *human* discussion," I said. "Honor killing violates both Israeli law and international human rights law, which upholds the dignity of all human beings – including women and girls."

"Honor is sacred to us, Miss Jones," Jabr said through clenched teeth. "It's *our* dignity, our law! We consider a woman our dignity–"

"You treat them disrespectfully to maintain control of them!"

"We are respectful of Druze women who are pious, chaste and obedient."

I laughed. "You don't respect people who obey you – you may be grateful for their servitude. Respect means that you look up to someone, that you refrain from harming them or ruling *over* them. Druze women only obey their men and behave like inferiors to try to protect themselves from assault! And because they've been brainwashed for an eon to buy into the whole sham."

He was shaking with contempt. "Women are *equals* in our society."

"They can't be, Jabr. They're not legal peers with men – they're minors their whole lives. They have to have a male blood relation as a legal guardian at all times. Women can only be custodians of children if they don't have any living male blood relatives. They're more akin to slaves."

He sneered. "Our founder abolished slavery *eight hundred years* before the West, Miss Jones!"

I was glad he was at a distance up on the porch, but didn't appreciate the implied superiority of his height over me. "Slaves are anyone owned by someone else – and that includes women," I said. "The *shaikhs* won't denounce honor killings, however immoral, because these crimes conveniently serve the Druze tried-and-true formula for survival by keeping women in their servile, compliant place. If women start making their own decisions, the whole jig'll be up!"

His face burnished with fury, he turned his body as though he were going to return to the house, but kept his eyes on me. "You think your men are so much better? What about U.S. soldiers raping female soldiers and other women in countries they're occupying? Druze hold women's honor in such esteem that in wartime, Druze have never been known to rape enemy females."

"But if your own women get raped, you kill them? Come on, Jabr. There's nothing sacred about honor – that's a smokescreen so nobody can criticize these murders."

He narrowed his eyes, his unibrow quivering. "Americans hold honor as sacred as anyone," he said. "Do you know what the last two words of the U.S. Declaration of Independence are?"

"Miss Jones." A commanding voice startled us both. The *shaikh* stood in the threshold of the front door. He put one hand on his grandson's shoulder and the other over his heart. "The sages believed that one's soul, the immortal part of one's being, is one's breath," he said. "Words, created by breath, come from the soul, so they are potent and sacred. As leaders, we mustn't forget this. As a writer of words, neither should you, Miss Jones…In our thousand years of persecution, we *Muwahhidoon* have never seen more peace than the years since Israel was formed. Please allow us to continue."

As I swept out of the yard, a branch of a bony old tree caught my sleeve. Without looking back at the two men, I untangled myself and rubbed out the droplets of blood that appeared on my arm as I hurried to the car.

Rushing back to the Valiant, I could no longer deny the distance I'd traveled from my 'live and let live' attitude about other ways of life. How I'd criticized the hypocrisy of my parents' missionary work, their 'target cultures,' all the losses of traditional beliefs, stories and languages. How was I any different now? Murder was far worse than mere interference in another culture, I told myself. And honor killing's just wrong. *Wrong.* I never thought I'd judge a culture so outright from my place of self-assigned superiority.

My chest and shoulders, which seemed to be my repository of guilt, felt as if they were in a vise as I pulled out into the road. The car moved sluggishly. I gave it some more gas, and then the car began to bounce as it ambled down the road. I pulled back over to the side and looked under the dashboard for the lever to pop the hood. Not that I would know what to look for, but maybe someone would help me. As I searched unsuccessfully for the lever, I noticed tiny beads and sequins on the floor mat, a trail of fairy dust Moshe inevitably left everywhere he went. I stepped out to look for a way to open the hood from the outside, but something seemed odd. The car was lower – much lower – to the ground. I climbed out and stepped back to look at the vehicle. My tires were flat. I walked around to the other side. They were all flat. I knelt down by one and picked up the frayed edges of a tire that had been slashed.

I stood up and looked around. No one on the street was looking my way. That's when a folded piece of paper jammed under one of the windshield wipers of the Valiant caught my eye. I pulled it out. Printed in English, in crude script was: "Leave Israel tonight or die with the others."

38

ith the others? Which others? The other women on the list? I called Moshe, who was none too happy to hear I'd rendered yet another vehicle unusable, especially one that didn't even belong to him. About the note he said, "Oh, that's just Arab exaggeration – they vent a lot, but don't follow through much."

I didn't believe him completely – after all, honor killings happened – but decided not to involve the police, as they could have been responsible for the tire slashing and note. Neither one of us had the wherewithal to get the Valiant towed and fixed, so I left it on Shaikh Hayyan's street and walked to the square to call a taxi. I was so torn: Should I get on the next flight? Or stay and finish this business, hoping Moshe was right that the threat wasn't serious? The list needed to be made public – very public – to both warn the women on it as well as disgrace the writers of it so much that they had to back down. And Qasim – I couldn't live with myself if he remained in custody for who knew how long and was convicted of murder. Even if he got out of prison in his teens or twenties, his soul would be irreparably broken. It might already be. I believed Fadi was innocent of murder, but I also felt that he knew more than he'd told me. If I could get it out of him, I could get Qasim released – and possibly put the real killer away. And there was still Leila's funeral and, now, the demonstration. Those were two things I felt reasonably confident I could pull off. But I had only enough money to stay in

Israel another three, maybe four days. I had hypothetical money coming from several media clients, but nothing had shown up yet. How was I going to get around?

When I got to the square and pulled out my phone to call a taxi, it was ringing. It was Duncan.

"I'm here," he said. "In Haifa."

"Oh, really? What for?" I asked sarcastically.

"To help you. And to try to buy back as many of Leila's paintings as possible to keep them in one public collection."

I wasn't sure what to say, or if I should trust him. I was still mad at him for leaving Israel abruptly and I certainly hadn't forgotten his role in Leila's dishonor that got her killed.

"I know it's late, but have you had lunch yet?" he asked. "My stomach is all confused with the time change."

"No, I haven't eaten."

"I'm staying at the Hotel Dan Carmel. Why don't you come and join me?"

Duncan sent his limo to get me, but I had the driver meet me just outside of Atabi to attract less attention.

Duncan's hotel was built just above the Bahá'í temple and gardens, affording a spectacular view of them, much to my chagrin – I still couldn't shake the memory of my brother.

He was staying in the penthouse suite that overlooked Haifa Bay and the Mediterranean. When I arrived, he was barefoot in faded blue jeans, hair still half-wet from a shower. Dressed down and without his glasses, he looked like the All-American boy.

"I took the liberty of ordering for us," he said, gesturing toward the dining table. "Jordan River trout roasted with a whole sprig of rosemary inside and grilled baby eggplants with fresh mint."

"I brought you something." I pulled Leila's secret love phone he'd given her out of my backpack. It took him a moment to recognize whose it was. His eyes got very wide and then he cradled it tenderly in his hands, fingering the buttons as though he were imagining Leila dialing. He looked at me sheepishly, then stuck the phone in his briefcase.

"Let's dine before it gets cold," he said.

As we ate, I caught him up to speed, sharing Moshe's and my plan to raid the *khalwe* to find the list.

"I'll go with you," he said.

This surprised me. "Aren't you afraid of getting implicated in Leila's murder somehow if you get caught?"

"I want to help. What else do you need?"

I felt uncomfortable and wished Moshe were here.

Duncan cut into his fish. "Would cash be helpful?"

"Well, if we're being frank, Moshe and I are both in dire straits with respect to cash flow."

"Whatever you need."

"And we don't have any transportation."

"Take my car and driver."

"Thank you," I said. "But I think the limo might stand out too much, you know?"

"We'll get you something else. An SUV?"

"Actually, if I could just get Moshe's van out of impound..."

Duncan's silverware clanked on his plate as he stood up to pull his wallet out of his back pocket. He fumbled and withdrew a wad of Israeli bills.

"Let me know if you need more," he said, handing me the stack. "It's a gift, not a loan."

After lunch, Duncan ordered us Egyptian chamomile tea and a platter of fruit and we moved out to the balcony under a blue umbrella.

"Leila remembered overhearing her parents talking about 'what to do with her' when she was a little kid," he said, staring out to the bay. "They both thought she should be killed, but her father decided to try making her stay in the house to see if that would help reduce the public scrutiny." He took a sip of tea and looked at me. "She said real death was not to be physically killed or injured, but to have to bear the judgment of others."

I nibbled on a spear of watermelon.

"You know, before I met her, she was sure she'd soon be dead," he said. "After she was forced to get engaged to Tamir, she decided she'd die before she'd marry him. She must've known from early on that marrying him was an option her parents were considering."

I remembered her "Initiation" painting, with the bride about to get raped in the marriage bed scented with spikenard, the ancient incense of sexual pleasure turned symbol of dying and grief.

"She had only one desire before she died," he went on. "To experience ecstatic love."

Duncan looked so vulnerable, so boyish, to say such words. I felt myself blush.

"She was determined to find the perfect lover for this," he said. "If she had a passionate love affair, she was certain she'd be swiftly killed by her family, thus saving her from committing suicide....and from marrying Tamir.

"When we met, she was searching for this lover. I don't know why, but of all people, she picked me. She proceeded with the seduction, without revealing her plan. But the whole thing felt dangerously out of whack to me. I slowed her down. I got to know her. I visited several times. She was the real deal, I tell you. I've dated heiresses, a prima ballerina and a senator. They couldn't compare. With all the covert stuff she had to do to survive, Leila was more authentic than anyone I've ever known. She lived each moment more consciously and gratefully than anyone."

Duncan took a sip of tea and held the cup in his palm. His gray eyes gleamed. "After I fell in love with her, she confessed her dying wish to me. I decided in that moment that I would save her. I'd take her to the U.S. and marry her. We decided to wait to be intimate until she was safely out of the country."

Duncan clenched his jaw and looked out to the sea. "If only I had trusted that she was really going to come with me to the U.S. and not cave and marry Tamir. My insecurity killed her."

While Duncan went to track down the other owners of Leila's paintings through Raziel, and to find out if Raziel had opened an account for Leila, I dialed the District Attorney and left her a message that I'd been assaulted, received a written threat against my life and had my vehicle vandalized. Would she be so kind as to call me back?

Duncan had given me US$2,000 in *shekels*. After talking to Moshe, I had the Valiant towed to a repair shop and got the van released. Duncan had invited Moshe and me to stay in his suite, which had an extra bedroom. I gratefully moved us in, then picked Moshe up from the train station in Haifa. We went to the *khalwe* on a reconnaissance mission to look at the lock on the door and other possible entrances, but there were about forty bearded Druze elders hovering around the outside of the building. We picked up the Valiant on the way to the hotel.

Back at the Dan, my father called, freaking out that "someone official" had paid Mom and him a visit, but he wouldn't elaborate. "If you don't get on the next plane out, I'm sending a lawyer to bring you home!" I noticed he wasn't coming himself.

Adam from Women's Legal Support called to report he'd heard a Druze women's organization in Atabi had abruptly disbanded, and many young women's driving privileges were being revoked because of my involvement, which was now being viewed as a community crisis. I'd tried to call Ru'yah a few times. I was afraid to drop by her house again.

Duncan returned to the hotel carrying four paintings of Leila's that he'd bought for obscenely inflated prices from other buyers whom he'd had to pay Raziel a hefty fee to put him in touch with. He'd spoken to Raziel about Leila's commissions and Raziel claimed he'd contacted his lawyer to arrange for a proper provision.

The paintings were exquisite. An abstract horned bull (symbol of goddess) in crimson. A circular canvas, like a Javanese mandala, of a fearsome Asherah threatening her way through the gates of the underworld, standing naked on a lion, holding a lotus flower, the symbol of life, in her right hand, and a pair of serpents, symbolizing life renewed, in the left. A diptych entitled *The Milky Way*, of Asherah with breasts overflowing with milk, streaming across the night sky. Leila had painted such beauty after so many unspeakable things had been done to her.

I rubbed my temples, exhausted from a long, intense day. Moshe jumped up from the couch. "Let's hang them all. *Right* now!"

Duncan nodded, reenergized by Moshe's enthusiasm. We soon discovered, however, that the art in the hotel suite was bolted to the walls, so we leaned Leila's paintings against the walls and furniture instead.

About 2:30 am, the three of us drove the Valiant past the *khalwe*, the Druze's religious meeting place. No one was around. It was quiet and dark. Duncan wanted him to park a block away.

"Shouldn't one of us hang out nearby in the car with the engine on, like the old Israeli bank robbers?" Moshe asked.

"Who wants to stay and be the getaway driver?" Duncan asked, looking at each of us. No one volunteered. "That's what I thought. Come on."

We parked on a side street and put on our hats – a nod to disguise should we be seen from afar. Moshe wore a black beanie like a ski cap, I tucked up my hair in my baseball cap and Duncan donned a fedora from Moshe's costume stash. We walked silently to the *khalwe*. Ever-present in my mind was the fact that if a woman were found in the men's side of the *khalwe*, she would be killed. My heart was pounding twice as fast as the tempo of my steps. *Keep walking, Fer. You're going to save many women's lives.* I shook off the fear as best I could and tried to focus on the task at hand.

The entrance was on the second floor, up some steps, along an ancient stone wall. A powder blue iron railing had been added in modern times, but Leila had told me the *khalwe* itself was built over 400 years ago.

It was so dark, I had to use the light from my phone to see the lock on the door. Duncan and I hovered closely to hide the light from outside eyes.

"At least it's old," Duncan said, ramming a screwdriver inside the lock and jamming it all around.

Behind us, Moshe was looking everywhere as nervous as a prairie dog sentinel. "Hurry up!" he whispered.

The lock wasn't giving. Duncan tried jamming the screwdriver between the door and its frame where the lock went in. He wiggled it around for a while, to no avail. I was starting to feel very vulnerable out there where we could be seen. Only one way out, down the stairs. Duncan bent the tool back, breaking the frame. A crack rang out in the night air. Moshe gave us an admonishing look, eyes like saucers. But the door was open. We each glanced behind us as we entered to make sure no one saw us going in. I couldn't believe what I was doing, but the adrenaline had taken over. Now or never.

219

Inside, Duncan pulled out his own phone and panned the light back and forth around the room. There were *divans* on the floor against the walls and some chairs and a small table in the center. It was large enough to hold a few hundred men. The only other furniture in the room was a tall cabinet resting against the wall to our right near the entrance. The whole chamber had just a few small windows, with one near the door.

"Moshe, stay by this window and tell us if you see anything outside we need to worry about," Duncan whispered.

Intuitively, Duncan and I both headed toward the cabinet. We each opened a door in the cabinet and began searching. I found stacks of papers, books, five small baskets, paper cups, keys, cleaning supplies, a bowl of walnuts and some dishes.

We must have had the same thought simultaneously.

"Do you know Arabic?" Duncan asked.

"Not enough," I said. "Do you?"

"Moshe!" Duncan whispered.

Moshe came over to help me look while Duncan stood lookout.

I was so scared, my fingers were shaking as I fumbled through papers, holding my cell phone's light for Moshe.

Duncan gasped. "A light went on in a house across the street!"

"Oh, shit! " I said. This was absurd. What were we thinking? It was like looking for a needle in a haystack. "Moshe, quick, do you see anything?"

"Hide your lights!" Duncan said.

"What do you see, Duncan?" Moshe whisper-squealed.

"Nothing," he said. "Hurry, guys."

"How are we supposed to find anything in the dark?" I asked.

"Just hurry!" he said.

My mind began looping doubt around my fears. *What if it's not here and I was set up so they could kill me with mitigating circumstances by catching me here? What if there is no list?* I tried to shake it off and borrowed Duncan's phone for light. Inside another cabinet door, I discovered a beautiful handmade book all by itself. I picked it up to examine it under the light.

"Moshe, what's this?"

He leaned over to read the calligraphy on the cover. "That's the *Kitab al-Hikma*," he said.

My heart stopped for a moment as panic swept over me. The holy book of the Druze. I was holding it in my bare hands. I quickly put it back in its place inside the cabinet.

"Isn't that what you've been looking all over for?" Moshe asked.

"Yes, but, but...let's stay focused on our task."

"I'm not seeing anything that looks like a list, Fer," Moshe said, worry rising in his voice.

"Come on, guys, we need to get going," Duncan said.

THE SEVEN PERFUMES OF SACRIFICE

"Should we just grab all the papers and take them with us?" Moshe said.

"I don't feel good about that," I said.

"You've already committed breaking and entering," Moshe said. I could sense him rolling his eyes.

"Oh no!" Duncan said. "Some people are running up the steps now!"

"To the *khalwe*?!" I said.

"Yes!"

"Oh my God! What are we going to do?" I felt like I was going to pee in my pants again, like in the bombing.

"Get on either side of the door and press yourself up against the wall. When they come in, we'll try to run out," Duncan said.

Moshe and I did as he said on the right side of the door. Duncan took the left. I felt paper against my cheek on the stone wall. Something was hanging there. I shone my phone light on it.

"Moshe!" I whispered.

"Quiet!" Duncan said. "Turn off your light!"

Moshe glanced at the paper, grabbing my phone from me for a closer look. I could hear the footsteps outside now and at least two men's voices. I felt tears coming to my eyes, my nerves were so unbearable. *They're going to kill me on sight.*

"This is it," Moshe said, and ripped the paper off the wall. "The list."

A lot of good it's going to do us now. Moshe turned off the phone light as I heard the men push open the door.

39

The men did not enter immediately. They must be scared, too, I hoped, my heart pounding so hard it must have been audible. Or they're preparing to pounce. I pictured Sultan Pasha Atrash's hundred warriors with braided hair and kohl-smudged eyes, wielding daggers and swords. I heard whispering. Suddenly, they burst in all at once, yelling in Arabic. I ran outside as soon as I saw they were out of the threshold, holding Moshe's hand so he wouldn't get left behind. (For one thing, he had the car keys.) Lights went on behind us; the men must have flicked the room switch on. I hoped Duncan was following. I'd never run so fast in my life – never had to. I heard the men yelling and running after us. I prayed Moshe wouldn't drop the list or the keys. Thank God it was dark out and my hair was hidden in a cap. I heard a loud noise and some grunting behind me, but I didn't want to turn around and lose time. *Please Duncan, make it!* Moshe and I finally got to the car and jumped in. Duncan was not far behind us. Another man was heading our way, too. I left the passenger door ajar for Duncan and we started moving. Moshe handed me the list and I white-knuckled it. I got down so the pursuer wouldn't see me if we drove past him. It was so hard not to look out, though. I felt Duncan jump in next to me, slam the door and Moshe gun it.

"Jesus, you almost hit him, Mosh!" Duncan said.

"Well, he was right in front of the car!" Moshe screeched.

"Watch out for the other two!"

The car swerved and I slid into Duncan.

"Why are you down like that?" Duncan said. I felt his hand on my back. "You okay?"

"Don't want them to see me," I said.

"Okay, they're all behind us now."

I sat up. We three were out of breath, freaked out and hauling out of Atabi.

"You got the list then?" Duncan said.

"Yeah," I said, showing it to him.

"I threw some trash cans down to block their path and two of them tripped and fell," Duncan said.

"Good thinking," I said.

"Lucky they were there," he answered. "We wouldn't have made it."

Moshe drove like a bank robber in a getaway car until we were well out of town.

"Why didn't you take the *Kitab*, too?" Moshe said to me.

"I just couldn't."

"Why not?"

I sighed. "No one's supposed to look at that book but the Druze initiates."

"You've been looking for the *Kitab* for weeks and you knew it was a private book."

"I thought I could get past it."

He rolled his eyes. "You broke into their *khalwe*, Fereby."

"That's different," I said. Though only by degrees.

We couldn't wait until we got back to the hotel to make Moshe translate the list, so he read as he drove. It was entitled, "Women Who Endanger the Community". There were six women's names, hand-written in black ink, only two of which we recognized. Ru'yah was third on the list. They were all Arabic names, except the very last one. When Moshe pointed to the name that was scrawled in blue ink at the bottom and translated, "Fereby McCullough Jones – The Corruptor," my heart sank.

None of us could sleep right away with all that adrenaline. I sat out on the balcony alone, thinking, not sipping a glass of pinot noir Duncan had poured me. A sliver of sand-colored moon cast a sweep of light across the sea. Now what was I going to do with this list? I obviously couldn't take it to the police. They wouldn't care. They'd just book me for breaking, entering and theft, or deport me. I would have to turn it over to a brave and responsible journalist. I wished so badly I could write the story for *The New York Times*, but I needed to remain anonymous as the list thief and it had to be an Israeli paper for the most local impact. Finally, to cover all my bases, I decided to make copies of the list and drop them off in the morning with a letter to *Al-Ittihad*, the national Arabic daily, *Haaretz*, the largest Hebrew daily and *The Jerusalem Post*. I wanted to omit my name from the list for privacy, but if I did, the writers of the list would know I had stolen it and given it to the papers.

After I'd worried long enough about what we'd done and my death sentence, my thoughts returned to Fadi, as they usually did. I had never felt anything before like I'd felt with him. The tension, hunger, tenderness, desire to know him so completely, inside and out. Unrequited passion. All our ambivalence – rage/love, fear/desire, trust/distrust – had flooded that bottomless kiss. We could never truly explore this connection, that was obvious. He made me feel both warm and whole as well as queasy and distraught.

After a short sleep, I was awakened by a call about 8 a.m. from the U.S. consul in Haifa, Shawn Collins. He said he'd heard about Leila's case and offered to help me. Elated, I invited him to the Dan at 10:30 am. I pulled myself together and Moshe took me to deliver the lists and letters to the newspaper offices.

I waited in the hotel's piano bar, sipping a virgin Bloody Mary. I was too wound up to eat. A fair man in an olive business suit approached me, followed by Joshua Shuman, the northern district commander of the Israeli police.

"Miss Jones?" the man said.

I stood up, glancing at Shuman in confusion. "Mr. Collins?"

"Pleasure to meet you."

I shook his hand absently. Why was Shuman here? Were the police finally going to take control of this situation? Or – my stomach clenching – did he find out about the *khalwe* break-in?

"Miss Jones, you know Commander Shuman."

"Yes, hello," I said, attempting to shake his hand, but he was less than enthusiastic doing so.

"Please sit," said Collins.

They took the pair of overstuffed burgundy chairs across from me. My heart began to hammer.

Collins smiled at me. "You have my sympathy, Miss Jones. You've been through quite an ordeal."

I looked back and forth at them.

"In light of what we've learned of your circumstances, the U.S. State department would like to provide you with complimentary air transportation back to California." He produced an envelope from his jacket pocket and handed it to me.

I was even more confused now. "You came to offer me a plane ticket home?"

"And free airport transfer," he said. "Tonight."

"Thank you, but I still have my own ticket and it's good for a long while." I handed it back. Now I was pissed. He wouldn't accept it, so I set it on the table between us and pushed it toward him.

Collins clasped his hands on his lap. "Miss Jones, we would be grateful if you could allow the very capable Israeli authorities to handle their own pursuit of justice. They mean well—"

"They haven't taken either case seriously yet – Leila's murder or my assault," I said, shooting a look at Shuman. "I have no plans to leave here until Qasim is released and Tamir Shahin and the person who killed Leila are arrested."

Shuman gritted his teeth. Collins glanced at him and looked back at me. *Yes, that's right. I'm going to be difficult.*

"Miss Jones, the authorities are confident they have the right suspect in custody," Collins said.

"Qasim is SIX years old, Sir. He was forced by his family to confess under duress and I'm positive he's not guilty," I said. "Why is this of interest to you anyway?"

Shuman cleared his throat. "Out of respect for you and our relationship with your country, we have asked the U.S. Embassy to step in and help before our immigration authorities must."

"Immigration?" I said. Metanis hadn't been joking.

They nodded in unison.

"Israel is thinking of deporting me?"

"We're here to encourage you to cooperate," Collins said.

"I'm not leaving yet." I stood up.

They got to their feet.

"We can take you right now," Shuman started. Collins put a hand on his arm to mollify him, but it didn't work. "You are suspected of obstruction of justice and may still constitute a danger –"

"I'm the only one who's *not* obstructing justice in Leila's case!" I said. "If anything, I should be suing *you guys* for lack of police protection and failure to arrest my attacker."

Collins leaned in closer to me, touching my arm. "Miss Jones, we're trying to avoid your further embarrassment—"

I pulled away from him. "I'm not ashamed of what I'm doing. But you two should be. You're afraid of your own humiliation when the truth comes out – once again it comes down to *honor*. You won't take me in right now because then the media *will* cover this story and you don't want that to happen. Your forcing me to leave would be the best thing for my cause."

I held out my wrists to be handcuffed. They looked at my wrists in unison.

"Miss Jones, we're aware *The New York Times* isn't even supporting you on this project," Collins said.

What was he talking about? "Sure they are," I said.

He smiled. "And you lied about your relationship to them to get sources to talk to you."

"I never lied about anything!" I said.

We all looked over to the corner as the pianist began playing an annoyingly upbeat jazz standard.

There was a wicked look in Collins' eyes. "Your family isn't supporting you, either. Evidently."

How could he know *that*? From the official that visited my parents? I willed my tears to stay in their ducts with every ounce of strength I had.

He looked at me with victorious pity. "What other options do you have?"

"I'm going to take this to the U.N.," I said.

He laughed. "You can't be serious."

"Oh, yes."

"They won't help you."

"Sure they will. And then the international media will have to cover it."

"With all due respect, Miss Jones, the U.N. has much more critical work to do –"

"Honor killing is a violation of internationally recognized human rights and the state bears responsibility if it systematically fails to try to prevent, investigate and punish it. Israel has violated this convention repeatedly."

"So, if these violations are as common as you claim, why would this situation warrant special attention by the media?" Collins asked.

I looked at him, at a loss for a few long seconds. Shuman was eyeing me to catch my moment of defeat.

"Maybe because it's the first time someone's raised hell about it," I said.

"Come on, Miss Jones," Collins said. "What's this all going to amount to? Israel will get – at best – a slap on the wrist. And we – Israel's greatest ally – get egg on our faces. I'm sure there is a much better – and more *diplomatic* – way to handle this."

"I'm not doing anything wrong." I turned to leave.

"Miss Jones, the Israeli government can revoke your stay whenever it wishes," Shuman said.

"And by the way," added Collins. "It's also been brought to my attention that you haven't submitted your journalistic work to the Israeli military censor for approval."

I paused behind my chair. "I'm not covering defense or national security."

"I think they're starting to see it otherwise, Miss Jones," said Shuman. "The work – or the author – must only *potentially* threaten national security to require it to be reviewed in advance."

I looked back and forth at them, standing in this swanky lounge, trying to intimidate me. "Good day, Mr. Collins, Commander."

40

Y ou carry your soul in your teeth, my friend," Moshe said, when I was back in Duncan's suite. "The Israeli authorities can arrest anyone anytime they want, no problem."

"Well, they didn't arrest me."

"Only because you're American media."

Still, I was in enough trouble with the authorities that I didn't know how I was going to pull off the funeral and demonstration now. As I rubbed the tension in my temples, Stephan, my editor from *The New York Times*, called. He was working rather late. At first, he sounded so distracted, it seemed more as if I'd called him and interrupted him on deadline.

"I'm making great progress on the story, Stephan – " I started.

"We've been contacted by several sources alleging that you've claimed to be on our staff in order to manipulate public officials in Israel –"

"*What?*"

" – that you've lied to people to trick them into giving you information about the murder case – "

"No!"

"—and you've given sexual favors to sources to get them to talk."

I laughed. "That's ridiculous, Stephan. Every one of them's a bald-faced lie. Who told you that?"

"I can't say, but they're credible enough."

227

"Commander Shuman? Wow, they're playing hardball now. They're all lies. I'm about to expose some serious corruption, Stephan. That's why they're saying these things."

"You must have mentioned *The Times* to someone."

"I only said I was submitting something, that was all. They evidently assumed a lot more."

"We're not going to consider any more of your stories until our investigation is complete," he said.

"You can't possibly believe any of this is true, Stephan!" I pleaded.

"Sorry."

Everything was falling apart. I paced the suite, stunned and humbled, Moshe and Duncan trying to talk some sense into me. I needed to clear my head and asked them to leave me alone on the balcony for a while.

I missed Fadi and pined for the comfort of his arms around me. Plus, it was time to try to talk him into telling me what he knew that could help me get Qasim freed. I called him.

"Hello, *habibi*," he said, after the first ring.

I smiled – *habibi* is Arabic for "sweetheart."

"I need to see you," I said.

"Come. I'm at the bar in Atabi."

It wasn't even lunchtime yet.

"Okay, I'll be there in ten."

I took the van in case the Valiant might be identified in Atabi as the getaway vehicle from last night. Duncan and Moshe didn't want me to go in light of my name being on the list, but I had to.

Fadi was leaning on his car in the parking lot when I drove up.

"How are you?" I asked, approaching gingerly, not knowing what to expect.

"I've come from visiting Khadija in the hospital."

He didn't try to touch me. I couldn't fathom what he was thinking.

"You've been drinking your breakfast."

"I just had a few." He scratched the back of his head.

"How's Khadija?"

"They moved her from intensive care to the neonatal unit yesterday. She'll be released soon."

She'd been in the hospital almost three weeks, her whole life so far. Since the night Leila died. The thought of Leila's soul reincarnated into Khadija's body passed through my mind. *The immortal soul flies out into empty space, to seek her fortune in some other place.* I looked at Fadi to see if I had quoted Ovid aloud.

He spun his car keys around one finger and looked off to the road. I feared his mood would shift and my last chance to talk to him before the funeral and demonstration would be gone. How could I get him talking?

"Would you take me to the woods where Leila was assaulted?" I asked.

He looked at me with his usual incalculable mix of emotions. "Why?"

"I'm curious…Where are they?"

"Behind my house."

We drove in silence. I wasn't crazy about letting him drive under the influence, but I didn't want to have an argument and blow this opportunity and he didn't seem impaired. When we got to the Azzams', he parked in the driveway as though it made no difference whatsoever for him to be seen with me. What had changed? Luckily, the only person outside was Ru'yah, sitting on her porch swing. She stood up when I emerged from the car.

Like the first night we met, I followed Fadi through the fig bower to the back of his house. I lost my balance on the path, as the loose stepping-stone had been removed. Fadi led me to the orchard and down the hill, dust kicking up between us and rows of lemon trees.

At the bottom, where the forest began, we entered under the canopy on a trail, our footfalls followed by snapping twigs and the crunching of dry leaves. I followed Fadi through the path as it wound along a ridge above a small creek.

"How did this part escape deforestation?" I asked.

"It's cool down here in the hot summers. We used to picnic or nap here a long time ago."

I wondered if they had stopped after Leila's attack.

It was a sultry trail along the creek, mottled with shadows. Crusty old pines, oaks, terebinths and sycamore figs. Vines with pink flowers. A wonderful, citrusy-smelling plant I couldn't identify. The deeper we moved into the forest, disturbing its floor, the richer the aroma it released, like a compost of muscatel and chocolate. I wondered if Leila's caul was buried nearby.

Fadi stopped. "Here."

I scanned the innocuous-looking ground before us. He hung his head, hands on his hips, enduring this field trip more than anything else. The forest was quiet. I thought of other places I'd been where atrocities had occurred, like Gettysburg and Auschwitz. As a child, I'd wondered if there was something perverse with God or nature or myself that these haunted places could seem peaceful years later, or ever. Much later, I read Oscar Wilde's explanation – "Where there is sorrow, there is holy ground" – but, twenty years after the fact, I'd still never been able to return to the Jaipur hotel where Cary died.

Fadi lifted his face to a beam of sunlight peering through the branches. A rivulet of tears trickled down his cheek. His face looked so naked. I looked away to give him privacy, pretending to survey the nature.

"Our family was destroyed by what Tamir did to Leila," he said, his voice straining.

I turned back to him.

"My mother locked her inside a room in the house and told her she could never come out. My father never spoke her name. Whenever I could, I'd go in and talk to her or play. Sometimes I would sneak her candies. I gave her a doll."

"Umniyah?" I asked.

He nodded, unsurprised I knew. "I watched her grow up inside that room."

"Did the isolation help your family's honor?"

He shook his head. "My parents decided to become religious. They thought maybe the village would accept them better. But my father still had trouble selling his produce and, after four years like this, my mother left poison in Leila's room and begged her to take it."

"What did she do?"

"She wanted to take it, but I begged her not to. I lied to her and made her believe there was *hope*."

Fadi covered his face with his hands and dropped to his knees, sobbing silently. I kneeled down beside him and tried putting my arms around him. Here, the earth smelled of black pepper and animal urine. A pine needle was making its way through the knee of my pants. Fadi let me draw him in.

"I brought her books and taught her to read," he said. "She'd never been to school. We never let her outside her room for nine years."

I thought of the woman living in the upper floor of the home Ru'yah showed me.

"Then, someone planted eggs under our olive trees to kill them. My father had to sell off half our land so we could survive. Everyone was affected...Iman, Qasim, once he was born."

"How was it for you?"

"Every day, people pushed me to do my 'duty'."

"To kill her?"

He nodded. "They looked at me as if I was disgusting, turned away from me on the street. I felt..." He looked up at me, searching. "Like I still existed, but in the worst possible way: not a true man. The code of honor is like the law of gravity. There's no choice."

I crossed my legs on the ground. "So, why didn't you go through with it?"

"I couldn't," he said, looking me in the eye. "She's my own flesh and blood. I love her. I didn't want to kill her."

"But you tried."

"On my sixteenth birthday, my mother gave my father a knife. He told me he'd kill me if I didn't do it."

"What did you do?"

"I couldn't. I just cut her a bit." He pointed to his abdomen. "As soon as I saw her blood, I dropped the knife and tried to stop the bleeding...My father left for a week. My mother didn't know where he was or if he was coming back. She had to explain my father's absence in the village. My parents were asked to leave the *khalwe*. I was afraid that when my father returned, he would kill Leila, me and, possibly, my mother. Leila wasn't even mad at me. She was apologizing *to me*! I hated myself."

"Was she okay?"

"She recovered at home."

Devrah had mentioned her chronic pain and ulcers. "You didn't go to jail."

"The police never officially knew."

We listened to crickets, a breeze blowing through the trees and a trickle of stream down below.

Fadi rubbed his forehead. "It was even worse than before. Everyone knew I'd failed. I couldn't wait to join the army to get away."

"Why didn't you just go live in Tel Aviv or something?" I thought of Moshe's solution.

"We have a very old saying: Paradise without people should not be entered because it is hell...I reminded Leila of that on the ride back to Atabi, when you were with us."

"Did you know about her boyfriend already?"

"No, but I knew something had happened. She was taking unusual risks...I was mad that day I picked you two up at school because I was afraid she was going to get herself in big trouble. Both of you were talking too loud so I knew she had been near the bombing in Jaffa, too."

We looked at each other for a long moment. I saw a man being pulled in two impossible directions, on the rack.

"Why does life here have to be so hard, Fadi?"

He picked up a handful of leaf litter and crushed it. "In my world, people will love you passionately and then kill you on the street like a bug."

"Huh," I said. "In America, there are people who will die for you but can't hold your hand."

He reached down and picked up my hand. He fixed his eyes on it for a long moment, then drew it closer to him, bringing it up to his face. He touched my hand to his lips and inhaled. I felt his breath, in and out, cool and warm, moisten my skin. He placed his cheek in my palm. The aliveness of his skin startled me, as if his unreachable soul had momentarily slipped out. He looked up at me with eyes more gentle than I'd ever seen from him. "What happened to you, Fereby?"

I knew what he meant, but wasn't sure if I could tell him. I looked back and forth at his eyes.

"Did somebody hurt you?" He said. "Long ago?"

I stared down at my lap and girded myself with a deep breath. "A boy. A teenager. My brother had just died. I was twelve...a complete mess. A walking wound. My parents were clueless, paying no attention to me. But Pat did. He quoted from things other than the Bible. I loved that. He promised making love to him would heal my pain. He recited something from Rumi to clench the deal. Unfortunately, it's stuck with me my whole life: 'Out beyond ideas of wrongdoing and rightdoing, there is a field. I will meet you there.' "

Fadi looked at me with such intensity, such tenderness. The way he held my hand was better than any sex I'd ever had. I looked up in the trees and found the sky. Some birds flapped in the canopy.

"I didn't resist much, and my father beat the hell out of me when he found out, so I didn't think of it as rape," I said. "But it was. I thought the loss of my virginity and the beating were God's punishments for me not saving Cary. Then my mother kind of went crazy. I believed I ruined my family."

Panic was rising in Fadi's eyes. He dropped my hands and covered his face. "It was my fault," he said, his voice cracking.

"What, Fadi?"

"I was there!" he cried, looking up at me, his face misshapen with pain.

"Where?"

"*Here!* In the woods!"

My mind raced forwards and backwards. "You were here...when Leila...?"

He nodded his head up and down, faster and faster, as if he wanted to hurt himself. Sobs came hurtling out of him. He braced himself with both hands on the ground like a laboring animal.

"Fadi?" I prayed he wasn't involved somehow. "Did you witness her assault? Tell me."

His mouth fell open gasping for air. "I was supposed to be with her, watching her!...but I went down to the stream to play with my friends." He pointed down the trail. "I thought I heard a scream, and I started to go back up, but I didn't hear anything else...just boys laughing, so I went back down to my friends."

A burning sensation started to fill my stomach. I struggled to stay present with him.

"A few minutes later, I heard another scream and I knew it was her...I went running back up...I could hear her crying and screaming, but I couldn't see her. I just saw the back of Tamir...he was on the ground in a weird sort of kneel. His pants were...*down*." Fadi gasped, his hands propped on his knees, rocking himself to stanch the memory. He shook his head like a boxer after a blow, determined to finish the round. "I had never seen a person like this before. Two of his friends – older boys than me – were there, too, watching and laughing and telling him to keep going. I was so confused about what I was seeing and the sounds I was hearing – there was both laughing and crying. When I got closer, I saw these little legs sticking out from under Tamir with Leila's yellow sandals on. I remember thinking how mad my mother was going to be because the white daisies on them had gotten dirty. I still didn't understand what they were doing...I moved so slowly."

I thought of myself on the bus after the bombing – a newborn baby in an alien world trying to figure everything out. Like floating in slow motion through a whirlwind.

"When I got closer, I saw Leila's face beneath him," he said. "Her eyes! *I can't ever stop seeing her eyes!...*" Fadi clutched his face with his fingernails. "They always come back in my dreams...and at other, awful, times...They were different. Not eyes of a child. There was terror, but Leila wasn't even *in* there. Like her soul had left..."

Fadi's face was crushed with anguish, his golden eyes possessed. I rested my hands on his knees, not knowing how to comfort him.

"Tamir's friends ran away...I started pounding Tamir in the head and the back, trying to make him stop, trying to pull him off her...but I wasn't strong enough."

Fadi buried his face in the leaves beside us, nails digging into the ground, grabbing handfuls of damp earth as though it would help with gravity. I pictured my brother's face...the last intolerable, sentient expression I saw on it before he lost consciousness: Terror. How useless and ashamed I was.

"You couldn't have saved her, Fadi." I felt tears hanging from my jaw. "He was so much bigger than you."

He looked up at me, lines of tears washing down his dirty face, his eyes, raw and wet as an open wound.

I stroked his back. It hurt to speak. "We can't always save the ones we love, Fadi."

He pulled himself out of the dirt and wiped his nose on his shirttail. We were kneeling opposite each other. He gulped air and grabbed my hands.

"There's more," he said, looking directly at me.

I braced myself. *Please...no...*

"When he got off of Leila...I could finally see her...she was bleeding, her little blue dress pushed up to her waist...her eyes rolled back...she must have fallen unconscious. I couldn't believe my eyes. When I looked up at Tamir, he hit me in the face so hard, I saw blood fly. I fell to the ground, the breath knocked out of me." Fadi regarded our hands, clutched in a mutual death grip. His voice trailed off into a whisper: "Then, he raped me."

41

We sat crying on the forest floor, which, among nature's dead things, seemed a fitting place to forsake old, rotting memories. I held him as he let his long hurt flow out. He'd kept the whole event buried until then. When he was finished, he held my face in his hands and kissed my eyelids first, my cheeks and then my lips. He wrapped his arms around me and laid us back down on the earth. In that pure embrace, I realized that Arabs are not the 'other.' What they do openly, we do covertly: I was victimized, too, but my family called it something else. The thought that I might never get to be in his arms like this again made me cling to him harder.

"What is it, Fereby?" he asked, stroking my hair.

"We can't do this. We can't be together."

"I know, but I can't stay away from you," he said, kissing my forehead.

I heard an owl hoot its first call to the twilight. The forest would soon be coming alive.

He held my head, breathing in the scent of my hair like nourishment. "I remember you," he said.

"What do you mean?"

"Have you ever had a strange feeling you've been somewhere or met someone before?"

"Like *déjà vu?*" I glanced up at him.

He looked uncertain.

"It means having this strong sense of familiarity, but at the same time, not knowing how," I said.

"Yes, that's your Old Mind showing you an ancient memory. I have them every time I see you."

"Really?" I smiled.

He took a deep breath. "Only I do have some recollection."

"Of what?"

We rolled on our sides toward each other in the fading daylight. His face, dirty and streaked with dried tears, was more tranquil than I'd ever seen it.

"We were together before....in another life."

"How did we know each other?" I asked, bemused.

Fadi caressed my cheek, tracing the trail of his fingers with his eyes. He picked up my hand and held it to his heart. "I think you were my wife."

A wave of pure energy rolled gently through me, our eyes locked on one another. I leaned in and touched his nose with mine. "How was it?" I whispered.

"Wonderful." He kissed me tenderly. "But we were lost from each other too soon."

I could have stayed with him in the woods all night; I was filled with an ebullience like nothing I'd ever known. As darkness fell, we knew we had to part and retraced our steps up through the trail.

It wasn't until later that evening, all alone back in the hotel suite, that the reality of Fadi's and my situation hit me. I hadn't asked him or learned anything that would help solve Leila's murder; I had utterly forgotten my focus. I was in love. But it couldn't go anywhere. The sensation of a jagged rip through my torso made me sit very still on the floor, leaning against the couch, for a long time. Movement required awareness, but awareness allowed in pain. I found that if I remained motionless, I could conjure a sort of waking numbness. I wondered if the yogis who can slow down their heart rates and breathing could will their hearts to stop beating altogether, too.

I was grateful for the distraction when Moshe and Duncan returned from dinner even though they were mad as hell at me. I'd been ignoring their texts and calls all day. They said all three newspapers had already published stories online about the list and my letter. I read the stories on the web, which mentioned the break-in at the *khalwe*. No telling what mayhem might break loose tomorrow. Moshe and I stayed up late preparing the ceremony for Leila's funeral before I collapsed in bed, exhausted.

The next day would have been Leila's eighteenth birthday. The day she would have escaped to America with Duncan and missed her forced wedding to Tamir and the second of many future rapes by him. The day she would, instead, have her belated funeral service.

I had invited Devrah, Fadi, Ru'yah, Duncan, Moshe, Adam, Badi'a, and Professor Binyamin to the funeral. "Whatever you do, do *not* bring flowers," I'd warned.

Moshe, Duncan and I got to the Atabi cemetery about ten minutes early. I was feeling anxious because of my name being on the list and the publicity of it. I felt as if I had a target on my forehead. The grounds were dotted in tiny purple blossoms that had opened since Leila's burial, like a quiet protest against the ban on funerary flowers. We located Leila's burial plot, which still looked fresh compared to the others, with young weeds just sprouting from the sandy soil. Duncan and I set several stones on top of it.

I glanced over and, to my amazement, saw Badi'a ambling towards us, a young Bedouin man holding her arm, helping her navigate her way through the weeds. I couldn't believe she had made it. And on time.

An owl hooted its persistent singular question and Badi'a stopped to look up in the enormous oak trees that encircled the graveyard. She pointed towards the sound with a crooked brown finger and cried out.

"How weird that it's awake now," I said, scanning the branches.

Badi'a shuffled over to us and, without saying hello, launched into a rant.

"She says Leila's blood is crying for revenge," Moshe said. "The owl is Leila's pissed-off, unavenged soul. She may haunt her murderer."

"Well, we can only hope so," I said. "That may be the only redress she gets."

Devrah and Adam arrived at the same time. Badi'a introduced her great-grandson Malik as Professor Binyamin came scurrying toward us, floating fluffy silver hair and all.

After brief introductions, we formed a semi-circle around Leila's grave. I was disappointed Fadi didn't find a way to attend. I thanked everyone for coming to celebrate Leila's extraordinary life and invited them to each say something about her.

Devrah expounded on Leila's artistic gift and what she had learned from her student, Leila's unusual compassion made all the more rare by her circumstances. "She mentioned on more than a few occasions the kindnesses of people from well over a decade ago."

Binyamin said Leila's talent echoed some of the great masters, but her courage far exceeded any of them. He pledged to donate his collection of her work to a public foundation for all to appreciate. Duncan glanced at me with a twinkle in his eye.

Badi'a started off with a flowery Muslim prayer, which puzzled me at first until I realized she was toeing the party line in front of her great-grandson. The last line Moshe translated from her, which I'll never forget, was, "And truth may walk through the world unarmed."

Duncan seemed uncomfortable in our odd group. He pulled a folded piece of paper out of his pocket with a shaky hand, but did not open it.

"I fell in love with Leila's paintings before I ever met her," he said. "I see a lot of art and it's rare for me to respond so powerfully to it. When I finally got to meet her, I saw she was not only brilliant and gifted, but beautiful...I was so nervous, it was like my first crush. I couldn't think of anything smart to ask her, but being the elegant creature she was, she led the conversation, and we got to know one another."

Duncan looked down while he spoke. I stared at the long shadows our circle of eight cast across the ground. Some aromatic plant had begun to release its sweet scent as the morning heated up.

"She courted the edge in everything she undertook," he continued. "Once, she was painting at home and her father surprised her. She only had time to lay out some paper over her canvas to pretend she was doing something for an art education class. She often took me to the best art museums in Israel and taught me many things. There were so many more experiences she longed for...to go to the National Gallery in D.C. to see Titian's 'Diana and Callisto'. She wanted to see Rembrandt's 'Susanna and the Elders' in the Hague. She wanted to buy a red bikini and wear it drinking a *mojito* on a Cuban beach – though three sips of alcohol made her tipsy. She wanted to paint openly. And drive...fast. You got the sense her childhood experiences would only be her first artistic inspirations...she wasn't going to be satisfied with repeating variations on that for long. She was a victim who never complained of it, just worked around it however she could. She marveled at the goodness of the world and enjoyed its every nuance." He laughed and looked up. "We had more fun during a driving lesson I gave her in the desert than most people do in a week enjoying New York's best attractions."

Laughter murmured through the group. Then, Duncan's voice changed.

"Our love caused me to see the world differently – as a good place. I imagined all the people's lives we might touch with our joy. I loved Leila, and I always will."

Duncan bent down and tucked the piece of paper under a stone on the grave. Moshe was unsuccessful in his effort to cry silently. With tears in my eyes, I put one arm around him and the other around Duncan and felt Devrah put hers across mine on the other side of him. Listening to Leila's inner circle extol her expansive nature on her birthday made me think of her painting "The Birth of Hawwah," Asherah giving birth to Eve and, thus, the promise of bounty for all women.

Then a searing pain shot through my right calf. My legs collapsed underneath me; I heard myself groan as Duncan and Devrah caught me on the way down. I grasped my leg, confounded by the pain. The others were surrounding me shouting in three languages. I looked behind me to see four teenage boys standing on the edge of the graveyard scowling. The tallest one threw a rock low that hit the ground three feet behind Devrah and skidded into her shin.

"Hey!" Duncan yelled. "You just hit them!"

News of the list's debut on the world stage had evidently reached the Druze...or else they just didn't like us here in the cemetery. With one eye on the boys, I checked on Devrah, who clutched her leg in pain. My calf still stung.

Another boy threw a stone. This time it hit Duncan in the hand, which he'd held up to his face to block.

"Stop!" Duncan yelled in a deep voice. His hand was bleeding.

"*Yu-af!*" I yelled. Stop!

Adam strode resolutely toward the youths shouting in Hebrew and then in Arabic. Binyamin began to follow him, but Duncan stopped him.

All four Druze boys were throwing rocks now. Adam guarded his face and ducked, but got pelted in the shoulder. One of the boys pitched a glass soda bottle over Adam's head that would have hit Badi'a had Malik not pulled her out of the way.

"Why are they doing this?" Moshe yelled to no one in particular.

"What do you expect from people who chant war songs at weddings?" Devrah shouted back.

Moshe put Badi'a behind several of us and placed himself in front of me. "I'm calling the police!" he cried.

A torrent of Semitic expletives raged across the graveyard. We couldn't escape since the boys were in front of the entrance and a high stone wall surrounded the rest of the cemetery. Adam couldn't get closer to the boys without risking further injury.

"Go back as far as you can," Duncan yelled at us.

Badi'a shook her finger in the air, cursing the owl, as Malik and I carried her towards the back wall. Moshe shouted into his phone to the police as he blocked Badi'a's back.

"Aaahhh!" Moshe screamed as his phone flew into the dirt. He dropped to his knees, holding the back of his head.

We sat Badi'a down and Devrah switched places with me as I went to Moshe's side. Blood oozed through his long fingers.

"Call an ambulance!" I yelled.

Devrah pulled off her lavender scarf and passed it to me. I peeled Moshe's fingers off the wound and pressed the scarf against his skull. The stones kept flying. Three more Druze boys appeared at the entrance to the cemetery, and I could see several men and a woman watching from across the street. Duncan was torn between defense and offense, wanting to protect Moshe and me on the ground as well as join Adam at the front. He pulled off his jacket and threw it to me for some cover for Moshe. The crowd behind the boys was growing in size and volume; many spectators yelled encouragement to the boys and even threw a few objects themselves.

I huddled over Moshe, assuring him help was on the way, hoping it was true. His face was pale. I yelled to Devrah to give me the Israeli equivalent of 9-1-1 and dialed it on my phone: 1-0-0.

Malik arranged Binyamin and Devrah in front of Badi'a by the wall and took off toward the front with a demented look on his face. He passed Duncan and Adam, picked up a handful of stones off a grave and began hurling them in rapid succession at the Druze boys. I saw two of them get hit, one in the face. He held his eye and I could see blood seeping through his fingers as he knelt down to the ground in agony. Another round from Malik skidded across the hood of a police cruiser just as it pulled up to the scene.

All stone-throwing ceased. Two cops jumped out of the car as a black military Jeep screeched to a stop in the middle of the street and four Border Police officers emerged, rifles drawn.

The Druze boys disappeared into the crowd. Duncan, Adam and Malik stood halfway between Leila's grave and the street.

"Put your hands on your heads and stand up," someone yelled through a loudspeaker in our three languages. The police remained behind their vehicles.

We all obeyed except for Moshe, who was in the fetal position on the ground losing consciousness.

The amplified voice boomed its command again. Moshe didn't move.

"He's hurt!" I called out, pointing to Moshe. "He's hurt!" *How the hell do you say that in Arabic?* It was unnerving being unable to communicate or help him.

Moshe tried to sit up and, when he did, the bloody scarf fell to the ground. Reflexively, he reached to retrieve it. A loud POP POP POP sound rang out, caroming past me. Moshe fell to the ground.

I screamed and it took everything in my being to keep my hands on my head. The Atabi cops and Border Police ran toward us with martial precision, weapons deployed. Two officers followed by two paramedics ran past me to Moshe. I felt my hands being jerked into handcuffs behind my back and then I was pushed toward the street. I cried out for Moshe, but couldn't see him behind the uniforms surrounding him. Once again, I found myself in the back of an Israeli police car in hysterics.

Even in the identical black uniforms and dark sunglasses of the Border Police, Fadi was unmistakable. He was expressionless as he cuffed Duncan and led him to the Jeep. I realized then that neither knew who the other one was. I couldn't see his eyes behind the glasses, and he didn't seem to even try to make eye contact with me. Had Fadi had a change of heart about me and set us up? Or was he just doing his job? Duncan caught my eye as he climbed into the Jeep.

Waves of long, low hoots sounded through the graveyard.

42

I t was my first arrest, but I was only half-heartedly paying attention as I was booked and jailed. I was inside myself, deep in a tunnel, praying for Moshe to live, second-guessing every decision I'd made in Israel so far and several from before that.

It wasn't as if I didn't know we were doing something the Druze wouldn't appreciate. I had crossed a line, culturally as well as spiritually. And more than one now. Stealing and going public with the list was one thing. With this funeral, though, I put my own need for reclamation and closure, as well as Leila's dignity, ahead of all other considerations. It was costly.

Except for Moshe, we all spent the night in adjacent jail cells, men in one, women in the other. The police never gave us any report on Moshe's condition, so I didn't know if he was alive or dead. I did meet the officer, whose name was Detective Khuri, who was on Leila's case, but he seemed no more helpful than Metanis.

After a medic wrapped Duncan's hand, Duncan joined the other men in the cell next to Devrah, Badi'a and me. While we couldn't see the men, we could hear each other and some of us talked late into the night. I kept to myself, horrified I was capable of bringing on such destruction. I was finished with this absurd pursuit.

Professor Binyamin, ever the optimist, tried to distract us with a charismatic recitation of the oldest surviving written story, the *Epic of Gilgamesh*. I'd read it in college and dreaded hearing a sad story under these circumstances, but this time I heard the whole thing differently: It was a quest in which the hero battles the Goddess for the secret to immortality, which he obtains in the end, only to have it stolen by a *serpent* before he dies.

Duncan insisted on posting bail for the group and Adam, being a lawyer, helped get the charges dropped for everyone except Malik, who had given the Druze boy a concussion and laceration requiring twenty stitches.

In the morning, upon my release, Adam was waiting for me in the lobby of the police station to tell me Moshe was stable and at Rambam Medical Center in Haifa. He'd only been shot in the forearm and his head injury from the stone was of more concern to the doctors than the gunshot wound. Adam had also heard Fadi was suspended from the Border Police following the incident yesterday, but didn't know why. I panicked: Had he been the one who shot Moshe?

Distressed anew, I called Moshe at the hospital. "I'm so sorry, Mosh! I never meant it to go this far. I'm quitting. I'm done. It's over."

"Quitting?" He was hoarse and groggy. "Don't. You. *Dare*, Fereby McCullough Jones!"

I could tell he was on painkillers, but his reaction took me by surprise.

"If you call off the demonstration, I will *never* forgive you," he said.

Badi'a was standing by the curb outside the police station when Adam and I walked out.

"How's she getting home?" I asked Adam.

"Another grandson is coming."

Badi'a spoke to Adam. He suppressed a smile as he turned to me. "She said that whenever one follows an owl, it leads one to ruin."

"Ask her what we're going to do about honor killing. And women's and girls' lives. Their basic rights."

They spoke for a minute and then Adam looked back to me.

"She says do nothing. Become present by paying attention to what's happening in the spaces between incidents. It's already happening."

I looked at Badi'a blankly.

She grabbed Adam's arm with her claw of a hand and spoke. He interrupted her to translate for me.

"What you see on the outside is the opposite of what is true on the inside. It's the men's joke on us that they flaunt these things in our faces and we do not see. But there are women who have begun a secret revolution. Haven't you noticed the trees?"

"What trees?" I said, glancing around.

"The sycamore figs," she said, sweeping a pointed finger across the sky. "They've planted many already."

I didn't know where I should look. "What's she talking about, Adam?"

"They're the *asherah* trees of the Bible," he said. "The first temples dedicated to Goddess. There were thousands of them in ancient times. She says women are planting them again, along with other sacred trees of Asherah…palms, olive, apple, cypress…it took a few thousand years to make people forget her; it will take time to help them remember."

I felt the hairs on one whole side of my body stand up. "Whatever happened to all the old *asherah* trees?"

"They were cut down ages ago," she said. "Their trunks were used for coffins."

Duncan's chauffeur gave us a ride to the hotel to take quick showers and pick up supplies for the demonstration. We grabbed newspapers in the lobby and found articles about the list in all of them, same as what was published last night online. Seeing it in newsprint, especially my own name, made it feel real. And chilling.

I considered calling Fadi, but was too scared to find out whether he shot Moshe or set us up. Instead, I tried calling the D.A. again.

"Why don't you just go home then?" Yael Simon said when I'd explained what I was facing. "That's probably the wisest solution." She sounded indifferent, like she told people this all day long.

"My friend's murderer is still at large and the police haven't even charged the man who assaulted me. They have a small child in custody for committing murder. I'm not leaving until somebody official appears to be working on this harder than I am."

"This is the honor killing case in Atabi? Victim Azzam?"

"Uh, yeah," I said.

"The suspect was released today."

My heart jumped. "What? Qasim Azzam?"

"Yes."

"Oh! That's fantastic news!"

Duncan looked up at my exclamation.

"Now you can leave," she said.

"There's still more work to be done," I said. "Could I please get some kind of protection?"

"Like police protection?"

"Uh, yeah."

"No, we wouldn't do that in this situation," she said.

"Why not?"

"The threat will discontinue if you just leave the country. You aren't a resident here."

Unbelievable. Just like the *shaikh* saying honor killing would end if the women would just obey the rules.

"Well, then, are you at least going to review these cases?" I asked.

"I'll look into it."

We couldn't have picked a hotter day for the demonstration, which we held right in front of Leila's house. I told myself the weather was the reason there was a lower turnout than I'd hoped for. About three dozen people showed up who'd probably read about it in the paper that morning. Most were older Jewish women, some were Christians who lived in the Carmel Druze villages and there were even several Muslims, both men and women. No Druze as far as I could tell.

No matter. I was ebullient about Qasim's release and gave interviews to the three newspaper reporters, including David Cohen for *The Jerusalem Post*, and the two TV stations that came. They all asked if this action was related to "the anonymous list" that had been published, which one of them showed me a copy of in the actual hard-copy newspaper. Somehow, things always seem more real in newsprint.

"We've had dozens of angry calls from Druze about that story," Cohen told me. "Some say it's fabricated. One guy wanted to add a few more names to the list and wondered if we'd publish that! Others are mad we published it and want the police to take the materials we received for forensic investigation to try to find out who broke into their prayer house. A few blamed you for stealing it and said you'd be killed for what you've done."

I put on a brave poker face, but I was reeling inside. Fortunately, the demonstration was very distracting. And Devrah was late. I looked and looked for her and kept checking my cell. She'd promised she'd come and, most importantly, bring the signs. Without them, all we'd have were several beautiful photographs of Leila that Duncan had blown up to poster size.

The Azzams' brown station wagon came roaring down the road and tore into their bumpy driveway, screeching to a stop. Kamil stepped out of the car and took a look at all of us standing in the road just outside his property line. He disappeared through the fig bower. I saw Qasim and Iman peeking through the curtains in the living room and my heart lunged with guilt. It was Qasim's first day home after being released from custody – and he had to see all this!

Kamil soon returned with a huge armload of firewood and piled it in the middle of the street, right where Leila's body had lain. He went back and forth, adding newspaper (today's *Haaretz* with a picture of Leila next to the story about the list, which he held up for the reporters to see and film), cardboard boxes and a broken chair to the pile. Duncan and I exchanged glances.

"He's hijacking our demonstration!" I said.

A TV reporter whom I'd spoken with earlier approached me. "Miss Jones, I just heard on the police scanner that the cops are on their way and they're escorting immigration security, who are looking for you."

It's over, I thought. *I'm either going to be deported or dead by the end of the day.* Somehow, that just fueled me with even more indignation.

I'd never even been to a real demonstration, only a candlelight peace vigil on the beach at home on the eve of the U.S. invasion of Iraq. Now my stomach churned with apprehension. I looked down the road. No cops yet, but there was Devrah running toward us, an armload of posters flapping, gold hoops bouncing, trepidation on her face.

"Where have you been?" I cried, pulling the signs out of her arms with Duncan's help.

Trying to catch her breath, she pointed to Kamil, who was adding more newspaper to his pile as if he were preparing for a ceremony. "He came...to school!"

"What?"

"This morning...he took all of Leila's things! Her paintings, sketches— "

"*What?!*" I yelled. "How did he find out?"

"He said Raziel sent him a check for Leila's work that he'd sold...Kamil went to the gallery to find out what was going on and Raziel sent him to me! I called security, but there was nothing they could do. Technically, everything belongs to her family now."

"Damn it, Devrah!" I yelled. "Why didn't you call me as soon as you knew?"

"I left so fast, I forgot my phone."

"Where are the paintings now?" Duncan asked.

"I don't know," she said.

All three of us looked over at the station wagon in the Azzams' driveway. Nothing inside the vehicle was in view from our angle, and we couldn't get closer without trespassing.

"He's going to burn her paintings right here in front of our demonstration!" I cried.

"The ultimate fuck-you," Devrah said.

Duncan had dread and fury in his eyes. "Like hell he is."

Kamil paused to appraise his pile as a woman protestor approached me.

"Some of my friends want to leave. They're afraid it's going to get out of hand, and there's only one road out." She glanced at the dead end past the Azzams' house.

I looked down at the forest, making a mental note of it as an alternative exit when the cops showed up. After we passed out Devrah's signs, I borrowed a scarf from a protestor and tucked all my hair up into it to make myself less recognizable. Druze neighbors were starting to come out of their homes, and others were walking up the street to see what was going on. Dima was watching everything from the porch swing across the street at Ru'yah's and Rushdi's.

An old white sedan drove down the road towards us, gradually making its way as people moved aside to let it pass. The car double-parked on the street since there were no more parking places available because of the small crowd that had come. Rushdi got out of the driver's seat looking very distressed at the commotion outside his home. He couldn't even get to his driveway because of the debris Kamil had piled in the road. He opened the front passenger door and Ru'yah emerged, squinting to read the protestors' signs. Our eyes locked for a second. She glanced down at the poster-size picture of Leila I held as if she might burst into tears. Rushdi opened the back car door and leaned inside. When he reemerged, he perched a small white bundle on his shoulder.

Khadija. Oh my God. They'd brought her home for the first time…in this chaos I created! Rushdi stood to one side where, as it happened, I could see the sleeping baby's face, chubby cheeks smushed against his shoulder. I inched closer. Khadija was mesmerizingly beautiful. I felt depraved.

I directed the protestors to stay back and be quiet. Sweat prickled the center of my back. I rubbed my throbbing temples and checked down the road again for police cars.

Kamil was digging something out of the back seat of his car and didn't seem to notice Khadija's arrival. Dima ran down the steps of the porch holding on to her *foutta* and hurried to Rushdi's car. She saw me, yelled something unintelligible to me in Arabic and tried to wave me away as if I would try to harm the child. I didn't move. Dima held out her hands, offering to take Khadija from Rushdi. He gently handed the baby over and Dima cradled her proudly in her arms. Within moments, Khadija's hands popped out of the blanket, her tiny purple fists foisted stiffly in the air. She was trembling, so much so that I could see it from several yards away. I took a few steps in their direction. Ru'yah and Rushdi watched their baby with a mix of puzzlement and concern. Then Khadija opened her eyes and tiny mouth and let out a bloodcurdling scream.

All eyes turned to Khadija. Rushdi reached for his daughter, but Dima turned to rebuff him. Her lips pulled into a taut line of embarrassment. She rocked Khadija back and forth, trying to shush her, but the infant screamed louder. Ru'yah offered to take Khadija, but Dima refused. She wasn't going to fail at this maternal task in such a public forum. Dima began to sing to Khadija and stroke the infant's head, but the more Dima tried to calm her, the harder Khadija bawled.

How peculiar. I was now just on the other side of Rushdi's car from them. Khadija was three weeks old, born a month premature. Barely six pounds now, I guessed. It was too early for stranger anxiety – and she'd scarcely been held by even her own mother yet. But she was terrified, that was unmistakable.

And then, as I watched, I had a wild thought: *That's Leila in there.* A warmth slid over me. Dima tilted her head and frowned at Khadija. Leila's triptych "Death of the Future," with the baby trying to nurse from its dead mother's breast in the moonlight, seemed to superimpose itself over the scene. The expression on their faces was identical. Leila painted it from memory...or prophecy. "The moon is feminine consciousness...both our inner child *and* our inner mother," she'd said. "Middle Eastern women have become completely disconnected from their ancient Mother."

In my mind, all the street noise ceased as if it had been sucked into a silent void. Professor Binyamin had said we'd know the tide of the Goddess was on the brink of turning back again when the battle had reached its lowest moral point. Hermes' prescient warning resounded in my head: "Into the Underworld goeth thine Soul."

Ru'yah's eyes were ablaze with revulsion and doubt as she covered her mouth with her hand. Rushdi watched his wife with bewilderment, looking back and forth at Ru'yah and Dima, not understanding what was happening.

The tense voices, the searing heat, the whereabouts of Leila's absconded paintings – every external concern disappeared off my radar screen. It was as if I'd grown a new sense, in the way that people born blind can "see" when they are out of their body during a near-death experience. There was nothing melodramatic or sanctimonious about the notion that came to me. It arrived calmly, like a mother's instinct. And that it was followed by a bolt of feeling so pure and so ordinary, I knew it had to be true.

Lines snaked across Dima's forehead; her lips disappeared into a taut thread. Self-conscious, she turned toward the house with the hysterical baby. Rushdi started to reach out for his daughter, then pulled back. He and Ru'yah exchanged helpless glances and followed her.

What could be a lower moral point than woman turning against woman? Mother turning against daughter?

"You killed Leila," I said loudly in Arabic, pointing at Dima.

They all swung around and gaped at me. Suddenly, Fadi came running up behind Rushdi, out of Dima's view. He glanced back and forth, trying to imagine what we could possibly be saying to each other.

I looked Dima in the eye still pointing at her. "You killed Leila."

She handed Khadija to Ru'yah, not as gently as she should have, and faced me. The bruise on her eye and cheek had turned yellowish green on the inside, outlined in blue and purple, like the battered woman in Leila's "Submission". Until now, her face had been as indecipherable as the bomber Hanan Barghouti's. Now she hid nothing.

"Why do you talk to me about death when you Americans don't know how to live?" she spat at me in her language, shaking a finger.

I understood enough. "You did it, Dima!" I yelled back in my kindergarten Arabic.

Fadi froze and stared at Dima.

Dima squared her hate-filled eyes on me, just as she must have done to Leila before murdering her. "If you were my daughter," she said. "I'd kill you, too."

A blast of heat struck me from behind. Nearly falling down, I turned to see Kamil backing away from the bonfire he'd just set. A long white dress lying on top of the pile went up in roaring flames like a *sati* on a Hindu funeral pyre: Leila's wedding dress! I bolted behind Rushdi's car. Some frightened demonstrators dropped their signs and raced down the road. Rushdi hurried his wife and baby into their home. Dima disappeared into the crowd.

Kamil sauntered over to his station wagon and popped open the back. He pulled out a rectangular black object that he threw on the fire. I stepped forward to see the flames devouring one of Leila's sketchbooks.

"No!" I screamed and lunged for it.

"Fereby, no!" Duncan yelled, grabbing me by the arm.

Kamil threw on another. He gripped a handful of paintbrushes and stood in front of the fire, pitching them in as if he were playing horseshoes. The crowd cheered. He pulled a paint-covered smock out of the back of his car and tossed that in, too. A strange, sweet-putrid smell arose from the bonfire. He lobbed tubes of paint that melted and exploded into gorgeous blue flames. Some of the Druze onlookers scattered. Next he flung Leila's box of incenses she'd used in her last series into the fire.

Duncan squeezed my arm. "He's got her paintings in the car, too!"

Kamil pulled a framed canvas out of the hatch and held it up for all to see. It was "Submission," the battered "La Grande Odalisque" woman. Fadi grabbed the painting out of his father's hands. They struggled in a tug-of-war exchanging Arabic obscenities.

I looked around desperately. Duncan pointed down the road. I couldn't believe it, but Moshe's purple van was working its way up the road toward us. The crowd parted to let the strange vehicle through.

"Shame on him," I said. Moshe was supposed to be recuperating.

Leaving the van in the middle of the road, Moshe hopped out of the driver's seat to gauge the situation. His left arm was in a sling and his head was bandaged on one side. Fadi screamed at him in Arabic. Moshe hurried to the back of the van and opened the doors with his good arm. Duncan, also one-handed, joined Fadi and pulled the painting away from Kamil, sending Kamil stumbling to the ground.

I ran to Kamil's car. As Fadi loaded "Submission" into Moshe's van, Devrah helped me pull out "Resurrection." We were headed for the van when Kamil pushed me so hard, I fell into Devrah and we both let go of the canvas on the way down.

Devrah screamed as Kamil wrested the painting and hurled it on the fire. Duncan got close enough to pull it out of the flames, but it was too hot. I remembered the book-burning Cohen had told me about, all the known copies of *Diary of a Young Druze Girl* being ritually incinerated. An enthusiastic bystander grabbed the poster with Leila's picture from where I'd set it down and delivered it to the fire. I watched the flames quickly consume her face.

Fadi produced a metal rake from somewhere and attempted to fish out the painting. Kamil tried to shove him as he'd done us, but Fadi didn't budge.

Undeterred, Kamil went back over to the car and pulled out "Sub Rosa Shame." As Duncan attempted to seize it from Kamil, Tamir suddenly showed up shouting and trying to shove Duncan aside. I braced myself for what he might do.

Fadi hauled "Resurrection" out of the fire. He and Devrah stomped on it to extinguish the flames. The photo poster had melted onto the top left corner of the painting, eerily adhering Leila's eyes into the sky. Fadi screamed at Moshe in Hebrew, and Moshe flew towards the van, jumping in the driver's seat. Fadi pitched the smoldering painting into the back of the van. While Kamil fought with Duncan and Tamir, Devrah and I grabbed a handful of Leila's unframed paintings from Kamil's car and loaded them into the van. Several men had come to Kamil's aid, but seemed confused about which side to fight on because Tamir was also trying to prevent the paintings from being burned.

I scoured the crowd for Dima, but she was gone.

"These are mine! She was *my wife!*" Tamir yelled at Duncan, throwing a punch to his left eye. Duncan, who probably didn't get in a lot of fistfights, was nevertheless a New Yorker and returned with a cuff to the chin that knocked Tamir to his knees.

Kamil was at the back of the van now, vehemently arguing with Fadi, who wouldn't let him get near anything inside. They began to push each other's chests. I could hear Moshe crying from the driver's seat, "LET'S GO!!! *YALLA!!!*"

I heard the howl of sirens and saw a blur of flashing red lights at the end of the road beyond the crowd. I rushed to Kamil's car and yanked out the last of Leila's works on paper, clutching them to my body. Two men tugged on them from each side, unaware they were thwarting each other more than me. I elbowed one guy as hard as I could in the ribs and racked the other with my knee. Duncan grabbed the paintings from me, but the first guy was still holding on and the edges ripped off. When he let go, I seized what remnants I could in the dust and ran for the van.

The fire raged, blowing blue and orange chemical smoke into the air and sending sparks and molten liquid up with every jar of detonating paint. I imagined Yahweh hurling fire down to honor Elijah's challenge to Baal, which supposedly happened only a few miles away.

Suddenly, strange and beautiful aromas began to fill the air...spice and balsam, musk, then cinnamon, citrus...something earthy like a fur coat. Leila's incense box had burst into flames. The puzzled crowd paused and lifted their chins to the alchemical sky, inhaling narcotic air. We were burning the seven perfumes of sacrifice: frankincense, malabathron, myrrh, nard, cassia, costus and styrax. Not exactly the ritual the ancients had intended to induce a meeting with the gods to negotiate immortality, but I bowed my head and said a quick prayer for Leila and myself anyway.

A woman screamed urgently. I looked around, frantic to find the source. Everyone's eyes were turned on the Azzams' house. A thick layer of dried leaves on the roof had gone up in an inferno.

"Qasim!" I cried, and ran towards the house.

Kamil and I collided on the front step, sending Leila's paint box he held flying through the air. My scarf fell in my eyes as Kamil stepped over me, tripping on the box and crunching a plastic roller.

"Iman's in there, too!" I yelled.

A smoke detector screeched as I crawled through the threshold, tossing the scarf aside. Kamil was nowhere in sight. I glanced down the hallway to the bedrooms and saw him just entering a room. Qasim was crouched in a corner of the living room. The ceiling was smoking and starting to crumble.

"Come on, sweetheart, *yalla*," I said as calmly as I could. I picked him up and carried him out the front door. He clung to me, his face against mine; a sweeter connection I may never know.

"Get in the van, Fereby!" Fadi commanded me in the doorway.

"Kamil and Iman are still inside," I shouted over the cacophony.

Fadi pulled Qasim from my arms and yelled instructions to him, pointing across the street where he'd be safer. Then Fadi grabbed my hand and pulled me through the tangle of the crowd. I wrenched my neck to catch Qasim's eye until the throng swallowed him. When I looked ahead again, Fadi was shoving me into the back of the van. Devrah and Duncan were squatting inside with the smoking ruins of the paintings, possessed looks in their eyes as if they'd just walked away from a plane crash.

Fadi pulled out a small brown paper bag that he'd evidently tucked into the back of his pants and tossed it to me without warning. Then, he slammed the van doors shut.

Moshe turned the van around in the bedlam, swearing all the while in three high-pitched languages. So many people were in the street, we couldn't go more than a few miles an hour. A line of police cars, two fire trucks and an ambulance, and their din of sirens, urged the crowd to let them through. I alternated watching between all the van's windows. From the back, I could see dark clouds of smoke billowing into the sky above the Azzams' blazing house. The gum tree overhanging the house didn't seem to be catching fire; I prayed it was the fire-resistant species often planted in Israel. Someone was trying to pull a hose across the street. Fadi stood still facing the bonfire. Wasn't he going to go back in for Kamil and Iman? At last, Moshe passed the emergency vehicles. As we sped away, I watched Fadi walk into the bonfire as if he was walking into the arms of his mother.

43

"Stop! Moshe! Stop!" I screamed.

Either he didn't hear me or couldn't respond quickly enough under the stress.

"MOSHE STOP!" I pounded on the roof of the van.

Moshe slammed on the brakes and Duncan, Devrah and I plowed into each other and the seatbacks. A tambourine jangled under the driver's seat.

I crawled over Leila's paintings and opened the back doors of the van.

"Go without me!" I jumped out, leaving the doors swinging, and sprinted back down the road, passing panicked people running away from the fire. The fig bower was up in flames.

Fadi was face down in the fire. Three men struggled to pull him out by the legs, his clothes still burning, and turned him over. The man spraying the hose on the Azzams' roof turned it on Fadi. I got down close to his face, steam rising from his raw head, the hair gone. Cold water drenched us both. I blinked hard to see him clearly as ash washed from his charred face. His eyes were seared shut.

"Fadi! My God!" I cried, reaching out to touch him, then paralyzed with fear to do so. I glanced at his body, burned so badly his clothes and skin were mixed together. There was that same unbearable smell from the bombing scene again. "Fadi…"

Paramedics surrounded us. Someone forced me to my feet and, weakly, I stumbled out of their way. Firefighters jumped from the engine and pulled out their hoses. I slipped into the frantic crowd that was trying to leave. The police attempted to establish a perimeter. People pushed and stomped my feet; I felt a wave of panic roll through me as if I were in the bus again after the bombing.

In what seemed like no time at all, the ambulance had turned around and was heading out with Fadi inside. A TV truck followed closely behind; when the driver had to slow down for the crowd in the street, I clawed my way up to his window to ask where the ambulance was headed: Rambam Medical Center, where Khadija had been until today.

I found my strength somewhere and sprinted to the highway. I hitched a ride with some soldiers who, as the ride progressed, became increasingly wary of me. Was my barbarity that transparent? With few words passed between us, they dropped me off a few blocks from the hospital.

I huddled in a chair in the over-air-conditioned waiting room of the trauma center, wet, muddy and shivering. Two reporters tried to talk to me until security came and made them leave. After another journalist called my cell, I was asked to turn it off while inside the hospital. A trauma nurse noticed my hands were burnt and insisted I get treatment. I guess I had grabbed some burning paintings, but I had no recollection of it. An administrator told me the Azzams' street and several others had been evacuated. She didn't know if Fadi's family had made it out safely or not. None of them had come to the hospital to see him.

Anxious exhaustion overwhelmed me. I hid my head in my knees, trying not to fall asleep or collapse into a leaky gap in my consciousness, afraid to lose my watchfulness, my self-reproach, and of horrible dreams I knew were awaiting me. I tried to think only of Fadi, Khadija and Qasim – the future – but the eyes of my brother, Cary, and Leila, the last time I saw each of them alive, kept intruding. I shook my head each time, unable to contain the images, and tried talking to myself out loud about anything else to ward off a recurrence. So, this is all insanity is, I thought. How simple. A short walk from any crisis we feel responsible for.

I buried my face in my hands at the next agonizing realization: I'd given up on my mother long ago, that's what I'd done. She had utterly failed me, that much was true. But what was my continuing hostility towards her for? Ongoing punishment for her unheroic response to tragedy? Indirect self-retribution? Or maybe it kept the crisis we'd never worked through at a safe distance.

Finally, after more than three hours, I was called back to speak with the doctor. A female surgeon and a younger male resident took me into a quiet examination room. Kind wrinkles splayed around her eyes. The guy stared at the linoleum.

"I'm sorry, Miss Jones," she said. "He passed away at three eighteen p.m."

44

Too disoriented to do the sensible thing and splurge for a taxi, I started walking from Rambam to the Dan Carmel. I breathed in gasps and coughs, crying as I walked, my hands bandaged as if I were wearing the oversized white gloves of a Disney character. Words of Mustafa from the House of Druze echoed through me: "A man must be killed if he attains his honor through his mother." She did his dirty work for him, but Fadi saved them the trouble of having to kill him. In sacrificing himself, he had finally gotten his wish: To be anonymous, invisible, exiled. To no longer sit between two worlds. To be free. I had been warned. Sorrow crystallized inside me like a white darkness.

I ended up at the Bahá'i gardens below the Dan. Every square inch of the sacred gardens was manicured precisely as they flowed toward the temple. I lay on a bench amidst whimsical, lumpy Korean grass, exposed to the full sun for I don't know how long, lucid dreaming about Cary, Leila, Fadi and Qasim. I believed I could will justice. I'd spent most of my life seeking the light, evading the dark. It was meant to be my path to perfection. But I wasn't mindful of my own darkness, my own fundamentalism running through a crack in my heart.

A security guard startled me and escorted me out. With difficulty, because of my hand injuries, I managed to turn my phone back on and call Duncan. He and Moshe had been wracked with anxiety since I hadn't been heard from for over five hours. They rode with Duncan's driver to pick me up and take me back to the hotel. When they arrived, I was hunched over on the curb, bandaged hands poking out, hair like a nest.

Leila's salvaged paintings were spread out around the hotel suite. Duncan had tried to assess the damage and restore what he could with makeshift tools and supplies. He and Moshe had begun the process of packing the paintings for shipping, only two useful hands between them.

Duncan held an icepack over his swollen eye as he ran a bath for me. Moshe poured me a glass of sauvignon blanc. One of them knocked on the bathroom door every ten minutes or so to check on me. I sat in the water with my bandaged hands on the sides of the tub until the water cooled off and the steam disappeared.

When I was drying off, I remembered it. In a panic, I pulled on the hotel robe and flew out to the living room.

"Where's the bag? Where's the bag?" I cried.

They looked up from "Resurrection." "What bag?" Duncan said.

"The bag – the *brown* bag! – the one Fadi handed me right before we left! Didn't you see it? He threw it in the van. Did you bring it in? Is it here?"

"I don't know. Just calm down," Moshe said. "Let's look for it, Fer."

"What was in it?" Duncan asked, looking around the suite.

"I don't know! That's what I want to know. I didn't get a chance to look."

We searched the suite to no avail. I was frantic.

"Maybe it's still in the van," I said. "You didn't throw anything away did you? God, I hope it didn't fall out of the van when I got out! Did you shut the doors before you took off?"

"Yes, yes, we shut the doors," Duncan said. "Let's go look."

I ran down with them to the parking lot in my robe and bare feet. We opened up the back of the van. The purple carpeting was melted and blackened in places. A couple of Moshe's costumes were torn and wadded in a corner. The tambourine had a tear in its drum. I crawled around, searching in crevices and beneath clothing. Under the front seat, I felt a plastic water bottle and possibly some beads. I rooted under the passenger seat and came upon something smooth and papery, but curved and hard underneath. The bag.

They gathered around me as I opened it. Inside was something hairy. The dressings on my hands made it hard to reach in, so Moshe pulled it out. A doll, about ten inches long, in a dirty white dress with blue embroidered flowers, with long, shiny dark hair and big brown eyes.

"A doll?" Duncan said, taking the bag from me so I could hold her.

"Umniyah," I whispered. I cradled her in my gauze-covered palms.

"Umniyah?" Moshe said.

"Fadi gave her to Leila when she was little and imprisoned in her room."
I stroked the doll's hair and imagined little Leila holding her against her cheek
in the room that was meant to be her tomb. Tears stung my eyes.

"Her name means 'wish' in Arabic," Moshe said.

I looked at Umniyah's face and imagined Leila naming her long ago,
keeping her dreams alive. Duncan pulled a folded piece of paper out of the
bag. I nodded at him to read it.

Fereby My One Love,

A new Rumi quote to replace the old one
you don't need anymore: "This is love: To fly
toward a secret sky, to cause a hundred veils to
fall each moment. First to let go of life. Finally,
to take a step without feet."

Fadi

45

M y friends didn't want me to, but I insisted on going alone to the Atabi police station to report Dima's confession. If there were any consequences for what had happened at the demonstration, I wanted to be the only one held accountable.

When I got out of Moshe's van, Detective Khuri, the new officer on Leila's case, was emerging from a police cruiser in front of the station.

"Detective!"

He glowered at me.

"Dima Azzam confessed to murdering Leila," I said.

He walked around the car to the rear passenger door.

I tried to look inside the cruiser, but the sun's glare blinded me. "Has she been arrested?"

Khuri opened the door and pulled out a handcuffed detainee who hung his head. His clothing was covered with blood and soot. When he glanced up, I saw it was Kamil, with hate-filled eyes. My breath caught.

"Go home now, Miss Jones," Khuri said, leading Leila's father toward the station.

"Not until I know Dima's been arrested and indicted for murder," I said.

He opened the station door for Kamil. "She's dead. Now leave our village."

46

D ima and Fadi are dead!" I screamed at David Cohen, who'd just pulled into the police station parking lot.

He rushed past me. "I know. I'm going to try to get a statement from Kamil."

I grabbed his arm. "What happened to Dima?"

"After Fadi was taken to the hospital, Dima ran away. Kamil found her in the *souk* and said, '*Insha'allah tmuti*' – 'it's best for you to die.' Then stabbed her in front of everyone."

I froze, my breath stuck inside my body. Cohen hurried into the station. Because of me, of my taunting Dima into confessing in public, everyone knew that it was she – a woman – who had finally restored the Azzam family's honor. Now the whole village knew the men weren't man enough to. I coughed and sputtered to catch my breath, as if I were so polluted, no clean air would go in and the bad air wasn't allowed out. This was the intersection of all my fears. I vomited behind Moshe's van and sat inside with the door open, dry-heaving. When Moshe phoned and heard me crying and talking nonsense, he and Duncan showed up within minutes. In the back of the limo, Moshe put one arm around me and held a plastic bag nearby in case I needed it, while Duncan followed behind in the van back to the hotel.

I lay face down in bed with the curtains wide open. Dark would have been terrifying. A hemorrhage had opened inside my soul. Moshe sat next to me and rubbed my back even though I told him to leave me alone. I didn't deserve kindness. Especially from someone I'd injured. Duncan arranged for us to fly back to New York together the next night and I didn't resist. Moshe squeezed my shoulder when he heard this and tears came to his eyes. How could he be sad I was leaving? He lay in the bed next to me all night, comforting me each time I woke up.

In the morning, we shared a solemn breakfast on the balcony with Devrah. Everyone looked haggard. There were more coffee-sipping sounds than conversations at first. Even Moshe was subdued.

Devrah put her cup down in the saucer she held in her lap. "A few days before her death, as she was finishing the 'Seven Perfumes,' Leila told me she'd learned something she didn't expect by painting them…but it was too late to put it in the series."

We all looked up at her. She pushed some frizzy hairs off her face as a breeze kicked up.

"She said of all the things women have lost, the ultimate sacrifice they've made is their support for one another."

I exchanged glances with Duncan and Moshe across the table. We sat in a long silence shaped by that prophetic epiphany. I suspected they were all thinking what I was: that I was among the guilty, failing to rescue Leila and inciting Dima's murder. And when Leila had saved my life at risk of her own! I got up and went to the balcony railing to face the sea and hide my shame.

"Fer?" Moshe said.

I waved him off. Duncan tried to change the subject to hotel laundry service, then got up to answer the suite phone.

I looked down the swath of green that led to the shrine of the Ba'b. Leila was right, of course. Giving up on each other, as Dima, Hanan, my would-be suicide bomber, and many others, in subtler, everyday kinds of ways, had done, was the greatest loss of all. Because, ironically, women's submission wouldn't be possible without their own cooperation. I wondered if it wasn't, in fact, when women finally abandoned the divine feminine – and thus, each other – that the transition to God was at last complete.

"You have visitors, Fereby," Duncan called.

A panic swept over me. *They're going to arrest me!* We looked at each other.

"Don't worry," Duncan said, smiling. "It's not immigration."

"Who?" I asked.

"You'll see."

After we'd all come in from the balcony, there was a knock at the door. I steeled myself as Duncan went to answer it. A nervous-looking Ru'yah walked in, holding an infant car seat. I couldn't believe it.

"I heard you're leaving tonight," she said. "I wanted to say goodbye."

I looked at Moshe, who seemed equally mystified, and motioned for her to come in. She turned the carrier around as she sat down on the sofa. Khadija was awake and making gurgling noises. I kneeled down next to her and ached at her beautiful sight.

"You came to see me, after…" I said to Ru'yah.

She smiled slightly.

"I'm so sorry, Ru'yah. I never meant this to happen."

She shook her head and looked down at her baby. "I wanted you to meet Khadija before you leave."

She unlatched the harness and picked up the baby, supporting her tiny head. Khadija was dressed in a pink cotton nightgown and wrapped in a cream-colored crocheted blanket. A little smirk appeared on her mouth as she sucked on one hand.

"Would you like to hold her?" Ru'yah asked.

I moved over closer and she put Khadija in my uneasy arms, helping me get her head to rest in the crook of my elbow. She was lighter than I expected and warmer, too. I leaned in so she might see me. She smelled at once like heaven and earth.

"I was afraid to tell Leila I was dreaming of her in my womb," Ru'yah said.

I looked at Khadija's sparkling blue eyes, newborn baby irises that hadn't settled on a color yet. She was so new, so flawless…a whole fresh life spread out before her. I prayed she wouldn't recall her past life and violent death. I rocked her and we exchanged some coos. Duncan and Moshe sat nearby, teasing me about motherhood. As I held her, I couldn't help but imagine being her mother. It was strangely easy to do so, and, yet, indescribably overwhelming. How did my mother hold me? Did I stop crying in her embrace? What did she feel then? How could a mother lose such a creature who embodies pure love so completely and *not* lose her mind?

After I gave her back to Ru'yah, I went and got Umniyah from my room.

"Fadi gave her to me yesterday."

Ru'yah regarded her with an expression I couldn't read. I handed her the doll.

"I remember her," she said, her eyes glistening.

"Would you like Khadija to have her?" I asked.

A tear skidded off her cheek onto Khadija's blanket. "You keep her."

That's when I began to understand that she had wanted to help me all along, but couldn't, not just because her own life was in danger, but because she couldn't publicly acknowledge who Khadija really was. Ru'yah needed to hide the past and break the chain of the dishonored lineage for her daughter.

~ ~ ~

While Duncan and Moshe took what was left of Leila's art to a shipping company before the authorities froze them, I went to see the *shaikh* one last time. His wife told me he was napping. I asked her to tell him goodbye for me.

Walking back towards the van, a stab of despair seized me. I went down to the main street and on towards the Azzams' road. On the corner, a sycamore fig I hadn't noticed before stood in the front yard of an old home. I ducked underneath and inhaled the musky scent in her shade. I felt the papery-thin, grey bark that was peeling off and revealing the greenish-yellow beneath. Her fruit was clumped on her trunk in sticky clusters of pinkish-brown balls. Several figs had fallen on the ground beneath her. I leaned down to tuck them in my jacket pocket.

I walked on to the home of the woman Ru'yah said had been hidden in the attic for decades. I watched the attic window as I approached. The white lace curtains were closed. Standing on the sidewalk in front of the house, I absently stuck my hands in my pockets and glanced down the road in both directions. No one was out. I surveyed the front door and equivocated. When I pulled my hands out of my pockets, one of the figs fell out and split open on the ground, revealing its flower and many seeds. I squatted down to pick it up and took a measured breath. *Truth may walk through the world unarmed*, Badi'a had said at Leila's funeral. I scraped a little hole in the pale, bare earth where the fig had landed. I squeezed the seeds out of the soft shell into the sandy womb. I covered them with soil and smoothed the ground.

When I turned to leave, I saw a smudge of motion out of the corner of my eye. I glanced up at the attic window in time to see the curtains fall back.

EPILOGUE

A year and a half later, Kamil was convicted of first-degree murder and received a sentence of life in prison. Four months after the trial, I was able to obtain a translation of the trial transcript.

Kamil told the court what happened the night Leila was killed: "The Druze guy who saw Duncan and Leila at the university told his mother. She gossiped to her friends and it got back to Tamir...I made Fadi take Miss Jones to the airport to try to prevent Leila's being killed. I was trying to save her...and Fadi. I didn't want Fadi to stay when I knew what was coming...I didn't want him to kill Leila. Dima asked me to do something. I knew what she meant – kill her. I wasn't ready to do that. I went back to our bedroom to try to clear my head alone. Leila left the house. Dima told me she went after Leila, had some words in the courtyard and then Dima said she hit Leila over the head with a stepping stone when she turned to flee. She fell after the first blow and Dima kept going several more times until she was sure Leila had to be dead. I only heard some pounding noises, like feet stomping a brief *debka*. No screaming.

"Then I heard Dima come inside, the water running in the kitchen. She came into our bedroom and said, 'It's done at last, praise God.' Then we heard Fadi arriving home. She told him Leila was dead, and he just fell apart like a stupid little girl. I closed our bedroom door so I wouldn't hear him.

"He held Leila's body for hours outside. Dima stayed up all night. I slept a little. Just before dawn, Dima got him to go to bed. She was angry that neither of us would drag the body out to the street to be found when it got light, so she did it herself. She said she thought about adding some stab wounds to make it bloodier so it would look more as if a man did it, but she lost her nerve. I backhanded her in the face as hard as I could for disrespecting my authority. She expected that one of us men would take the blame for the killing. But the police were making it so easy with their hit-and-run theory, no one had to confess. Miss Jones was something we never planned for…then everything started to come apart."

There were a number of inheritance issues once Raziel sent that check to Kamil and the paintings were discovered. One of Leila's notebooks we salvaged from the fire contained a sort of homemade will in the form of a journal entry. The Druze courts spent eleven months trying to figure out if it was valid. Tamir tried to get the *qadis*, the Druze judges, to follow Moslem laws of inheritance in absence of an official/valid will so he might receive half of Leila's estate. Khazna, an organization that sprung up after I left Israel to fight honor killings, put public pressure on the judges in favor of validity of her will until they finally consented.

Leila left all her artwork to Duncan, and all her money to Qasim, about US$24,000, which was fortunate for Qasim because Kamil and Dima had squandered almost every *shekel* they had on Leila's wedding to Tamir.

Tamir sued the state for the money, and sued Duncan and his foundation for the paintings. Since Leila's consent to the marriage to Tamir was coerced with a death threat, it was ultimately ruled invalid. Tamir still tried to argue that the Azzams owed him something since they were responsible for her death, but the judge wouldn't go for it since Tamir incited the death with hearsay. Tamir got sentenced to eight months in prison himself for that, the strongest message ever sent by Israel to those who would impel an honor killing.

Not surprisingly, the police never found enough evidence to charge him with assaulting me. The cop who shot Moshe was never charged or disciplined, either. It wasn't Fadi.

Since their mother and brother were dead and their father was in prison (not to mention their home burned down), Iman and Qasim went to live with Ru'yah, Rushdi and Khadija. If it weren't for the giant fire-resistant gum tree behind the Azzams' house, the orchard would likely have been consumed, as well.

When Tamir got out of prison, he married Iman.

Adam filed a complaint to the Attorney General with a request to prosecute Jabr Hayyan, the *shaikh*'s grandson, for incitement to commit murder in his media statement. An indictment never followed, but Jabr was forced to resign the town council.

David Cohen, the *Jerusalem Post* reporter, was indicted on three counts of failing to report a felony for the various police crimes he ignored; he was given immunity by testifying against the Atabi police and the Northern

District. Amir Metanis, his boss Safwan Sa'd el Din, two other cops and the medical examiner were sentenced to prison for one to three years each for obstruction of justice. Joshua Shuman got off scot-free.

No one was arrested for writing the list, but I am gratified no one on it has been killed yet.

Duncan had a show of Leila's work, a major fundraiser in New York City, to help Khazna. For the opening night of the show, oriental rugs covered every inch of the foundation gallery's floor, diaphanous Shile draperies hung like veils from the high windows and rose incense filled the air. Divans with *crêpe de Chine* cushions were created in nooks. I'd sent Duncan the photographs I'd taken of Leila (including the one with Fadi in the light of the moonbow), which he blew up artfully in black and white and had displayed by candlelight throughout the gallery. Umniyah, Leila's doll, was on display, too, the piece of green yarn I took from Mother of Rags tied to her wrist.

A gorgeous belly-dance troupe gave an understated performance to a live Syrian band. (Moshe declined, saying his style was inappropriate for the intention of the show.)

I brought Duncan a rare, antique, hand-sewn English edition of Muhyiddin Ibn al-'Arabi's *Turjuman al-Ashwaq, The Translator of Desires* – the book of love poems Leila was going to give him when they left for the U.S. He carried it in his hand the entire evening.

Devrah and Professor Binyamin also came. Binyamin lent his paintings of Leila's indefinitely to the foundation. A handful of celebrities who care about human rights attended, as well as dozens of journalists, politicians, and non-governmental organizations.

Duncan netted $450,000 for Khazna from the fundraiser and matched it with personal funds to launch a spectacular Druze women and children's shelter in Haifa called The Leila Azzam Safe House, administered by Khazna. He plans to pay for Qasim's and Khadija's higher educations, if they so desire, but he says nothing can undo his unbearable burden.

A month after I left Israel, Moshe got a lead role in the gay, Hebraicized version of "Brigadoon." I gave him two first class international plane tickets with my airline miles. He used one to come to the fundraiser in New York and the other to visit me in California. On his way back, he stopped in Vegas and got a role in a new Arabian-themed Cirque-du-Soleil show at Luxor, basically playing himself to the tenth power.

Ru'yah sends me e-mails every so often, sometimes with pictures of Khadija, who is predictably turning out to be quite a handful. For her first birthday, I sent a handmade, organic satin blanket, with her name and birthdate embroidered in Arabic next to a smiling full moon.

Qasim has been slow to adjust to all the loss and change. I've wanted to write to him, or send him something, but nothing seems like enough, and I think it would just cause him more pain and confusion.

I took a break from traveling abroad and moved back into my parents' house for several months. I helped my mother clean out some closets and plant some fruit trees. I went down to Baja to the orphanage with her and held some of the babies. We've begun a long, hard journey home.

The New York Times found me innocent of all the charges and will soon publish a four-part series I wrote about Leila and honor killing featuring all my controversial findings, including the origins of the practice and the destruction and return of the Goddess. My editors are uneasy about the repercussions.

Back at home, I recently met someone special named Henry and enrolled in a belly dance class I get to more often than not. I'm considering other international investigative pieces, but I'm taking my time. I haven't seen any more moonbows since I left Israel, but I haven't really been looking.

ABOUT THE AUTHOR

Amy Logan's writing and/or photography has been published in *The New York Times Magazine*, *The Los Angeles Times*, *The Dallas Morning News*, *The Denver Post*, *Vegetarian Times*, *Natural Solutions* magazine and many others. She wrote a nationally syndicated travel column for Tribune Media Services and contributed an essay to the 2008 anthology *Mothering Heights' Manual for Motherhood, Vol. 1: What We Wish We Knew Before We Became a ~~Milk Machine,~~ ~~Short Order Cook, Shuttle Driver, Laundress~~ MOTHER* (Mothering Heights' Press), which became an Amazon #1 best-seller in the Motherhood category. She has studied creative writing with Booker Prize finalist Arnost Lustig, Pulitzer Prize-winning poet Henry Taylor and National Book Award finalist Andre Dubus III and attended the 2006 and 2008 Squaw Valley Fiction Writers Workshops. *The Seven Perfumes of Sacrifice* is her first novel. She may be reached at www.7perfumes.com.